SICKO MODE

A Novel By
Keisha R. Ervin

Sicko Mode Synopsis

Cam and Gray tried their hardest to make their marriage work but miscommunication, lies, cheating, exes who wouldn't let go and acting impulsively tore them apart. Gray always thought that Cam would be there to catch her when she fell but when she needed him the most he literally slammed the door in her face. Now she's facing life on her own for the first time since her early twenties. Love no longer lives in her heart for Cam only malice. The same can be said for him. You were either with him or against him, and when we last saw Cam, he was being placed in handcuffs, thinking that Gray, the love of his life, had betrayed him in the worst way possible. For a nigga like Cam, there's only one way to pay his beautiful wife back for her treachery . . . death.

Color Me Pynk Publications is accepting manuscripts from aspiring or experienced fiction, romance, interracial, urban, black woman/white man, alpha male, erotic, supernatural and fantasy authors. The review process can take up to three weeks. We will contact you once a decision has been reached. NO PREVIOUSLY PUBLISHED MANUSCRIPTS WILL BE ACCEPTED.

WHAT WILL SET YOU APART FROM THE REST:

The ultimate alpha male. He's drool worthy, confident, arrogant, strong, great in bed, complicated and flawed. He messes up but is willing to change to better his life and his woman's.

Female leads that are sassy, sweet, loving, ambitious, funny yet beautifully imperfect. She puts up with drama to a certain extent but learns to stick up for herself and what she believes in.

A story that is dramatic, shocking, action packed, sexy, hilarious, romantic and tear jerking.

If you'd like to join the Color Me Pynk fam, dare to be different! There is no story that hasn't already been written so make it fresh and new by adding a new twist to it. We want stories that our readers will read twenty years from

3

now. To be considered please email the first five chapters of your manuscript, synopsis and contact information to colormepynksubmission@gmail.com

Follow us:

IG:
ColorMePynkPublications/https://www.instagram.com/colormepynkpublications/

Other Titles by Keisha Ervin

The Untold Stories by Chyna Black

Cashmere Mafia (Material Girl Spin-off)

Material Girl 3: Secrets & Betrayals

Paper Heart

Pure Heroine (Sequel to Me and My Boyfriend)

Emotionally Unavailable (Chyna Black 2)

Heartless (Chyna Black 3)

Radio Silence (Chyna Black 4)

Smells Like Teen Spirit Vol 1: Heiress

Mina's Joint 2: The Perfect Illusion

Cranes in the Sky (Messiah & Shyhiem Book 1)

Postcards from the Edge (Messiah & Shyhiem Book 2)

Such A Fuckin' Lady (Chyna Black 5)

First Wives Club Vol. Melanin Magic (Chyna, Mo & Gray)

Beast Mode (Gray Book 2)

Sicko Mode (Gray Book 3)

Sicko Mode Playlist

Cardi B "Money"

Iyla "Shampoo"

Mullato "Bitch From Da South"

Meek Mill feat Cardi B "On Me"

Blueface feat Cardi B "Thotiana"

Normani feat 6lack "Waves"

Iyla "Juice"

City Girls "Act Up"

Travis Scott feat Drake "Sicko Mode"

DJ ESCO feat O.T. Genasis & Future "Bring It Out"

Alex Isley "Loss For Words"

Raiche "047"

Etta Bond "He's Mine"

Etta Bond feat SiR "More Than A Lover"

H.E.R. "Changes"

Meek Mill "Respect The Game"

Dawn Richard "Sauce"

Waka Flocka Flame feat Drake "Round of Applause"

Tank "Dirty"

Emmit Fenn "Painting Greys"

Sheck Wes "Mo Bamba"

Brandy "Broken Hearted"

Brandy "Nothing"

Alex Isley "Road to You"

Etta Bond "Teleport"

James Arthur "Falling Like the Stars"

Kenny Lattimore "For You"

Alex Isley "Water & Air"

Dedication

To Cliff Dixon, I never personally knew you but somehow our souls connected in a supernatural way. Your existence on earth gave me so much inspiration. Thank you for being the physical muse for Cam. From your honey dew skin, freckles, heavenly smile, sex appeal and swag you were pure perfection. I am so sorry that your time in this world was cut so short, but you made such an impact on not only my life but so many others. In wake of your untimely passing, I learned that much like Cam you were equally as funny and such a loving, caring friend. You were just dope. You poured into me in ways you never knew. Your memory will never die. It will live on through my most iconic character Cam forever.

Previously in Beast Mode

Sleep never came easy to Cam. Nights where he stared absently at the ceiling was natural to him. Most nights he asked God to forgive him for all his sins or plotted revenge on his enemies. Devin, or better yet Devin, lay next to him on her stomach with her naked ass propped in the air. She made sure he had easy access to her pussy at all times of the night. Cam had worn her ass out. For hours, he drilled into her like a maniac. All the anger he wanted to take out on Gray, she got for three hours straight. She was wore out, but Devin being the freak she was, seemed to always be down for more, but Cam was off that. She'd came multiple times, but he wasn't able to bust one nut. The convo between him and Gray replayed like a song stuck in his head on repeat. She'd come there to tell him she was pregnant. Cam didn't believe her at first. He kinda still didn't now. Gray no longer being able to bear children was one of the sore spots of their marriage. Now all of a sudden, after he'd broken up with her she was pregnant. What a convenient coincidence. Cam honestly didn't know what to think. That's why he found it hard to even lay in peace. He couldn't rest easy knowing she might be pregnant with his seed. Having a kid had always been a dream of his. Gray knew this. She wouldn't play on that emotion for sympathy or for a place back in his heart or would she? Cam didn't put shit past her at that point. After seeing her with Gunz, his entire opinion of her had changed. Gray was scandalous as fuck. It had become clear that there were no good females in the world. The only way he would know for sure if she was telling the truth was if he made her pee on a stick his self. Even then, if she was indeed pregnant, that still left the question if the baby was his or not.

He'd come in and found her and Gunz kissing. Who's to say they hadn't already smashed before then. Finding out if she was really pregnant was the first step in all of this madness. He'd figure out the rest after that. But first, he had to go take care of business. It was March 12th. The day of his last big shipment. Thirty kilos of cocaine had been transported from South America to a local convenience store hidden inside fresh pineapples. At least that's what it would look like from the naked eye. When the box of fruit was opened from the outside, it would look like a regular shipment of pineapples. But when the shell was removed, you'd see the inside had been hollowed out and filled with cocaine compacted into cylinders. The cocaine cylinders, which carried between 800 and 1,000 grams each, were coated in a yellow waxy substance. The wax coating helped to conceal any odor the chemical product might contain. The storeowner had no idea that drugs were inside the containers. He simply accepted payment for the drop-offs and minded his own business.

Since Cam had taken over as Lieutenant, he'd had several successful shipments brought in. He and his crew had been flying under the radar. That day would be no different. He'd ensure that all the kilos were accounted for then go holla at Gray. He might not fuck with her like he used to but the way he'd spoken to her the night before didn't sit well in his spirit. Cam kept seeing the look of complete devastation on her face. He'd never be able to get the vision out of his head. He'd decimated her. In the moment it felt good to make her hurt. Maybe then she'd know how she'd made him feel. Witnessing her kiss, the very man that killed Diggy was the equivalent of finding out his mother had passed away. It was the death of their relationship or maybe their marriage had ended the moment he stuck his dick in LaLa. Either way, marriage wasn't suitable for either one of them. They'd both failed each other. Him more than her, but in the game of love and war, there were no winners.

Cam hurried and got dressed. His day would be shit, until he talked to Gray. He had to hurry up and handle his business so he could get to her and they could figure this shit out. Fully clothed, he made his way out of the bathroom and looked at Devin. It was 4:00 a.m. and she was wide awake. On her side, she lay naked with desire in her eyes. He still hadn't gotten over the fact that she was one of the many girls Gunz had cheated on Gray with. St. Louis was small as fuck. If he would've known that bit of information before hitting her up, he would've never taken it there with her. He wasn't that spiteful of a nigga, but the deed had already been done. He couldn't take it back. He'd been bustin' Devin down for weeks.

"Where you going dressed in all black like an omen?"

"I gotta go take care of some business." He grabbed his phone and keys.

"You want me to wait on you to come back?" She purred, rubbing the space where he once laid.

"You can do that." Cam licked his bottom lip.

His dick was starting to brick up, but he didn't have time to dick her down again. He had to go. Gray's face kept dancing in his head. Fuckin' Devin could wait. And yes, he was going to continue to mess with her. Whether Gray was pregnant with his baby or not, divorce was still on the table. He and Gray were toxic or maybe it was just him that was the bad seed. Regardless, they needed to leave each other alone. Neither of their sins could ever be forgiven so it was over.

11

"It's food in the fridge. I'll be back." Cam left out without giving her the kiss she so badly wanted.

He and Devin weren't like that. Right now, she was just something warm for him to lay next to at night. Cam jogged leisurely down the steps. He was only inches away from the door when it was forcefully kicked in. Without warning, several federal agents came barreling through the door with weapons drawn on him.

"Get on the ground!" One of the agents yelled.

Knowing it was best that he comply, Cam slowly made his way to the floor. He quickly learned that an indictment had been issued with allegations of an international cocaine ring that he and other members of the Gonzalez Cartel allegedly distributed throughout Missouri, Illinois, Michigan and Ohio. According to the indictment, they'd confiscated 30 kilos of cocaine found at a convenience store through a confidential informant.

Cam knew for a fact none of his boys had snitched. Hell, they were probably being ran down on too. Only one person had the motive to drop a dime on him . . . Gray. It took everything in him not to start spazzing out. Yeah, they were in a bad place. He'd violated her, and in front of Devin of all people, but was taking away his freedom the only way to get back at him? No way had Gray done this to him. There had to be someone else who hated him just as much but who? Cam had so many enemies he could hardly keep count. None of his enemies knew the exact date or location of his final shipment. It wasn't by accident that he'd cussed Gray out and then the next day his house was being raided by the Feds. Cam needed answers and fast.

After being handcuffed and read his rights, he and a now clothed Devin sat against the wall as federal and local law enforcement agents spent hours raiding his home in search of narcotics they wouldn't find. Cam wasn't dumb. He would never have drugs in his home. Linking him to the cocaine they'd found would be damn near impossible. Cam had made sure that if anything went down the drugs couldn't be traced back to him or his crew. The cops did, however, find two pounds of marijuana and three unregistered handguns. Because he was a convicted felon, Cam was prohibited from legally purchasing a gun. Now that they'd found something they could pin on him, he was escorted in a squad car to the DEA building. Since she was innocent, Devin was released.

Inside the interrogation room, Cam was handcuffed to the table. The cold steel dug into his wrists. At this point, most criminals folded but not Cam. He'd been here before. No matter what they threw at him, he wasn't saying a word. The agents tried to scare him into confessing the drugs were his, but Cam was no fool. No response was the best response. The Federal agent eventually grew tired of his nonchalant attitude and arrogance and gave up. After that, everything happened so fast. Cam's lawyer arrived and he was arraigned. Locked in handcuffs, he stood before the judge as he ran down his charges. Cam thought he was going to be hit with a barrage of criminal acts. The way the FEDS had been talking, he was going to be put underneath the jail. To his surprise, he was only charged with felony possession of a firearm. The prosecutor tried to stick him with a 924 C which was misconduct involving a federal drug trafficking offense, but his lawyer immediately had that thrown out.

"In the case of Cameron Parthens Jr., you are being charged with felony possession of a firearm. How do you plead?" The judge asked.

"Not guilty."

Cam took the charge with a grin on his face. A possession of a firearm charge was far better than a drug charge. Whoever had snitched on him had fucked up. He'd be out of jail in no time, and as soon as he was released, Cam was coming for blood.

"Your honor." The prosecutor interjected. "The defendant is a powerful man. He's a flight risk and is still a part of an ongoing investigation of being associated with the Gonzalez Cartel. He's also a known gang member. I ask that his bond be denied."

"I agree. Bond denied." The judge threw down his gavel.

"The fuck!" Cam growled as he was escorted out of the courtroom.

"I'm gonna get you out of this." His lawyer assured.

Cam was livid. He just knew he'd bail. His lawyer was good, but he wasn't that good. The fact still remained he was on probation. By law, he would have to serve time. He, along with several other prisoners, were transported to St. Louis County Jail. After changing his clothes and being placed in a brown jumpsuit, Cam finally got to make a phone call. Questions needed to be answered and only Gray could answer them. Standing at the payphone, he dialed her number. Cam held the phone up to his ear, waiting to hear her voice. He had to hear her voice. It was the only way he'd be able to calm his suspicions, but Gray didn't answer. The sound of the operator clicked in.

I'm sorry, you have reached a number that has been disconnected or no longer in service. Please hang up and try your call again.

Dread sat in the pit of his stomach, tying it up into a knot. Dismay set into his face like rigor mortis, causing his jaw to clench tight. Fear creeped up his spine like a poisonous spider leaving a path of silk in its wake. Frozen in space, his feet were stuck to the ground as if they had been submerged in concrete. All Cam could do was pray things began to make sense because he was about to blow. Quickly, he called Quan.

"What's the word?" He answered on the first ring.

"Gun charge."

"Fuck. They got Priest too."

Cam dropped his head. That was the last thing he wanted to hear.

"You talk to Gray?" Quan questioned.

"Nah, I called her, and the line was disconnected. I was about to ask you if Kema spoke to her."

"She called her too and got the same thing. We went by the crib to make sure she was straight but she ain't answer the door. Her car was in the driveway though so Kema used her key to go inside. She was freaking out and shit, thinkin' something had happened to her, but when we got in . . . no one was there. All of her shit was there, but the majority of her and the girls' clothes were gone. The dogs were gone too."

All of Cam's suspicions were confirmed. Gray had betrayed him in the worst way possible. Cam morphed into one giant ball of fury. Without warning, his breathing turned from steady to a labored gasp. He sucked in air like it had abruptly become thick and too hard to lure in. Cam immediately became deaf to Quan calling out his name. His rage was irreparable. Using the receiver as a weapon, he smashed it into the payphone repeatedly, prompting the guards to tackle him to the ground. By the time they got him on the floor, the payphone was dangling from the wall. Cam roared like a lion as a heavy knee was placed into his back. Because of Gray, this was how his life would be. He'd be shackled and imprisoned away with no doors or windows. Every day would be hell. There was no place to run or hide. He'd be surrounded by guards and four white walls. Cam could already feel his lungs start to cave in.

He would hate Gray forever for this. Revenge ate away at his soul. It festered like a poisoned wound. Gray would pay for this. Her day was coming. An untimely death was in her future. Until he could get his hands on her, Cam would bear a grudge until the day of his release. As soon as those prison doors opened, there would be no mercy. He was going straight sicko mode.

And now…

1

"Leave one wolf alive and the sheep are never safe."- Arya Stark, "Game of Thrones"

1,186 days had passed since Cam last seen or heard from Gray. The divorce papers taped to the bottom of the bunkbed above him was the only way he knew she was alive. He'd received the papers a few weeks after being sentenced to three years in prison. After she'd disappeared in the wee hours of the morning, no one knew where she'd gone. Cam still didn't know. He'd tried getting information out of Kema, but she wasn't giving anything up. Gray was like her sister. She'd die before she snitched. Cam eventually gave up on trying to figure out her whereabouts. He'd see her eventually. The only thing that stood between them was time and steel bars.

Like every other day since he'd been imprisoned, he lay on his back, legs crossed at the ankle with his hands behind his head while staring at the papers. Every day he zeroed in and studied the document. Irreconcilable differences was the reason she cited for the divorce. The shit made Cam laugh. She knew it went far deeper than that. She'd betrayed him in the worst way possible and for that she'd pay dearly. Cam glared at the black words on the white sheet of paper. On days where he wanted to give up the divorce decree gave him a sense of purpose. It kept him going during the dark times in prison. It was a symbolism of the hate he harbored in his soul for Gray. For 1,186 days he'd been biding his time and waiting patiently till he saw her again. If she thought divorce would be the end of them she had another thing coming. He wasn't letting her off that easy. She had to pay for the hell she'd put him through. The betrayal she'd bestowed upon him was of biblical proportion. He'd never get over it. To toy with her mind, he refused to sign the papers. Not because he still loved her and wanted their marriage to work. He refused because divorce would be giving Gray what she wanted. It was an easy way out. If he had to live in hell so would she. He wasn't going to let her go on with life, living carefree after she'd set him up. If she was going to hold up his life, he for damn sure was going to return the favor. Every day he spent in the cold dank cell had been torturous. He'd barely survived the hellhole. Not having any doors, windows or a way out nearly killed him. He was a man that was used to coming and going as he pleased. He cherished his privacy. Not having it was something he'd barely gotten used to. Having to shower, sleep and eat with other niggas was not the move. Every minute of confinement tap danced on his nerves. In the beginning it felt like his lungs were going to cave in. There was no place for him to run or hide. No weed, liquor, pills or pussy to distract him from his demons. He was forced to deal with his PTSD and night terrors head on.

Cam's reputation for being a savage killa proceeded him when he entered prison. He had to live up to his name. He couldn't look weak. If word spread that he couldn't even sleep without waking in a panic he'd become prey, he'd be eaten alive, so Cam did what he had to do. He beat an inmate mercilessly with a tray and was involved in a race war that resulted in him stabbing a member of the Aryan Nation. The bad behavior got four months added to his sentence and him sent to solitary confinement which was his goal. He needed the alone time to get his disorder in check. At first it felt like he was losing his mind. Cam had never considered suicide until he was forced to face his demons head on. Visons of his mother and battle buddies faces haunted his sleep. Day after day he woke screaming in terror. Sweat covered him from head to toe. The sounds of their voices were so crisp and clear he swore they were there. Cam didn't know if he'd be able to make it. Dealing with his anxiety and Gray's betrayal was almost too much for him to handle. It was hard but with time, meditation, breathing exercises and not cowering to the horrific memories of his mother and battle buddies deaths, helped him cope. Not having his usual vices at his fingertips to distract him showed how dependent he'd become upon them. By the time he was released from the hole, Cam had learned how to sleep a few hours at a time without his mind running wild and him waking in panic. He still struggled but being clean of alcohol and weed gave him a better outlook on life. It, however, didn't numb his hatred for Gray. Every time he looked around at the beige chipped paint, blinking lights, stale disgusting food, racist guards and orange jumpsuits, he thought of her.

Cam never thought he would hate Gray. At one point she was his heart and soul. He would've moved heaven and earth for her. He thought the feeling was mutual. She'd claimed to love him and like a fool he took her word. Then within a blink of an eye everything changed, and their love turned to hate. She morphed from his lover to someone he no longer trusted or recognized. That night on the porch of their forever home, he'd decimated her with the cruel words he'd spewed but everything he said was justified. Whether Aoki called Gunz over or not, it still didn't take away the fact that he'd caught Gunz and Gray in a passionate kiss on their couch. His biggest fear from the beginning was that she still loved Gunz and would eventually go back. That night confirmed his suspicions had been right. Gray wasn't as over him as she claimed to be. Maybe it was his fault that she sought comfort from Gunz. Cam hadn't been a perfect husband. He'd tried and failed despite his numerous efforts at making her happy. But Cam would've rather she stabbed him in the heart than cheat on him with the same nigga that killed his best friend, shot his other pot'nah five times and attempted to take his life. And no, he hadn't been an angel. He'd cheated as well but for Cam he no longer gave a fuck about that. He couldn't. In his mind, Gray's betrayal was far worse. He'd gone to war with Gunz for her, had nearly lost his life because of it and this was how she thanked him? To make matters worse, all because of a misunderstanding with Aoki and because he didn't want Gray anymore, she got him locked up. Nah, the bitch had to die.

Quan and Kema tried to make him believe that she had nothing to do with him being locked up. Cam wasn't having it. The motive was there. He'd destroyed her and told her he wanted a divorce in front of her nemesis Devin. Hours later, the Feds swoop down on him. That wasn't a coincidence. All signs pointed to Gray. She was a liar and a manipulator. She played on people's emotions and used their weaknesses against them. On top of that, Cam still hadn't heard shit about her having a baby. The fact that she'd played on his past trauma for sympathy only made him loath her more. Any love he had for her died and was consumed with bitterness and hate.

Because of her, he was separated from his family and best friends. Because of her, he was locked behind bars in a lonely cell. Prison was a dark, unforgiving place. Men were imported and exported like cattle. The only thing that kept him sane was the fantasies he'd created in his mind of how he would seek revenge. Each one was more elaborate and gruesome than the last. But no matter how much he tried to escape through fantasies of killing her, it still didn't negate the fact that he was alone. He had no one but himself to keep him company. Sure, he received letters and made phone calls home, but at some point, prison breaks every man. The voices he'd quieted began to get louder, screaming for attention. He tried to ignore their cries, but the voices in his head returned, blurring his reality. Cam had to seek help. One of the OG's suggested he try prayer. He was a lifer who had found God through Allah. At first, Cam turned down the offer. He and God hadn't seen eye-to-eye since he was thirteen. Let Cam tell it, they were mortal enemies. God had taken away everything he'd ever loved. He couldn't trust that nigga no more than he could trust a crack head on the street but the demons in his head wouldn't go away. They started to take over his psyche, so he decided to make a truce with God and try things his way.

To his surprise, attending bible study and learning how to pray actually helped silence the negative thoughts in his mind. He found God to be a comfort. The relationship he forged with him helped heal all the old wounds from his past that kept him hindered as an adult. There wouldn't be a day where he didn't miss his mother, but Cam had to forgive his self for not telling her the truth about his father's infidelity. He finally realized that his father's sins weren't his. He was a child. He'd done nothing wrong. He also could no longer blame his self for his battle buddies passing. He'd done all he could do. It wasn't by mistake or punishment that he'd survived. His story wasn't done being told. There was still so much more that God wanted to do with him. Cam had no reason to be discouraged or dismayed. God was with him every step of the way.

After three years and four months in jail, Cam was a new man. He wasn't the same easily angered, impulsive, nutcase he was when he entered. He was more centered and levelheaded. Through prayer and exercise he found peace. His family, Quan especially, were so happy with the progress he'd made. Seeing how much he'd changed, Quan tried to get him to drop his vendetta against Gray but that was the one thing he couldn't do. The need for revenge was like a sewer rat gnawing at his guts. It was unyielding and never-ending. Killing Gray couldn't be stopped. Her betrayal was like a septic wound and the only effective antidote was hard cold revenge. Cam had a kill list and she was number one on it; Gunz number two. He wouldn't rest until both of them were six-feet deep.

"Parthens! Let's go! It's time for your release." The prison guard opened his cell.

Cam rose from the creaky bed and cracked his back. The muscles in his arms protruded like mountain peaks. He was overjoyed that he would no longer have to sleep on the flat, smelly mattress. The memory foam, king-size mattress and bed at his home was calling his name. Ripping the divorce papers from the bed, he placed them inside his pocket and stood up. His time in prison was over. He was finally going home. As his life hit the reset button, another life was about to come to an end. Death was a sin. Romans 12:19 said, "Beloved, never avenge yourselves, but leave it to the wrath of God, for it is written, Vengeance is mine, I will repay, says the Lord." Cam should sit back and let God hold true to his word, but he couldn't. He had to take matters into his own hands. Gray's time was up. Death was right around the corner and nothing or no one would be able to stop him or save her. As he walked out of his cell, Cam prayed that through prayer and repentance God would be able to forgive him. Prayerfully, God would have compassion and cast his sins into the depth of the sea. For Gray's last day on earth had finally come.

2

"I was born to flex. Diamonds on my neck. I like boardin'
jets. I like morning sex but nothing in this world I love
more than checks. "- Cardi B, "Money"

      With her game face on, Gray placed her delicate
hand inside the driver's open palm and stepped out of the
Rolls Royce Phantom into the warm July sun. Looking
around she took in her environment. Nothing had changed
but everything felt different. Maybe, it was her energy that
had shifted. It had been 3 years and four months since she
last stepped foot in St. Louis. She hadn't missed the god
forsaken city at all, only the people in it. The only family
she had was there. She truly missed seeing and spending
time with her three best friends but living in St. Louis was
no longer an option for her. After her and Cam's last
conversation, if you'd call it that, it was more of a
murdering of her soul, a stab wound to her integrity, and an
evisceration of her character. She was depleted mentally,
physically and emotionally. She was drained of every
feeling known to man. She'd been beaten down to nothing.
Gray felt like a walking corpse. After dealing with an
absentee father, a rapist best friend, the loss of her mother,
a devil of a fiancé and an emotionally immature husband,
she'd gone through everything a person could go through.
The only thing left was death. If she would've stayed in St.
Louis a day longer, she was sure to have slit her wrist
sideways. For the sake of her children she had to push the
demonic thoughts from her mind and figure out her next
best option. The only thing she could think of was to move.

She had to get out. She had to find a place where she could rebuild. Another place where she could be who she wanted to be. It needed to be a place where no one knew her face. New York and California were too close. Cam could find her there. No, it had to be further. After doing some quick thinking she decided that Paris, France would be the place she'd have her new beginning.

It was by far the best decision she'd made since leaving Gunz and Cam behind. Gray found her footing in Paris. She explored the city, ate the food, submersed herself in the culture, made new friends and lived her life to the fullest. In the beginning adjusting was tough, especially for Aoki. She didn't want to leave her father or friends behind. She hated her mother even more than she already did, but with persistence and therapy, she and Gray were able to repair their relationship. The dreaded conversation about her paternity was finally tackled. Gray explained her side of the story in full detail. She didn't leave one piece of the horrid incident out, no matter how uncomfortable it made her. She had to make sure Aoki understood why she'd kept who her father was a secret. All she wanted was for Aoki to be raised in a two-parent household. It was something she didn't have and desperately craved as a child. In doing that, she exposed her children to infidelity, mental and physical abuse. Taking responsibility for her part in the chaos her children were raised in, Gray profusely apologized for her lack of judgement. The last thing she ever wanted was for her kids to suffer, and in the end, Aoki had suffered the most. Her daughter was hurting deeply. Gray couldn't help but feel like it was all her fault. She felt like she'd failed as a mother. Plenty nights, she cried herself to sleep. Finding her worth as a woman and as a mother wasn't easy. Being in a new country alone with her children was scary as hell. Gray had always had her mom, Gunz, her friends and even Cam to fall back on. Now she was by herself. For the first time in her life, she had to be her own savoir. Finding the strength to be a single mom, running a household alone and navigating her career was strenuous. Gray often found herself wanting to throw in the towel but having her girls there to depend on her kept her moving forward.

There was plenty push back from Aoki, and even Press at times, but as the months passed their wounds began to heal. Gray never gave up on her daughters. Despite the anger and pain, she continued to pour love into them. She refused to have two broken girls searching for love in such a cruel world. Little girls yearning for love was a dangerous thing. It could lead to underage dating, promiscuity, teenage pregnancy, drug use and more.

Three years and four months later things were better than ever. Gray was killing it career wise and personally. Her girls were thriving in the city of lights. They'd learned to speak fluent French, was on the soccer team and discovered a genuine love for the arts. For the first time in years, Gray was genuinely happy. She'd never been more at peace with her life. She and her girls were closer than ever before. The bond she'd created with Aoki and Press was unbreakable. They were her best friends. They did everything together. Gray was on cloud 9. She'd never felt more confident or self-assured in her life. Nothing or no one could tear her down. Gray didn't take shit from anyone anymore. Disrespect was not tolerated. If something or someone brought negativity into her life, she immediately removed the source. If you came to her wrong you were getting checked off rip. No Chill was her new middle name. She was over people taking advantage of her and toying with her heart. She was that bitch. Fuck being humble. If no one else was going to amp her up, she was going to be her own cheering section. You couldn't tell Gray nothing. She was the shit and she knew it. The stares and cat calls she got as she sashayed slowly into the restaurant proved it.

Kema, Heidi and Tee-Tee's mouths dropped to the floor when they saw her. Gray's swag was on a hundred. They barely recognized her. Sis, exuded power. She was a brand-new bitch. The old Gray had a quiet beauty and elegance about her. The new and improved Gray dripped with cockiness and sass. There was no denying she was a boss bitch. The platinum blonde shag cut she rocked fit her heart shaped face perfectly. Rose gold, Oliver Peoples shades covered her ice blue eyes. $60,000 diamond drop earrings that she'd purchased herself dangled from each of her ears. On her curvaceous size 18 frame was a fire orange, spaghetti strap, latex Thierry Mugler dress that stopped at her knees. The skin-tight dress cupped her 32 D boobs and hugged her wide hips. Gray had body for days. She was every man's wet dream. Men all over the world fantasized about making her their girl. Every man in the restaurant, whether single or taken, couldn't take their eyes off of her. Nude Christian Louboutin 'So Kate' pumps and a camel colored Birkin bag completed her rich bitch attire. Gray looked like a bag of money. Her successful career as a plus-size model had paid off in dividends. She'd graced major magazine covers such as Vogue, Elle, Cosmopolitan and Glamour. She'd walked shows for Dolce and Gabbana, Christian Siriano, Michael Kors and Victoria's Secret. She'd done collaborations with brands such as Fashion Nova, Pretty Little Things and Forever 21. Her first makeup collaboration with Too Faced had launched earlier that year and sold out within thirty minutes. Gray was on top of the world. She was all about her coin. Her gross net went from 8 mill to 20. In the words of Lil' Duval she was living her best life. She prayed that coming home after three years wouldn't ruin the momentum and peace she'd gained.

"Give me body!" Tee-Tee snapped his fingers in the air. "Category is . . . faaaaaace, tittsssss and assssss."

Going into model mode, Gray did a fierce runway walk, pose and a twirl. From every angle she exuded sex appeal.

"Bitch! You look good girl!" Kema jumped out her seat to give her a hug.

"You too friend." Gray hugged her tight.

Tears stung her eyes. She never wanted to let go. Kema was more than her best friend, she was her sister. They had a closer bond than blood relatives. Kema knew all of her deep dark secrets. The same went for Heidi and Tee-Tee. Outside of her kids, they were the only real family she had. Living in Paris, she had no support. Phone calls home to them kept her afloat. They were her sounding board when she had moments of doubt and despair. Without them she would've lost it. After hugging each of her friends for what felt like an eternity they all sat down.

"We got you a X-Rated Martini." Heidi smiled, happy to see her friend.

For the past three years they'd only saw each other through Facetime.

"Ooh I missed these." Gray smacked her lips after taking a small sip. "Let's make a toast." She held up her glass. "To Kema, may your wedding week be everything you've ever dreamed of and more."

"Cheers!" They all clinked glasses.

Gray closed her eyes and took a long swig of her drink. The cold alcoholic beverage gave her the much-needed buzz she'd been dying for since she got off the plane. She tried to act like she wasn't worried but being back in St. Louis had her shook. All of the old demons she'd buried would soon bubble to the surface.

"What's been up wit' you?" Gray asked Heidi. "Every time I call you, you on the phone cakin' wit' your li'l boo."

"I think this might be the one ya'll."

"You say that about every nigga you meet." Tee-Tee rolled his eyes.

"I know but this one is different."

"You been fuckin' wit' this nigga for months and still ain't been to his house." Kema put her on blast.

"You always trying to make something out of nothing. I told you he said it was being renovated. He don't want me to see it until everything is finished."

"I don't know friend. That sound fishy to me." Gray argued.

"And the only time ya'll talk is when he calls you." Kema continued to spill the beans.

"I swear I ain't telling you shit else." Heidi threw the lime in her drink at her.

"He yo' man but you can't call him?" Gray quizzed.

"He works crazy hours." Heidi tried her best to explain.

"Nah, I'ma need to meet this nigga."

"I invited him to the bachelor, bachelorette party but while we're talking about niggas when yo' boo coming?"

Gray's face broke into a cheery smile.

"He'll be here later on this week."

"Oh, you really like him." Tee-Tee arched his brow. "Let me find out you finally bust it wide open."

"I did!" Gray bounced up and down.

"How was it?"

Gray threw her head back dramatically and sighed.

"Lets just say I went back for seconds and thirds."

"That's what I'm talkin' about!" Tee-Tee gave her a high-five.

"Bout time you gotta new man." Kema congratulated her friend.

"Right. That pussy was about to be on cardiac arrest." Tee-Tee joked.

"I had to make things right with my girls and focus on me before I brought a new man into my life."

"Which is admirable. You did the right thing, but that puss was starving honey." Kema pointed out.

"Enough about my vagina." Gray flicked her wrist. "Are you nervous?"

Kema crossed her leg and gave a thoughtful smile.

"Not really. Just excited. Me and Quan have been together for over four years. I've built a life with him and Li'l Quan. Like who would've ever thought my ghetto-ass would be somebody's mama. Like I love that li'l boy ya'll. You can't tell me he ain't my son. I can't wait to make this shit official so I can get pregnant and give him a li'l brother or sister. That's all we talk about."

"I know Quan can't wait to knock yo' ass up."

"Girl, he been tryin' for years, but I wasn't having that shit. I'll be damned if I was gon' be somebody baby mama. No disrespect Heidi and Gray."

"None taken." They both replied.

"I know that's right." Tee-Tee agreed. "Why buy the milk when you already got the goat."

"It's the cow jack-ass." Gray laughed.

"That nigga too."

"Like sometimes I have to pinch myself." Kema continued. "I can't believe I'm gonna be somebody's wife. Marriage was never important to me, but Quan changed all of that. As soon as that man laid eyes on me, he was determined to make me his forever."

"And yo' ass fought him tooth and nail." Heidi pointed out.

"I sure did. I wasn't looking for love. Even the thought of being someone's girlfriend gave me hives. Then Quan ole persistent ass fell out the sky and bogarted his way into my cold black heart. Who would've ever thought that I would be the one to tame him. Quan slang more dick than I gave up pussy. It astonishes me how much he's changed. Like he a whole new nigga. I'm so proud of him, ya'll. He's such a good man. He's always telling me how thankful he is to have me in his life and how much he loves me. I have never vibed with a man like I have with him. He gets me. He doesn't judge me or try to change me. He accepts me for who I am. That's how I knew he was the one. You know niggas stay trying to change and control a bitch. Quan ain't did none of that. Instead of trying to change me, he uplifted me and upgraded my life."

"Like a real nigga should." Tee-Tee nodded his head.

"I'm so happy for you friend." Gray smiled from ear to ear. "You deserve this moment in your life."

"Thank you. I really am happy."

"So, what you got planned for us this week 'cause I'm ready to turn up. Does anybody still say turn up?" Gray asked her friends.

"No." Tee-Tee shot her a deadpan expression.

"Well." Kema pulled out her bridal book.

It was as thick as an encyclopedia.

"First we have the barbeque, then we have the bridal shower, the coed bachelor/bachelorette party, the rehearsal dinner and then the wedding! I'm so excited ya'll. Gray, I can't wait for you to see my new dress."

"Wait a minute. I thought you were going with the Vera Wang ball gown."

"Nah, girl. I changed my mind last week."

"You are insane. Are the alterations gon' be done on time?"

"For the seamstress sake they better be. I would hate to have to bring the old Kema out."

"Old Kema?" Heidi pursed her lips. "Bitch you just cussed out a cashier at McDonald's yesterday cause there wasn't enough salt on your fries."

"And?" Kema rolled her neck. "You know black folks need they MSG."

"How are my god babies?" Gray laughed.

"Ooh chile. Gaga done got so big. She's starting to sprout titties. I had to buy her ass a training bra and everything." Tee-Tee showed her a recent pic of his daughter.

"How is Harlem, Heidi?"

"Grown as hell. You know he just got his license so that nigga feeling his self."

"Wow. We getting old."

"Speak for yourself. The Botox in my face says I'm twenty-one." Tee-Tee pursed his lips.

"More like sixty-one." Gray joked.

"Choke on a dildo." Tee-Tee threw up the middle finger.

"Ya'll, I'm so stressed out." Kema sighed heavily while rubbing her temples.

"I told you. We got you boo." Gray rubbed the back of her hand.

"I just want everything to be perfect. I have planned every detail of this week down to a T. I don't want nothing messing this up."

"Everything will be fine." Heidi assured.

"You sure 'cause if you know who gets out of jail this week, like he's supposed to, shit gon' go left real quick." Kema glanced over at Gray.

For a moment, everyone at the table got quiet. The elephant in the room had finally been addressed.

"You askin' me if I'm nervous and I should be askin' you that."

"Yeah friend. What you gon' do if he show up?" Tee-Tee asked concerned.

"You know she ain't gon' do nothin' but whine and throw up." Heidi added her two cents.

"First of all, fuck you and fuck you too. I ain't no punk no more. I been stopped throwin' up."

"The bitch might look different, but she still be lyin'." Tee-Tee cracked up.

"Whatever."

"Forget them. Straight up. What you gon' do?" Kema questioned.

Gray shrugged her shoulder. Talking about Cam was the last thing she wanted to do. He was not only a sore subject for her, but he also represented a dark space in her life that she never wanted to revisit. The night she told him she was pregnant would forever be a scar on her heart. She would've rather he sliced her pretty face than speak the hateful words he'd spoken to her. Cam spoke to her as if she were a stranger, when in reality they'd been closer than two people could possibly be. He drew a line in the sand that night. He was on one side and she the other. They were no longer husband and wife, friends and lovers. They were mortal enemies. Gray hoped time and prayer would heal her broken heart, but the crack was still there. No amount of daily affirmations, clothes, magazine covers, and laughter could heal the dull ache in her chest. It was constant. It followed her around like a lost puppy. Underneath the makeup, designer duds and smiles, the devastation he caused gnawed away at her soul.

"I mean what can I do? We're not together anymore. I sent him the divorce papers. He refused to sign them which I don't understand why. I know for some idiotic reason he thinks I snitched on him which is fuckin' stupid. But this is Cam we're talkin' about, so I don't expect much from him. He's an asshole that I want nothing to do with. If he is released this week, my main objective is to get him to sign these divorce papers so I can continue on with my life. That's all I want." Gray looked around the table.

The doubtful expressions on her friends faces said it all. A) she was delusional and B) she was fucked.

"I hear what you're saying, and I hope you get your wish friend, but we all know it ain't gon' be that simple. You and Cam got some unfinished business, sis, and I don't know how ya'll gon' make it through this. Hell, even Iyanla can't fix this shit." Kema gulped down the rest of her drink then signaled the waitress for another.

3

"The heart lies, and the head plays tricks with us, but the eyes see true."- George R.R. Martin, "The Game of Thrones"

It's only a week, Gray kept telling herself as she entered the Airbnb she'd be living in during her stay. *Just one week and I'm out of here.* She loved Kema dearly, but she couldn't wait to get back to Paris. St. Louis held way too many bad memories. Kicking off her heels, she flexed her foot and popped her toes. No matter how much she wore heels, strutting around in 5-inch stilettos never got easy. The latex dress she wore wasn't helping either. After a few hours she started to feel like she was suffocating. Being out in the sweltering heat with her friends all day had her feeling a hot sticky mess. A steaming hot shower was calling her name but first she had to take inventory of the place she'd be laying her head. Her assistant, Melody, was the one who'd booked the lavish mansion. Judging by the looks of things, she'd done a good job. From the marble foyer with its private elevator, to the unrivalled grand ballroom, to the library with a marble and glass fireplace, to the sumptuous 7-room master suite—every detail was considered in its conception. The second level of the home boast a sky-lit entertaining space and colossal outdoor oasis extending the full length of the building. The 4700+/-SF terrace, with its copper molding and painstakingly constructed parapet provided unmatched privacy. The third-floor observatory opened onto a 950SF terrace with spectacular panoramic views of the city. All the finest quality materials, smart home technology and luxury amenities were incorporated to create a regal lifestyle for the outstanding residence.

Gray loved every inch of the home and was sure the girls would too. After turning every light in the spacious mansion on, she headed upstairs to get cleaned up. Stripping down to nothing she stepped into the shower. Her toes flinched as they touched the cold marble floor. This was what she needed; a moment of peace and quiet to take a deep breath. Steam filled the bathroom as she let the hot water beat down onto her caramel skin. Gray closed her eyes as her mind faded into dullness and everything became a muddled illusion. The sensation of the steamy water calmed her achy bones. The thirteen-hour flight from Paris was no joke. She couldn't wait to cook dinner and go to bed. Standing underneath the showerhead her mind began to swirl with exhaustion. Just as she was about to dose off, she heard a creaking sound that startled her awake. On high alert, she stood still to see if she heard anything else. If someone had broken into the house, she had no way of fighting them off. She was in the shower soaking wet with no weapon. When she didn't hear anything else, she quickly rinsed the sudsy water off, powered down the shower and got out. Gray's heart was beating wildly. This was the reason she'd turned on every light in the house. She hated being in huge spaces alone. With a white body towel wrapped around her figure, she poked her head out the bathroom door to see if she saw anyone, but no one was there. Dizzy with fear she slowly tiptoed down the hall until she hit the top of the staircase. Looking over the banister, she gazed down onto the main floor. There wasn't a person or a shadow in sight. *Girl you trippin'. Ain't nobody in here. Calm down. You just don't like being back in St. Louis,* she tried to tell herself. Figuring it was all in her mind, she went into her bedroom where the maid service she'd hired had already stored her clothes. Taking her time, she lathered her body in Jo Malone body oil and slipped on a gray cardigan, white lace bralette, cut-off jogging shorts and socks that said *fuck you pay me* written on them.

The silence surrounding her caressed her skin like a cool summer breeze as she made her way to the first level of the home. It had been a fun day filled with laughter and catching up with her friends. Now all she needed was a cool glass of wine and soothing music to help her wind down. The haunting sound of Moses Sumney was her musical choice for the night. His rich, raspy voice filled the kitchen as she surveyed the rustic space. Dark wooden shelves with spice jars, pots, pans and cutlery filled the walls. Underneath the shelving was a long counter space with a farmhouse sink, stove, built-in microwave and dishwasher. In the center of the room was a gorgeous restored dining table with chairs on one side and a bench on the other. Gray wouldn't mind making meals for her family in the spectacular kitchen at all that week. The kids would be arriving in a few hours. She had to get dinner on the table quick, but she couldn't help but feel like someone was watching her. The hairs on the back of her neck were standing up. Goosebumps covered her arms. The pit of her stomach was in knots. Grabbing a butcher's knife, she cautiously stepped into the living area. Gray felt like she was in a real live horror film as she looked around. Once again, she saw no one but the feeling of having eyes on her was still there. Maybe someone was outside. The mansion was made of stone and floor-to-ceiling glass. Any random person from out on the street could see in. The sun hadn't all the way gone down so she peeked out the window to see if anyone was lurking about but nothing odd stuck out to her.

After double checking the locks, she relaxed her shoulders and headed back to the kitchen. *Everything is*

okay, Gray. It's all in your head. No one is out to get you,
she took a deep breath. She knew being back home would
be stressful, but she had no idea that her fears would weigh
on her this heavily. Slipping the butcher's knife back into
its holder, she opened the stainless-steel refrigerator door.
She was happy to find a fully stocked fridge. There was
chicken breast, steak, lamb chops, cod, shrimp and more to
chose from for protein. Bending down she checked the
vegetable tray and found tomatoes, onion, asparagus,
broccoli, squash and yams. It was a no brainer. She was
going to make seared lamb chops, asparagus and mashed
yams. Gray collected the vegetables and meat into her arms
and stood up. She wasn't in the upright position two
seconds before someone creeped up behind her and placed
a white cloth over her mouth. In the grip of silent panic, she
dropped the produce and kicked and screamed for her life.
Her eyes were wide with fear. Adrenaline flooded her
system. It felt like her heart was about to explode. She
knew she had heard someone in the house. Flapping her
arms wildly, she tried to fight back but the person's hold on
her was too strong. With each breath she took, the cloth
drenched in chloroform seeped into her lungs making her
drowsy. Gray's eyes started to flutter. The harder she
fought the sleepier she became. As she kicked, her legs
started to feel like jello. She was fading fast. This was
confirmation that coming back to St. Louis was a mistake.
She should've listened to her first mind and stayed in Paris.
Lord please don't let me die, she prayed as her body went
limp and everything around her faded to black.

———

Cam tried telling himself that Gray had made her
bed and now she had to lie in it, but the longer he stared at
her sleeping face, the more he started to doubt his self. She
sat before him, head rested to the side, sleeping peacefully.
She'd been knocked out for almost an hour. Any minute,

she'd awake and find herself tied to a chair. Cam had bound her hands and feet. There was no place for her to go but heaven. Gray had no idea that from the moment she stepped off the plane she was being watched. There wasn't a move she made that Cam didn't know about. She tried to keep her being back in town on the low, but Cam learned she was coming back through Priest. Kema told Quan when she'd be arriving, Quan told Priest and then he relayed the news to Cam. Little did Kema or Quan know but they'd unknowingly led Gray to slaughter. Neither of them even knew Cam was out of prison. No one knew except Priest. He was the one who had picked him up from jail. Under normal circumstances, Quan would've been the person he chose but Cam didn't feel like hearing him try to talk him out of killing Gray. She'd sealed her fate three years and four months ago.

At least, that's what he tried to tell his self. As he sat on the gray velvet couch smoking a blunt, staring at her angelic face, the malice he harbored slowly drained away. All the feelings he thought died while in prison rushed him like a tidal wave. A lovely sight sat before him in all her curvaceous glory. He never envisioned Gray with blonde hair, but the color fit her well. Now that he'd seen her with it, he couldn't see her without it. Soft blonde wet curls fell over her eyes and touched her long black lashes. Blemish free wheat colored skin covered her flawless face. The freckles he used to adore covered her nose and cheeks like brown snowflakes. She was fucking adorable. Even after years apart, she still was the most gorgeous woman that had ever graced the planet. Cam hated what she did to him. Only she made his heart skip a beat and his temperature boil. The lace midriff top she wore showed off her taut and toned stomach. From where Cam sat he saw no sign of her bearing another child. Her body looked better than it had three years ago, which made his anger arise. It reminded

40

him that she was nothing but a liar and manipulator. Gray couldn't be trusted. All of his suspicions were being verified. She wasn't even wearing her wedding rings. He didn't know why he expected her to have them on. She'd filed for divorce as soon as he was sentenced. She'd made it known that she wanted nothing to do with him. A part of him hoped that it was all a front and that she still loved him but the missing rings and covered tattoo on her ring finger showed any feelings she had for him were gone. Their wedding date had been replaced with hearts. He wondered was his name still tattooed on the face of her pussy. What was he thinking . . . of course, it wasn't. She'd erased every sign of him from her life. Any remorse he started to feel for killing her vanished. Fuck Gray. Cam didn't even know why he cared. It didn't matter if she still loved him or not. There were foes and this was war. She'd crossed the line. Cam wouldn't rest until dirt was being shoveled over her casket. Taking small draws from the blunt, he watched closely as her sapphire eyes slowly opened.

Gray could feel him before she saw him. At first, she didn't know who her attacker was, but the scent of Cam's Tom Ford Ombre Leather cologne revealed his identity. Over the past three years she had moments where she swore she smelled notes of violet leaf, jasmine sambac, black leather, cardamom, patchouli and white moss in the air. Whenever it happened, she'd search for him then she'd be reminded that he was locked in a cage a million miles away. This time she wasn't hallucinating. He was actually there. Gray strained her eyes to look at him, but her vision was extremely foggy. It felt like she had sand in her eyes. On top of that, her mouth was as dry as the Sahara desert and the pounding ache in her head needed extra strength pain medicine to heal.

"Bout time you woke yo' snake-ass up." Cam quipped.

Gray could feel his eyes bore into her. They were the same eyes she felt earlier.

"What?" She panted.

Gray felt like she'd been run over by a Mack truck.

"Shocked . . . confused?" He taunted. "That's the same way I felt when you had me locked up."

"What are you talkin' about?" She tried to sit up straight.

It was hard. Her arms and legs were heavy like sandbags.

"What the hell did you do to me?" She groaned as her vision started to clear.

Cam sat before her with his legs cocked wide open. His diamond shaped, coffee colored eyes were at half mast as he glared back at her. Gray's heartrate increased as she took him in. Even in the mist of confusion he was beautiful. The night she left their forever home was the last time she physically saw his face. Time in prison had changed him but not in a bad way. Prison had brought out the beast in him. Cam was a tall man. He stood at 6 feet 4 inches. Before serving time he had an athletic build but now his body was ripped with muscles. His arms were so big that they stuck out like wings. His broad chest reminded her of a block of concrete. She would bet money that the six pack of abs that once graced his stomach had now doubled to an 8 pack. Cam was cock diesel. She hated that the sight of him alone made her nipples hard. She hoped he couldn't tell but the cocky grin on his face showed he did. Gray rolled her eyes feeling ashamed. She had to remember that she hated him. Cam was the enemy; the man who'd stomped on her heart and left it bruised and battered on the floor. Fuck him and his thick brows, hypnotizing eyes with flecks of gold, freckles that mirrored hers, perfect lips for kissing, strong hands that used to knead her breasts and 11-inch crooked dick that rested against his solid thigh. She would not be a slave to his devilish good looks. The new Gray demanded more from a man than a gorgeous smile and a hard dick. As she rushed to get up, she realized her hands and feet were tied.

"What the fu— Have you lost your damn mind? Untie me now!" She rocked back-and- forth.

Cam ignored her demand and asked, "Where Aoki and Press?"

"Why? You gon' try to kidnap them too?"

"I see that mouth ain't changed. I'm not gon' ask you again. Where are they?"

"Somewhere safe away from your crazy ass." She spat.

Cam shot her a sinister grin and chuckled.

"Ain't nobody safe from me. You ain't even safe from me."

"Why are you doing this?"

"Don't act dumb, Gray. You had to know this day was coming."

"I knew you were getting out of jail, but I didn't think you would do this. I thought we would be able to sit down and have an adult conversation but obviously prison didn't help you mature not one bit." She shot with venom.

"Actually, it did. The old me would've been shot you in the head, but in order for me to start my new life, I need to get rid of some old baggage and tie up some loose ends."

It was then that Gray noticed the Glock resting on his lap. A crippling fear soared through her veins. She couldn't believe things between them had gotten so bad that he'd hold her captive and threaten her life. This wasn't the Cam who'd asked her to marry him. This man was the devil.

"So now I'm old baggage? You got to be fuckin' kidding me. Get the fuck out my house. You treat me like shit but somehow you're the victim? Typical Cam. Untie me before I slap the shit out of you."

Cam glared at her, took another slow pull from the blunt then exhaled the smoke into her face.

"I see you still got me fucked up."

Gray turned her head to the side and coughed profusely. Once she got her breath back she said, "And I see you're still stupid as hell." She snarled, pissed. "Despite what you think, I didn't have anything to do with you getting locked up."

"Yo' ass stay lyin'. Who else did it, Gray? If it wasn't you who was it? Press . . . Kilo . . . Gram. Where the fuck my dogs at anyway? You fuckin' thief! You just like your damn thieving-ass daughter."

"They're in Paris and after everything we've been through you really think this little of me? That's fucked up, Cam. It really goes to show that you never loved me. You couldn't have 'cause this shit right here ain't love. This is toxic. This is sick."

"Exactly. I don't love you." He tried to convince his self. "Just like you don't love me. If you did, you wouldn't have turned me over to the FEDS. I never took you for the vindictive type. But I guess you never know about a muthafucka until you hurt they feelings. That shit still fuck me up that you would get in your feelings 'cause I said I didn't want you or that fake-ass baby you lied and said you was carrying. Then you gon' go snitch?"

"On my mama and on my kids, I did not—"

"SHUT THE FUCK UP!" Cam charged forward and got in her face. "Lying-ass bitch! You can't bullshit a bullshitter. I know you did it! You the only person that had motive!"

"Oh, I'm certain that's not true. It's plenty muthafuckas out here that hate you more than I do."

"Now we getting somewhere." Cam egged her on. "You admit it. You hate me?"

"With every fiber of my fuckin' being." She lied. "I hate you. You ruined my life. You broke things in me I'll never be able to fix again."

"Feelings fuckin' mutual."

Tears stung the brim of Gray's eyes. She tried her best not to let a tear fall but the stab wound to her heart wouldn't let her. All the strength she'd gained over the last three years went out the window as tears dripped down her flushed cheeks. Gray felt stupid as fuck for crying over him. He didn't deserve her tears but hearing him say he hated her with a gun pointed at her face made the words all too real. Cam could see the look of hurt in her ocean blue orbs but pretended like the evidence wasn't there. If he did, he wouldn't be able to go through with killing her.

"You got a lot of fuckin' nerves. You really gon' sit up here and cry like I ain't catch you kissing that nigga. You was damn near fuckin' him on the couch, but let you tell it, you hated him right? You hated him so much, but you couldn't even tell us apart."

45

"I told you I was drunk!" Gray's entire body trembled.

"Drunk my ass! I got into a war with that nigga for you! I stepped in and played daddy to your fuckin' kids 'cause yo' weak-ass baby daddy would rather play war games wit' me than be a daddy to them! I gave up the game for you! I gave up millions to make yo' ungrateful-ass happy. My best friend got killed cause of you! Stacy almost died cause of yo' lyin' ass! I went to jail for over three fuckin' years 'cause of you bitch! And you had the nerve to kiss that nigga in the place I lay my head at?" Cam eyed her with disgust.

All the hate he'd bottled came spilling out like vomit. It was as if a demonic figure had taken over his body. Sweat poured from his flesh. He couldn't contain his anger. The woman before him was no longer the girl he promised to love and protect. She was the op. Cam could barely stand looking at her tear-stained face. He hadn't felt this kind of rage since the club shooting, but this was worse. He'd actually loved Gray, so her betrayal was far worse than any other he'd ever experienced. She took what was left of his soul the day he caught her with Gunz.

"You wanna talk about hurt? Bitch, you destroyed me! I gave my all to you. I would have done anything for you! I practically gave up my whole entire life for you! I would've died for you! Shit, I almost did! And while I sat in jail, you was out here tryin' to be a fake-ass Tyra Banks. You ain't even send me a letter or put money on my books but you could send me some punk-ass divorce papers?" His bottom lip quaked.

With his watery eyes narrowed to slits, Cam jumped up and paced the floor in front of Gray. His fist was so tight that he could feel his nails cutting his skin. The Glock in his other hand was being tapped against his leg as he thought back on everything she'd done. Sweat rained down his tight face and spit sprayed from his mouth as he continued.

"I wasn't even in that bitch a week before you filed for divorce!" He halted his steps and pounded his chest with his fist. "You couldn't wait. You left me for dead like I ain't mean shit to you. Like I ain't love you and try to take care of you. You worse than LaLa. Least that bitch was loyal! You turned your back on me as soon as shit didn't go your fuckin' way. As soon as you saw that I wasn't fuckin' wit' you no more, you gon' go and drop a dime on me."

Gray's throat ached as she listened to him. Her mouth was dry, and in this tragic moment, she was reluctant to say anything. The only thing she could say to calm him was, "Cam—"

He slammed the Glock against his leg and barked at her through gritted teeth. "Shut the fuck up, bitch! I don't want to hear shit you got to say."

Cam's chest heaved in and out. Sweat dripped down his spine. Every inch of him trembled with hate. Every time he looked at Gray or heard the sound of her voice he got angrier. Cam could literally feel the devil on his shoulder as his index finger curled around the trigger. That quick, he'd gone from a child of God to a demon. All those days of listening to and studying the word were pushed to the back of his subconscious. Cam had gave into the devil's demonic ways. The temptation to end Gray's life with one single bullet to the brain could no longer be ignored. He hated her. Who cared if she had kids that would miss her or that God would send him straight to hell. With all the dirt he'd done, he was going there anyway.

47

Furious, Cam quickly smacked away a lone tear that had slipped from his eye. This moment pained him more than Gray would ever know. There were still so many unanswered questions, and he needed answers from Gray now. "Where the fuck the baby at, Gray? I ain't seen or heard shit about no fuckin' baby. Lyin' ass bitch! You was that desperate to get me back that you gon' lie about being pregnant?"

Cam wanted to hide his emotions, so he spun around to avoid eye contact with Gray. His hands were placed behind his head; thoughts were running a mile a minute. He blinked his eyes to clear them, but the sound of Gray's voice again caused more rage and fury to set in.

"Can you stop yellin', listen and let me explain?" She said cautiously.

He swung around with the look of pure evil washed over his face. Thick, sweaty wrinkles lined his forehead and a dagger from his eye sliced Gray's broken heart as he spoke.

"Listen to your lies about the baby? Or do you want to *explain* that you a grimy-ass bitch! *Explain* how you ruined my fuckin' life? *Explain* that you took away three-and-a-half years of my life away. I can't ever get that shit back. You know how many nights I wished that I could go back and unmarry yo' trifling ass? I should've never gave you my fuckin' last name. I should've nutted in yo' mouth, let that shit drip and walk away. But it's all good. Lesson learned. After today, I'm puttin' all this shit behind me. I ain't gon' never have to deal wit' yo' ass again."

Cam was gone. His eyes twitched as he slowly lifted the gun in his trembling hand and pressed it against the center of Gray's forehead. She shut her fluttering eyes, but quickly opened them to stare down the man who once

48

claimed to love her so much, but would soon be classified as her killer. Their eyes connected without a single blink. Pure silence fell over the room, and from Cam's position, nothing else needed to be said. His moment had arrived. Nothing would satisfy him more than to see the bitch who had abandoned him and snitched on him brains splattered all over the place.

"Do it," Gray said to his surprise. Tears streamed down her face; her body shook uncontrollably. "Stop wasting my fuckin' time and kill me nigga! If this is what you've waited years to do, don't stand there like a fuckin' bitch! Do it and get this shit over with!"

The old Gray would've coward at his brazen attempt to end her life, but the new Gray wasn't backing down from no man. If Cam wanted to kill her then so fuckin' be it. She'd go out with her head held high knowing she'd stayed true to herself.

Cam always knew Gray had guts. Her braveness caused a smirk to form on his face. He toyed with the trigger, before pressing the gun harder against her head. Gray clenched her jaw thinking if she could, she'd claw his fucking eyes out.

"Bitch, you think this a game? Now ain't the time to talk shit! You need to be begging for yo' fuckin' life. Not that it matters, 'cause I'm still—"

"Then do it!" Gray cried out so loud that it pierced Cam's ears. "And after you shoot me, you sick bastard, be sure to shoot your fuckin' self too. How about we both die and resume this fucked up union in heaven? Maybe we'll have better luck there, 'cause we damn sure couldn't get it right here. Notice I said *we*. I fucked up too, and breaking news nigga, so did you! Regardless, I never would've snitched on you. Never, and for you to even think I would prove how sick yo' ass is."

Gray's feisty words caused Cam to straighten his spine and inch back. He cocked his neck from side-to-side while holding the gun steady.

"Sick? You got the nerve to call me sick, but you the one who let that nigga Gunz cheat on you, have a baby on you, beat yo' ass, treat you like shit and—"

"You're right. I did let him get away with hella shit and maybe you can call me sick too. But we . . ."

Cam tuned her out. He was agitated. He wasn't there to reconcile with Gray or listen to her confession. She had said too much, and he could hear the devil telling him to man up and silence her now.

"Don't be a fuckin' pussy." The devil said. "You know she did it. Kill her. It's the only way you'll feel better."

Cam inhaled deep. It wasn't that hard of a task. He'd murdered plenty of people before. Gray should be no different than anyone else he'd killed but she was. This was his baby. This was his Star. This was the woman whose freckles he used to count for fun, the woman who he used to rush to get home to, the woman that made him fall in love with her two kids, the woman who gave him a family that was all his. All he had to do was apply a little more pressure to the trigger and she'd be gone.

"I can see it in your eyes," Gray said with gobs of snot seeping from her red nose. Deep inside, she feared for her fucking life, but she refused to let Cam see it. "You're almost there, *Boo*. I know how proud of yourself you'll be, after this is done."

Cam had heard enough. His face was twisted as he shoved the gun in Gray's mouth to silence her.

"I said shut the fuck up!"

Gray looked at him with wide eyes. Cam positioned the gun sideways in her mouth and searched into her beautiful eyes with a heavy heart.

"Will you listen to yo bitch, nigga?" Satan yelled. "She said kill her. Get rid of her. We've been waiting too long for this. She took away three years and four months of your life. She deserves to die. She hurt you remember. Kill her!"

Another lone tear slipped from the corner of Cam's eye. Despite his anger, a deep-rooted love for Gray was tattooed on his heart. It would make killing her far worse, but it had to be done. By street code alone she had to die. If so, why couldn't he pull the trigger? Gray had invited him to do it, but another voice whispered in his right ear and captured his attention.

"The enemy is tryin' to kill you but I'm here to talk to your belly. I'ma talk to your insides, Cam. I'ma reach way down and communicate with you on another level. 'Cause the frequency you're on won't allow you to hear me any other way. All you hear is the enemy saying kill her. So now I have to bypass your understanding and talk to your spirit. I will not let the devil do what he's trying to do to you in this situation. You . . . will . . . not . . . lose your mind! You . . . will . . . not!"

Emotional pain flowed from every crevice of Cam's body. A battle of spiritual warfare was being waged on his soul and it was making him sick. His temperature had rose to 106 degrees. He'd begun to feel dizzy. *What the fuck is happening to me?*

"I'm guarding your head. The devil is trying to drive you crazy, but I will not let him win. I have let the devil feed on you long enough. You are my child. You were created from the dust of the earth, but you can't make anything out of dust. You need water. Water and dust make clay. I'm the potter, you're the clay. When you choose to worship me, you have a will. Which means if there are areas of your life you don't want me in, those areas lack water and therefore are dusty. So, I gave the enemy the legal right to feed on anything that isn't submitted from the water of the word. So, don't get mad and upset with Gray. She is not your enemy. If you wanna know where this hate comes from, check your will. The hurt inside of you is what's stopping you from healing."

Cam pondered God's words and wondered were they true. He'd been so busy blaming Gray for everything that he'd neglected to acknowledge the broken areas of his life he'd suppressed.

"Don't listen to this fool. If God was gon' heal you, he would've done it by now. Just kill her, Cam. I'm your salvation. He's a hypocrite. He's a liar and a fake. Where was God when she ruined your life? Where was God when Stacy got shot up? Where was God when Diggy got killed? Where was he all those lonely nights in jail? Where was God when your mother died in that plane crash? You can't believe shit he say. Choose me. I ain't never steered you wrong. I was always there for you. Kill her, Cam. Kill her." Satan hissed in his ear.

This was the moment of the truth. Cam could either forsake the relationship he'd built with God while in jail, cleave to the devil or choose God as his savior. All his life he'd chosen to be bad. Being bad came easy, especially when he felt there was no good in the world. But Cam no longer wanted to live a life filled with hate. It felt better to love and be loved. The love he and Gray once shared was pure. The love he felt when he prayed to God and he answered couldn't be replaced. It couldn't be defined. It was unchanging, unwavering, all-knowing. If he truly wanted to change his life, he couldn't seek revenge.

"Vengeance is mine." God spoke sternly.

A flood of tears clouded Cam's vision. He felt defeated, yet relieved. Killing Gray would be the easy way out. Forgiveness would be harder. Walking away knowing she'd fucked him over and still was able to walk this earth would torture his soul. It would make him feel like a bitch, but it was the right thing to do. He eased the gun from Gray's mouth and dropped to his knees beside her. His arms were wrapped over his head, and while shielding his face he released thunderous cries that echoed throughout the room. He rocked back-and-forth on his knees as he felt God covering him. The cries he'd held in since his mother's death came pouring out. Releasing all that he'd felt inside, he pounded the floor with his fist and cried for what seemed like an eternity. Gray had never seen Cam like this. He was in pure agony. A part of Gray wanted to comfort him, but she needed comfort too. They both wailed until nothing but emptiness and sorrow remained. In the midst of Cam's awakening and Gray's second chance at life, he crawled closer to the chair she sat in and untied her. As soon as he freed her, he heard the front door unlock. He rushed to his feet, and with fiery, red eyes he aimed his gun at the door. Gray had arrived in St. Louis alone so no one should be entering the home. His breath hitched when in walked Aoki, Press, some young chick, and three toddlers that looked just like him. Cam stood in awe. His mouth was wide open, and a loud thud occurred when the gun slipped from his hand and hit the floor.

4

"Some old wounds never truly heal, and bleed again at the slightest word."- George R.R. Martin, "The Game of Thrones"

"Papa!" Press ran towards Cam at lightning speed.

"Cam!" Aoki followed her sister's lead.

Shocked to see not one or two but five kids enter the home, Cam frantically picked up the gun and tucked it under the couch cushion. He pulled the girls into his arms. A whirlwind of emotions swarmed him as he hugged them. Tears streamed from his eyes. If he would've given into the devil and killed Gray, the girls would've walked in and found her dead body. Cam would've never forgiven himself. The guilt would've been so heavy he would've, without a doubt, turned the gun on himself.

"I'm sorry, God. I'm so sorry." He cried as he held the girls tight.

This was the meaning of happiness. Happiness couldn't exist around negative emotions. Anything done for pure and positive motivation will fill you with happiness and begin healing. Having Press and Aoki back in his life would motivate Cam to lead with love and not hate. They always brought out the best parts of him.

"We missed you." Both girls wept.

"I missed you too." Cam ran his hands through their hair then kissed their foreheads.

Extending his arms, he held them at arm's length so he could look at their faces. Aoki and Press had gotten so big. They were no longer the little girls he met almost four years before. Aoki was thirteen now. She'd grown at least three inches. She was tall as hell. Her big blue eyes no longer held sadness. They were bright and expressive. Long, full curly hair reached the middle of her back, and Cam would be damned if she didn't have titties. He didn't know how he was going to be able to handle a teenage Aoki. She was already a handful at the age of ten. She was sure to give him hell now. Cam looked over at Press. The sight of her face made his heart smile. While in prison he tried not to think much about her. He couldn't take the pain of knowing he wasn't going to see her. Seeing her there live in the flesh showed him just how much he'd actually missed her. The little precocious six-year-old he'd left behind was now nine. Like her big sister, she'd grown too. Her once long hair had been cut above her shoulders. The new cut looked cute on her. Press could rock any hairstyle tho. She was that beautiful. She and Aoki had blossomed into gorgeous young ladies. While away, Cam had always wondered how they felt about him. He and Gray ended things on such bad terms, but despite their beef, he held true to his word and tried to be there for the girls as best as he could. There wasn't a birthday, Valentine's Day or Christmas that went by where he didn't have gifts sent through Kema from him. Judging by their reaction to seeing him, and the fact that they still wore the Tiffany necklaces he'd bought them years ago, the girls hadn't thrown his love away like he'd done their mother's.

"When did you get home?" Press rubbed his face.

"Today." Cam hugged her again.

"Ughn. You ain't been home five minutes and you and mama already on some freaky shit." Aoki looked at the ropes on the floor, next to where Gray stood in silence. "Get a room. Ya'll can play cops and robbers later."

Thinking about what had just happened, the blood in Cam's face drained away. If the girls knew the truth about why he was really there, they'd hate him forever.

"Ms. Rose, are you okay?" Gray's assistant asked cautiously.

As soon as Gray gave her the go ahead, she was calling the police. There was no denying that something sinister had taken place. The energy in the house was all off. Gray's face was covered in tears. Snot dripped from her nose. The man who she assumed was the kids' father was dressed in an all-black Champion jogging suit like a killer. Plus, she couldn't ignore the gun she'd seen him put underneath the couch.

"I'm fine," Gray lied as she attempted to gather herself.

She wiped her tear-stained face and straightened her clothes. Melody knew Gray was lying. Fear was etched on her face. Gray's entire body was trembling. Melody didn't know what was going on, but she knew that it was bad.

"Are you sure you're okay?" She spoke in a low tone so only Gray could hear. "Are we safe?"

Gray displayed a fake smile as the triplets stood close to her.

"We're fine. We were just having a little miscommunication."

"I got 911 on speed dial. Just blink twice if you need me to make that call."

"You ain't gotta whisper," Cam quipped. He kept examining the triplets while trying to make Melody believe everything was fine as Gray had suggested. "Gray good, but if she was in trouble, she would be dead fuckin' around wit' yo' non-whispering ass."

"Yeah, sis. You gotta work on that 'cause I heard you having phone sex with that one man the other night." Aoki added.

"You got muthafuckas having phone sex around my kids?" Cam scowled at Gray.

"Your kids?" She exclaimed.

"Yeah nigga, my kids." His eyes shifted to the triplets again then back at Gray. "My kids. I ain't Rueben Studdard."

Rising to his feet, he made his way over to the triplets. With each step Cam took, it felt like his heart was damn near about to explode out of his chest. *I got fuckin' kids,* he thought as he stooped down and looked at their faces. No DNA test was necessary. These kids were his. Around each of their necks were a gold chain with one of Gray's wedding rings attached. Cam swallowed the tennis ball size lump in his throat. Here he was thinking she'd discarded the rings when really she'd given them to their children. At a loss for words, he examined every feature on their tiny bodies. They all had two eyes, ten fingers and he prayed ten toes. They were as close to perfect as three children could be. Cam was truly stunned. It was like three mystical creatures stood before him. Having children was something he'd always dreamed of. Unbeknownst to him, he had three and didn't even know that they existed. Once again, Gray had fucked him over in the worst way. Maybe he should've killed her after all.

57

"What's your name?" He asked the little girl standing to the left of him.

"Sky." She shyly twisted from side-to-side.

Tears stung the brim of Cam's eyes. Sky was an exact replica of her mother and Aoki. She had jet black curly hair, tan skin, slanted blue eyes, high cheekbones and heart shaped lips. She might've looked like Gray and Aoki, but her personality was soft and subdued like Press. There was a gentleness to Sky that he immediately connected to.

"Why you not ask me my name, daddy?" The energetic little girl next to Sky spoke up.

Cam almost stopped breathing. Hearing her call him daddy was the last thing he expected. He wondered how she knew who he was.

"My bad doll face." He sniffled. "What's your name?"

"Guess what, daddy?" She jumped up and down, ignoring his question. "We rode on a big spaceshift in the sky. I got to see all da clouds."

Cam chuckled. This little girl was gon' be a problem. Unlike Sky, her sister was spunky. Her black hair was pulled away from her face in two French braids. She had perfectly arched brows, mischievous brown eyes and a wicked grin like her father. Her Korean features weren't as prominent as Sky's, but you could still tell they were sisters.

"I think you mean spaceship." He corrected her.

"I know what I said, daddy. It's a spaceshift. Mama, tell daddy it's a spaceshift."

58

"Your daddy's right, Bee. It's a spaceship." Gray replied, feeling groggy as hell.

"Your name is Bee?" Cam toyed with one of her braids.

"No silly butt. It's Beaux like what Santa puts on da presents. His name Reign." She pointed to her brother.

"Shut up stupid! I can say it myself!" Reign balled up his face.

He hated when his sister spoke for him. Being the only boy in the family, he sometimes felt gained up on by his sisters.

"Oooooooh, mama, Reign said shut up." Beaux snitched on her brother.

"It's be quiet, Reigny, remember?" Gray rubbed her skin.

Rope burns were all over her wrists. She'd need ointment to deal with the sting. Cam examined his son. Reign was the perfect mixture of him and Gray. Like his sisters, he had curly hair but his was cut into a neat box. Angry brows hovered over a set of doe shaped blue eyes. A galaxy of freckles decorated his button nose. Like Cam, he had pink juicy lips and a scowl so mean he'd scare any kid on the playground.

"You know that I'm your daddy?" He looked at Reign.

"Yes." He answered while nodding his head at the same time. "Mommy tells us stories about you all da time."

A new set of tears dripped down Cam's face. This was too much for a man fresh out of jail to handle. He was experiencing sensory overload. For three years and four months he'd thought Gray lied about being pregnant. He'd read numerous articles about her and not once had she mentioned having triplets. The whole thing was confusing as hell. Then suddenly, something dawned on him.

"Hold up." He stood up straight and looked at her. "You named our kids Reign, Beaux, Sky?"

"Sure did. You got a problem with that?" She quipped with an attitude.

Cam actually didn't have a problem with it. He kinda thought it was dope. The names fit the triplets perfectly. Shell shocked, he took in all five of his kids. He didn't deserve the blessing God had bestowed upon him. For three years his heart was on E. Now it was filled to capacity. No matter how happy he was, it didn't take away the fact that Gray had kept him away from his kids. Because of her, he'd missed out on their first word, the first time they crawled, their first birthday. It quickly dawned on Cam that he didn't even know how old the triplets were.

"You had fuckin' triplets and wasn't gon' tell me?" The anger he stifled erupted all over again.

"Who wants ice cream?" Gray ignored Cam's outburst.

"You know I do girlfriend." Beaux tooted her little lips.

"Melody, will you take the kids for ice cream, please?"

"Yes ma'am."

"Ooh, mama, can I get chocolate with sprinkles on top?" Sky asked.

"You sure can, my love." Gray brushed her hair back.

"Yay!"

"Do I have to go?" Aoki asked her mother. "I wanna stay and chop it up with the big homey."

"You'll get to talk to Cam soon, I promise. Just do me a favor and keep an eye on your brother and sisters."

"Don't I always?"

"You sure do, and I love you for it. You're such a blessing to me." Gray kissed her cheek.

Cam watched as Aoki fell into her mother's embrace. The resistance and anger that was once there was no more. Any anger and animosity she used to harbor towards Gray was gone. The two seemed like they were closer than ever.

"Love you too mommy." She wrapped her arms around her mother's waist.

"Papa, will you be here when it's time for me to go to bed?" Press asked on the verge of tears.

The last thing she wanted to do was get ice cream. She wanted to spend every waking moment with Cam. She'd missed him something terrible while he was in jail. She couldn't risk leaving and him disappearing again.

"There isn't any other place I'd rather be." He pinched her cheek.

"Cam won't be staying tonight baby girl, but you'll see him soon okay?" Gray assured.

"Fuck what yo' mama talkin' about. I'll be here to put you to bed." Cam shot Gray a look of pure disdain.

61

"You heard what the fuck I said. No, you won't." She spat back.

"Who the fuck you talkin' to?" Cam inched closer to her.

"I'm talkin' to you!" She stood firm.

"Umm, c'mon kids. Mommy and daddy need to talk." Melody rushed the kids out the door.

"Mama, you straight?" Aoki asked TTG.

She was always trained to go. She loved Cam but nobody was going to disrespect her mother.

"I'm fine baby. I swear." Gray guaranteed.

"A'ight and no more of that Fifty Shades of Grey nonsense. It's nasty." Aoki shot them one last look before walking out.

"Bye Papa." Press waved her hand.

"I'll be right here when you get back, pretty girl."

"I swear this nigga hard headed." Gray mumbled under her breath.

Once the door was closed and the car had backed out of the driveway, Cam turned around and wasted no time going in on her.

"Three kids! Three fuckin' kids, Gray! You trifling as fuck, dawg. You hate me that much that you was gon' keep three fuckin' kids away from me?"

Gray stood silent and glared at him with contempt. The thin line between love and hate had been broached. Soon, she would loath his mere existence.

62

"Three kids, Gray? Not one but three! When was you gon' tell me or were you not gon' tell me at all?"

"For your information, I was gon' tell you as soon as you were released but let's be clear nigga. I don't owe you shit!"

Cam stormed over and got in her face. He was so tall that he towered over her 5'7 frame.

"Fuck you mean you don't owe me shit! You lost your fuckin' mind? Them my fuckin' kids too! You selfish as fuck! I done missed my kids being born, crawling, their first words, their first steps cause you wanna be fuckin' spiteful! I don't even know how old they are! I don't know shit! You know how fucked up that is? You was that mad cause I didn't want your lyin', sleazy-ass that you was gon' keep my kids away from me? That's why I don't fuck wit' you now. Now I wish I would've shot yo' ass!"

For a second there was nothing but silence. If hatred was visible, the air would have been scarlet red.

"You fuckin' bitch!" Gray balled her fist and punched him in the face with all her might.

The blow almost knocked Cam off his feet. Enraged with hate she kept swinging, connecting hit after hit to his face. Gray rained down blows as if she meant to smash his face into the earth. She was over being misused and disrespected by the men in her life. There would be no more of that. Cam was going to learn to respect her one way or another. She didn't care if he was a man that could physically decimate her. He'd pulled a gun on her with the intent to pull the trigger, which was a big mistake. Cam should've killed her when he had the chance 'cause now she was going to do everything in her power to end his life. Not wanting to hit her back, Cam tried to block her swings, but Gray was so charged up that she landed a hard jab to

63

his throat. Winded by the punch, he grabbed his neck, giving Gray the opportunity to knock him in the eye. Gray was ten times smaller than him but packed a powerful punch. Cam was almost sure she'd given him a black eye. Tired of her beating his ass, he forcefully took her into his arms and slammed her down onto the couch. Gray's head bounced off the couch cushion.

"Calm yo' dumb-ass down!" He growled violently.

"Fuck you!" She harked up a glob of spit and spat in his face.

A string of saliva slid down his nose. Cam closed his eyes and tried to compose his anger. He could literally see himself choking Gray until her eyes rolled to the back of her head. Getting spit on was the ultimate sign of disrespect. Niggas had died for less than that. Getting spit on by Gray made it ten times worse. Letting her go, Cam got up before he hurt her. At this point, things between him and Gray would never be fixed. Their relationship was irreparable.

"You betta be glad dawg." He shook his head as he wiped his face with his shirt.

"I better be glad what?" Gray shot up, still wanting to fight.

She'd been waiting for this moment for over three years.

"You gon' cuss me out some more? You gon' put another gun in my mouth? Of course I kept my fuckin' kids away from you. You're a fuckin' monster! All you care about is yourself!"

"That's not true and you know it!" He barked.

64

"Oh, it's not?" Gray drew her neck back. "Get a fuckin' abortion. Fall down the steps, put a hanger up your coochie. Remember that?"

Not a day went by where Gray didn't recall that conversation in her head. Cam's brain stuttered for a minute. He'd completely forgotten about all the cruel things he'd said to Gray that fateful night she'd told him she was pregnant.

"Oh no! Don't get quiet now! Keep that same energy muthafucka! I was lyin' remember? I was desperate? If it wasn't your baby it was Gunz! According to you, I was probably fuckin' him the whole time! You dirty, lousy, trifling bitch! Fuck you! Them my fuckin' kids! I was the one on bedrest for five fuckin' months wit' high blood pressure while you was in jail lickin' ass!"

"Aye hold up." Cam looked at her like she was crazy.

"No, you hold up!" Gray pointed her finger in his face. "I almost died giving birth to your children! I was the one pregnant with quads, had a C-section and only heard three of my babies cry!"

"What?" Cam's heart stopped.

"Yeah, bitch, we had four kids not three. Our third baby girl was stillborn, but you didn't know that 'cause you called me a liar. I was the one that buried her alone. I was the one that had to explain to Aoki and Press why their little sister wasn't here anymore. I was the one that was in the NICU day after day praying that my other three babies didn't die. I was the one that had to take care of three newborns that had Respiratory Distress Syndrome! Do you know what it's like to see your baby in a fuckin' incubator with tubes all down their throat 'cause they can't breathe? No, you don't!" A tsunami of tears swarmed her eyes.

"I was alone! I didn't have you. I didn't have my mother. I didn't have my friends. All I had was my muthafuckin' self so don't say shit to me about them being yo' kids. I don't want shit to do wit' you and neither do they! You gon' blow my damn brains out and take me away from my kids that I raised by myself for damn near three years while yo' faggot ass was droppin the soap on purpose and letting niggas nut on your freckles! You fuckin' pussy!" She pushed Cam hard in the chest.

Fury raced through her veins at lightening speed. Blacking his eye and spitting in his face wasn't good enough. She needed to cause him pain. She needed him to experience the same pain he'd caused her three years ago.

"And just so you know, don't nobody want you. I was done wit' your bitch-ass the night I showed up on your fuckin' doorstep! You ain't no fuckin' prize. You tall lanky bitch! Yo' scary-ass can't even sleep at night. Talkin' about I ruined your fuckin' life. Nigga, you ruined mine! That pregnancy was the worst nine months of my life!"

Cam didn't know what to say or do. Gray was hitting him with a barrage of shit he had no idea about. His head developed a cramp from all the information. More importantly, his heart was placed in a chokehold. For the first time since everything had gone down, he got out of his own feelings and saw things from her perspective. Cam had done a number on Gray. It wasn't until he'd pushed her to the edge that he saw just how bad he'd fucked her over. Seeing how much she hated him made his soul cry.

"And let's not forget nigga you was the one who cheated on me!"

Shocked by her confession, Cam's eyes grew wide. He thought he'd take fuckin' LaLa to the grave.

"Yeah, I know *allllllllllll* about you fuckin' that skanky, slutty, big forehead having, shitty mole above her hairy ass lip wearing, wide pussy, Doc McStuffins lookin' ass bitch!" Gray mushed him in the head with every word. "I knew it that night I told you I was pregnant. And you stood there on your high fuckin' horse, talkin' all that shit while knowing damn well you stuck your dick in that bitch! In a pissy-ass bathroom no less. I know you got a staph infection behind that shit. Nasty muthafucka. I could've sprayed yo' ass that night but I didn't. You wanna know why?"

"Not really." Cam mumbled.

He always knew that she had pain inside but to see it so visible on her face fucked with his psyche. He couldn't take it. Hearing Gray talk to him like he was a nigga off the street was worse than getting shot or going to jail. Seeing how disappointed and disgusted with him she was would haunt him till the end of his days.

"Well, I'm gon' tell you anyway." Gray backed him up into a corner.

Cam's back hit the wall as he looked into her stormy caerulean eyes.

"I didn't say anything cause you don't fuckin' matter to me. I was done with you then, and after the stunt you pulled tonight, I'm most certainly done with you now. Ain't no more Cam and Gray. On my kids' lives, I wish I never met you. I don't want my son to grow up and be bitch made like you. Using excuses that you're a motherless child as to why you're such a fuck up. Yo mama ain't got shit to do with that and neither do your dead-ass army brothers. It's your fault why you lose everybody you love. You still ain't even got the balls to tell your family you got an illegitimate brother, but you supposed to be so tough.

You weak-ass bitch. You a grown-ass man and can't find a way to get a goodnight sleep. What the fuck these niggas even respect you for? You talk all that rah-rah shit, talkin' about you Killa Cam. Nigga you Bitch Cam! If it wasn't for Quan, yo' bitch ass wouldn't even be standing here. You talk all that shit about Gunz, but I bet if the shoe was on the other foot, he wouldn't have let Diggy die that night and Stacy for damn sure wouldn't have got shot five times."

Nausea churned in the pit of Cam's stomach. His head swam with half-formed regret. His heart felt as if his blood had become thick as tar. A black cloud of rain poured over him and Gray. Nothing else had to be said. The bullet that he'd intended for her had been lodged into his own heart. Gray had officially killed him. Cam wanted to hit her with a couple of truths of his own but there was no point. They'd destroyed each other enough. He didn't have the energy to fight her anymore. The girl with the pretty blue eyes, sweet smile and forgiving heart had changed. She was harder now. All the softness he used to love about her was gone. Cam had no one else to blame but himself. He'd done this to her. He'd made her this way. She was a savage. He'd turned her into a beast just like him.

"All of this is your fault!" She continued to chip away at his heart with an icepick. "Not mine! I never once disrespected you. I never cheated on you and oh please believe me, nigga, I could've. Niggas was *DYING* to get wit' me. I had mad niggas in my DM's including Drake, but I didn't fuck wit' none of them 'cause I called myself loving you. I loved you so much that I looked past all of your bullshit and your excuses. I married you on a whim not even thinkin' about how it was going to affect my kids. Aoki hated you, you wouldn't even tell me you loved me, you slept at that bitch house and like a dummy I still kept you around and tried to be the best fuckin' wife and mother I could be. I should've left yo' ass then but nooooo instead of listening to my head, I went with my stupid-ass heart and tried to love you anyway. But loving you ain't get me shit but being cheated on, a dead baby and a gun in my fuckin' mouth!"

It was then that Cam saw the innocence leave her eyes. He'd fallen short of everything he said he was about and destroyed her and them in the process. Neither him or Gray had won this war. They were both losers. They'd lost in the game of love and ended up despising each other. Grief surged with every expelled breath Cam took. How they would coexist and raise five children after this was beyond him.

"Now, I'm gon' tell you how this shit gon' go. Don't call me, don't text me, don't climb your stupid, crazy-ass through my fuckin' window. You fuckin' cat burglar. If you see me, walk past me like I'm the air you breathe. You will see *my* kids on *my* terms and not a second sooner. Other than that, don't say shit to me. I don't exist to you 'cause you for damn sure don't exist to me. I don't want no contact with you. If it's concerning the kids reach out to my fuckin' assistant. Other than that, this conversation is over. Now, I'ma say this one last time. Get the fuck out *my* house!"

On everything Cam loved, he didn't want to leave but he'd caused enough chaos for one night. Retrieving his gun, he tucked it in the back of his jeans and left out the door without saying another word. Gray hurriedly locked the door behind him, and with her back against the door, she broke down into a heap of tears and sobbed.

#5

"I left my tee shirt on the edge of your king bed. I tell myself that I'm not stupid. Your hungry heart was over feed. Said you made your bed you gotta lie in it, but you lied to me instead."- Iyla, "Shampoo"

Gray cried for what seemed like hours and fell into a deep comatose like sleep. She'd been physically and emotionally drained by Cam. The time difference, jet lag and being chloroformed by her psychopath husband added to making her weary. Her body needed rest, so she slept. She lay in a deep, heavy sleep allowing her mind to escape the day's events. What was supposed to be an hour nap turned into her sleeping through half the night. By the time her eyes blinked open the moon was in full glow. The sky was onyx serenity married to a poetry of stars. Stretching her arms and legs, Gray tried to remember where she was. The room she was in wasn't hers and the mattress she lay on was softer than the one she owned. Sitting up, she groggily looked around until her eyes landed on the suitcases by the door. Suddenly, she remembered everything. Every sordid detail of the day came flooding back. Flashbacks of Cam holding her at gunpoint bombarded her mind. Her entire body became hot with dread all over again. Gray's heartrate increased as her breathing became a struggle. Holding her chest, she fought to catch her breath. She'd never had a panic attack before, but she was sure this was what it felt like. Inhaling and exhaling slow, she focused on the clock to calm herself down. It was almost 2:00 a.m.

"Fuccccccccck." She groaned, dropping her head between her legs.

She hadn't cooked dinner, given the kids baths or put them to-bed. This was not how she wanted Kema's wedding week to start off. She was supposed to be enjoying her time back. She was supposed to be having fun but no. Here she was having a fuckin' anxiety attack at two o'clock in the morning because of Cam. This was all his fault. He'd done this to her. He'd come out of nowhere and turned her world upside down. Now she was a nervous wreck, wondering at every turn would she take her last breath. The notion that Cam had almost killed her really rattled her brain. If he would've pulled the trigger, she would be lying in a morgue as her kids and friends mourned her death. Her children would be motherless, and she'd be buried six-feet deep covered in ants and maggots. Gray would never forgive Cam for what he'd done to her. She didn't care that, at the last minute, he changed his mind and didn't pull the trigger. The fact still remained that he tried.

"Fuck him." She hissed, rising from the bed.

She had to go check on her kids. Cam's paranoid, insecure ass was not a priority on her list. In order to survive her time back home he'd have to be the last person she thought of. Walking out of the bedroom, she listened for voices but heard nothing. The house was completely still. If Melody hadn't put the little kids to bed, she was sure Aoki had. She'd been Gray's mini me since they moved to Paris. Being that Gray had no familial help, and didn't believe in hiring nannies to take care of her kids, Aoki stepped up to the plate. She helped Press with her homework, made bottles, changed diapers and burped the babies. Gray was so thankful for her. Without Aoki, she would've crumbled. Raising two kids was hard but five nearly took her out. She never envisioned herself as a single mother and was fearful at first she'd fail. There were days where the crying, poopy diapers and spit up became too much. Gray wanted to drink a fifth of Jack and say fuck it, but she couldn't. Her babies big and small depended on her. In the end, she was glad she didn't give up. A strength she didn't know she possessed evolved and now she was stronger and more self-confident than ever.

By the time she made it across the hall to the triplet's room, her breathing had regulated. But once she stepped inside and found an empty room, shortness of breath resumed. Gray's eyes darted from bed to bed in desperate search of her kids. In panic mode, she raced next door to Press' room to find that she too was missing.

"No-no-no-no-no-no." Her heart thumped so loud she could hear it in her ears.

Frantically, she rushed down the hall to Aoki's room, nearly tripping over her feet. *Please, let her be there,* she begged as she pushed open the door ready to explode. She was stopped dead in her tracks. The sight before her not only calmed her worried spirit but made her heart melt. All five kids were there, including her estranged husband. Cam's large frame took up half the space in the queen size bed. He rested on his back in nothing but a pair of black jogging pants. His arms were stretched wide to cradle each of their kids. Gray took in the rhythmic rise and fall of his chest. Cam looked peaceful. The features of his face were much softer when he was asleep. The mean scowl he donned on a daily was replaced by a youthful glow. If she were a fool, she would've almost thought he was an angel but thankfully she wasn't. The coldhearted murderer from earlier was still there under the surface. It was just a matter of time before he returned.

Aoki and Press lay on one side of him while the triplets lay snuggled up against him on the other. Cam and

Reign lay shirtless snoring. One let out air simultaneous to the other breathing it in. Sky's little chest pumped up and down as she slept in her Frozen princess dress. She'd have a hissy fit if she didn't wear it to bed each night. Beaux lay in-between Reign and Sky with a naughty grin on her face. She was just like her father. Aoki's full hair was sprawled across the pillow as she held Press close so she wouldn't fall out of the bed. Even though the visual was precious, Gray was pissed that Cam had disregarded her warning not to return. The evil part of her wanted to wake him up and make him leave. She didn't want him there. He was violating her space. His disobedience showed that her words had gone in one ear and out the other. Cam still didn't respect her. It was obvious he still took her as a joke, but she'd deal with him later. This was bigger than her. She had to put her feelings to the side. The kids deserved time with their father. No matter how upset she was with him, she wouldn't take that away from them. Gray would never admit it out loud but secretly she'd prayed for a moment like this. Despite how bad Cam had done her, she'd always wanted him to be apart of their kids' lives. That's why she made it her business to include him in the triplets' lives as much as possible, without him physically being there. She told them stories, showed them pictures/home videos and gave them gifts that she said was from him.

Even after the way he'd done her, the plan was always to unite him with his children once he was released from prison. Gray figured there was no point in proving she was telling the truth while he was locked down because she was never going to introduce the triplets to their father through a thick coat of plexiglass. She, nor her kids, would ever step foot in a prison. They would never have to suffer because of the idiotic choices their father made. Some would argue she'd kept the children away out of spite and those people would be right. Gray was mad as hell. She didn't want to play nice. Everyone always stepped on her feelings. In the past she'd take it and try to be the bigger person. Those days were over. Gray had tapped into her malicious side. Cam had done her dirty. She wasn't going to kiss his ass and cater to his bruised ego. He'd said fuck her and she'd return the favor tenfold.

But regardless of how he'd failed her as a husband, deep down she knew he'd be a phenomenal father. Watching him lay sound asleep with their babies proved it. *Wait a minute. He's asleep,* she thought. Cam was actually sleeping and peacefully at that. She wondered how that had come about. In the past he couldn't rest without, tossing, turning, twitching or waking in a violent state. He seemed to be doing fine now. Gray would, however, keep a close eye on him throughout the night. It wasn't like she'd be going back to bed. Knowing that Cam was only a few feet away made her jumpy. Plus, she was hungry. She hadn't eaten since lunch with her friends. Quietly, she pulled the door up but didn't close it. She needed to be able to get to her babies in case Cam did have a night terror and she had to fuck him up.

———

The air was thick with the scent of coffee as Gray held her favorite mug up to her lips. She was on her third cup. Coffee wasn't good when your nerves were already bad, but it was better than drowning her worries in alcohol. Plus, she needed something to keep her awake. She'd been on high alert all night, anticipating Cam having a night terror. Taking a sip, she winced as the piping hot brew burned her tongue. Deciding she'd had enough, Gray put the cup down and looked out the window. The night sky had melted away. The sun filtered through the clouds signaling the dawn of a new day. The morning horizon was filled with hues of lavender, neon pink and peach. The colors merged together soothing her troubled heart. She couldn't remember the last time she'd watched the sun come up. Rampant thoughts of Cam and their fucked-up marriage filled her mind. She'd talked to Melody and learned that when she returned with the kids, Cam was there. Despite her warning he'd broken back in. Concerned for Gray and the kids' safety, Melody checked in on Gray and found her sound asleep. Unsure about Cam, she decided to stay and keep an eye on him as he cooked dinner and got to know the kids. To her surprise the children were 100 percent comfortable around him. Talking and laughter filled the air. After a while, she saw that they were safe in his hands and decided to leave but not before telling Aoki to call her if anything funny went down.

Gray was pleased that the kids got to spend time with their father, but a divorce was a must. She and Cam were no good together. Their relationship was unhealthy. It was a sinking ship and both of them were sure to drown. They couldn't continue to do the same thing expecting things to be different. That way of thinking was the definition of insanity. Gray refused to be stuck in a toxic cycle of distrust, disappointment, lies, cheating and hate. She was determined to move on. By the time she left St. Louis the divorce papers she served him years before would be signed.

"Let me get these kids up so they can eat." She unfolded her legs.

Because she was on edge, Gray had fixed a smorgasbord of food. She needed to do something to keep herself busy. On the table was Belgian waffles, freshly cut strawberries, blueberries, sliced bananas, bacon, sausage, eggs, grits and orange juice. She had to make it up to the kids, since she'd failed to fix them dinner the night before. The sound of her bare feet slapping against the wooden floor lingered in the air as she made her way to Aoki's room. She and her siblings were still bundled together in bed. Cam, however, was missing. Gray screwed up her face, wondering where could he be. She'd been up all morning. There was no way he'd walked past her and left. Climbing onto the bed, she kissed each of her kids' cheeks and nudged them awake. Each of them rose one by one yawning and rubbing their eyes. The first thing out of Press' mouth was where is Papa. Gray wanted to roll her eyes but didn't.

"I want daddy." Sky whined already attached.

"Go wash your face and brush your teeth while I go find him." Gray rubbed her baby girl's back.

Cam hadn't been around 24 hours and he already had her little girl wrapped around his finger. Sky used to beg for her in the morning. Now Gray was nothing but chopped liver. All the kids scooted out of bed and made their way to the bathroom to handle their hygiene. Gray walked out and checked the other seven bedrooms, library and terrace. Cam wasn't in either. *Where the hell is this nigga?* Something told her to check her room. The sound of the shower running, and the hypnotic smell of Saint Laurent body wash swarmed her as soon as she walked in. The scent took her back to a time when things were good between them. She used to enjoy lathering every inch of his sculpted physique with soap. Cam would teasingly caress his chest, arms and steel rod as he washed himself off in front of her. He knew how much Gray loved to ogle his tall frame. Showering together always led to sex. They'd fuck for what seemed like hours and he'd make her come more times than she could count. Those days were long gone tho. She could give a fuck less about Cam or his muscles. She wanted him gone so she could enjoy breakfast alone with her kids. Thankfully, they seemed to be on the same page.

76

A new white tee, Marcelo Burton slim fit jeans, Emporio Armani boxer briefs, socks and Valentino Garavani sneakers lay on the edge of the king-sized bed. Gray wondered when he'd smuggled in a change of clothes as she scooted the items over and awaited his arrival. Seconds later, the water stopped running. A cloud of steam followed Cam as he walked out as naked as the day he was born.

"Putain." The word goddamn slipped from Gray's mouth in French.

When they'd met, Cam's body had definition, but he wasn't cock diesel. She used to make jokes about him being tall and lanky but now he was buff as fuck. The nigga knew it too. There was a cockiness in his stride that hardened her clit. The arrogant muthafucka didn't even bother toweling off. Beads of water leisurely strolled down his burly chest as his long, meaty, crooked cock swung back-and-forth hitting his muscular thighs. Gray unconsciously ran her tongue across her upper lip. She was so turned on by him that she didn't even notice the eye she'd hit him in was black. The man was a mountain of rolling muscle. His oversized arms hung like threatening weapons from his broad shoulders. The eight pack of muscles in the center of his stomach reminded her of a set of stacked bricks. The sight was nothing short of sinful. Cam was the virtual image of an African god, a superhuman figure of enormous strength and brawn. A multitude of tattoos covered his neck, chest, arms and back. She wanted to lick each one with the tip of her tongue. The tattoo of her name was still etched into the skin on the side of his forehead. She didn't know how he'd done it, but somehow he'd managed to set off a mini orgasm from her clit to her core. The seat of Gray's panties were drenched as she squeezed her legs tight. Her entire body shuttered from the eruption. She prayed to God Cam hadn't noticed the way her upper half quaked but of course he did. Cam saw the flash of excitement in her expressive blue eyes.

"It's still yours." He smirked, standing before her. "Go head. Get you a taste."

His dick was right in front of her face. It dangled like a slab of beef. If Gray wanted to, all she had to do was lean forward and the tip of his dick would be in her mouth. The erratic thump in her clit was begging her too. She used to get off on sucking his dick. There were times when she'd climax just from giving him head alone. Gray clenched her jaw and swallowed. Cam's cock was so hard and thick. She'd be lying if she said she didn't miss it, but the devil was lie. She would not fall into temptation.

"Grab it. I know you want to."

"You wish." She rolled her eyes, trying to remain stoic but somehow ended up blushing any way.

"Are you blushing?" He unconsciously caressed her cheek with his thumb.

Cam and Gray's bond was weird. There was so much animosity, so much distrust between them but somehow their souls wouldn't untether themselves to the other. Spell bounded by his touch, Gray leaned into his stroke.

"Black people don't blush."

"You ain't black." The pad of Cam's thumb glided over the numerous freckles on her cheeks.

"Fuck you." She blinked, coming back to reality.

"Anytime."

"Nigga please." She pushed his hand out the way. "You or your dick will never be in me again. Now move."

78

She scooted past him. "And what the hell are you doing in my house anyway? I told your crazy-ass not to climb through my fuckin' window."

"I didn't. I walked through the door after I picked it." Cam tried to act like the touch of her hand didn't make his dick throb with desire.

"How? I set the alarm."

"And I disabled the shit." He slipped on his underwear to Gray's disappointment.

"You are a psychopath. I'm callin' your probation officer."

"You betta call the morgue too while you at it 'cause if you do I'ma shoot you in the fuckin' throat."

Gray stilled. Her heartrate slowed. How dare he say something like that to her after what had taken place. Back in the day, Cam threatening to shoot her was all fun and games, but now that he'd actually almost done it, there was nothing humorous about it. The only thing he'd succeeded in doing was refueling the anger she harbored for him. She found him attractive, yes. There would always be sexual tension between them. It had been there from the start, but she didn't trust him. She didn't know him anymore. He was a complete stranger. Once more, Cam reminded her that they weren't what they used to be. They were adversaries.

"You got five seconds to get your black-ass the fuck out my house." She shot him a look of disgust before exiting the room.

Cam twisted his neck from side-to-side until it popped. He'd gone too far and needed to apologize but how do you apologize to someone for trying to kill them? There wasn't an apology for that, but in order for them to co-parent he and Gray had to find some kind of common ground. How that would occur was beyond his understanding. She hated him and he dispised her. She'd kept his fuckin' kids away from him for god sake. A simple 'I'm Sorry' wouldn't take away the pain he felt. Gray had pulled the wool over his eyes and made him think she was this innocent, wounded little bird. In reality, she was just as vindictive as the killers he dealt with on the streets.

Gray's body was hot with rage as she stomped towards the kitchen. She needed to get away from Cam. He was driving her insane. Her hands shook with rage, but as soon as she got around the kids, she dropped her anger and put a fake smile on her face. Gray had been putting on a front for her kids for as long as she could remember. She never wanted them to see her down or depressed. For them, she'd pretend to be happy and act like everything was okay.

"Is Papa still here?" Press asked with hope in her eyes.

"Unfortunately." Gray frowned. "Who's hungry?" She plastered on a bogus smile.

"Meeeeeee!" The triplets raised their hands.

"I swear ya'll greedy." Aoki helped them into their highchairs.

Over the years, she'd become a second mom to her siblings. She'd witnessed firsthand her mom running a household of six alone with grace and class. Gray never whined or complained. In Aoki's eyes that made her a superhero. She'd gone through hell and back but never once did she crumble. She took it all on the chin and powered on.

"Me want food! Me want food!" Reign banged his fork and spoon to the beat.

"GET. . . IN. . . MY. . . *BELLY*!" Beaux growled like a monster.

"Why are they so weird?" Press screwed up her face. "I swear they need Ritalin."

"You used to act the same way." Gray assured.

"Lies you tell. You was drinking while you was pregnant wit' them."

"What's shaking?" Cam strolled into the kitchen fully dressed. "It smell good up in here. Who gon' fix daddy a plate?" He took a seat at the table.

Speechless, Gray glared at the back of his head. The devil was a lie. He was not joining them for breakfast. He'd just tried to kill her less than 24 hours before. No way was he about to sit and break bread with her like nothing had happened.

"Are you dumb?" She snapped, annoyed by his presence.

"Ya'll sleep good?" Cam ignored her statement.

"Daddy, you too tall. You hogged all da bed." Beaux poked out her bottom lip.

"Yeah, you gotta sleep with mommy next time." Sky shimmied her shoulders.

"Shiiiiiiiiiit." Gray grimaced, rolling her eyes.

"Nah, mommy got bed bugs. I ain't fuckin' wit' her." Cam fixed himself a glass of orange juice.

"Eww, mama, for real? How you get that? Don't they travel?" Press began to scratch herself.

"Uh ah. You gon' have to call an exterminator 'cause I ain't got time for that." Aoki stepped far away from her mother.

"Aoki, you know damn well I ain't got no bed bugs." Gray hit her with the dish towel.

"Daddy, why yo' eye so black?" Sky pointed out.

"Yo mama don't know how to keep her fuckin' hands to herself."

"And if you don't want another black eye, I suggest you do us both a favor and leave." Gray walked past and bumped him on purpose.

"Get knocked out." Cam disregarded her threat yet again.

"Suck a dick." She said loud enough for only him to hear.

"You first. I'm always available for them Chinese lips, Ling-Ling."

"Nigga, I got your fuckin' Ling-Ling."

"C'mon, ya'll, let's say grace 'cause the devil fasho up in here." Cam ordered.

"Who gon' say it 'cause me and God beefin'?" Aoki pursed her lips.

"I will!" Beaux yelled excitedly.

"That's my girl." Cam ruffled her hair still amazed she even existed.

Cam and all the kids joined hands and bowed their heads. Gray stood off to the side. She didn't want to be anywhere near Cam. Beaux licked her tiny lips and said, "Bless this meat. Now let's eat."

"Amen!" The family cheered.

Cam sat back in his seat dumbfounded by the blasphemy.

"You got to be fuckin' kidding me. You still ain't taught these kids how to pray?" He scowled at Gray.

"What?" She shrugged.

"You need to be fuckin' shame of yourself. Ain't you like fifty? Got these kids talkin' bless this meat, let's eat. You need yo ass beat. That's that Polynesian shit. C'mon ya'll. We can do better than that." He made the kids join hands once more.

"Huuuuuuuh." They all groaned.

Their bellies were grumbling. They didn't want to pray anymore.

"Daddy, you mean." Sky pouted.

"Yeah, you not my friend." Reign furrowed his brows.

"Bow your head for me li'l man." Cam kissed the top of his son's head.

I gotta son, he thought. Reign was an exact clone of him. Just like his father, he was easily angered and annoyed. Once everyone's eyes were closed, Cam started to pray.

"Bless us, O Lord, and Thy gifts which we are about to receive from Thy bounty. Thank you for blessing us to come together in fellowship. Father we thank you for this food. We thank you for the ones who prepared it. Lord we appreciate the matriarch of this family. If it wasn't for her, I wouldn't have these five beautiful kids."

Gray bit her lower lip and tried to seem indifferent to his kind words. She couldn't let him being nice get to her, but damn did it feel good to hear him thank God for her.

"Father, I thank you for my children big and small." He squeezed Press and Reign's hand. "I can't say thank you enough for them. They are the best thing that has ever happened to me. Even though I missed out on a lot 'cause someone in this room was all in her fee-fee's, tryin' to be petty, like she wasn't fuckin' wit' the op—"

"Wrap it up!" Gray interrupted.

"Anyway . . . I swear I'm gon' be the best father I can possibly be. I love my kids, God. With all of my heart. I know a nigga ain't perfect but I'm working on it. And I know I ain't seen them in the last couple of years 'cause Jackie Chan wanna be spiteful and set a nigga up—"

"Cam!"

"A'ight-a'ight. In Jesus name, Amen."

"Bout time." Beaux rolled her big animated eyes.

"Long-ass prayer." Aoki muttered.

"When you get so soft, Papa? I thought that you was a bad bitch?" Press placed her napkin on her lap.

"He a bitch alright." Gray cut up the triplets' waffles.

"Don't fuck up my vibe after I just said that nice-ass prayer." Cam warned.

"Yeah okay, Satan. And since when you become Pastor Jamal Bryant?"

She'd never heard Cam speak about the lord so eloquently and passionately. She'd almost forgotten how much of a degenerate he could be.

"Just 'cause yo' heathen-ass don't know the lord." Cam popped a banana in his mouth.

"And neither do you. Let's not forget about yesterday."

"Stop bringing up old shit. It ain't even that deep." He waved her off.

"It ain't that—" Gray lost her breath. "You know what? Get out." She tried to keep her composure in front of the kids.

Cam tuned her out and took a piece of banana off his son's plate and ate it. He was determined to make up for all the time he lost.

"Why you taking my nana? I don't even know you like that homey." Reign screwed up his face.

"What I tell you about your mouth?" Gray scolded him.

"But he took my nana." Reign pouted.

"Here man." Cam fed him another piece.

Reign's attitude instantly improved.

"You gon' have to chill with all that whining tho dawg. Big boys don't whine, okay?"

"I'm sorry, daddy." Reign leaned his head against his father's arm.

"It's okay man." Cam kissed his forehead.

Every time the triplets called him dad fucked with his head. He still hadn't fully grasped that he was in fact a father.

"Aoki, eat your eggs." Gray eyed her.

Aoki eyed her plate repulsed. If she even touched the eggs she'd vomit.

"Mama, I told you a recent study said that eggs aren't good for you. If I wanna grow up and be a world-famous DJ and artiste I have to eat food that nourishes my body."

"I don't care what the study said. Eggs are good for you."

"Tell that to the chicken that just lost a child." Aoki folded her arms.

"Well, my appetite is ruined." Press pushed her plate away.

"Daddy, you want some bacon?" Sky dangled a piece in his face.

"No pork on my fork, pretty girl. And ya'll need to stop eating that bullshit too. It's bad for you. Matter of fact, starting today ain't gon' be no more oink-oink."

"To hell wit' that." Aoki looked at him like he was crazy. "We eat everything from the roota to the toota around here."

"I forgot ya'll mama be having ya'll eating that freaky shit."

"Just 'cause your hood-ass ain't cultured." Gray finished making the triplets' plates.

"That ain't got shit to do wit' it. You clogging up my babies arties. You heard what the fuck I said. Don't feed them no more pork. I don't even want them eating beef. The shit ain't good for you either."

"Let me tell you something, you fake-ass Suge Knight." Gray pointed a sharp knife in his direction. "You ain't coming up in here regulating shit. I will feed them whatever the fuck I want to. Matter of fact, why are you still here? Get the fuck out!" She shouted.

Gray was truly on the brink of losing her shit. Visions of Cam with a gun tap danced on her subconscious. He had no idea how traumatized she was.

"Why you yellin'?" He drew his head back perplexed. "Do she always yell like this?"

"Yes!" All the kids said in unison.

"Really?" Gray side-eyed them all.

"Well, mama, you do." Press pointed out.

"Aoki was right. You are a traitor."

"I told you she was the op. She just like her damn one-eyed daddy." Aoki rolled her eyes.

Caught off guard by her statement, Cam choked on a piece of fruit.

"Oh shit." He smacked his chest.

"Don't talk about my daddy!" Press shrilled.

"Aoki, that's enough. Watch your mouth." Gray warned as her hands shook with anger and trepidation.

87

She needed Cam out of her space asap.

"A'ight, I'ma chill." Aoki held up her hands in mock surrender.

"I thought *he* was our daddy?" Sky asked confused.

"I am. I'm all ya'll daddy." Cam clarified.

And for Aoki this was true. Cam had been more of a father figure to her in the last three years than the man who had raised her majority of her life.

"Thank you again for all the stuff you sent us while you were away. You didn't have to do that, but you did. I got mad respect for you for that OG. Whatever you need I got. Word is bond." She said sincerely.

"We wanted to come see you Papa, but we were too far away." Press said solemnly.

Suddenly, her appetite had disappeared.

"I told you I was gon' be there for ya'll forever." Cam planted a loving kiss on her forehead.

"True." Aoki nodded. "But you can't believe shit these niggas say now-a-days."

"Facts." Gray absently agreed. "Hold on. What the hell I tell you about all that cursing?"

"I'm just keepin' it a hunnid, ma. Cam a real one. He showed us the real from the fake. He did more for us than that nigga my sister share her DNA wit'."

"Least I gotta daddy!" Press shot back.

"That's enough! Aoki apologize to your sister."

Gunz was a touchy subject in their home. Whenever his name came up, Press immediately became sad. A well of tears sat on the edge of her big brown eyes begging to fall.

"Sorry." She mumbled, slumping down in her seat.

"You okay, pretty girl?" Cam pulled Press close.

His heart ached to see her cry. Press was his world. He'd kill a muthafucka behind her, including Aoki's bad ass.

"Now that you're back, I'm okay. Are you gonna move back in wit' us?" She hoped and prayed he said yes.

Uh ah, Gray thought. The conversation had gone left quick.

"Hell, to the nah. Absolutely the fuck not. Ya'll say goodbye to your daddy." She rose from her seat.

This was not a topic she was willing to discuss.

"Goodbye these nuts. I ain't going no fuckin' where." Cam balled up his face.

"It's time for you to leave."

"Gray, sit yo' ass down and eat. You know you hungry. Slap into a Slim Jim muthafucka." Cam pushed the platter of Belgian waffles in her direction.

"Cameron!" She stated sternly.

"Liar!" He arched his brow.

"On my mama I will call the cops if you don't get up and leave." Gray cautioned for the last time.

She was done playing with Cam. It was time for him to go. There was only so much of his shit she could take. He'd disturbed her life enough. Cam squinted his eyes. He wanted to rip Gray's pretty little face off. He'd missed out on every second of his kids' lives. The least she could do was let him eat breakfast with them. She wasn't playing fair, but could he blame her? He'd set the tone for their relationship when he'd attempted to put a bullet through her brain.

"You worse than my brother Kerry and Mrs. Mariam but I forgot snitching is in your blood. That's what you do." He got up, pissed.

"No mama. Why he gotta leave?" Press whined.

"Daddy, don't go." Sky broke out in tears which caused Beaux and Reign to cry too.

They finally had their father there in real life, not in a picture or a video. Gray's heart sank down to her toes. She hated to see her babies cry but she couldn't pretend like things were all good with her Cam when they weren't.

"It's cool, pretty girl. I'ma get up wit' ya'll tomorrow at the barbeque okay?" He kissed her goodbye then picked up the triplets one by one to say goodbye.

Cam held them close and bounced them up and down until they calmed. Gray felt like shit for making her children cry but boundaries had to be set between her and Cam.

"This shit ain't over." He stepped into her personal space. "Me and you need to talk, and I better see my kids tomorrow or that's your ass."

"Just go, Cam." She said exasperated.

Cam wanted to press the subject but the appearance of despair on Gray's face stopped him. She couldn't even look him in the eye. There was so much built up anger and resentment between him and her. The love they once shared seemed like it was light years ago. With all they'd done to one another had they ever loved one another? That was the question that plagued his mind. Love wasn't malicious or vengeful. They both played games and pushed each other's buttons. Out of anger and hurt he and Gray had done their worst to one another. He'd tried to kill her, and she'd kept him in the dark about giving birth to his kids. The path to clarity and forgiveness seemed farfetched. Cam couldn't shift his hate. Every time he looked at the triplets tiny little faces it ebbed and multiplied.

#6

"Everyone who isn't us is an enemy."- Cersei Lannister, "A Game of Thrones"

The last 24 hours of Cam's life had been a whirlwind. Never in a million years did he expect to come home to three small children. He thought by now he'd be sipping on a glass of Hennessy as word spread that Gray was dead. For 1,186 days he dreamt and damn near salivated over how he'd kill her. He thought about strangling her, stabbing her with a hot poker, snapping her neck or running her over with a car. There were so many different scenarios that none of them seemed self-serving enough. Ending Gray's life had been his number one goal, but his plans quickly changed as soon as he saw her face. When his diamond shaped eyes landed on her sky-blue ones the world stopped. His heart thudded like a bass drum on an R&B beat. Gray's eyes, freckles like confetti, defined cheekbones and Cover Girl smile reminded him of all the reasons why he fell in love with her. At one point in time she was his muse, his reason for living. He'd found life in her kisses, triumph in her courage and hope in the way she loved him. Their morning talks used to put his troubled mind at ease. She was his anchor, his rib, the Ruby Dee to his Ossie Davis. He loved her; more than he thought a fucked-up individual like him could. Cam tried to be the man she wanted him to be. He tried to be a good husband, even though he had absolutely no idea what the hell he was doing. There wasn't a map, guide or blueprint on how to uphold your wife. His own father didn't stay true to the vows he told his mother. Every man he knew was a piece of shit. They all lied and cheated. He tried to be different for Gray. He didn't want to follow in his father's footsteps. He didn't want to repeat Quan's mistakes. He didn't want to mishandle her heart. After everything Gray had been through, she of all people deserved her happily ever after. Instead, she and Cam's marriage crashed and burned faster than when they said, 'I do'. Now here they were years later living in a nightmare they once called love.

Cam didn't know what to think or feel. A part of him wanted to believe that she had nothing to do with him getting locked up, but even after all the tears and her rage-filled rant he still didn't 100% believe her. All the signs were there. He'd be a fool to ignore them. But the look of sadness and devastation on her face as she pleaded for her life told him otherwise. Gray was genuinely shocked that he would think such a thing of her. The only other time he'd seen her look so disappointed in him was when they broke up on New Year's Eve. The look she gave him then and the look she gave him the night before would forever be etched in his brain. It shook him to his core. Cam hated to see her hurt but the distrust and resentment he'd built regarding her wouldn't allow him to care. She'd taken the most precious thing away from him . . . his kids. He never thought Gray could be so cruel. And yes, she told him she was pregnant but considering the timing, circumstances of their relationship and her tubes being tied, of course he wouldn't think she was telling the truth. Chicks always cried pregnant as soon as a nigga broke up with them. In his mind, Gray was no different than any other desperate female trying to get her man back.

It didn't matter how upset or done with him she was, she should've followed up with him, but she didn't. Instead, she kept their triplets a secret and sent him divorce papers. Cam thought LaLa lying about Kamryn being his was fucked up, but Gray's deceit took the cake. She'd literally destroyed any hope or faith he had in the opposite sex. All these bitches were fake. Gray's betrayal confirmed that true love was a myth. Everybody wanted it but no one really cared to cherish it. People jumped in and out of relationships like a game of hopscotch. Humans were selfish creatures. They made decisions based on how the outcome would affect them and not the others around them. Gray knew keeping the kids away from him would be the ultimate revenge. She knew it would kill him and it did. Cam was emotionally dead inside. Knowing that he'd missed out on Reign, Beaux and Sky's birth was worse than any prison sentence a judge could give. He'd missed the pivotal parts of his children being newborns and toddlers. He'd never get that time back and it was all because of Gray.

Now that he knew about the babies, every aspect of his life had changed. Cam couldn't move like he used to. He had to make some major life changes and fast. After Gray put him out, he immediately hopped in the car with Priest who had been waiting outside. Unbeknownst to his estranged wife but Cam already had plans on leaving after breakfast. He had shit to take care of. Dire issues that couldn't wait.

The car ride to Victor Gonzalez's estate had been a quiet one. Cam sat stewing in his thoughts as Priest whipped his Nipsey Blue boxed Chevy through the city streets. Cam appreciated that his cousin didn't bother him with a barrage of questions. Priest didn't speak much anyway. He preferred silence. He only talked when it was necessary. He was the opposite of his big cousin. Priest wasn't flashy and didn't care to be seen. He kept to himself and kept his mouth shut.

Slouched down in the passenger seat, Cam gazed out the window at the mansions that lined Billionaire's Row. Only the wealthy and elite stayed in the reclusive subdivision. Cam was rich but the people that lived on Billionaire's Row were wealthy. He'd always dreamed of owning a home in the exclusive neighborhood, but he'd be selling coke until he was a hundred to get there. Jefe Victor Gonzalez was born into wealth. He'd taken his family's notorious cartel and turned it into a 10-billion-dollar empire. Once they reached their destination, Priest slowly pulled up to the large gate that was flanked by two armed guards. After announcing their arrival, being patted down and a full sweep of the car, they were allowed through the gate. Cam looked around. There were strategically placed armed guards on the roof and on the grounds. Victor didn't take any chances when it came to the safety of his family. Although he didn't like another man touching him, Cam couldn't do anything but respect it. He would do the same thing if he was in his position.

The expansive gates opened to a 30-car courtyard surrounded by 40-foot-tall Canary Island palms and a setting worthy of the best Italian palazzo. Walking inside the mega mansion was like stepping into the Taj Mahal. It was enormous. Cam had only been there a few times and each time was like the first. The home was worth $165,000,000 and sat on seven acres of land. The mansion was approximately 20,000 square feet and afforded every possible amenity from high ceilings to large and formal gathering areas to small and intimate spaces. A four-plus acre backyard offered views to a pool, pool house, two-story guesthouse, tennis court and a walking/jogging trail that surrounded the estate.

Two armed guards escorted Cam into Victor's office. Priest was left in the foyer to sit and wait. Cam inhaled deep and exhaled a slow anxious breath. Stepping into Victor's office, he didn't know what to expect. He could either walk out of the meeting alive or be carried out in a body bag. Victor was a fair man, but he was also a businessman. He'd given Cam a prominent position in the Gonzalez cartel and he'd brought nothing but heat from the FEDS down onto the organization. Even though Cam had paid back the money he owed for the confiscated bricks, he still had to face the music. He'd fucked up and Victor Gonzalez didn't tolerate fuck ups.

He was a man that exuded power and respect. As soon as Cam entered his office, he felt the energy shift. Victor rose from his leather chair and placed his large hands inside the pocket of his dress pants. Based off his hard expression, Cam couldn't tell what he was thinking or feeling. Victor wasn't a man that smiled or joked around. He was all about his family and his paper. Anything or anyone that stood in-between it would be erased. He was a heartless, cold, son-of-a-bitch. The word cruel took on a new meaning when associated with him. It was funny because based off his looks, you wouldn't think he was a stone-cold ruthless killer or boss of a cartel. The man could've easily been a model. Women fantasized about him when they played with their pussies at night. He was over six feet of caramel muscle. His African and Puerto Rican roots mixed together well to make one fine specimen of a man. He donned a low-cut Caesar with a part just like the rapper Nas. Thick bushy brows hovered over deep earthy brown eyes. He had a brood prominent nose, full lips and a smooth beard. Covering his solid chest and protruding arms was a pale blue button up, gray and white plaid vest and a navy and white polka dot tie. Navy blue fitted slacks, two-tone brown leather oxford shoes and a 1.8-million-dollar Frank Muller watch finished off his dapper look. Nothing about his outfit or watch was glitzy. There wasn't a label or diamond in sight but every article of clothing or jewelry he wore cost more than what most people would ever make in a lifetime.

"It's good to have you home." Victor stepped around his desk and gave Cam a warm hug.

Relieved that he hadn't greeted him with a bullet to his cranium, Cam hugged him back and said, "It's good to be home."

"Have a seat."

"Thank you." Cam eased down into the chair.

It was one of the comfiest chairs he'd ever sat in. He wondered was that a part of Victor's lure. He'd sit his prey in the seat, make them feel comfortable, get them to let their guard down and then go in for the kill.

"Care for a drink?" Victor strolled over to his bar.

"Nah, I'm good."

Cam had made a vow to himself while in prison that he was going to cut back on drinking. Drinking had been a crutch to help him deal with his PTSD. Not anymore. He'd use therapy, meditation, prayer and his meds to cope from now on. The only time he'd indulge in alcohol would be during social settings or when he wanted to unwind. With a fresh tumbler of Scotch in his hand, Victor retook his seat behind his desk and glared at Cam.

"So . . . how are you adjusting?"

"Man, I don't even fuckin' know. So much shit has happened in the last 24 hours. If I would've known I was coming home to all this shit, I would've stayed my black-ass in jail."

"What's good? Talk to me." Victor leaned back in his chair and took a sip of his drink.

"Turns out I got three fuckin' kids."

Victor paused mid gulp then swallowed.

"Say that again?" He placed down his glass.

"Yeah, me and Gray got triplets."

"Wow." Victor scratched the hair on his chin. "And you ain't know nothin' about this?"

"Nope. I found out about'em last night when I broke in her crib to kill her."

"Did you?"

"Kill her?"

"Yeah."

"Nah." Cam looked off to the side. "I couldn't do it."

"So, did she set you up or not?"

"I don't know who did it. All I know is somebody gotta die." Cam flexed his hand then balled up his fist.

"I agree 'cause shit ain't adding up and it's making me look bad."

Not knowing who the rat was caused a major threat to Victor, Cam and the entire Gonzalez organization. The person could have more information on them that could get them locked up or killed. The pit of Cam's stomach stirred with irritation. This was the part of the conversation he'd been dreading. Victor wasn't going to let him off without a punishment. Cam would have to pay for the drama he'd caused but he refused to be a bitch about it. He was going to take whatever Victor dished out, whether that be cutting off a limb or death like a man. Sitting up straight, he looked him square in the eyes.

"You know you brought a lot of unwanted attention my way, Archibald. I don't know what you and your people were used to in the past, but I don't run no Mickey Mouse orperation. This shit between you and Gunz is fuckin' asinine. It's childish. When I heard that ya'll were going to war over a fuckin' girl—"

"With all due respect Jefe." Cam said pissed that he'd called him by his middle name. "She's not just no girl. She's my wife."

"I don't give a fuck who she is. She's a fuckin' problem and you know I like eliminating problems."

"C'mon man." Cam shuffled around in his seat.

If it were anyone else disrespecting him, he would've dived across the desk and beat the shit out of 'em, but he couldn't. He'd be dead before he took one step.

"Ever since you met her, you've been off your game." Victor resumed speaking. "It's very disappointing because at one point you were my star pupil. Dame handpicked you to take his place. I didn't even consider any other candidates. I chose you to be my second in command 'cause you were focused. You weren't easily distracted. My revenue increased, the death rate went down, my monthly profits doubled, and we expanded to several more cities because of you. But as soon you put your dick into that Korean bitch you lost your fuckin' mind. You started causing scenes, having fights, gauging out eyes and busting out bitches' windows like you Jazmine Sullivan or some shit. You not only embarrassed yourself, but you embarrassed the Gonzalez name and I can't have that. I have worked too hard to let some puta come ruin everything I've built—"

"She ain't no fuckin' bitch." Cam cut him off only for a pistol to be placed at the back of his head.

"Excuse me." Victor narrowed his eyes and cocked his head to the side.

Cam stopped breathing as the sound of the safety being clicked off pierced his ears.

"What was that?" Victor taunted him.

He wouldn't hesitate to have his man pull the trigger. Cam's brain matter would be splattered on the floor if he stepped out of line once more. Heated, Cam kept quiet as his chest heaved up and down. If he would've had a gun on him, he would've shot Victor point blank in the face. He was testing his manhood and Cam didn't like it one bit. He wasn't the kind of nigga to let another man disrespect him. Let alone put a gun to his head. It went against everything he stood for as a man.

"Nothing." Cam sucked his teeth then clenched his jaw.

"That's what I thought. Never interrupt me again. Have I made myself clear?"

"Yeah." Cam fumed with anger.

Silence followed as he and Victor stared each other down. Victor could smell a pussy nigga from a mile away. If he thought for one second that Cam was bitch-made, he'd be laid out on his ass in seconds. Cam held his head high and showed him that he would not be easily intimidated. For a brief second, Cam saw a glimmer of respect in Victor's eyes, but it disappeared as fast as it appeared. Seeing that they had an understanding, Victor signaled to his henchmen to back off.

"Now back to what I was saying. Had you not been sloppy and pillow talkin' wit' your so-called wife we wouldn't even be in this situation. I love Mina to the moon and back. She's my everything. There isn't anything I wouldn't do for my wife *except* involve her in my business. I don't give a fuck how mad at me she is. That shit come with the territory. Mina and my business are separate. She don't know shit about what the fuck I do. And you should've had that same mentality when you were at the cemetery telling all your business like a fuckin' niñita."

Cam's face contorted into a confused scowl. He and Gray had been alone that day or so he thought. He knew Victor's reach was long but damn. The nigga really had eyes and ears everywhere. No one was safe under his watch.

"You ain't gotta disrespect me by callin' me no li'l girl. I fucked up but this shit with Gunz run way deeper than what you know. Only reason why I stepped to that nigga is because he put his hands on her—"

"Do I look like I give a fuck about your personal problems with Gunz?!" Victor slammed his fist down onto the table, causing his drink to rattle. "I don't give a rat's ass about that shit. I stopped giving a fuck about both of ya'll niggas the minute you became a liability to my operation. Either ya'll gon' dead this shit or one of ya'll need to kill the other. 'Cause this petty school girl beef ya'll got is interfering with my business."

"I just got home. I ain't even trippin' off that nigga. I got too much other shit on my plate." Cam groaned, thinking about his children and his and Gray's impending divorce.

He had every intention on getting at Gunz but first he had to get his relationship with Gray and the kids situated.

"As long as that nigga don't start wit' me, we good." He lied.

Victor side-eyed him and shook his head.

"Lying is never good. Especially, when you're lying to me." He warned with a sinister glare.

What the fuck? Is this nigga Jesus, Cam thought?

"Now that you're home, the number one thing on your list is to find out who set you up. Whoever did it put my organization at a disadvantage. That can't go unpunished."

"I'ma find out."

"Oh, I know you are. Matter of fact because I like you, I'm gonna give you until the wedding."

"The wedding is next Sunday. I need more time than that."

"Nueve dias or I'm going to be forced to take matters into my own hands." Victor cryptically responded while lighting a blunt.

A soft panic rose inside of Cam. Fear flooded his system. His breathing instantly became shallow. His body wanted to lunge into an attack but instead he remained seated.

"What that mean?"

Victor took a long pull from the blunt. Taking his time, he leaned his head back and let the smoke seep into his cells before exhaling. Satisfied with the way he felt, his hooded eyes looked in Cam's direction.

"It means, I'm going to eliminate the main suspect. It means your baby mother won't make it back to Paris."

A muscle twitched involuntarily at the corner of Cam's right eye. A cold sweat glistened on his wrinkled brow. His mouth formed a rigid grimace as his heart pounded inside his chest.

"She's the mother of my kids'."

"Anyone that isn't us is the enemy so if you want her to live, I suggest you get on your job." Victor replied, coolly.

Knowing his back was against the wall, Cam had no choice but to comply. No, he and Gray weren't getting along. They weren't on the best of terms. He wasn't feeling her at all. He still thought she might've been the one to get him locked up but until he knew for sure, he had to keep her safe. She was the mother of his kids. He couldn't let anything happen to her.

"A'ight man. I got you. I'm on it but after this I'm done. I want out. I got five kids to live for."

The laugh hit Victor's eyes before it bellowed out his mouth. Cam's facial expression was one of absolute disdain. He hated to be made fun of or laughed it. Niggas knew not to test him in that way but up against Victor he didn't stand a chance. He couldn't do shit but sit back and take his ridicule like a battered wife.

"Tu escuchas este nigga."

You hear this nigga is what Victor asked in Spanish. The two henchmen inside the room laughed too.

"Nigga, when I say you're out, you're out and not a second sooner. Keep it up, Cameron. I would hate for you to end up a single father of three."

The skin of Cam's face became ash grey. His mouth hung with lips slightly parted. His eyes were as wide as they could stretch.

"Wooooow that's fucked up Jefe."

"Yeah, whatever." Victor waved him off. "Get the fuck out my office. I don't want to see your face again until this shit is resolved."

#7

"I throw that ass back to see if he gon' catch it."- Mulatto,
"Bitch From Da South"

"Ooooh yeah, muthafucka." Tia gripped the sheets
and threw her ass back into her baby daddy's shaft.

The way he was dicking her down should've been
against the law. He'd forced the perfect arch into her spine
as he gripped her tiny waist. Sweat trickled from his brow,
down his neck and onto his chiseled chest. The room was
hot from the sexual heat they'd created. The top of Tia's
head nearly collided with the headboard with each push of
his hips. In and out, out and in. He tapped danced on her G-
spot like he was Kanye West making a beat. He was
fucking her like a man who'd lost all sense of control. The
sound of his skin slapping against her thighs fueled his
passionate thrust. Their fuck session was supposed to be no
longer than fifteen minutes. It was the middle of the day.
They both had things they needed to do but they'd been
going at for nearly two hours. He couldn't get enough of
her and vice versa. It was as if their bodies had fused
together. Where his dark cocoa skin ended hers began. Tia
and her man were a match made in heaven. From the
moment she laid eyes on him she had to have him. No
matter the cost he would be hers. She didn't care that he
was taken or that he was much older. Tia knew what she
wanted, and she wanted him with every inch of her being.
Zero fucks were given. She went after him with a
vengeance. Anyone in her way be damned. It took a

minute. There was a lot of plotting and planning, nights spent alone craving his presence, frequently shed tears and unkept promises but with time, patience, mind-blowing sex and a child that would bind them together forever, he finally became hers.

Now here they were fucking each other's brains out like there was no tomorrow. Let them tell it, the world would end as soon as they came. Tia couldn't get enough. She loved this dick. She'd fight a bitch for the dick, serve FED time for the dick, rob, still and kill for the dick. Forsake all others for the dick. Hell, Tia would give up her family for the dick. It was addictive. It was mouthwatering delicious. Like greasy food or sugary sweets, she knew it was bad for her. Nothing good came from fucking it or sucking it. His dick was wicked. It was ten-inches of unmitigated sin wrapped up in rigid hard flesh.

The ripples in her ass cheeks reminded her baby daddy of beach waves as he took her savagely from behind. His long, slick, cock slid in and out of her wet hole at a feverish pace. She was sure, by the time they were done her clit would be beaten, damaged and bruised. His pussy pounding hurt but she liked the sensation. Electrical currents swarmed her lower half as she bit into her lower lip. Erotic lust and desire filled the air. Any limitations and boundaries be damn. This was what she'd came for. Fuck that he was supposed to be off limits. The pleasure he gave her was too good to give up. For days, her body begged and pleaded for this release. The release that only he could give.

"Ooooh yes! Fuck me, Kingston! Fuck me!" Her thighs began to shake as her face kissed the sheets.

The orgasm she was experiencing was so strong she couldn't even hold herself up. Her soul had skyrocketed to the moon. Twinkling stars clouded her vision as her entire body shook violently. Kingston's long locs fell over his eyes. The sight of her creamy cum flooding his cock caused his ass cheeks to clench. He got off on seeing her cum. It was a beautiful vision to see. The inside of her womb would be coated with his milky white seed. Spent from their strenuous sexapade, he fell onto her back and tried to catch his fading breath.

"Get yo' big ass off of me. You heavy." She reached back and swatted him with her hand.

Placing a small kiss on her shoulder blade, Kingston rolled over onto his side and took her petite frame into his strong arms. Tia was the opposite of her Aunt LaLa whom he had a son with as well. LaLa was high yellow with big fat juicy lips, oversized breast implants, wide hips and a booty like Serena. Tia took after her mother. She had smooth cinnamon skin, almond shaped eyes, moderately sized lips, chest and arm tattoos, rock hard breast implants, surgically enhanced hips and ass. She was his sexy chocolate bunny. There wasn't anything he wouldn't do for her, except be her man. No one could ever find out that he'd been dicking her down since she was seventeen. She was twenty-two now and they shared a three-year-old son who was named after the man everyone thought was his father. Kingston hated that both of his sons were named after men that weren't him. LaLa had done it without his permission and refused to change it. Tia named their son Gavin Jr. cause Gunz, his friend, wouldn't have it any other way. He'd dreamt of the day he'd have a son that he could mold into the image of himself. There were plenty of times when Kingston wanted the truth to come out but revealing their deceit would wreck too many lives. LaLa would be out for blood and Gunz would kill them both without blinking an eye. Kingston valued his life too much to have it cut short. For everyone's sake, it was detrimental that the paternity of Gavin Jr. be kept a secret.

"What time is it?" Tia moaned, still reeling from her explosive orgasm.

Her entire body tingled from the aftershock of pleasure. Kingston lifted his head and glanced at the clock.

"2:20."

"Shit!" She hopped out of bed like it was on fire.

"What's wrong?"

"I gotta go." She haphazardly threw on her discarded clothes. "Gunz thinks I'm at the gym."

Kingston chuckled, turning over onto his back. Her sticky cum coated his half erect dick like whipped cream.

"You better hurry then. I ain't tryna fuck up ya' happy home."

"My home ain't happy if you ain't in it." She sniped.

If Tia could have things her way, she and Kingston would've been together from the start. She didn't give a damn that she was seventeen at the time or that he was her aunt's baby daddy. Kingston was walking sex on a stick. He looked just like Shooter from Love and Hip-Hop Atlanta. She couldn't fight her sexual urges. She had to know what it felt like to have him between her thighs. It didn't take much to get him to fuck her. Even though she was young, Tia was shaped like an Instagram THOT. Kingston being the dog-ass nigga he was wasn't turning down no pussy. Morally, it was wrong to fuck his baby mama's niece, but he couldn't care less about LaLa's feelings. She wasn't his girl. She had a whole nigga when they started fucking around. Fucking Tia was supposed to be a onetime thing, but the pussy was so good he kept doubling back for more. Over the years they both messed

108

with other people, but no matter who they pledged themselves to they always found their way back to each other. When Tia became pregnant it was a no brainer who her child's father was. She and Gunz always used condoms. Whenever she smashed Kingston it was always unprotected. She just knew that when she told him she was carrying his baby they'd be together but her dreams of them being a family were quickly dashed. Kingston refused to step up and let the world know that he was in fact her baby's daddy. He was too chicken shit to suffer the consequences of their forbidden tryst. Thinking he would eventually come around, Tia decided to keep the baby. It didn't take her long to see that he wasn't going to change his mind, so with her back up against the wall, she told Gunz the baby was his. The only reason why he believed her was because they had a few instances where the condom had broken.

"C'mon ma. We talked about this." Kingston groaned, staring at the ceiling.

The last thing he wanted to do was talk about their relationship. If you would even call it that. In her mind, they were together but for him they were just fuckin'. She wasn't shit but his baby's mom. He was never going to make her his girl. She was untrustworthy. She couldn't even be loyal to her aunt and her nigga. Why would he ever think she'd be loyal to him?

"I know. I know. No one can know." Tia rolled her eyes. "But ain't you tired of sneaking around? I am. Fuck St. Louis. Why can't we just move away? That way we don't have to deal with LaLa or Gunz."

"You know I can't do that. All of my businesses are here."

"It's always about you and what you want. When is it gon' be about me? I'm tired of sneaking around. I want everyone to know you belong to me. Gavin should know that you're his dad."

"You know how many lives we'll fuck up if people knew the truth? I love you. I swear to God I do but I ain't trying to lose my life behind no pussy. No matter how good it is."

"Tell me how you really feel." Tia screwed up her face.

"I ain't tryin' to hurt you but it is what it is. It's just not the right time."

"Seems to me like it'll never be."

"It will." He held each of her hands. "You just gotta be patient."

"I've been being patient since I was seventeen." She sneered, angrily.

"I just need a li'l more time." He lied.

"How much? I don't know how much more of this I can take. I hate going home to that nigga. Ever since he lost his fuckin' eye, all he do is bitch and complain like a fuckin' old man—"

"He is an old man." Kingston reminded her.

"Whatever. You know what I mean. We don't do shit no more. All he wanna do is stay in the house, eat, fuck and talk shit about Gray and them raggedy-ass kids. I swear if this nigga compare me to that big bitch one more time I'ma explode."

"What he be sayin'?" Kingston wiped off his dick and laughed.

"He compares the way I cook to her; the way I clean the house and the way I take care of Gavin. In his eyes I can't do shit right. He act like that bitch is God or something. This muthafucka even had the nerve to give me pointers on how to suck his dick like her." She slipped on her sneakers.

"That nigga Gunz wild." Kingston chuckled, discarding the soiled rag.

"That shit ain't funny." Tia hit him in the face with a pillow. "That nigga crazy for real. If he ain't talkin' about Gray, he plotting revenge against Cam. I'll be glad when one of 'em kills the other 'cause I'm tired of this shit."

"Ain't that nigga out the pen? My old bird told me he was coming home soon."

"How yo' mama know?" Tia eyed him quizzically.

"She cool wit' his old dude."

"Mmm." She pondered his confession.

Tia had no idea that Kingston's mom and Cam's dad knew each other.

"Anyway. Fuck all that. What are we doing? I'm not playin' Kingston. I'm tired of this. You ain't gon' keep jerkin' me around. We need to tell the truth. Fuck Gunz and LaLa."

"So, you don't care how this gon' affect your aunt?"

"No. She grown and LaLa don't give a damn about nobody but herself. I love the bitch, but my feelings come first. Period."

"You cold-blooded."

111

"Nah, I'm fed up with the bullshit. That's what I am." Tia put her foot down.

"Look." Kingston stood up and gazed down into her angry brown eyes. "I want shit to be different too but you gotta give me more time."

"How much time do you need? Our son is fuckin' three and he's starting to look more and more like you every day. The only thing that's keeping my black ass alive is the fact that he's dark skinned and Gunz is dark skinned too."

"What you want me to do? You knew what it was from the start, and when you saw shit wasn't going your way, you started fuckin' wit' my nigga to make me jealous—"

"And it worked! How you think we got Gavin? Didn't nobody tell you to nut up in me!"

"Bottom line shorty. Can't nobody know." He turned his back on her.

"Why?" She made him face her. "Why can't nobody know? Let you tell it, you don't even fuck wit' LaLa like that and we both know Gunz ain't even your homeboy for real. I'm the one that's got the most to lose. So, what's really good? Let me find out you got feelings for her?"

"Feelings for who?" Kingston mean-mugged her.

"My aunt nigga!"

"C'mon. You on that bullshit. You know damn well I don't give a fuck about LaLa big head ass."

"Put that on Gavin."

"What the fuck I look like? I ain't doing that childish-ass shit."

"Do it." Tia stood her ground.

"What's next? You want me to pinky swear too?"

"I'm not playin'. Put that on your son. Matter of fact, put that on both of your sons."

"Man, watch out." He pushed her out the way. "You doing too much."

"Nah, nigga, I ain't doing enough! Put that on your son or I swear to God I'm going home and tellin' Gunz everything!"

Kingston paused midstride. Tia was pulling out all the stops. She wasn't going to let him off easily this time. His back was against the wall. If he didn't tell her what she wanted to hear the countdown to him taking his last breath would begin.

"A'ight man, shit. I put that on my son. You happy now?"

"Yep." She giddily pecked his lips.

"Get the fuck out my face." He side-stepped her.

"I love you too." She grabbed her purse and headed towards the door.

"Yeah-yeah-yeah. Kiss my son for me when you get home!"

8

"Three bad bitches, fuckin' on me. Top floor at my penthouse. Young rich nigga, I'm on my roll."- Meek Mill feat Cardi B, "On Me"

Cam thought finding out he had triplets was a mind fuck, but after his conversation with Victor, he felt like someone had nutted on his brain. What the hell was he going to do? If Gray wasn't the person who snitched on him, and he didn't find the culprit by the following Sunday she'd be dead. Their children would also be motherless just like him. It was too much. He wanted to place his face out the car window and scream. He wanted to bash somebody's face in. It was too much shit going on at once. For the first time in his life, Cam couldn't keep up. He felt trampled on. Life was much simpler in jail. He'd come home to nothing by chaos. Cam was deeply troubled. Being conflicted wasn't new to him, but when he was facing life, sober things seemed ten times more stressful. He needed a quiet space, a blunt and a glass of Hennessy immediately. There wasn't a man on the planet who could face his troubles without knocking back a drink or two. He wasn't going to go back to his old ways by using alcohol as a crutch, but his nerves were a mess. Thankfully, he'd pulled up to his new crib. The ride home from Victor's had been a long one. It was sunny out when they'd left and now night had come. Cam wondered what his babies were doing. Did they miss him as much as he missed them? It felt like he'd left half his heart back at Gray's crib. They would have to figure out their living situation soon because he couldn't imagine going to sleep each night without his kids.

"A'ight fam." He gave Priest a handshake. "I'ma get up wit' you tomor."

"Yep." Priest said ready to go home.

For him, it had been a long day too. Cam hopped out and headed inside his building. While in prison he had Quan sell his old apartment and find him a new place to lay his head. He could've gone to his and Gray's forever home, but after everything that had gone down, he didn't want to return there. The mansion held too many bad memories. He didn't want to return unless he had Gray and the kids by his side. The way things were looking that would never happen. It was best he sell it. His new condo was on the 20th floor and was the most expensive in the building. He couldn't wait to get inside and unwind. Using his key, he unlocked the door and found Devin and a room full of strippers awaiting his arrival.

"Welcome home baby." She held out her arms.

Cam didn't know what to think. His brain expressed no thoughts other than to register he was shocked. He wasn't really in the mood or prepared for this. He couldn't speak and wasn't even given anytime to take in the atmosphere before *Thotiana* by Blueface came on. The strippers turned their backs to him and started shaking their asses to the hip hop beat. All Cam could focus on was ten different asses wiggling, bouncing and popping. There were an array of colors and silhouettes inside the living room. Some girls had skin the shade of sand, others ground coffee. Devin stood in the center of the buxom beauties dressed in nothing but a Cartier diamond necklace, white waist-length fur, white lace bra and panties. An iced-out Rolex gleamed like a fallen star from her wrist. Her hair was styled in a warm brown bob that stopped at her chin. Cam's dick instantly got hard. Devin was a gorgeous looking woman. Cinnamon colored skin graced her toned body. She was 5'3 of Godiva chocolate goodness. Her natural breasts fit perfectly inside Cam's large hands. Her flat stomach, curvy hips and thick legs added to her unstoppable sex appeal.

She and Gray were complete opposites physically and mentally. She wasn't a go-getter or self-sufficient. Devin was all about her man and his needs. Whatever Cam asked of her she did. She held him down the entire time he was locked up. She took his phone calls, sent him letters and broke her neck to see him. She let it be known that she was unabashedly in love with Cam. She loved how fine he was. How niggas feared him. He, however, had love for her but wasn't nowhere near in love. Only one woman had access to his heart in that way. No other female would ever get that close to him again. He felt bad because Devin was a sweet girl. She was loyal to a fault and held him down. For that he officially made her his lady halfway through his prison sentence.

The only reason he'd done it was because she was easy to get along with and he craved companionship. Cam hated to be alone. He always needed a woman by his side. That was part of the reason he ran to her after finding Gray kissing Gunz. Devin was the type of woman he was used to dealing with. She was codependent and needy. She idolized him like he was a god. She was the kind of girl niggas like him adored. She fed his ego. She was easy to handle. She didn't challenge him. She made him feel like he was the ruler of the world. Gray always made him feel like she would be good with or without him. Cam never felt like a permanent fixture in her life. He never felt as if he truly had every piece of her heart. She always had one foot out the door.

Cam would practically have to push Devin in front of a moving car to get her to leave him alone. After being there for him his entire bid, Cam had to show her his appreciation. That's why he copped her the necklace, watch, a whole new wardrobe and a few Celine bags. If that wasn't enough, he told her she could move in, but now that he hadn't killed Gray and the kids were involved, the dynamics of he and Devin's relationship was about to change. She was going to be pissed when she found out Gray was in town and they had three kids. Cam had every intention on telling her as soon as he walked in the crib but with the display of asses in his face he couldn't concentrate. Cam hadn't had sex in almost four years. He was ready to break a bitch in a half. He secretly wished that woman could've been Gray. He missed everything about her honey colored flesh and curvaceous silky-smooth frame. But he would never fuck with her on that level. He loathed her mere existence now.

"You miss me?" Devin sauntered over to him seductively.

"If I said no would it matter?" He took in the features of her makeup covered face.

"Yeah." She slid the tip of her stiletto nail down the side of his face. "Cause I know it would be a lie."

"Is that right?"

"Your hard dick tells me otherwise." She grinned wickedly while stroking his throbbing cock through his jeans.

Devin was so turned on that her juices began to trickle down her inner thigh.

"Oh, you actin' up." Cam roughly drew her into his strong embrace.

"You gon' punish me?" She wrapped her arms around his neck and tried to pull him in for a kiss.

Cam jerked his head back. He would never put his mouth on another woman's lips. Gray would be the last chick to know what his lips tasted like.

"Kiss my dick instead."

"Anything for you baby."

Never taking her eyes off him, Devin eased down onto her knees and unzipped his jeans. Her tiny hand reached inside his boxer/brief and pulled out his 11-inch, brown dick. Precum dripped from his tip. Devin eagerly lapped up the salty liquid. The first lick sent Cam into a tailspin. It had been ages since he had his dick sucked. He'd forgot how good it felt. Leaned against the wall, he allowed her to have her way with him. Their eyes were locked on each other as the taste buds of her tongue glided up and down his veiny shaft. Her poetic expression of oral display made his manhood hard as a brick. This wasn't what he expected to come home to, but Cam wanted this feeling to last all night. The music and the strippers dancing erotically added to the experience. Most of the girls kept it professional and danced as if he wasn't getting his dick sucked by the door. Two of the dancers, however, couldn't keep their eyes off his ginormous crooked dick. Cam could practically see the drool drip from their lips.

"You want some?" He grinned arrogantly.

Both girls nodded their heads.

"Come get a taste."

Seconds later, Devin and the two strippers were all on their knees taking turns sucking his dick. Homegirl didn't even care that he was making her share. Devin

118

started to go harder when the two girls joined in. By the sound of her moans and the way she sucked and slurped his dick, Cam could tell she enjoyed every second of the illicit act. She'd deep throat his cock then place it in one of the other girl's mouths. Back-and-forth this went, until Cam started to feel his orgasm approach. Devin's pupils began to dilate as she felt his dick inflate. She absolutely loved sucking Cam's dick. He was her favorite flavor. Twirling her tongue around his steel mushroom tip, the two other girls ran their wet tongues across the side of his shaft.

"Mmm." She moaned, cupping his heavy ball sack.

Cam groaned in pleasure. Saliva dripped from his pulsating cock. Devin stroked his massive instrument with her tiny wet hands. Fisting his dick, she massaged his balls in a clockwise motion. Cam's leg began to shake. She and the two strippers were driving him insane. At any minute he would go over the edge.

"Fuuuuuuuuuuck." He growled, gripping the back of her neck.

Taking her mouth off his cock, Devin tongue kissed one of the strippers. The other stripper had begun playing with her pussy, making her quake. Devin was soaked. With hooded eyes, she continued to stroke Cam's dick until milky cum sputtered onto her face. His orgasm was wild and uncontrollably. Curse words spewed from his slacked jaw. His skin burned hot with lust. All night long this went on until the girls tapped out. Cam fucked them in every position ever created. They'd done missionary, doggystyle, 69, plow, elephant and more. Devin ate the girls out and they returned the erotic act. Three boxes of Trojan Magnum condoms were used that night. Cam had cum so much that he was sure he didn't have any sperm left. He was exhausted after but there was a conversation that still needed to be had. Alone in bed, Devin lay snuggled next to him with her head on his chest. The sun hid behind a haze of black clouds. Twinkling stars of all shapes and sizes beamed in the night sky reminding him of the greatest star of them all. . . Gray. The room was quiet. The commotion of the day gone. Cam wondered had Devin fallen asleep until she said, "What's the matter and what the hell happened to your eye?"

"I got something to tell you."

Devin's body stilled. She didn't know what he was about to say but somehow she knew it was bad. The whole time during their foursome his mind seemed elsewhere. Physically he was into it but mentally his mind seemed a million miles away.

"I don't even know if you can handle this shit."

"Just say it." She prepared herself for the worst.

"Gray and my kids in town for the wedding."

"You claim her kids?" She snarled confused.

"Yeah, I do but I ain't talking about them."

"Well, who you talkin' about then?" She sat up abruptly and glared at him.

Cam ran his hands down his face and sighed.

"Remember that night Gray came to the crib saying she was pregnant."

"Yeah." Her heart raced.

"She wasn't lying."

"So, you telling me ya'll gotta baby."

"Not a baby. Three babies."

"Three babies? How the fuck is that even possible?"

"Well, when a man—"

"Don't play wit' me." She smacked his bare chest.

"Let that be the last time you put your hands on me." Cam said in a menacing tone.

He didn't play that putting your hands-on people shit. A tingling sensation crept up Devin's spine as they glared at each other. She'd never feared him until that moment.

"I'm sorry. It won't happen again, but I'm backed in a corner here. I expected you to come home and it just be me and you. Now you tell me there are three kids added to the equation. Put yourself in my position. How would you feel if you were me?"

"I'm not you. This is about me, and to be honest wit' you, I'm not concerned about nobody's feelings except my kids."

"Wow. . ." Devin threw the covers off her body and stood up. "After everything I've done for you, this is the thanks I get."

"Lay yo' ass back down." Cam demanded.

She wanted to put up a fight, but Devin knew better. Seeing he wasn't playing, she begrudgingly climbed back into bed. Not in the mood for her antics, Cam took her by the hand and pulled her next to him. Devin resumed her position and lay her head on his solid chest.

"I know you wasn't expecting this shit. Neither was I, but this is where we are. As stressful as this situation may be, I'ma be there for my kids regardless. That's nonnegotiable so if it's too much for you, I understand."

"It's not." She said eagerly.

She and Cam had finally been reunited after almost three and a half years. She'd be damned if she lost him in less than 24 hours.

"But . . . how do you know they're even yours."

"When you see 'em you'll know why."

"When I see 'em?" Her body went rigid again.

"They're coming to the barbeque tomor." Cam stroked her arm to soothe her. "Just chill out. Everything is gonna be fine."

"If you say so." Devin muttered, knowing things wouldn't be that easy.

9

"We ended long ago. I should be numb to these emotions."-
Normani feat 6lack, "Waves"

Kema and Quan's wedding week had officially
begun. That Sunday the entire wedding party, family and
friends joined together at Forest Park. The park was 1,300
acres and was filled with 45,000 trees. There were hills,
plains, concrete filled pathways and bikeways. Park
benches were placed sporadically for people to lounge and
take in the atmosphere. Flower hedges and bushes gave the
park a relaxing and attractive feel. Several lakes, a
boathouse, The Muny, Saint Louis Zoo and The Saint
Louis Art Museum were just some of the attractions the
park had to offer. A warm July breeze rustled the leaves,
making some fall to the ground. Beams of light from the
sun shined down onto Cam's caramel face. *GET DOWN!*
GET DOWN! Gunshots cracked in the air as loud as
thunder. Cam's mind had transported back to Afghanistan.
His squad members bullet riddled bodies lay sprawled in
the dirt. The memory was so vivid it was like he was there.
His heart rate slowed to the point he thought he was going
to die. Fear took over every crevice of his body. Counting
backwards from ten, he closed his eyes and tried to calm
his nerves. The sun was still one of his biggest PTSD
triggers. In jail, he didn't have to spend much time outside.
Since he was out, he'd have to learn to adjust being
exposed to the sun. In the past, it was something he used to
dodge at all cost, but Cam no longer wanted to let his

anxiety rule his life. He had small children now. They would want to go outside, have fun and play with their father. Taking a deep full breath, he allowed the oxygen to flow to his lungs before exhaling slow. Repeatedly, he did this in hopes that he no longer felt like his chest was being squeezed with a noose.

"You good?" Quan placed his hand on his shoulder.

The feel of his friend's firm hand gave Cam the comfort he urgently needed.

"I'm tryin' to be." He answered truthfully.

The glare from the sun was not only triggering him but the weight of having Victor on his back, and three kids he knew nothing about, was messing with his mental. Cam released a slow precise breath and tried to loosen his limbs by walking back-and-forth. Rolling his head around in a circle, he rotated his shoulders while shaking out his arms and legs. He had to get the spirit of fear off of him. *Fear is nothing but false evidence appearing real,* he repeated over and over again.

"Your anxiety actin' up?"

"Yeah." Cam bent over and rested his hands on his knees.

"I got somebody that might be able to help you with that. Edris!" Quan called out. "You talked to LaLa?" He asked to distract him from his flare up.

"Not since I've been home. While I was locked down the bitch wrote me every week and was putting money on my books." Cam laughed.

Hopefully talking shit with his friends would take his mind off the glare from the sun.

"Did you hit her back?"

"Fuck, nah."

"She shouldn't have even been hitting you up. Her ho-ass begged me for your info, but she knew damn well I wasn't giving up shit, so she got Stacy ole loose lip ass to do it. Nigga can't hold water for shit."

"Aye." Cam stood up straight. "I'ma need you to look into my case. I need to find out who dropped the dime on me asap."

"I got you." Quan slapped his hand.

"Yo, these ribs bout to put ya'll niggas on ya' back." Stacy walked over with a chef apron on.

"I told you, I don't eat that shit no more." Cam said.

"Oh yeah, I forgot you a Muslim now. Ole alakazam-ass nigga."

"It's As-Salaam-Alaikum you fool and I ain't Muslim."

"My bad you a born again Christian." Stacy made air quotes with his hands.

"You need Jesus."

"And you full of shit. I don't trust no nigga that found religion after prison."

"You ignorant as fuck dawg." Cam couldn't help but laugh. "Straight up. I'm cutting out all the bullshit. All that meat and shit ain't good for you. You need to change your diet too fat boy." Cam patted Stacy's solid stomach.

After almost losing him years before to gunshot wounds, Cam would do anything to keep his friend alive.

"We getting old, nigga."

"Speak for yourself."

"Nigga, I'm good. That nut I bust last night on that stripper's titties said I'm fourteen."

"What stripper?" Quan asked confused.

He wasn't clued in that Devin had a welcome home orgy for Cam.

"Before you tell me, Cam this is Edris. Edris this is my best friend Cam."

Cam gave the guy a once over glance to size him up. He and Edris were the same height, but the nigga looked mad young. Edris had a baby face but was every bit of 32. He was 6'4 with a chestnut skin complexion, curly box and a goatee. From what Cam could see the dude was pretty clean cut. He didn't have any tattoos on his arms or legs. The white tee, black jogging shorts, Vans socks, matching sneakers and small iced-out chains gave him the edge he desperately needed.

"What's good?" Cam gave him a pound.

"What's going on fam? Welcome home." Edris gave him a one-armed hug.

"Preciate it. Aye yo. Ya'll gon' shoot over to the cemetery wit' me tomorrow?"

"Yeah." Stacy and Quan agreed.

"Bet, but look . . . I walk in the crib last night and its bitches and titties everywhere! All I saw was ass-ass-ass and more ass. I'm talkin' pussy galore."

"Whoa-whoa. Wait a minute." Quan said taken aback by the conversation.

"Nah, let 'em finish. He gotta paint the picture nigga." Stacy grinned.

"As I was sayin'. My li'l mama had on the white fur and shit. You know it was her first time seeing the kid since I got home so she come over and tried to give me a kiss and I'm like hold up. You know I don't play them type of games. The last bitch I kissed got me sent up state."

"Facts and she stole yo' dogs too." Stacy agreed.

"Indeed, so instead of kissing my mouth I told her to kiss my dick." Cam grinned devilishly. "I was just talking shit. I ain't really think she was gon' do it, but before I could blink, she was down on her knees. She had my whole dick in her mouth. Straight up. My dick was all the way down her esophagus. I felt all her throat glands and shit."

"Cam!" Quan interjected once more.

"Then I let two of the stripper bitches join in and them ho's got to tag-teaming my dick. It was like boing-boing-boing-boing." He humped the air like he was fucking their mouths.

"Nigga, will you shut up! This ain't just the homie. This is Pastor Edris. He's standing in for his father Bishop John and officiating the wedding." Quan finally explained.

"Oh shit." Cam put his hand up to his mouth. "My bad preach. I ain't mean no disrespect. Nigga, you should've said that off rip."

"I tried."

"It's all good, my brother." Pastor Edris held up his hands. "No judgement here. I've had a few of those wild nights in the past."

127

"Oh word?"

"The operative word is past. After being out here in the streets and getting shot three times, I decided to change my life around."

"You was a street nigga?" Cam said skeptically.

"Yeah, I was in a gang, sold dope, rained down on cats and all that. It's not something I'm proud of, but if I didn't go through what I went through, I wouldn't be standing here right now. I almost died when I got shot. I flatlined on the table and everything."

"Damn." Cam replied shocked.

"Now why do you think God gave me a second chance at life?" Pastor Edris looked around at the fellas.

They all shrugged.

"It's because he had a plan for me. I always knew I had a calling to lead people but the choices I was making pulled me further and further away from my calling. I knew I was supposed to be more than just a hustler. Nothing good would come from that life. Sure, the money, women, cars and jewels gave me instant gratification, but my soul was empty when I laid down to rest at night. I had no peace. It wasn't until I was at death's door that I decided to change my life and devote the energy I put towards destroying my community to building God's kingdom."

"That's what's up. That's some deep shit." Cam nodded his head.

He couldn't do nothing but respect Pastor Edris' testimony. If meeting him taught him anything it was never to judge a book by it's cover.

"I'm still a boss. I just do it for God. You can be on the same path to righteous if you put some of that energy towards Christ and the church."

"I'm good. I got God on speed dial."

"I talk to that nigga long distance." Stacy massaged the back of his neck, feeling like a heathen.

"Ya'll silly." Pastor Edris chuckled. "On the real, you should consider coming down to the church."

"I mean, I was considering finding a church home." Cam opened his self-up to the idea. "While I was locked up, I was attending bible study and it really calmed a nigga. I realized Jesus ain't so bad after all. That nigga be having my back for real. Even when I don't deserve it."

"The bible said before you were born, before you were conceived in your mother's womb, he knew you. He knew everything you would become. From your bad decisions down to the number of hairs on your head and he still died for you. That makes you worth it."

"Amen!" Stacy shouted like he was in church.

"I'm liking what you talkin' Preach. You might get me down to your church after all. With everything I got going on, I need God more than ever." Cam let out an exasperated sigh as Devin walked over and circled her arms around his waist.

"What ya'll talking about? You was tellin' them about the foursome we had last night?"

"And if you come, bring her too." Pastor Edris eyed Devin with disdain.

"Yo, watch your mouth. This Pastor Edris." Cam scolded.

"Oh, I'm sorry. Nice to meet you. I'm Devin." She shook his hand.

"Pleasure is all mine. You two make a gorgeous looking couple. Can I assume you'll be the next couple to jump the broom?"

"I hope so." Devin gazed lovingly at Cam.

"Hell no." He clarified.

"Really babe?" She gasped.

Stacy cleared his throat.

"You can't get married when you're already married. But come to think about it, the way Devin get down, she might consider it."

"I might share his penis every once in a while, but I will never share his heart or his last name." She checked him.

"Too late." Stacy coughed into his hand.

"So, you're married?" Pastor Edris inquired confused.

"Yeah, unfortunately." Cam groaned, thinking about Gray.

She and the kids would be arriving soon. He couldn't wait to see all five of his shorties. Facetiming them before bed and that morning wasn't enough. He needed to see their faces, hold them in his arms and bath in their laughter. Seeing Gray was another thing. He'd been anticipating and dreading her arrival all day. They despised each other, but whenever he was within ten feet of her, his heart started to pitter patter like a li'l bitch. The effect she had on him was crazy. She could either piss him off or make his dick throb with undying need to be inside of her.

130

"I'm sorry to hear that. Are you two considering divorce?" Pastor Edris asked.

"Not considering . . . doing."

"No disrespect to your current situation but I would highly recommend you try marriage counseling before you go through with the divorce."

"I don't know about that, Preach. Too much shit done went down between me and ole girl. Our marriage is a lost cause."

"Yeah, she's the one who blacked his eye." Stacy added.

"Stop bringing up old shit."

"Old shit?" Stacy drew his head back "It just happened the day before yesterday."

"Oh, so she's the one that blacked your eye." Devin raised one of her brows.

"Domestic violence is never okay but something that I've learned about love is you will have your heartbroken a million times. We all go into love expecting our partners to be these perfect human beings that are going to come into our lives and heal everything that's broken. The thing about it is nobody's perfect. We think that just because we fall in love and that people love us, they're going to be perfect for us. And that they're always gonna make us feel as good as they did in the beginning of the relationship 'cause that's the thing we're all trying to hold onto. But love isn't perfect. It hurts, it's disappointing, it can be devastatingly bruising to our pride and ego." Pastor Edris spoke with conviction. "Love equals forgiveness. The two can't be separated. To truly love, you must forgive. To truly forgive, you must love. God taught us that. Just as we

131

mess up over and over again, he still loves us and never turns his back on us. So, isn't it hypercritical of us to expect someone to love us despite our flaws, even when we don't offer that same kind of commitment to God? Now, I don't know what has happened between you and your wife, but real love will never return to you void. If what you shared was real, don't give up on her."

Forgiveness was something Cam struggled with his whole life. He struggled with it even more now. How could he make amends with someone who had possibly betrayed him not once but twice? Each time he thought about Gray's deciet the wound cut deep. While in jail, he'd read somewhere that forgiveness is letting go of all negative emotions and memories. It was moving on with whatever positive remained, and if nothing remained, then the relationship was all negative. That wasn't true for him and Gray. Their relationship was 85% good. Yes, they had moments of discord. They lacked trust and didn't know how to communicate. But sometimes the hardest part about loving Gray was being away from her. Cam missed her the moment he walked out of the door each day. There were times where he'd lay awake holding her at night wondering what he'd done in life to deserve her. Women like Gray were a rarity. She might not have been his first love, but she was the love that made all other love irrelevant.

"Here's my card. Give it some thought." Pastor Edris held out his hand.

"I don't think that's necessary." Devin snatched the card from his grasp. "He's very happy where he's at. Ain't that right babe?"

"I mean . . . we good." Cam shrugged his shoulders.

"This bitch suck dick so good she got this nigga lying to a pastor. I swear these bitches be the devil. Straight treacherous!" Stacy joked with a hint of seriousness.

"Babe, we're better than good." Devin squeezed him tight. "You're finally home. We got our own place. We can finally start our life together. Like what more could we possibly ask for?"

"Ugh, gag me with a spoon." Kema curled her upper lip.

She'd been listening in on the guys' conversation. Each time Devin spoke it made her insides churn. She couldn't stand the bitch. Not only was Devin a whore, she was a leech and a viper. The bitch was worse than LaLa in her eyes. At least LaLa never switched up. She was who she was whether bad or good. She didn't pretend to be anything but a selfish, hateful, spiteful cunt. Devin was the kind of chick whose treachery sneaked up on you. It wasn't in your face. She wanted people to think she was a good person when really the chick had no identity. The only goal she had in life was to be wifey. She was so thirsty to be a man's main chick that she would dumb herself down and adapt to the situation to be what the man she was dealing with needed her to be. Kema would never have respect for her. Any woman that willingly messed with a man that she knew had a girl wasn't and would never be shit in her eyes.

"Slit my throat and drink it." Mo exclaimed a few feet away.

Kema turned in her direction. It was like she was seeing a unicorn for the first time. She'd heard stories and seen pictures of the infamous Mo but seeing her face-to-face was an experience she wasn't prepared for. Her body was insane. She was tall like a supermodel. She had mesmerizing 32 DD breasts, full hips and a round ass from

133

bearing six children. If her body wasn't intimidating enough, her gorgeous face took Kema's breath away. She fully understood now why Quan was so obsessed with her. Her skin reminded her of rich fudge. It was silky smooth and chocolate. Whiskey brown, almond shaped eyes, high cheekbones that were so sharp they resembled blades, and plump, luscious lips made up the features of her heart stopping face.

In the beginning of Kema and Quan's relationship she felt like she was living in Mo's shadows. Quan would go on and on about how great of a woman she was. Kema didn't know where she fit into his life. It seemed like he had no use for her except to fulfil his sexual needs, so she fell back. Falling back was the best thing she could've done. She had to show him that she would not play second fiddle to another woman, especially not the memory of his ex. Kema gave Quan a run for his money. She went out on dates with other men and showed him that she wasn't no slouch. She too was hard to get and keep. Quan quickly recognized her worth and got it together. He realized that he could no longer live in the past. He had a woman in his life that was down for him and loved him flaws and all. Once they got on the same page, they were unstoppable. With God, time and prayer they were about to say, 'I do'. Staring at each other, the two ladies burst out and laughed.

"Girl!"

"She getting on your nerves too?" Mo eased her way.

"Getting? She stomping on them muthafuckas. I'm just waiting for her to say something out of pocket so I can drag her ass. I've been waiting thirteen years to fuck her up." Kema burned a hole in the back of Devin's head as she cracked her knuckles.

"I don't know what in the hell my brother sees in her."

"You know damn well what he sees in her. A fat ass, a deep throat and some pussy."

"And don't forget threesomes."

"No bitch it was a foursome."

"You lyin'!" Mo's mouth dropped wide open.

"I wish I was but I'm not. I used to be a ho' but that bitch ain't got no shame. You know she used to mess with Gunz too."

"I think I heard that." Mo glared at Devin with contempt.

"Yeah, when Gray and Gunz first started dating she was his side bitch."

"Please tell me she didn't know about Gray."

"Of course, her rat-ass did. She ain't give a fuck. The bitch wanted him so bad she even lied about being pregnant."

"Ooh girl. This is too much tea for me to digest!" Mo placed her hand on her chest.

She knew all too well about shiesty bitches going after men that were taken. For a second, Kema sat silent and stared at her with a blank expression.

"What? I got something on my face?" Mo wiped her mouth.

"You ain't too bad after all. I didn't know how I was gon' feel meeting you."

"Really?" Mo said genuinely surprised.

"You are the notorious Mo. The one who got away."

"Girl, I didn't get away. I ran away. No fuck that. I took a helicopter out that bitch."

"He was that bad?" Kema laughed.

"You don't even wanna know but I'm happy to say Quan has done a complete 180. You got a good one now. Back then it would've been a completely different story. I'm so glad he's found you. He needed a good woman in his life. For so long, he punished himself for the way he did me, but I had been moved on as you can see." Mo looked over at her six children Ryan, Makiah, King, Zaire, Deoni and Khadeen.

"None of the stuff we went through affected me anymore. We were kids. We didn't know what the hell we were doing. He loved me the best he could at the time and vice versa but with you it's different." Mo took Kema's hand in hers. "I see the way he looks at you. That man adores you, and when he talks about you, he lights up in a way I've never seen before."

"That means a lot coming from you. You know it's been hard living in your shadow. I didn't know what to think when Quan made it clear that you were always going to be in his life. That was very intimidating but with time I saw that I had nothing to worry about. I'm happy that you two are still good friends. Without you, he wouldn't be the man he is today."

This was how two grown women who loved the same man at different stages of their lives conversed. This was a big girl moment that Kema didn't know she needed until the conversation began. Any insecurities she might've had about Quan and Mo were completely put to rest. She was happily married, and Quan was so in love with Kema that in a few short days she'd be donning his last name. Mo was the last thing she had to worry about. Her only concern now was making sure her wedding went off without a hitch. As if the devil read her mind, out of nowhere Devin sat across from them and interrupted their chat. Kema rolled her eyes. She knew, without a doubt, that Devin was about to say something to piss her off.

"So, girl are you nervous?"

"Kema." She spoke flatly.

"Huh?" Devin replied perplexed.

"Kema. My name is Kema not girl. We ain't friends. If it wasn't for my man's best friend, you wouldn't even be here, so don't get it twisted."

"Mmm, excuse me. Well, *Kema.*" Devin stressed her name. "As I was saying, are you nervous? Considering you're marrying a serial cheater."

"Not at all. Considering he's marrying a serial killer. Now keep fuckin' with me."

"I mean, I don't understand why you're getting so upset. Let's not pretend, it's no secret your man like to lay it low and spread it wide. Ask Mo, she knows firsthand."

"Hold up bitch—" Mo jumped off the bench only for Kema to hold her back.

"Uh ah. This light work, sis. I got it."

"Sis? Ya'll sister wives? Mmm . . . that's nasty. I ain't even know black people was into shit like that."

"You know all too well bitch. Having foursomes and shit." Mo spat.

"Mo, chill. I got it." Kema stressed.

"Well, you betta get her 'cause I'm about to slap the shit out this bitch."

"Let's be clear." Kema leaned forward and shot Devin a threatening glare. "You don't know shit about my nigga."

"You're right, sis, I don't. I just know he's not always . . . *your* nigga."

"Oh god. Oh Lord. BOSS!" Mo called out for her husband. "Get the bail money ready 'cause I'm about to go to jail!"

"Ten, nine, eight, seven." Kema bounced her right leg at a rapid speed. "Ooh Jesus. Don't fuck her up. It's your wedding week. You cannot go to jail."

"Don't let the devil use you. She ain't worth it Miss Celie. She ain't worth it." Mo said it just like Oprah Winfrey in the Color Purple.

"Nah, you might need to fuck her up." Heidi announced ready to fight.

She'd heard all the foul shit that came out of Devin's mouth.

"Babe? Who all is in this wedding?" Devin ignored the girls theatrics.

"Me, Stacy, Li'l Quan then Kema got Heidi, this nigga name Tee-Tee—"

"Where the fuck that fruity-ass nigga at anyway?" Stacy interrupted.

"Don't talk about my friend." Kema spat. "He's away on business. He'll be here for the rest of the festivities."

"So that's the whole wedding party?" Devin continued her line of questioning.

"And my baby mama, Gray." Cam replied in a daze.

The notion that Gray was his baby mama hit him like a ton of bricks. From the second he laid eyes on her, he wanted her to be the mother of his kids. He couldn't see himself having children with anyone else.

"Ugh, don't even bring her up." Devin groaned, repulsed. "I still can't get over what she did. What mother keeps their children away from their father?"

"She had her reasons." Heidi jumped in.

"What could possibly be the reason? Outside of her being a selfish bitch?"

"The same reason." Kema started to take off her earrings. "You about to catch these hands."

"Aww shit. C'mon babe. Not today." Quan rushed over to stop her.

"Nah, let her go." Stacy urged. "C'mon Killa Kem! I ain't seen Killa Kem whoop ass in a minute!"

"Don't sweat your weave out getting all rachet. It was just a question." Devin smirked.

She loved that she was getting under Kema's skin.

"Don't fuckin' worry about why she ain't tell 'em! It ain't none of your fuckin' business!" Quan held her back. "You just a bitch he's fuckin'. At the end of the day, that's between husband and wife. Last I checked you wasn't neither. Don't mistake a keyring for a wedding ring, bitch." Kema waved her left hand. "And let's be clear, my bitch can take her husband back anytime, anyplace, anywhere, any city, any state, any country or any continent! The only reason why you wit 'em is because she don't want 'em!"

"Get her bitch!" Mo gave Kema a high-five.

"Aye." Cam furrowed his brows and frowned. "Leave me outta this."

"And you better pray that don't change 'cause the minute it do it's a wrap for you and your big ass forehead."

"Go Kema! Go Kema! It's your wedding day! It's your wedding day!" Stacy sang doing the Prep.

"Stacy shut yo dumb-ass up!" Cam shot.

"Aww shit. Start packing your bags Quack-Quack. Looks like that day came early. Cam, your wife just pulled up." Mo beamed brightly.

Everyone turned and focused on the black SUV pulling up. Once the car was parked, the driver got out and opened the back door. Aoki and Press stepped out first. Upon seeing their faces, Cam smiled. It was the first time that day he honestly felt happy. Being around the kids made him feel complete in ways money, pussy or power couldn't. Like a magnet he was connected to each of their souls. Cam didn't even realize he'd started walking their way until Gray came into full view. Any anxiety from earlier vanished. Time stood still. She appeared like the angel of death stopping him dead in his tracks. Somehow, she'd sucked him into her wicked vortex. English became a foreign language. The palms of his hands became misty with sweat. Birds stopped chirping. Leaves stopped falling. The sun shined down exclusively on her like a spotlight. It was clear. She was there to take what was left of his heart and destroy it. Cam's chestnut orbs connected to her ocean blue ones. Gray was classically beautiful in a way that was reminiscent of Nancy Wilson, Diahann Carroll or Joyce

140

Bryant. Her eyes were passion in ice. It was damn near impossible for him not to be held prisoner by them. Her rosy cheekbones were highlighted with some gold shit that made them gleam under the sunlight. Gray's face was perfect. Every square inch was symmetrical. The short blonde haircut she rocked framed it stunningly. Rose gold eyeshadow decorated her eyes while pink lip-gloss adorned her heart shaped lips. Normally, her facial features were what drove Cam crazy but that hot July afternoon it was what she barely wore that nearly put him in his grave. The Gray he'd met years before was the kind of girl that rocked two-piece Ashely Stewart suits to the club during the middle of August. This femme fatale holding one of his kids on her hip had on just enough clothes not to get arrested. She literally only wore a nude bandeau bra and high-waisted panties. What made the look an actual outfit was the nude crochet crop top and skirt that stopped at her ankles. Yeezy PVC pumps and a Chanel beach purse topped everything off. The full swell of her bronzed breasts bounced with each step she took. Cam's throat became drier the closer she neared. Sex was written all over her face. He could taste it on his tongue. The sweet, clean scent of her perfume caused his cock to pulsate against the seam of his cotton shorts. Cam wanted to kill her. He was two seconds away from choking her out. In the past, Gray would've never disrespected him by wearing no bullshit like this around his friends.

"Fuck you got on?" He scowled.

"Clothes." She snapped back not liking his sour attitude.

"You really tryin' me, Gray."

"Boy move." She tried to push him out the way.

"Go home and change." Cam blocked her path.

141

"You funny." She attempted to side step him again.

"I ain't fuckin' playin' and I ain't in the business of repeating myself."

"I don't give a fuck. You better get the hell out my face. You don't run shit over here."

"On God, Gray. Go home." Cam shot her a look that let her know he wasn't playing.

"You betta move before I black yo' other eye." She handed him a sleeping Sky and bogarted her way past him.

Gray quickly regretted her decision. She should've stayed hidden behind Cam's large frame. All the reasons not to come back to St. Louis were there staring her in the face. Some expressions were of love and admiration, others scorn and disappointment. A blanket of panic covered her as she swallowed the lump in her throat. She'd been avoiding this moment since she decided not to tell Cam, or anyone connected to him about the triplets. She knew they all would hate her for what she'd done. She couldn't blame them. What she'd done was wrong, but the only person Gray had to protect her was herself. She had to do what was best for her, her kids, her mental health and her heart. At least that's what she kept telling herself.

"Auntie Kema! Auntie Heidi!" Aoki and Press ran over and gave them both a big hug.

"Look at you two. Ya'll got so big." Heidi placed a kiss on Aoki's forehead as she held her close.

Mo looked on with tears in her eyes. Aoki, Press and the triplets were her nieces and nephew and she had no connection with them at all.

"Ya'll remember me?" Her voice croaked as she tried to keep it together.

"Hi Mrs. Mo." Both girls gave her a warm hug.

Mo's heart sank. She wished the girls felt comfortable enough to call her auntie too.

"Is Ryan and Makiah here?" Aoki asked eagerly.

She missed her frenemies.

"They're over there playing with the other kids." Mo pointed. "Press, King is over there too."

Press gave her a nervous smile and followed slowly behind her sister. Harlem, Makiah, Ryan, King, Zaire, Deoni, Khadeen, Li'l Quan, Diggy Jr., his sister Taylani and their little brother Bronx and Stacy's daughter, Kayla, were all in the grass having a ball. She'd been hysterically nervous about seeing King since they arrived back in the states. He used to be her best friend. Whose to say he didn't have a new best friend now. What if he didn't remember her? Even worse, what if he no longer wanted to be her friend? Press' little feeble heart wouldn't be able to handle it. King was not only her best friend but her protector. When the kids at school used to make fun of her for being too sweet, ditzy and naive, he was the one who stood up for her. No one could touch her. Anyone that tried to bully her, King would pound into the ground. He was her hero. The knight in shining armor she read about in fairytales.

At the age of six, she didn't know what her feelings for King were. All she knew was that she became profoundly happy whenever he was around. At the age of nine, Press was older, wiser and certain. She knew without a shadow of a doubt how she felt about King. He wasn't just a childhood friend. He was her first crush. Her true north star. She loved him then and now as she watched him run down the field the love she felt for him blazed hotter than a million suns. He was her soulmate. The boy who would grow up to be the man she'd marry. As if it were her

143

first-time laying eyes on him, Press became smitten all over again. King was so handsome he rendered her speechless. He was no longer the scrawny little, Godiva chocolate boy with long wavy hair. His ravenous, wild, curly mane blew in the wind as he ran at full speed to catch the football Pastor Edris tossed to him. On gangly thin limbs, he raised his hands in the air and captured the ball, scoring a touchdown.

All the kids yelled and screamed, excited that he'd scored his team extra points. King relished the attention. Press wondered when he'd become so sociable. When they were little, he was a loner that wasn't particularly friendly. He was all about his schoolwork and selling candy on the playground. He didn't even care that all the girls in their class swooned over him. He never paid them any attention. He only had eyes for her. Press was pretty sure she was the only person he was nice to. They were inseparable but as some girl with skin the shade of black Hawaiian sand approached him with a congratulatory kiss on the cheek, Press realized that the raven-haired boy she once knew had found someone more special than her and it broke her heart. Completely crushed, she turned to walk away before he could spot her.

"Press!" Aoki called out. "Where you going?"

Now that she'd been exposed, Press had no choice but to face the music.

"Ooh King! There go yo' li'l girlfriend!" His big sister, Makiah, teased.

King turned to see what his sister was talking about. When his eyes landed on Press, a smile gradually crept onto his face. Suddenly, the air grew thick with a tenderness that couldn't be faked. King's hypnotic brown eyes took in every inch of Press. Her hair was shorter, but

144

she was still as pretty as he remembered if not prettier. Slowly, he walked over to her leaving his admirer behind. Mad that he left, the girl folded her arms across her chest angrily. Within seconds, King was in her personal space. Press' breath hitched as soon as the toe of their sneakers touched.

"You ain't gon' speak?"

Press looked down and shuffled her feet. King was not only bigger, but his voice was an octave deeper. His smooth baritone echoed through her bones, making her swoon with unexpected emotion.

"Look at me when I'm talking to you." King placed his index and thumb on her chin and tilted her head back.

He'd waited almost four years to look into those pretty brown eyes again. He wasn't going to allow her to make him miss a moment. Press forgot how to speak as she gazed absently at his face. There wasn't a hint of acne in sight. Skin as velvety as his wouldn't allow it.

"Hi." She spoke shyly.

"Much better." King smirked, holding her chin between his fingertips. "You know I'm mad at you right?"

"Why?" Her voice croaked.

"You didn't call or text."

"I wanted to. I did but my mama said I couldn't." Press said regrettably.

The last thing she wanted was for King to be mad at her the entire trip. She wanted her friend back. She wanted him to like her and not the girl that was giving her the evil eye behind him.

"Don't let it happen again or I'm gon' have to find me a new best friend."

"It look like you already got one." She glanced over his shoulder.

King looked back at the girl.

"Don't worry about her. She a stalker. Everybody know I only got eyes for you."

Press shyly hung her head. She could feel the heat growing on her cheeks. Unwilling to let her hide from him or herself, King lifted her head again. He enjoyed seeing the color pink spread across her face like wild fire.

Under the pavilion, Mo eased towards two of the triplets in awe. When she heard that her brother and Gray had triplets, she was stunned to say the least, but to see them live in the flesh blew her fucking mind. The kids were gorgeous. They were the perfect blend of both their parents. All the kids were fresh to death. Reign wore a Givenchy fitted tracksuit and Bred 1's. Sky and Beaux were dressed just alike in Givenchy track jackets, white camisoles, Givenchy skirts, socks and Bred 1's.

"What's your name, pretty girl?" She asked Beaux.

"Mama, who is this lady?" Beaux asked her mother instead of giving her name.

"Baby, that's your Auntie Mo." Gray stood nervously behind her daughter and son.

She was the most anxious about seeing Mo. They'd begun to grow close before her sudden departure. If it hadn't been for Mo, she wouldn't have even known she was pregnant. Gray wanted to tell her about the triplets, but fear of her telling Cam kept her at bay. No matter how cool they were, Mo's loyalty would always be with her brother.

146

"Tell her your name." She gave Beaux a little nudge.

"My name Beaux and his name Reign." She pointed to her brother. "Mommy named us after the rainbow in da sky."

"I see and what a pretty name." Mo touched a tendril of her hair. "They're beautiful Gray. You did a great job."

"Thank you."

"I just wish I could've been involved in their lives from the beginning. We all do." She gestured to her brother, husband, Quan and the rest of the crew.

If Mo's mission was to make Gray feel bad, she'd succeeded. Gray wanted nothing more than to curl into a tiny ball and disappear. Yes, she was stronger now but having the people she cared for upset with her was never a good feeling. She hated it, especially since she knew she was the cause of everyone's pain. Sensing her apprehension, Mo reached out and caressed her arm.

"It's all good. I understand why you did what you did. I know my brother. I know how he can get. The nigga is crazy. I would've ran too if I had a baby by Stringer Bell." She joked, causing Gray to laugh.

"I needed that laugh. Thank you Mo and I'm so sorry. My intentions were never to hurt anyone. I just did what I felt was best at the time and that was to protect me and my kids."

"Good fuckin' job. Everything is always about you." Cam held a sleeping Sky in his arms.

Her soft hair rubbed against the side of his neck. It amazed him that Gray could apologize to his sister but not give him the same courtesy. He was the one she'd hurt deeply.

"Mind your business, Cam." Mo ordered.

"Nah, fuck that. You know I'm not wrong. What she did was fucked up. You shouldn't even be talkin' to her. You're my blood."

"You know what? I'ma just go." Gray decided before she blew up.

"No, the hell you ain't." Kema spoke up. "This my damn party."

"I get that friend, but I didn't come here to cause all this drama."

"Ya'll got three kids together—"

"Five." Cam cut her off.

"Okay five. With that being said, ya'll gon' have to learn how to coexist. So, I would advise both of you to get out of your feelings and act like fuckin' adults for the sake of these kids."

"Period." Mo added.

"Cam my nigga but you know us big people gotta stick together." Stacy gave Gray a friendly hug.

Quan stood back. He couldn't pretend that he didn't feel some type of way about what Gray had done. He'd been sticking up for her the past three and a half years, only to learn she was a snake in the grass. He felt played. Cam was his boy. She'd hurt him. Therefore, she'd hurt Quan as well. He couldn't forgive that so easily.

"C'mon, Gray." Mo linked her arm with hers. "Let's go get some of these ribs before Stacy fat-ass eat 'em up."

"Shit, Mo, we the same size." Stacy clowned.

"Yo' don't make me fuck yo' big-ass up." Boss warned.

Everybody knew he didn't play about his wife. Over at the food table Mo and Gray fixed their plates in silence. There was so much food it was hard to choose from. Macaroni and cheese, potato salad, baked beans, coleslaw, hot dogs, bratwurst, barbequed chicken, pork steaks, rib tips and more had been prepared. Even though Gray was starving, her spirit wasn't at peace. Guilt washed over her like a cold wet cloth. The guilt she harbored weighed heavily on her chest. It was like gasoline to her guts. Gray tried to remind herself that she couldn't undo her misdeeds. Over the years, she told herself that even if she couldn't forgive herself in God's eyes her slate was clean. But in that moment, she knew in order to function, she had to make amends.

"Mo, I know you said everything was cool but I really wanna apologize again. Looking back on it, I wish I would've told you what was going on. But after the last conversation me and your brother had, the only thing I could do was remove myself from his life and anyone associated with him."

"Really? It was that bad?"

"It was worse. He fuckin' destroyed me and I'm not sayin' this to gain sympathy. My mindset was just really fucked up at the time. Between everything I went through with Gunz and then Cam, I had to get myself together. My life was hanging on by a thread." Gray replied truthfully.

"I get it. I've been there. I'm just happy you're in a better place now and prayerfully you'll allow me to build a relationship with my nieces and nephew. And by nieces, I mean Aoki and Press too."

"Of course." Gray wrapped her arms around her for an embrace. "I really appreciate that you want to be apart of my girls' lives. That means the world to me."

When their plates were full, the sister-in-laws headed over to the table everyone congregated around. Gray was happy to be amongst all her old friends, until she spotted Cam and his little girlfriend. Sky had awakened and was laughing heartily as her father tickled her stomach. Cam's entire face lit up with joy. Devin latched herself to him like a blood sucking leach. Adoringly, she watched him play with his daughter through long, thick, false lashes. Every other second, she'd throw out a bogus giggle like she was Sky's age, making Gray ill. She didn't want her anywhere near her kids or Cam. And no, she shouldn't care that he was with someone else. He was moving on with his life and so was she. They'd ended long ago so she should be numb to these emotions, but she wasn't. Envy swarmed her like killer bees. A part of her wished it was her by his side. Gray quickly checked herself. She and Cam were over for a reason. It was best he be with someone like Devin. Cam needed a chick like her. She'd feed his male pride in ways Gray wouldn't. She'd be the perfect submissive wife, but seeing her husband so close to another woman almost sent Gray off the deep end. He was the only man that had the power to control her emotions. One minute she blamed him for the demise of their marriage, then in the next breath, she needed him as much as the sun needed hydrogen to function. For three years and four months she hated his guts, but as she took in his handsome features, she began to crash. Someone needed to make it illegal for a man to look so good. A black cap rested low over the

150

hickory colored eyes she'd pay money to see. A simple diamond chain rested on the chest of the crème Adidas Calabasas sweatshirt he donned. Black shorts trimmed in white hung low off his waist. Off-White socks and low-top canvas sneakers finished off his athletic leisure wear.

Gray wanted him in nasty, freaky ways she shouldn't. It was hard to explain her feelings. Her hard nipples strained against the fabric of her top, but her mind kept reminding her that he'd nearly killed her 48 hours before. That incident alone proved that Cam was no good for her. They were in over their heads when they ran off and said, 'I do.' She was tired of hurting behind his erratic behavior. She couldn't let his relationship with her arch nemesis affect her. In order for her to get through the day she needed to pretend like Devin wasn't there, but she couldn't. Her eyes stayed stuck to her like glue. Gray wanted to stab her in the eye with a fork. She hated Devin with a passion. Her presence annoyed her to no end. It didn't help that the bitch was drop dead gorgeous. Her lush cocoa skin looked pretty even with sweat covering her brow. The perspiration gave her skin a healthy glow. If Gray started to sweat, she'd look like a wet, mangy dog.

"Stop staring. Don't even give that bitch the satisfaction." Mo whispered in her ear.

"I can't. I'm jealous. Is this how it feels when other girls look at me?"

"And here I thought my brother was vain." Mo laughed as they took a seat.

With each bite of food Gray took, her heavy heart weighed her down. She was beyond uncomfortable being around Cam and Devin. It was pure torture watching him introduce her to their kids. Gray wanted to object but didn't want to come across like a silly jealous bitch. She couldn't let on that she was pressed. She had a whole man who'd she introduced to Aoki and Press. She could've introduced him to the triplets, but out of respect for Cam's feelings, she didn't. Now she wished she had. *You can do this,* she coached herself. Gray inhaled the fresh summer air. If she could get through this week, she could get through anything. Cam wasn't making it easy tho. He acted as if she didn't exist. His dismissal of her presence almost made her want to cry. He was supposed to love her forever. Now, he sat inches away from her grinning in another woman's face like the vows they said before God hadn't taken place.

"So, Gray, how you been?" Stacy wanted to know.

"Good. I'm honestly the happiest I've ever been."

Gray's confession wasn't aimed to hurt Cam but to know she'd been at her happiest without him was a huge slap in the face.

"Life has been treating me well. After having the babies, I had to take some time off from modeling, but when I started back, it was like I never left. It's been one campaign after another. I have my own makeup line with Too Face cosmetics and several capsule collections with Fashion Nova and Forever 21." She sneered at Devin. "Me and the kids have built quite a life for ourselves in Paris. Press and Aoki are on the soccer team. All of the kids are taking French lessons."

"Quel est ton nom?" Cam asked Sky what's your name in French.

"It's Sky daddy." She giggled, tugging on his beard.

"Donc vous connaissez le François aussi? (So, you know French too?)" Gray quizzed astonished.

"Si vous vous y teniez assez longtemps, vous le sauriez peut-être. (If you would have stuck around long enough, maybe you would know that.)" He replied without giving her eye contact.

"Peu importe. Cela ne fait que confirmer Je ne t'ai jamais connu du tout. (Whatever. This just confirms I never knew you at all.)"

"Uh ah. Speak English. We wanna argue too." Mo grinned.

"Daddy." Sky placed her hands on her father's cheeks. "Be nice to mommy."

"I'm sorry, pretty girl." He kissed her forehead lovingly.

"Maintenant, dis que tu l'aimes. (Now tell her you love her.)"

All the color drained from Gray's face. If Cam said he loved her, she'd throw up or faint.

"Daddy can't do that baby girl."

"Now, daddy! Say it now!" Beaux screamed at the top of her lungs.

"Oh, she crazy-crazy." Stacy drew his head back afraid.

"Okay. Okay. Je t'taime." Cam groaned with a scowl.

"What you say?" Devin asked paranoid.

"Say it back, mommy." Beaux demanded.

"Say what back?" Devin looked back-and-forth between Cam and Gray frantically. "Somebody tell me what he said."

She was so fearful she was about to piss on herself.

"Do I have to?" Gray whined.

"Now, mommy!" Beaux growled like a monster.

"Cam, what did you say?" Devin hyperventilated.

Gray sucked her teeth. She would rather have her tongue cut off with kitchen shears than say it, but the words came out her mouth before she could stop herself.

"Je t'taime aussi."

"What does that mean?" Devin pleaded.

"I knew ya'll still loved each other." Stacy said with a shit-eating grin on his face.

"What?" Devin screeched. "Did you just say you loved her? Please tell me you didn't say that."

"Stop yellin."

"No!"

"Scream again and I swear to God I'ma rip your esophagus out." Cam warned agitated.

Knowing he wasn't playing, Devin closed her mouth and sat back upset with an attitude.

"Trouble in paradise." Mo smirked, taking a swig of water.

"Pastor Edris." Kema broke up the tension. "Let me introduce you to my matron of honor and best friend, Gray."

154

"Nice to meet you." He said mesmerized by her beauty. "No one told me you were so beautiful."

"She a'ight." Cam said out of nowhere.

Gray might've thought he wasn't paying her any attention, but she had more of his attention than she knew.

"Nigga, you a hater. You know yo' bitch bad." Stacy laughed.

"Well, his bitch is right here so thank you." Devin sneered.

"Don't mind them, Pastor Edris. Gray is his soon-to-be ex-wife." Kema explained.

"It's a pleasure, Gray." He shook her hand. "I was telling your husband earlier that I offer marriage counseling."

"You and Cam should go. His father counseled me and Quan." Kema winked at her fiancé.

"You and Cam should come see me. He mentioned you all are seeking a divorce. I always tell couples to exhaust all options before considering permanent separation."

"Thank you but I'm already exhausted." Gray pushed her plate away. She'd lost her appetite.

"And I already told you that won't be necessary." Devin quipped. "He's happy where he's at, remember?"

"What is she doing here?" Heidi said fed up. "Ain't there a shoe sale going on at a Payless you should be attending?"

"I wouldn't know. My nigga keep Giuseppe's on my feet." Devin rolled her neck. "And judging by them

155

dusty, dingy-ass slides you got on, you would know more about a sale at Payless than I would."

"Yo . . . I ain't wanna say nothin' but I was lookin' at them joints earlier." Stacy looked down and side-eyed Heidi's feet.

"Shut the fuck up, Stacy!" She smacked his chest.

"I swear bitches get a few designer outfits and lose they mind." Kema rolled her eyes. "Let's not forget everything in your closet cost $7 with your employee discount. Miss Forever 21."

"And got the nerve to be sitting her talking shit like she ain't 35 and a damn store manager." Gray backed up her friend.

"I'm sorry, and how is your magazine company doing?" Devin cocked her head to the side.

"Yo, this bitch gotta die!" Mo shouted irritated beyond belief.

"Bitch, don't act like you don't see my face all over your store." Gray shot.

"I don't go over to the obese section."

"Sock her, Gray." Stacy took off his apron. "I swear to God I'ma follow up."

"Bitch, you just lost weight. You was a cheeseburger away from having a heart attack. And since you wanna bring up my magazine, how is your invisible baby?"

"Checkmate!" Heidi chuckled.

"Huh? You gotta baby?" Cam said confused.

"Oh, she ain't tell you? She like to lie about being pregnant, so niggas won't leave her. Be careful hubby when you finally get tired of running through that stretched out, salami looking—"

"Wide as all outside—" Kema joined in.

"Deep as the Pacific Ocean—" Heidi added.

"Fish market smelling—" Mo joned.

"Now that you mentioned fish market." Stacy fanned his nose. "Kema, I think I smell something."

"I smell that shit too, bro."

"Yeah, it's lingering over here too babe." Quan covered his nose and mouth.

All Cam could do was close his eyes and shake his head because he knew what was coming.

"I don't smell anything." Pastor Edris sniffed under his arm.

"Please don't ask." Cam begged with dread.

"What ya'll smell?" Pastor Edris questioned anyway.

"Shit." Cam groaned.

"I smell. I smell . . . PUSSY!" The whole crew said in unison then doubled over dying laughing.

Mortified, Devin sat frozen stiff. Tears the size of lemon drops stung the brim of her eyes. She couldn't believe what had just happened and in front of everyone no less. Traumatized by their cruel behavior, she absorbed their heckles as her head began to swim. No matter how hard she tried, she'd never be able to live this down. She'd

157

be reminded of their mean jokes every time she came around and it was all Gray's fault.

"Ya'll need to grow up. Talkin' about this woman pussy." Cam consoled her. "Gray, you of all people should know better. You too old to be bullying somebody."

"She don't know better. You know them foreigners ain't got no home training." Devin wiped her face.

"Bitch, is your last name Parthens?" Gray narrowed her eyes. "I mean, let me know 'cause last I checked my husband was talking to me."

"Now he's your husband? He wasn't your husband when you kept him away from his kids the last three and a half years."

"Watch your fuckin' mouth." Cam ice grilled her.

"It's the truth. She's foul as fuck and if no one else here is going to tell her I will."

"Fuck this." Mo threw down her fork. "Just give me the word, Gray. I'll fuck her up if you want me to."

"No, I got this." She assured before giving Devin her full attention. "You got a lot to say so speak up. What's on your mind?"

"Okay." Devin sat up straight. "I think you're selfish, immature, a liar, a manipulator and frankly . . . an obese whore. God knows if these are even his kids."

"What?"

"You heard me. Who pops up almost four years later saying they have kids by someone? That's sus as fuck. For all any of us know, these could be Gunz's kids. We know how you get down, sis. Remember, I know you."

158

"Oh, you know me?"

"Of course, I do."

"Well, since you know me so well did you know I was gon' do this?" Gray picked up her plate and threw it at her face.

"Or that her best friend was gon' do this?" Kema reared her hand back and tossed her plate at her too.

"And you for damn sure didn't think her sister wife was gon' do this!" Mo followed up with a throw of her own.

"Sister wife?" Boss tuned up his face confused.

One after another, Devin got smacked with plates of soul food. Some of it even got on Cam as well. Devin was so stunned that she had no time to dodge either throw. Mac and cheese, baked beans, green beans, potato salad, and ribs dripped down her shocked face and onto her lap. She was covered in food to the point she felt like she was drowning. Every time she breathed in, she sucked in an air full of cheese, mayo and barbeque sauce.

"FOOD FIGHT!" Stacy dumped a whole aluminum pan of coleslaw on her head.

Devin shrieked at the top of her lungs. She couldn't even open her eyes. Her hair, face and clothes were drenched in slaw.

"If that's your girl, I suggest you train that bitch." Gray warned Cam as she snatched Sky from his arms. "Aoki and Press get your brother and sister! We getting ready to go!"

"Where you think you going?" Cam followed behind her.

"I ain't got time for this shit. I'm going home." She grabbed her purse.

"You can go home but you ain't taking my kids."

"Watch me."

"Think it's a game. I ain't fuckin' playin' wit' you." Cam took Sky from her arms.

"Cam, stop!" She pleaded with a hint of desperation in her voice.

Gray felt like he'd snatched a piece of her soul. Her kids were her lifeline. Without them she had no reason to continue on.

"No, you stop! You dead fuckin' wrong! You ain't have no business doing that girl like that? You on some real childish shit."

"Ain't that the pot calling the kettle black." Gray scoffed. "You been doing childish shit since we met."

"This ain't about me. You somebody whole mama and out here throwing food on people like you on Love and Hip Hop. You should be embarrassed."

"Are you really about to defend her right now? I was minding my fuckin' business. She came at me."

"So! What the fuck are you five? It's always tit for tat wit' yo' ass. Be the bigger fuckin' person!" He yelled irate. "You lucky I ain't let her fuck you up."

"Ha!" Gray chuckled. "Bitch please. Picture that. You already know how my hands work."

"TALK HEAVY GRAY! I SWEAR TO GOD THAT'S MY BITCH!" Stacy pumped his fist in the air.

"Cam! I can't see out my eye." Devin wailed. "I think I'm blind!"

"See what you did!" Cam barked. "You sittin' there letting your friends hype you up. That's why I don't want nothin' to do with your ass now."

"Nigga, are you high? *I don't want to be with you neither.*" Gray squealed. "Now give me back my daughter so we can go!" She tugged on his arm.

"No." He pushed her back almost causing her to fall.

Cam didn't want to put his hands on her, but she'd pushed him too far. She'd kept his kids away from him long enough.

"You heard what the fuck I said. You can go wherever the fuck you want to but my kids staying here with me. And by kids, I mean all 'em."

"I fuckin' hate you." Gray's spat.

"The feeling is fuckin' mutual." He hissed in her face.

Neither of them said anything as their chest heaved up and down. The air was thick with animosity. Gray's entire body flooded with heat. Grief drained through her rather than gliding over her skin. It trekked through every cell until she was numb. How could two people who loved each other immensely become mortal enemies? They'd ruined each other. *Don't you dare fuckin' cry,* she mentally scolded herself. Using all the strength she had, she swallowed back her tears. Cam had seen her cry enough.

"Ooh I wish you would just sign the papers so we can get divorced!"

161

"It's funny how you wanna divorce me when you was the one caught sucking face with your one-eyed baby daddy."

"And you letting that minimum wage, food court eating, I gotta get to the club before 10 so I can get in for free bitch suck your dick now so we're even."

"Quan, get the strap!" Cam ordered.

"For what? You gon' shoot her?"

"Fuck yeah. Everybody dyin'!"

"You gon' shoot her and the baby?" Quan said nervously.

"No, I'ma just gon' put a cap in her ass."

"Fuck you. You ain't gon' do shit but eat my ass and die." Gray shot back.

"Pause, Cam you eat ass?" Stacy quizzed.

"Shut the fuck up, Stacy!" Cam bounced Sky up and down as she began to cry.

"See, look what you did! You're making her cry! Give her to me so we can go!" Gray tried to reach for her again.

"You are not keeping me away from my fuckin' kids!"

Fed up, Gray threw her hands up in the air.

"Okay daddy dearest, keep 'em but what you won't do is have them around that bitch!" Gray pointed in Devin's direction, letting her emotions get the best of her.

Cam looked at her like she had two heads. Anger boiled deep in his system. Gray was making it increasingly hard for him to even want to protect her from Victor. She had life fucked up if she thought she was going to dictate how he parented his kids. If it wasn't for her selfish-ass behavior they wouldn't even be in this position.

"You think after keeping my kids away from me for three and a half years you in the position to tell me what I am and ain't gon' do. You betta get yo stupid-ass outta here. You got life fucked up, Gray. You been over there with them Parisian muthafuckas too long. You must've forgot who the fuck I am."

"Oh, I know exactly who you are. You're the same muthafucka that broke—"

Refusing to let him get the best of her, Gray did a mental woosah. She would not let Cam get her riled up. His bitch had pissed her off enough.

"You know what? You not even fuckin' worth it. Keep the kids. I'll come get 'em later." She stormed off, leaving him standing there with an angry look on his face.

Gray refused to give him, his bitch or their marriage anymore of her energy. She was done with anything that brought her unhappiness.

#10

"I wasn't lookin' for you when you came along. When you came in. Where did you come from like . . . out the sky into my life now."- Iyla, "Juice"

The last time Gray stepped foot on 22nd street she'd received some of the worst news of her life. Learning about Cam's infidelity was pretty much the nail in the coffin of their destructive relationship. Once she left that day from getting her hair braided, she swore she would never come back again. Any good memories she and Cam created were instantly replaced with ones that would haunt her for the rest of her days. When she first moved to Paris, she replayed what she overheard over and over again. *Gray was just sittin' there the whole game cheesing like her and Cam were the shit. I'm lookin' like girl! Yo' nigga just fucked his ex the night before in the men's restroom!* The shocking news hurt then and still hurt now. What made the memory even more painful was, upon further reflection, Gray realized the only reason Cam said he loved her was out of guilt. Now she was left to wonder if he ever loved her at all. Had she been in a one-sided relationship the whole time? The notion made her sick to her stomach. It made her dislike him even more. Cam not only betrayed her, he left her heart in an array of shattered pieces. Gray would never be whole again.

Pulling up on 22nd Street, she parked her rental car and looked around. It was one of St. Louis ten worst neighborhoods. The high crime rate, low to intermediate income, high unemployment rate and low home value were just a few of the reasons it ranked on the list. Outsiders weren't welcome. If you infiltrated the block, you were liable to end up dead. Although it was a crime ridden area, the residents on 22nd Street were a close-knit group of people who came up together. They all looked out for each other. Bloods ran the neighborhood but looked out for the older residents and kids. The houses might've been run down, grass was pretty much nonexistent, litter was everywhere, and potholes filled the streets, but despite the poverty, there was love on the small city block. Laughter and music livened up the depressing looking housing. Children ran up and down the block playing. The matriarchs of the street held court on the porch policing every move the kids made.

A mob of gangstas draped in red hung out in front of Aunt Vickie's house. Red rags were tied around their heads, hung under their caps or from the back of their pockets. Shit talking ensued as they played a heated game of dice in the driveway. Gray searched the crowd for Cam but couldn't find him in the sea of muscle-bound tattooed men. Carefully, she stepped out of the electric blue Mercedes G-Class. The rust-orange, six-inch, Christian Louboutin heels she rocked were super thin. It was like she was walking on stilts. The last thing she wanted to do is bust her ass in front of a crowd full of niggas. She wouldn't hear the last of it. Cam would take pleasure in roasting her for doing the most. After leaving the barbeque, she went home, took a shower and changed. She'd gotten some of the food she threw at Devin on herself. She'd changed into a burnt orange and white polka dot bandeau top with a ruffle sleeve that showcased her bountiful breasts perfectly. Ripped, Rag & Bone skinny leg jeans hung low off her waist showing her toned stomach. Gold hoop earrings and a Cartier watch shined brightly from her ears and wrist.

Gray didn't have any reason to get so dressed up. She wasn't even supposed to be over there. Cam reached out and said he'd bring the kids home, but Gray wanted to be petty and pop up looking cute to piss him off. Cam would most definitely have a fit when he saw her. Securely, out of the vehicle she closed the door and chirped the alarm. The loud noise caused several of the guys to look her way. Gray swallowed hard. The eyes of gang bangers, dope boys, jackers, killers and thieves glared back at her. They all gave her the look of death. Gray thought she was frightened the first time she came on the block, now she was afraid she wouldn't make it home alive. *This what yo' ass get. You should've stayed the fuck at home,* she thought trying to contain her fear. These men were like dogs. If they smelled her fear they'd pounce.

"Aye yo. Who is this mark-ass bitch pulling up in this flu ride?" A cock diesel dude that looked like Mack 10 balled up his fist.

The rest of the men turned around. All Gray saw was a sea of red, muscles and scowls. She felt like a lamb being led to slaughter.

"She must be stupid, pullin' up in this truck like she won't get shot." Another guy said with venom.

"Her big ass must wanna catch a fade?"

"She big but she bute as fuck. Who you here for baby girl?" A dark-skinned cutie licked his lips and grabbed his dick.

"I don't give a fuck if she bute or not! This blood territory! We the real Piru! Coming up in our hood like she all comfortable! You play with this shit, you gon' get hit up!" The Mack 10 look alike lifted his shirt to reveal a gun.

166

"Sue woo! Fruit nation!" They all threw up blood signs.

"I'm sorry. Play with what? Hit what?" Gray held up her hands up in the surrender position.

She swiftly understood that popping up uninvited was a huge mistake. She hadn't been around in years. None of these guys knew who she was.

"Fuck that!" A big, stocky man that resembled Dub C creeped up behind her. "Get the heat blood!"

"Oh my God. Please don't kill me." Gray cowered in fear.

The air in her lungs came out in struggled breaths. It felt as if someone was choking her. All she wanted to do was curl up in a ball and wait for someone to come save her, but no one would. Gray didn't recognize any of the guys in Aunt Vickie's driveway.

"What set you claim?" One of the guys asked. "Who you ride for?"

"You a brip bitch?" Dub C's twin hemmed her up.

"No!" Gray shrilled about to shit on herself.

"Who sent you?"

"Nobody! I swear! I did not come into your jurisdiction to cause problems! I'm here to pick up my kids!"

"*Jurisdiction? Jurisdiction?* This bitch think she funny blood. Get the strap."

A choked cry for help forced itself up Gray's throat.

"CAM!" She screamed hysterically.

Not even a second later, he came rushing to the door holding Reign. Beaux and Sky were right behind him. Gray and Cam might not have left off on the best of terms when she exited the barbeque, but she couldn't have been happier to see him. Her stubborn lustful heart wouldn't permit her to ignore how good he looked. He still wore the outfit from earlier, but he'd discarded his shirt. Cam was in the best shape of his life. The eight pack of abs and mural of tattoos on his upper body made the heartbeat in her clit come alive.

"Fuck is going on out here?" He stepped onto the porch.

"Go back in the house wit' your family, OG! We got this shit under control! This intruder about to be 6F!"

"Pussy, that ain't no fuckin' intruder! That's my baby mom! Get yo' fat-ass back!" Cam put Reign down and power walked across the lawn.

The gang member quickly let Gray go.

"My bad, OG. She came through in the flu ride. I ain't know what was up."

"What's up is yo' ass about to be 6F." He griped the guy up. "Now apologize."

"My bad baby girl—"

"It's Mrs. Gray, nigga!" Cam knocked him upside the head.

"I'm sorry, Mrs. Gray. I ain't mean no disrespect." The grown man whimpered like a child.

"Shut up! You idiot!" She gave him a smack upside the head too. "Do I look like a brip? And what the hell is a brip?"

"A crip, Gray." Cam explained.

"Oh." She replied feeling dumb.

"You ever come near her again, you and your thick-ass neck gon' be 6F, ya dig? Now get the fuck outta here." Cam shoved the guy with force, causing him to fall to the hard concrete. "Got me actin' all uncouth in front of my kids. Ya'll bitch-ass niggas apologize too."

"Sorry Mrs. Gray!" The men said in harmony.

Pleased with their response, Cam turned his wrath on his ex.

"And why the fuck you even over here? Didn't I tell you I would bring them home?"

"You don't dictate when I pick up my kids. Check yo' bitch. Don't check me." Gray folded her arms underneath her breasts, unintentionally pushing them up.

Cam's eyes traveled from her plush pink lips to her collarbone to her ample chest. There was nothing more bewitching than Gray's natural D cup breasts. If given the chance, he wouldn't hesitate to take one of her warm brown nipples into his mouth and flicker his tongue until it pebbled from his ferocious licks.

"Speaking of your bitch. Where is that Garbage Pail Kid?"

"At our crib getting the coleslaw out of her hair."

"Ya'll live together?" Gray prayed to God she'd heard wrong.

"Yeah."

"Figures." She shook her head, repulsed.

"You mad?"

"As if."

"There you go lying again. Tell the truth, Gray. You still got feelings for a nigga. That's why you came over here to see me." He stepped into her personal space and grinned.

Cam was onto Gray. He could see the outline of her pussy print from a mile away. The print was fat and sweet. Cam yearned to bury his 11-inch dick deep inside her warm hole.

"Boy please. Ain't nobody thinking about you." She stepped back so he wouldn't overpower her.

"Then why you come over dressed like a sexy senorita and shit?"

"You think I'm sexy?" She replied, caught off guard by his compliment.

"You stay missing the point."

"Whatever. Where are Aoki and Press?"

"Up the street playing with Mo bad ass kids."

Gray looked past him and spotted them by the stop sign jumping rope.

"Aoki and Press, c'mon!"

The girls stopped turning the old telephone cord they used as a rope and ran to their mother.

"Hi mama." Aoki barreled into her and hugged her waist.

"Hi." Gray squeezed her back.

"Can we stay?"

"Yeah mama! *Pleeeeease*! We having fun." Press jumped up and down.

"You can stay, pretty girl." Cam responded, rubbing her hair.

"Umm, no they cannot."

"Yes, they can . . . and they are. The fuck." Cam screwed up his face. "Ya'll go back and play."

"Yay! Thank you, Papa!" Press gave him a quick hug then took off running.

"Yeah, Pop, you the real MVP." Aoki gave him a high-five.

She didn't even realize that she'd called him Pop. Cam had and it touched his heart in ways she'd never know or understand.

"Did she just—"

"Yeah." Cam grinned from ear-to-ear.

"Wow. I wasn't expecting that." Gray said, astonished.

"Me either."

Gray knew Aoki's feelings for Cam had grown over the years, but she hadn't expected her to call him dad so soon after their return. She'd apparently misjudged how much her feelings towards Gunz had changed. In the past, she was such a daddy's girl. She would fight you tooth and nail if you said something about Gunz she didn't like. No other man came before her daddy. She idolized everything about him. At one point in time, she preferred him over Gray. Things, however, were different. His absence in her and Press' lives had obviously altered her opinion of him. The fact that Cam didn't let being locked behind bars keep him from being in the girls' lives showed Aoki that a man can call himself dad, but without his presence, it was simply just a word that didn't mean a thing. Gray wished she would've felt this way three years ago. When she wanted Aoki to like Cam, she couldn't stand him. Every chance she got, she had something slick to say. She and Cam used to fight like cats and dogs. It was pretty funny that she'd start to like him now that they weren't together.

"I'm happy that you and Aoki are getting along but that doesn't change anything. I'm still taking the kids home. They've been with you majority of the day."

"What the fuck is a day compared to three and a half years?" Cam barked. "You betta gon' somewhere with that bullshit, Gray. I ain't in the mood for your shit today."

"I ain't in the mood for your shit either." She rolled her neck.

"Bye, Gray. I don't get paid to argue wit' you." Cam gave her his sculpted back.

"Don't turn your back on me. You big bitch." She pushed him.

"Now, as soon I touch you, you gon' be cryin' and callin' the police."

"I ain't a rat!"

"Sure, you're not."

"I don't snitch."

"The police report says different." He lied to see her reaction.

"I don't give a fuck what your stupid-ass police report said. I ain't have shit to do with you getting arrested. That was on you and you know it. Maybe if you got a real job, you wouldn't have to worry about nobody snitching on you."

Cam's nostrils flared as he stalked towards her slowly. Face-to-face, he methodically licked his bottom lip. Gray tried to seem unbothered, but he could see a hint of fear in her blue irises.

"Real shit. I ain't gon' kill you 'cause I be talkin' to God now and shit, but I will shoot you in your fuckin' pinky toe. Try me. Say something else."

"Something else." She challenged.

"Daddy! Push me!" Beaux demanded, patting his leg.

Cam had bought the triplets customized Jeep Wranglers. They hadn't quite figured how to drive them, so they made him push them.

"You betta be glad." He gave their mother one last look before walking off.

"Ain't nobody scared of you." Gray said under her breath as she stomped past the group of men and took a seat on the porch steps.

It didn't look like she'd be going anywhere. She was stuck in the middle of ghetto hell. For the sake of her kids, she'd suffer through the agony as long as they were happy, and they were. There wasn't a sad face amongst the group. Reign giggled, waving his arms for Cam to pick him up. With little to no effort, he hoisted him up and tossed him into the air. Gray held her breath praying he didn't accidently drop him. She had nothing to worry about tho. Cam would never allow any of his kids to be hurt under his watch. He speedily caught Reign in his arms and placed loving kisses all over his face. Happiness radiated from their son, warming his skin like rays from the sun. Reign's usual ominous scowl erupted into a glowing grin that Gray had never seen before. He was the quiet one that didn't show much emotion except anger. He was so much like Cam it was scary. Suddenly, it dawned on her. Maybe what he'd been craving the whole time was his father. It seemed that way. Gray felt horrible. Had she been depriving her baby boy of the father figure he apparently needed? Gray thought she'd be hindering her kids if she exposed them to Cam while he was in jail. She didn't want them to see him locked up like some caged animal. She wanted them to view him as the hero she'd built him up to be in their minds. What she failed to realize is that the kids didn't care about any of that. They simply wanted a father. They loved Cam imperfections and all. As she watched them play, Gray grew to regret her decision. She prayed to God that her kids, and prayerfully Cam, would one day forgive her for the sin she'd committed. She should've never kept the triplets away from their father. When the time was right, she'd apologize but, in that moment, under the warm July sun everything seemed to be right in the world. Reign had

174

Cam and Cam had him. Father and son reunited. They'd made the best out of a bitter sweet situation.

"Aye." Cam got the Mack 10 lookalike attention. "You do what I tell you?"

"We put the word out but niggas ain't talkin' yet." Twan replied.

"Listen, I need this info like yesterday. Let muthafuckas know I got a hunnid k for whoever drop a name. Tell them I want that shit accurate. No fucks ups or that's yo' ass." Cam warned.

"No worries boss man. I got you." Twan dapped him up.

Cam had been digging around as well, but he too came up short. He prayed that his case file and reward didn't turn out to be dead ends too. Since she had a minute to herself, Gray decided to take the opportunity to get in a few chapters of her favorite author Chyna Black's book *Such A Fuckin' Lady*. It was a book based on the author's crazy, whirlwind life. Chyna was a character who always found herself in weird, chaotic circumstances. She jumped from one relationship to another, but in this story, she seemed to have finally found her match in an old love interest by the name of Basil Damian Shaw.

"There you go on that weird shit again." Cam snatched her phone from her hand.

"Give me back my phone!" She leaped up to snatch it back.

"You bet not be reading no fuckin' porn in front of my kids." Cam held it over his head so she couldn't reach it.

175

"Of course not, dip shit."

"I'll be the judge of that." He read the first paragraph on the page. "Oh, you reading Such A Fuckin' Lady. You late. I been read this." He handed her phone back.

"You read a book? I thought the Berenstain Bears was as high as your vocabulary went."

"Ya'll niggas gon' quit playin' me like I'm dumb."

"I mean, if the shoe fits." Gray mumbled, sitting back down.

"Say one more thing and yo' ass gon' be laid out in this driveway."

"You really read this book?" She ignored his threat.

"Yeah, nigga. You act like I don't know how to read."

"Then what happened?" She twisted her lips to the side.

"She ran up on LA in Cali and found out he married ole girl, lost her shit, came back to Saint Louis, got on her ho shit, went out with a few bogus-ass niggas, then met up with Dame in Chicago after twenty years—"

"Oh shit. You really did read it." Gray cut him off, amazed.

"I told you, I did. Chyna did her thing. I read a lot while I was in the pen. Quan sent me a ton of books. I read all of Chyna shit, Takerra Allen and this broad name Love Belvin that don't like to show her face and shit."

"I love her work, especially her *Ezra* series."

"You would. You fuckin' freak." Cam sucked his teeth.

"Shut up." Gray laughed, leaning back. "You know what you should read?"

"What?"

"I think you would like *Crime and Punishment*. It focuses on the mental anguish and moral dilemmas of an impoverished ex-student in Saint Petersburg who formulates a plan to kill an unscrupulous pawnbroker for her money."

"That do sound like some shit I would like. I'ma check out." Cam took a seat next to her. "Have you read *The Great Gatsby*?"

"Nah but I saw the movie."

"The movie was good, but it don't do the book no justice. The book captured the mood of the 1920's, especially the moral emptiness of a postwar society. America became obsessed with wealth and status. The first time I read it, I thought the book was about the decline of the American dream in the 1920's, but after several reads, I realized that *The Great Gatsby* is a story of the thwarted love affair between a man and a woman."

"Well, look at you sounding all smart shit."

"I did graduate at the top of my class." Cam ran his tongue across his top teeth.

"I didn't know that."

"Yeah, I got accepted to Duke, Wash U, Wharton and Vanderbilt but I chose the army instead. My brother Kerry likes to pretend that he's the smart one 'cause he built his own investment firm but that nigga struggled in school. He barely passed his SAT."

Who is this man, Gray wondered? Her so-called husband had gotten into some of the best universities in America and said it like he'd gotten accepted to Forest Park Community College.

"That's why he can't stand you?"

"Pretty much. Also, I think lowkey 'cause I was my mom's favorite."

"I'm certain she loved all her kids equally."

"She did. I'm just fuckin' wit' you."

"What other books you like?" Gray asked fascinated by the conversation.

It was a rarity that Cam let people inside his brain.

"I fucks wit' *To Kill A Mockingbird, Song of Solomon, War and Peace* and *The Adventures of Huckleberry Finn* heavy."

"You read *Song of Solomon?*"

"Gray, you gon' quit coming at me crazy. My mother actually used to read books to us every night before bed. She would gather us all in one room and read a chapter a night. Every time we finished a book, she'd make us write a report on what we learned. I hated writing those fucking reports, but after she died, I would've given my right hand to write a report for her again." Cam gazed sadly into the distance.

His mother was always a sore subject for him. Gray felt his sadness. Back in the day, she would've comforted him but visions of Cam holding her at gunpoint flashed through her brain, dulling any compassion she had.

"Toni Morrison was one of her favorite authors. When she came to Saint Louis for a book signing, she drug me and Mo with her. The line was long as fuck. I remember complaining the whole time but the look on my mother's face, when she got her book signed, made waiting almost two hours worth it. From that day on I became a huge fan of her work. I've read *The Bluest Eye* and *Jazz* so many times I've lost count."

"Wow. You learn something new every day. Who knew Killa Cam would be a Toni Morrison fan?"

"I would think by now that you would know there's more to me than being a crazy-ass nigga that sell dope and like to smoke weed."

"That's the thing, Cam. We didn't know each other then and we really don't know each other now. We met, had sex, got married, moved into together and broke up all within' seven months."

"Yeah, we did move hella fast, but I don't wanna talk about that shit right now." He dismissively flicked his wrist.

Whenever their marriage was brought up things went left quick.

"You know what you need to read?" He changed the subject back to books.

Books were a safe zone.

"What?"

179

"The *Ethic* series by Ashley Antionette."

"What you know about *Ethic*?" Gray challenged.

"More than you. That nigga Messiah act just like me."

"He sure do, and I was dumb and in love just like Morgan." She shook her head, ashamed.

"You wasn't dumb. You just fell in love with a real one."

"If you consider cheating and accusing me of sending you to jail real."

The jab didn't stagger Cam, but it damn sure did sting. With no comeback of his own, he sat silent and so did Gray. Neither of them said a word. Silence caressed their skin like a cool summer breeze. It lingered in the air, thick and heavy like a blanket. That Sunday had been a rough day for both of them. Being so close to each other was weird as hell. Gray didn't know what to do with herself. She didn't know whether to bite him in the face or lean into his warmth. Cam made her feel a million emotions at once, some she wished she didn't feel at all. Her stomach muscles tightened at the thought of running her nose up his tattooed neck and inhaling his manly scent. Cam's Tom Ford cologne was like a drug to her. It always sent her body ablaze with the desire to have him pounding into her slow. Cam placed his elbows on his knees and steepled his hands under his chin. Gray's uneasy energy leaped off her skin and onto him. He didn't like that he made her feel this way. They used to be best friends. In the past they would sit and talk for hours about any and everything. Now it was a struggle to have a decent conversation without things becoming awkward or shit from the past being thrown in each other's faces. Thank God they had their kids to break up the monotony.

"Mommy, Beaux did something bad." Reign stumbled over his little feet to get to her.

"Stop running and be careful."

Reign did as he was told and took his time.

"Now what did Beaux do?" Gray asked once he reached her.

"She . . . she . . ." He huffed all riled up. "She got marker on her face."

"Oh, she did? Beaux Parthens! Get your butt over here right now!"

"What I tell you about snitching li'l man?" Cam picked his son up and sat him on his lap.

"Snitches get stiches." He placed his head on his daddy's shoulder.

"Exactly. Nobody likes a snitch. That's why me and yo' mama don't get along."

"Keep my name out your mouth li'l boy." Gray snapped as Beaux approached them slowly with her head down.

Once she got in arms reach of her mother, she instantly started to cry.

"Don't start crying now. Let me see your face."

Beaux lifted her head at a snails pace. Sure enough, there was red marker all over her cute little face. She had marks on her forehead, eyes, nose and cheeks.

"It was an *ac*-cident." She whined.

"You accidently did that to your face?" Gray quizzed, knowing she was lying.

"Yeah." She pouted.

"Where did you even get a marker from?"

"Uncle Stacy gave me one so I can draw."

Gray looked up. She didn't even know Stacy was there but found him standing on the sidewalk waving at her like a fool. Pissed, she threw up the middle finger and returned her attention to Beaux.

"Now let me get this straight. You accidently took a marker and colored all over your face?"

"Hmm?" Beaux acted like she couldn't hear her.

"Look at me." Gray grabbed her chin and glared into her heart-stopping coffee colored eyes. "This was an accident?"

"Yeah." Beaux grinned like a Cheshire cat.

"Excuse me. This is not funny li'l girl. Are you telling the truth?"

"Mmm hmm." Beaux nodded her head.

"I don't think it was an accident. I think you did it on purpose and you know better. Did you do this on purpose Beaux?"

"Yes." She finally admitted.

Cam cracked up laughing. Beaux and Reign were his mini-me's for real. It was crazy to watch Gray mother

182

their kids. *I got kids,* he thought once again. He still hadn't fully digested that they were a legit family now. Cam didn't know what he was doing. Being a stepdad to Aoki and Press was one thing. There was a limit to what he could and could not do. He didn't have to take on the responsibility of being a full-fledged parent. He just had to be there whenever they needed him. It wasn't like he had the tools to be a father anyway. His own father had been a blip on the surface of his childhood. Cam Sr. never said I love you. He wasn't one of those fun parents that gave you piggyback rides or tickled your stomach until you almost pee'd. For him, the definition of being a father was going to work and providing for his kids. The only time Cam spent time with him was when he made him his scapegoat so he could fuck his mistress. He never gave him advice, unless he asked for it. Other than that, he never really talked to Cam or his brothers, unless they spoke to him first. Any love or affection he had to offer was saved for Mo and their mom. Cam prayed to God he'd be a better father than him. His biggest fear was failing as a parent. He'd need all the help he could get. The natural thing to do would be to ask Gray for advice. She made parenting look easy. The kids looked at her like she was their hero. He hoped one day they would look at him the same way too.

"Why did you do it, Beaux?" Gray continued her line of questioning.

"Because I do that on purpose." She shrugged her shoulders.

"But you know you're not supposed to do that, right?

"Uh huh."

"We don't color on our face. We only color on paper, right?"

"Yeah. Not on da *wall*, not on our hands, not on da *furniture*, and not on our dolls. And not on da phones!"

Gray tried her best not to laugh but Beaux was so darn adorable it was nearly impossible.

"And not on our faces?" She reminded her.

"No. Not on our *nose*. Not our *eyes*. Not our *eyebrows*." Beaux smiled proud of herself for getting it right.

"You are a mess li'l girl. C'mon, let's get you cleaned up." Gray rose to her feet then looked at Cam. "Oops my bad. Can I go in your auntie's house? If I remember correctly, you told me not to step foot in her house again."

"If you don't get yo' ass out my face. Wit' yo' Lane Bryant jeans on." He admired the swell of her ass.

"Shut up. They're from Boo Hoo."

"Well, boo-hoo yo' ass on in the house and clean up my fuckin' daughter."

"Whatever." Gray tried her hardest not to blush.

She hated that Cam's sarcasm turned her on. As she picked up Beaux and walked in the house, Cam took one last look at her round behind. The jeans she wore were like a second skin they were so tight. The jeans did nothing to hide how big her ass was. If she was still his, Cam would've made her go home and change but he couldn't, so he kept quiet and acted like his dick hadn't grown several inches inside his shorts.

184

Down the way Aoki, Press, Ryan, Makiah and some of the other neighborhood girls played Double Dutch while the boys tossed the pigskin in the middle of the street. Aoki was having the time of her life. Her friends back in Paris were cool but they didn't get her cocky attitude and ratchet behavior like her American friends did. Now that they were older, she and the twins got along much better. As soon as they linked up at the park, they were inseparable. All three girls were on the same level. They all knew what it felt like to be the prettiest and most popular girls in their class. Makiah and Ryan were chocolate goddesses like their mother. They were tall and slim with natural curly hair that reached past their shoulders. The twins were the perfect combination of bad and bougie. Like Aoki, most people underestimated them because of their beauty. For some reason society thought that a girl who was beautiful couldn't be smart, driven, funny and tough. You either had to be one or the other. Aoki and the twins were all that and more.

The afternoon sun warmed her skin as music from the radio became the soundtrack to their perfect summer day. Aoki stopped and took in the sky. It was one of those powder-blue skies. Pristine white clouds formed shapes that resembled cotton candy while tree branches performed like marionettes. The day was postcard perfect. The concrete was hot under the soles of Aoki's feet. Closing her eyes, she took in the sounds of the hood. She could hear loud chatter, trap music, police sirens, ambulance wails, honking horns and construction. All of it was music to her ears. She missed this. Being in the city invigorated her. Out of all the sounds the one that stuck out the most was the low growl of a classic muscle car. The engine purred like a sex fiend kitten. Aoki opened her eyes and let the daylight flood back in then focused on the car. It was sleek and stunning. She'd never seen a 1950's Chevrolet Camaro SS up close. It was black with bold white stripes on the hood. Aoki tried not to get too hyped. Over the years she'd become obsessed with old school cars. When she turned sixteen, she wanted a 1960's fire engine red Mustang. Aoki was so enamored with the car that she didn't even notice she was still standing in the middle of the street until the driver laid his hand on the horn. The deafening sound quickly brought her back to reality.

In a daze, she dreamily stepped back and watched as the car parked across the street. Then time slowed. It was just like in those cheesy 90's movies her mom liked to watch. The boy of her dreams eased out of his car in slow motion. As he came into full view, Aoki's heart stopped beating inside her chest. This dude had the kind of face that stopped chicks dead in their tracks. His hair was in a short, cropped, curly box with tapered sides. His brown eyes shimmered like blood diamonds. His slender nose and pink kissable lips were symmetrical to the other features of his face. Plain and simple he was fine as fuck! The portrait of tattoos on his neck, chest, arms and back complimented his peanut butter complexion beautifully. He had so many tattoos that they all began to form one big giant tat. Not only was he handsome as hell, his body was to die for. There wasn't an ounce of fat on his rock-solid frame. Shirtless, a pair of Balmain jeans sagged low revealing the Calvin Klein boxer/briefs that cupped his firm ass. A fresh pair of 6-inch, wheat Timbs with the laces untied covered his feet. This nigga made Aoki's young-ass want to do tricks on his dick. She'd most definitely let him eat it until his mouth was lock jaw. He had her sweating in places she shouldn't. Then just like in the movies he looked at her. His cinnamon colored eyes connected to her glacier blue hue and Aoki melted into a pool of nothing. His eyes were like windows. She saw galaxies instead of pupils. When he looked at her, Aoki felt every ounce of breath in her lungs become extinct. Then he smiled and the whole world stopped. Aoki swore this was what falling in love felt like. If this was the beginning of their fairytale love affair, she never wanted the story to end.

"Stop drooling, ma. That nigga don't want you." Ryan stood shoulder to shoulder with her.

"How you know? Who is he?" Aoki tried to control her breathing but to no avail.

"That's our cousin Priest."

"Priest." Aoki let the name roll off her tongue and into the atmosphere.

"Yeah Priest. *Our* cousin, remember?"

"Let's be clear, sis. He's *your* cousin, not mine."

"He's still too old for you."

"How old is he?" Aoki twisted her mouth to the side.

"Twenty-three."

"Fuck." Her heart dropped.

Because of their age difference, Aoki knew she stood no chance of getting with him. That still didn't explain what she was supposed to do with the riot brewing in the pit of her belly. She'd never felt this way before. This feeling was bizarre. It stretched throughout her whole body. It was overwhelming, but it made her feel complete. There was no hiding from it. It had no length, no bound or depth. The only thing Aoki could equate it to was being in a roaring fire but feeling completely safe at the same time. Priest gave her peace. She wanted him to kiss her, touch her, taste her, tease her. She needed him to lick her in places that a man his age shouldn't. He was all that and then some. Seeing the hardcore criminals on the block, including Cam, show him love and respect was better than a seat at the popular table. Just that quickly, she became obsessed with him. Aoki had liked boys her age, but none of them made her feel like this. Priest was a grown-ass man, but she didn't care. She was in love. She had to have him.

"ICE CREAM!" Like a stampede all of the kids started running up the street.

The Bomb Pop truck had finally made its way into the neighborhood. As the colorful truck drifted past them, Aoki could already see kids running in the house to beg their parents for money. The children who did have change raced behind the truck with the hope of being first in line. By the time Aoki made it up the street, hordes of kids surrounded the truck, eagerly waving their money in the air.

"Daddy, I want ice cream." Sky begged.

"I got you li'l mama."

Cam went over to the truck and gave the driver enough money to cover all the kids on the block. The triplets wanted ice cream cones, so he got them the flavors they wanted. He even got Gray a cone too. On the porch they sat together as a family and enjoyed their ice cream. But after only a few minutes in the sun the ice cream began to melt.

"I don't know if you're free or not but tomor I'm taking the kids to see The Wiggles if you wanna come." Gray wiped the corner of her mouth.

"Hell, yeah, I wanna go. I ain't tryin' to miss shit else."

Gray swallowed hard. His comment wasn't meant to send a pang in her heart, but it did.

"Mommy, I want yours 'cause mine is . . . mine is melting." Beaux reached for Gray's cone.

"Mommy, I wanna switch too." Reign then took the one Beaux gave Gray and gave her his.

"Daddy, can you switch with me?" Sky asked for Cam's.

"Here, pretty girl." He swapped cones.

Sky eagerly took a lick and savored the sugary treat. Ice cream covered her, and her sibling's faces. It dripped down their chins and onto the steps. Cam savored every minute of them making a mess.

"I want yours, daddy." Beaux bounced up and down on her mom's lap.

"Here, baby girl." Cam handed her his cone only to realize he'd ended up with Gray's.
"Ain't this about a bitch."

"But we have to share with people, daddy." Sky scolded him. "Sharing is caring."

"You're right." Cam chuckled, surprised by her statement. "Daddy's sorry."

"Yeah, don't do me." Gray rolled her eyes. "I'm the one that needs to be worried. Lord knows where your mouth has been. I heard all about your li'l nasty foursome."

"That shit was lit. You should'a been there."

"You are disgusting. I would've never been there."

"You act like when I was fuckin' you, I couldn't get you to do anything."

"You couldn't." Gray pretended like he wasn't telling the truth.

"So, I ain't have my dick in yo' ass?"

"Nope." She covered Beaux's ears.

"I ain't have my belt wrapped around your throat?"

"I have no recollection your honor."

"You a muthafuckin' lie." Cam held his head back and laughed.

"Mommy, you a muthafuckin' lie?" Reign repeated, sounding just like his daddy.

"No and don't say that no more."

"It's mommy told a story." Cam explained.

"What's the difference? It's the same thing." Gray challenged.

"Call any elder I know a liar and see what happen."

"You know I got slapped in the mouth for calling my mama a liar when I was a li'l girl."

"You should've."

"No, I shouldn't have. That was abuse." Gray joked.

"Yes, you should've. Yo' mama was making up for all the lies you was gon' tell in the future. She knew yo' ass wasn't nothing but a liar in training."

"I am not a liar. I just try to protect other people's feelings."

"You just lied again. You lie to protect yourself."

"Cam, I have never lied to you. Did I do things that maybe could've been thought out more? Yes. Anything I did that ended up hurting you came from me having good intentions." She said sincerely.

Cam absorbed her words. He believed what she was saying. Gray wasn't a horrible person. She wasn't an evil villain. She had a good heart. She just did stupid shit.

"Look at ya' dumb-ass. You don't even know how to eat ice cream. Sitting up here making a mess." He lifted her hand to his mouth and licked the ice cream off her fingers.

Everything happened so fast that he didn't even realize he'd crossed an invisible line until he'd done it. Gray stilled. She had every intention on checking him for invading her personal space but the wet flicker of his tongue on her skin elicited sparks of lust she'd tried her best to ignore. Why did he have to go there? This was too much. She could feel her heartbeat . . . every single pound in her chest. It was fast and commanding. The acceleration didn't have anything to do with anger but everything to do with what her body craved. Refusing to let him see her sweat, she looked the other way and allowed the world to gain her attention. It didn't matter where she adverted her eyes, Cam could still read her like a book. He knew she was mentally freaking out. With a gentle finger, he turned her face to his so he could receive the gaze she didn't want to give to him. There wasn't a hint of a smile on his lips, only the scorching intensity of a glare that would start a blazing inferno.

Blood rushed to Gray's ears. She tried to swallow back her emotions, but her mouth was too dry to produce saliva. Gray could barely function. Cam was making it hard for her to speak, let alone think. The seat of her panties were drenched in juices that only he could extract. If she didn't stop him now, she'd be off somewhere bent over as he gripped her waist and fucked her hard from behind.

"Stop." She released a whispered plea as her body trembled.

"You're right. I'm trippin'." Cam sat Reign next to Sky and got up.

What the fuck am I doing, he thought shook. She'd just ripped him to shreds with her venomous words two days before. He'd just tried to kill her. If it wasn't for his relationship with God, she wouldn't even be alive. How had he gone from wanting to murder her in cold blood to wanting to stick his tongue down her throat? Cam missed being balls deep inside her pussy, but sex had never been a problem for them. Their sexual chemistry was always undeniable. All the other components that made a relationship successful is where they struggled. He had to get his mind right. He had to get away from her. He was with Devin now. No, she wasn't the woman of his dreams. He cared for her deeply, but he'd never love or marry her. She was simply someone to be with for right now. She was a safe bet. He'd never have to worry about her hurting him because he'd never give her the chance to. Gray, on the other hand, would always hold his heart in the palm of her hand. Instead of licking ice cream off her fingers, he needed to remember all the foul shit she'd said to him. Not to mention he wasn't sure if she was the one who set him up or not. The countdown to Victor killing her had begun. Cam didn't have time to think about wanting to kiss or fuck her. It was best he keep his distance and focus all of his attention on the kids and finding the culprit who snitched.

On the other end of the street, all the older kids had demolished their ice cream and were now jamming to City Girls. Aoki really tried to put on a show, since her crush Priest was only a few feet away. Tossing her long sandy brown hair over her shoulder, she placed her hands on her knees and started to act up. Twerkin' was her specialty. She could shake her ass better than most exotic dancers. The twins hyped her up as she rapped JT's part:

Real ass bitch, give a fuck 'bout a nigga
Big Birkin bag, hold five, six figures
Stripes on my ass so he call this pussy Tigger
Fuckin' on a scammin' ass, rich ass nigga

At home she and Press always rap the song together, so when Yung Miami verse started, Press joined in.

Same group of bitches, ain't no adding to the
picture
Drop a couple racks, watch this ass get bigger
Drinkin' on liquor, and I'm lookin' at your nigger
If his money right, he can eat it like a Snicker

When Aoki saw that she had Priest's attention, she started performing like she was on stage. She bounced what little ass she had like a stripper at Magic City. Aoki could pop her ass and shake her titties better than Aliya Janell. Like her mom, she loved to dance and always went extra hard when a song she loved came on. Aoki thought Priest liked watching her dance but really, he was wondering who this fast-ass li'l girl was. He had no idea that Aoki was the same little girl he used to guard from a distance years before. Not to be outdone by her big sister, Press did the Floss and ended with a Stripper Bop of her own.

"Look at her. She can't even dance wit' her ugly-ass." Sanya, the little girl who had kissed King at the park sneered.

"Right, she think she cute 'cause she got good hair." Her friend Nisha looked her up and down.

"I should snatch it out the root."

Hearing what she said, King threw down the football and said, "You ain't gon' do shit."

"Why? Cause you like her?" Sanya got in his face.

"Nah, that's the homey but that don't mean you gotta disrespect her."

Hurt covered Press like an invisible cloak. Her mood went from outrageously happy to melancholy within seconds. A black cloud of sadness hovered over her head. That quickly the entire trip had been ruined. King was one of the only reasons she wanted to come back to Saint Louis. She wanted to see if they could pick up where they left off but clearly things had changed. This wasn't the King she used to know. The King who was her best friend at the age of six would've never played her like this. Silvery tears lined the brim of her eyes as she took in his betrayal.

"Oh my God. Are you really about to cry 'cause he don't like you?" Nisha taunted her.

"Where you find this bitch?" Sanya placed her hand on her hip. "She weak as fuck. Bye crybaby. Take yo' ass back to Paris or wherever you came from."

194

"*Wee-wee.*" Nisha quipped, snapping her finger.

Press cast her teary eyes down to the ground. It felt like someone had turned on a furnace inside her system. Her bronzed skin slowly turned ghostly white. The warmth in her body turned into a full-blown scorching heatwave bursting through her pores, triggering her to cry. Press wasn't like her big sister. She wasn't confrontational. Fighting wasn't her thing. She was soft-hearted, meek and quiet. She hated when people didn't like her, whereas Aoki thrived off the hate. At school, kids made fun of Press because of how ditzy and clumsy she was. They cracked jokes because she needed glasses to read, loved to learn and was the teacher's pet. School was where she learned in life you were either a bully or a victim. Either you brushed your shoulders off and kept it moving when it came to bullies or you broke down and succumbed to the teasing. Press tried to be strong. She tried to remind herself that embarrassment wasn't an emotion. It was a weapon used without a trace of pity, but in that moment, that mantra didn't work. Her tiny chest had already started to heave up and down. Hyperventilating was something she did when she became upset. Salty tears dripped down her face and past her chin as she prayed King would stick up for her, but he didn't. He just stood there as Sanya and her friend's snickers continued on.

"Are you dumb? Why you still standing here?" Sanya mushed her in the forehead.

Press' mind was telling her to tuck her tail between her legs and walk away but her feet were frozen in place. She was too shocked and embarrassed to move. A throaty sob ripped through her bones and guts and spilled out onto her rosy cheeks.

"Yo chill. That ain't even necessary." King pulled Sanya back.

He didn't wanna see Press cry, but King was only nine. He'd be ten in two months. He didn't know what to do. He was stuck between a rock and a hard place. He liked Sanya. They'd been vibing since the beginning of the school year. She was a cute girl with a lot of sass that he liked but the feelings he had for Press ran deeper than the Red Sea. He liked her so much it scared him. A girl like Press seemed unnatural. She was so perfect that she didn't fit into such a corrupt society. The world was too small for her. She needed room to breathe. Goodness oozed from her pores. He knew at the age of six that she was more than just a friend that he liked to play Legos, hide-and-go-seek and house with. He wanted to grow up and make her his wife. Outside of his mother, she was the most beautiful person he'd ever seen. But what was he supposed to do when he had feelings for two girls? He didn't want to hurt either one, but by the look on Press' face, he already had.

"Well, you need to tell her to gon' before I slap her in her stupid face." Sanya yanked her arm away.

"You gon' slap who?" Aoki loomed over the little girl.

Unprepared for someone bigger and badder to check her, Sanya eased back.

"Nobody." She whispered.

"Cause I know you ain't talkin' to my li'l sister."

"And if she was? What you gon' do about it?" Sanya's sixteen-year-old sister, Damya, walked up on Aoki.

What neither she or Press knew was that Sanya and Damya were their father's new girlfriend nieces. Tia was their aunt. Like their aunt, Sanya and Damya were raised by Mama Lucy. Unfazed by her height and age, Aoki looked the girl up and down. Damya was a pretty honey colored girl that towered over her by at least several inches. Her body was slender, but she had full boobs, curvy hips and a round ass. If Aoki didn't know any better, she'd think she was a grown-ass woman. The fact that she chose to check Aoki instead of checking her li'l sister showed that she was nothing but an ignorant teenager. Aoki didn't give a damn how old or how big she was. There wasn't a bitch on earth that pumped fear in her heart.

"Bitch, I'll beat both of ya'll asses. Don't let the cute face fool you." She snapped.

"Cute? You think you cute 'cause you mixed and got long hair? Bitch you ain't cute. You a mutt. You ain't got shit on me or my sister. I'll dog walk yo' ass."

"Bitch, ya'll ugly as shit. Fuckin' project baby. You got a whole mustache which means you probably got hair on your vagina. Wolf pussy!"

"And it stink!" Makiah jumped in.

"And ya'll got roaches and ya'll grandma on WIC and welfare!" Ryan added.

"While ya'll talking, ya'll need to go find ya'll crackhead-ass mama and yo' nonexistent daddy." Makiah told all their business.

"At least I ain't no fuckin' rape baby." Damya spat with venom.

If hatred was visible it would be scarlet red. Rage grew inside of Aoki to the point you could practically see flames roaring in her eyes.

"Yeah bitch. I said it. What the fuck you gon' do? Rape baby." Damya pushed Aoki in her chest hard as hell.

Aoki weighed eighty-five pounds soaking wet, so the shove sent her skidding backwards on the ground. The rough concrete scratched the back of her bare legs, causing her to bleed. The scraps were so deep she immediately felt the burn. On her butt, she glared up at Damya who was laughing her ass off.

"Talk that shit now bitch, wit' yo' scary ass."

Fuming, Aoki rose from the ground and examined her legs. Half of the skin on her calves were gone. All she saw was pink flesh. Aoki stood up straight and zeroed in on Damya's stupid grin. In her silly mind she really thought she'd been victorious at taking Aoki down. Little did she know but Aoki was just getting started. A vein popped in her forehead as she clenched her fist, reached up and punched Damya in the face with so much strength she saw stars. Light headed from the punch, her legs gave way and she fell to the ground. Seeing red, Aoki hovered over Damya and rained down one blow after another. Damya tried to block her hits by covering her face, but Aoki wasn't having it. She was going to fuck her up. By the time she was done with her, Damya or her sister wouldn't bother anyone else again.

"Beat her ass, Aoki!" Makiah coached.

"You bet not let her get the best of you!" Ryan yelled out.

"Papa!" Press raced up the street.

198

Her feet pounded against the pavement as she sprinted at full speed. Once she reached him, she was out of breath. Cam peeped her distress and took her by the shoulders.

"What's wrong, pretty girl?"

"Aoki fighting!"

Nothing else had to be said. Cam immediately took off in her direction. Stacy and Priest were hot on his tail. Gray had the triplets, so she was forced to stay on the porch. When Cam got to Aoki, she was on top of Damya slamming her fist into her face. Blood covered her hands as she savagely beat the girl like she was a grown woman. Before he could even grab her up, Priest took her by the arms and pulled her back. He didn't know she was Cam's step daughter at first but now that he did, he couldn't let her be outside fighting.

"Let me go!" Aoki kicked and screamed, trying to break loose.
"Relax Blue Eyes. I got you." He bear hugged her from behind.

The sweet sound of his voice promptly caused Aoki to stop putting up a fight. Gazing up, she took in the handsome features of his face. He was just as beautiful up close as he was from afar. All the anger she felt instantly melted away. It was like she was staring into the face of a god. *If I gotta beat a bitch-ass to get him to hold me, then I'ma be beating ass every day,* she swooned, loving every second of being in his arms. Priest's rock solid chest was pressed against her back. She could feel every muscle and groove like it was a second layer of skin.

"Relax slim. You too pretty to be all riled up." He shot her a seductive grin.

At least, that's what she told herself he did as her Powerpuff Girls panties soaked with juices she didn't even know she could produce.

"WHAT THE FUCK IS GOING ON?" Cam roared.

"She called Aoki a rape baby, Uncle Cam!" Ryan tattle tailed.

"She what? What the fuck you say?" He grabbed Damya by the arm, yanked her off the ground and commenced to giving her an old school ass whooping with his hand.

"Fuck her li'l dirty-ass up!" Stacy egged him on.

"Cam, stop!" Gray pleaded.

She'd left Press and the triplets back at the house with Aunt Vickie.

"You can't whoop somebody else's kid!"

"Who gon' stop me?"

When Gray didn't have a reply, he resumed spanking a weeping Damya.

"What in the hell is going on here?" Mama Lucy slammed her rickety screen door and stepped out onto the porch.

All she had on was a housecoat and slippers. A lit cigarette hung from the corner of her lips. What made it even worse was she didn't have her wig on. Several rows of straight back braids lined her hair.

"He hit me!" Damya cried like a li'l baby.

"I thought they got rid of you." Mama Lucy spat.

200

"What?" Cam let Damya go.

"I mean, I thought you were in jail." She corrected herself.

"Don't worry about where the fuck I was at. Worry about yo' bald-head-ass grandbaby. The li'l bitch betta watch her fuckin' mouth or I'ma have my daughter beat her ass again." He warned before turning his attention to Aoki.

Priest had already put her down. She was still as mad as a bull, but her breathing had regulated.

"C'mon Li'l Boosie Bad Ass." Cam took her by the hand.

Gray wanted to be the one to comfort her daughter but now wasn't the time to pull rank. Instead of being a mother hen, she fell back and let Cam handle the situation.

"Where my sister?" Aoki looked around for Press.

"At the house."

The walk up the street seemed to take forever. Aoki hated it. Even though she'd won the fight, she wanted to go home and lick her wounds. The long walk was giving her too much time to think. Whenever she was reminded about her paternity, anger erupted in her as hot as a volcano. Rape wasn't something to make fun of. Her mother had suffered dearly behind the actions of the man who raped her. When anyone called Aoki a rape baby, it was not only a slap in the face to her but a gut punch to her mother as well. Aoki would be damned if she let anyone disrespect Gray. She'd been through enough. Huffing and puffing she eyed Cam. He had a stone-cold expression on his face. She prayed to God he wasn't upset with her. The news would be too much for her to handle.

"You mad at me?" She held her breath and waited for his reply.

"No."

Aoki let out a sigh of relief. She never wanted Cam to look at her the way he did when she was caught stealing. She respected him now. She wanted his approval and validation. She needed him to give her the love that her biological father wasn't alive to give and the man who raised her took away.

"Why would I be mad at you for sticking up for yourself and your sister? I would be mad if you didn't. You're supposed to have her back. Never let anyone disrespect you or your family. But don't let these dusty bitches knock you off your square either. Muthafuckas gon' try you wit' that rape shit for the rest of your life. You can't spazz out every time somebody bring it up or you gon' end up behind bars just like me."

"Uh ah. I ain't going to jail. I ain't lettin' nobody play with my booty."

"Pause. What you trying to say?"

"I ain't mean no disrespect, big homie." Aoki cracked up.

"You bet not. You can't whoop my ass."

"Wanna bet?" She put up her dukes.

"Nah, I don't want no smoke killa." Cam pretended like he was afraid.

"That's what I thought." Aoki slid her hand back in his. "Thanks Pop— I mean Cam for everything."

Cam tried to appear relaxed even though his heart was beating out of his chest.

"You can call me Pop if you want to."

Joy filled Aoki so much it overflowed. Being near Cam lit up her insides. The breaths she took were now full because he was back. Cam may not have been the man that created her or the man that raised her, but he was by far the greatest example of a father she had.

"Say less . . . I would be honored to call you Pop, Cam."

"Young LaFlame, he in sicko mode."- Travis Scott feat
Drake, "Sicko Mode"

"Oh my God. Where is this nigga at?" Gray paced
the floor.

She'd been waiting on Cam to arrive for over an
hour. Before leaving Aunt Vickie's house, he said he'd be
over an hour before it was time to leave for the concert so
he could help her bathe and dress the kids. She told him she
could handle it on her own, but he insisted that he wanted
to help. He even went as far as to tell the kids what time
he'd be over. They were all super excited to see him. All
morning long they'd been talking about seeing their daddy.
All Gray heard was daddy this, daddy that. She didn't
wanna be a hater, but she missed the days where she was
the center of her children's world. The kids big and small
loved their daddy endlessly, which made his absence
worse. It was one thing not to help her get the kids ready.
Gray could get over that, but leaving them stranded was a
whole other story. Instead of using her driver, Cam
demanded that he be the one to take them to the concert.
Now, here she was blowing up his phone waiting for him to
answer. It wasn't like him to just blow her off but that was
the old Cam. The Cam she meet and married was totally
different than the one she'd been dealing with since his
prison release. The new Cam was cold and callous. Gray's
feelings weren't a priority for him anymore. He had a new
life and a new woman. Gray prayed he didn't pull a Gunz

and forsake his old family for a new shiner one. Aoki and Press wouldn't be able to handle it, and neither would she. What was left of her battered heart would surely die.

Gray checked the clock. It was 12:50. The show started at 1:00. Because of Cam they'd miss the first half of the concert. Pissed, she hung up and dialed his number again. She never thought Cam would be the kind of dad to dish out broken promises but that's what it was beginning to look like.

"Mommy, I'm ready to go." Beaux tugged on the hem of her skirt.

"In a minute baby."

"No minute. Now mommy!"

"Li'l girl, you betta get somewhere and sit down." Gray warned, arching her brow.

Beaux continued to pout and marched away stomping her tiny feet. Gray had all the kids dressed and ready to go. Beaux and Sky had their Emma costumes on, and the signature Emma yellow bow in their hair. Reign wore a Wiggles' t-shirt and jeans. They'd been waiting in the living room for Cam's arrival. Gray tried calling him several times. The phone just rang and then went to voicemail. He didn't even have the decency to face the music and answer. He was probably somewhere fucking off with Devin's, ho ass. Fed up with Cam and his bullshit, Gray ended the call. *I should've never invited his ass no way,* she thought. She was beyond annoyed. Cam talked a good game. He made it seem like he wanted to be in the kids' lives, but the first opportunity he got to spend quality time as a family, he gave them his ass to kiss. No one could say Gray didn't try. She tried putting her emotions to the side so Cam could spend time with his kids. She could've gone to the concert alone and not told him a thing, but she

205

felt guilty for keeping him away from the triplets so long. Now she wondered had she made the right decision to separate him from their lives.

With no driver, Gray mentally prepared herself to load five kids, a big diaper bag and a huge triplet stroller into the truck herself. She could've called Melody for help, but she'd given her the afternoon off. She assumed based off Cam's persistence that he'd be there. It was cool tho. She could do this all by herself. She'd been doing it for almost four years anyway. She didn't need Cam. She didn't need anyone. She was good alone.

An hour earlier

Cam stepped out his brand-new, state of the art, tricked out, black Cadillac Escalade. He wasn't really into black vehicles. All of his other cars were red but in order to accommodate his new large family he had to make some adjustments. His red cars represented his blood affiliation. Cam couldn't risk his enemies or rival gang members recognizing his car when he was out with the kids. In order to keep them safe, he needed to be able to fly under the radar. He needed a car that was durable, spacious and comfortable for him and the children. That Monday afternoon, he'd be picking Gray and the kids up to go to the Wiggles concert. He didn't know who the fuck the Wiggles were, but he was down to go. As long as he was around his babies that was all that mattered but first, he had to pay respect to his brother. Taking one last lug from the blunt, he let the soul scorching smoke fill his lungs then exhaled it slow. The blunt was pretty much done. It was the size of a roach, so he flicked it to the ground. Quan and Stacy followed suit and hopped out the truck. They'd rode with him to the graveyard. The last time Cam visited Diggy was the day of his funeral. There wasn't a minute while he was locked down that he didn't think about him. He hated not being there for Quan and his family during such a trying time. He could only imagine how it felt to lose a sibling. Twenty-eight years had passed since his mother's death and he was still reeling from it. God only knew how Quan was feeling. Cam prayed to God he'd never have to find out. Even though he wasn't particularly close to his brothers, he didn't want to see any of them die. For the specific reason that he hated cemeteries. Walking over bones of the dead never felt right to him. As they walked through the graveyard, tombstones surrounded them with their faded engraving. Some were old and withered because of time and climate conditions while others were smooth, shiny and new. Stiff, cold bodies lay in coffins covered in dirt, ants and maggots. They were no longer people just soulless corpses. Knowing this made Cam feel uneasy. Yet, under the clear blue sky, the air scented with newly cut grass, a sense of calm washed over him. There was no need to fret. Amongst the dearly deceased he had time to contemplate and mourn in peace.

Standing before Diggy's grave, he reached out his calloused fingers to touch the headstone. Three years had gone by since Diggy's passing but it still seemed unreal. Leisurely, the pads of Cam's fingertips traced the white engraved lettering. Somehow, the cool feel of the stone gave him comfort. The gravestone had held up well under the harsh elements. It was still as polished and smooth as the day he was buried. Quan had spared no expense at getting his baby brother the most expensive option the funeral home had to offer. It took all of Cam's will not to cry. Quan and Stacy could sense his emotions bubbling to the surface. They'd been to visit quite a few times so the experience wasn't as hard on them as it had been in the beginning. Stacy gripped Cam's shoulder. The feel of his hand should've given him relief, but it didn't. The tears Cam tried to hold within escaped from the brim of his eyes and landed on his cheeks. Till this day, he still felt like Diggy's death was his fault. His beef with Gunz caused his best friend's little brother to die. Cam still didn't know how Quan was able to be friends with him after everything. Never once did he blame him for Diggy's murder. He chalked it up to a consequence of the game. Honestly, it didn't even matter if Quan blamed him or not. Cam blamed his self. He'd live the rest of his life knowing that because of him Diggy was dead. He just wished that Gunz would've finished him off when he had the chance to. Instead of coming for him, Diggy was targeted and murdered. This did nothing but fuel Cam's hatred of Gunz. The nigga thought he was a true OG, but he didn't know the true meaning of war or friendship. Cam would've traded places with Diggy in a heartbeat that fateful night. He would've left his family, Gray and the girls behind if it meant keeping his pot'nah alive.

"Sorry, I ain't been to see you in a minute. It's been mad crazy out here. A nigga just got home but I had to come pay my respect. Ain't a day that go by where I don't think about you or miss you. Shit ain't been the same without you dawg. I wish you were here, but I know you're in a better place." Cam gave a thoughtful glance up at the sky. "Check this shit out. You ain't gon' never believe this shit. Me and Gray got three polyamorous kids—"

"Polynesian, my nigga." Quan corrected him. "Polynesian."

"Whatever. It's the same thing. Them niggas look just like me blood. I can't believe it. I'ma daddy. Our kids the same fuckin' age. Taylani and Bronx are beautiful man. They lookin' more and more like you every day. On my mama we got 'em. They ain't gon' never have to worry about shit. I love you and I miss you dawg." Cam kissed the palm of his hand and laid it on the headstone once more before stepping back.

Quan took his place and stood in front of Diggy's gravestone.

"What's up li'l bro? I've been holding everything down like I said I would. Taylani and Bronx good. They ask about you all the time. I make sure I keep your memory alive by talking to them and telling them stories about you. Tara dating some lame-ass nigga. I checked him out so far, he straight but if the nigga get to actin' up, you know I'ma handle it." Quan scratched his temple.

A ball of tears crept up his throat.

"Mommy alive but she ain't been living since you passed. The only time she's somewhat happy is when we're all around. I try to spend as much time with her as I can, but no amount of time can replace losing you." He started to cry.

"FUCK!" He shouted enraged. "Why the fuck you have to die? You would still be alive if you never tried to be like me. This street shit was never for you. I should've made you go to college like mommy begged me to."

Quan's silent sobbing was worse than any tantrum or wailing a child could throw. His eyes welled up with a sadness a man his age shouldn't possess. The hush of his cry was unnerving, like it was a trait he'd been forced to learn. Seeing his best friend in such a vulnerable state fucked Cam up even more. He wanted to ease his pain. He wanted him to know it was okay to cry out loud but there was nothing he could say or do. Quan was a hood nigga to the heart. A mere mortal wouldn't be able to help him. It would take the strength of God to mend a soul so damaged. Since the mass shooting occurred where Diggy became a casualty of Cam and Gunz's war, Quan had been wanting to seek revenge. He thought about it every second of the day but Gunz was hidden away somewhere where no one could find him. The streets barely saw him. After Cam burned down all of his businesses and crib, he went off the grid. No one knew where he lived. He hadn't opened any new restaurants. The nigga literally became a fucking ghost.

"I miss you li'l bro." Stacy laid a bouquet of flowers on his grave.

Time went by where the three best friends stood, deep in their own thoughts. Even though it had been nearly four years since Diggy's brutal murder, Cam's grief still hadn't ceased. Sorrow was in his limbs as much as his mind. Things he once found funny no longer fascinated him. Diggy should've been there to laugh and crack jokes with them. He should've been at the barbeque playing with his kids. He should've been the one to stand by his brother's side on his wedding day, but he wasn't. There was no trace of him, just a memory and a gravestone with his name carved. In the past, Cam used to be uncertain about his faith in God. Now he knew without a shadow of a doubt that God would take care of Diggy and reunite them when his time on earth had come to an end. For no human being could simply vanish. Diggy was in heaven waiting on them to arrive. Cam had never been so sure of anything in his life. Taking his focus off the headstone he asked Quan, "Did you find any info on my case?"

"I reached out to your lawyer. He's on vacation but he's supposed to get me your paperwork before the end of the week."

"A'ight." Cam groaned, frustrated.

He hoped that something inside the case file would give him a tip on who'd snitched on him. He didn't have time to be waiting.

"What time is it?"

Stacy glanced down at his Patek Phillipe watch.

"11:30."

"Yo I'm trippin'. I gotta hurry up and get to Gray."

"Please tell me you ain't hitting that again. Ya'll niggas worse than Whitney and Bobby."

"Nah, we on our co-parenting shit today. We taking the kids to go see some li'l gay niggas called the Wiggles."

"Yo the Wiggles are the shit. They got some bops, for real. *Hot Potato! Hot Potato!*" Stacy sang joyously while doing the Hokey Pokey. "*Hot Potato! Hot Potato! Potato . . . potato-potato-potato!* That used to be my shit. Kayla used to love them, especially that fine-ass white bitch named Emma."

"I swear if I hadn't known you since third grade, we wouldn't be friends." Cam shook his head.

"Nigga, you know you love me."

"So how you feeling about all of this? Cause I'ma be honest wit' you. I ain't really feeling how ole girl handled the situation." Quan referred to Gray.

"Shit me neither. Every time I look at her I wanna snap her fuckin' neck."

"Now you know she ain't got no neck." Stacy joked.

"You stupid bro." Cam laughed. "I know I be on some wild shit. I know we ended things not on the best of terms. Matter of fact, fuck that we ended things horribly but what she did was mad corny. What's fucked up is she don't even think what she did was wrong."

"Yeah, that was crazy. She gon' apologize to Mo and not you. I'm lookin' like was you fuckin' her? Did you say vows to her? I like Gray but that's some nut shit. I ain't feelin' that." Quan spoke his peace.

"Ya'll not gon' talk about my li'l big sister." Stacy chimed in.

"Fuck yo' sister. If she's wrong, she's wrong." Cam argued.

"And where did you go wrong?"

"I went wrong when I married her lyin' ass. That's the only place I went wrong. You feel me?" He raised his hand for Quan to give him a five.

"Nah, I ain't sayin' all that." He shook his head. "Gray got some shit wit' her, but you fucked up too."

"Yeah nigga, let's not forget who slept over LaLa's house." Stacy added.

"Outta spite." Quan reminded him.

"Then fucked her in the bathroom."

"Out of spite again." Quan nodded.

"Then after all that . . . gon' have the nerve to cuss Gray out . . . on *their* porch . . . in front of his new bitch."

"Out of spite yet again."

"Do you see a pattern here?" Stacy arched his brow.

"Man, get yo' fat-ass out my face." Cam pushed him in the stomach.

"Niggas don't like to hear the truth."

"Man, fuck both of ya'll. Keep talkin' shit and see how you gon' get home." He warned.

"This nigga act like I ain't got a whole fiancé that won't pick me up." Quan chuckled.

Laughing, the guys made their way to the car in a better mood than when they came. Inside the whip, Cam started up the engine. Placing his foot on the brake, he took the car out of park and pulled off. He'd be a little late meeting up with Gray, but he'd rather be late than never show up at all. After explaining why, he was sure she'd understand the reason he didn't arrive on time. Bumping DJ ESCO feat O.T. Genasis and Future *Bring It Out* he bobbed his head to the beat and rapped along.

Got a lotta cash, still move fast
Dope in the pot, spoon in the trash
I'm addicted to the pace, I'ma trap nigga
Why you talk behind my back, you should act nigga
Make the money come back like a lap nigga
Treat you like ya' did good 'cause I clap niggas
I got shooters on deck and its real fun
Put your fingers in the air, get a real gun
Heard you got a bitch nigga, get a trill one
Couple days in a month I hit a million
I done had too much to drink I done fell on her
Had a foursome with my bitch, put Chanel on her
I'm still married to the game, got my ring out,
Long clip in this bitch, we can bang out

Vibing to the song, Cam relished the blessing of being behind the wheel again. It felt good to have his life back. Nothing or no one would ever send him back to the

213

pen. He'd die before he ever was locked behind bars again. As he whipped the Escalade through the winding road, he spotted a blacked-out car parked sideways in the middle of the street.

"The fuck." He scowled, blowing his horn.

The car didn't move.

"What the fuck are they doing?" Quan sat up straight on high alert.

The words weren't even good out of his mouth before all four doors of the vehicle opened and four masked men dressed in black pulled out semi-automatic weapons. Cam wondered if Victor had forgone his threat and sent his shooters to come kill him instead, until he noticed the letters MCM written on the four guys' masks.

"Oh shit! Pull off!" Stacy yelled.

Memories of the day he got shot flashed before his eyes. He was always down to shoot a fair one, but Stacy was getting too old to be constantly putting his life on the line. He had a daughter to live for. This street shit was cool when he was coming up, but he was forty-one now. Times had changed. It was now a young man's game. His mission every night was to make it home to his baby girl. All she had was him. Now that Cam had children of his own, he was certain he felt the same way. Cam put the gear shift in reverse and prepared to drive backwards only to see another black vehicle behind them with four more men. With nowhere to go he placed the car in park and sparked up a blunt. Leaned back in his seat, he took a long pull. The smoke was hot as he drew it into his lungs. Filled to capacity, he relished the light headed but pleasant feeling the Cali Kush gave him. Needing to exhale, he gradually blew the smoke out his mouth and nose.

"What the fuck are you doing?" Quan looked at him like he was crazy. "These niggas about to get to bustin'! Kema gon' kill me if I die!"

"You strapped?" Cam asked nonchalantly.

"Are you dumb? Yeah. Why are you gettin' high when we about to die?"

"Real talk, I ain't got time for your shit right now. You done already got me shot five times." Stacy went off.

"You trust me?" Cam asked him.

"No, nigga. You sittin' here smoking like it's a game."

"Do you trust me?" He looked at Quan.

"Sometimes. I don't know." He yelped unsure.

He wasn't in the mood to practice trust exercises with his best friend. Guns were aimed at the front and back windshield. Quan's heartbeat pounded inside his chest. The blood in his veins felt as if it were on fire. Cam apparently had something up his sleeve because he was as cool as a cucumber. He didn't even bat a lash as the members of MCM started letting off rounds into the car. Quan and Stacy ducked for cover. Cam didn't budge. Before his military training, gunshots used to make him jump but not anymore. They were as omnipresent as the sun just not as nourishing. He sat perfectly still smoking his blunt like he didn't have a care in the world. Gunshots cracked in the air as loud as thunder. Bullets spurted and cut through the air oblivious to their purpose. Each tore into something whether it be a gravestone or tree but not the truck. What Gunz or his pussy-ass hittas didn't know was that the truck was bulletproof. Cam was no dummy. He'd learned his lesson the hard way once Diggy died. He knew the war with Gunz was far from over, so he had all of his cars turned into armored vehicles. All of the windows were replaced with bulletproof glass and layers of military armored plates were inserted into the body panels. The hitmen hired dumped bullets from an Ak-47 but their shells still weren't getting through. The windshield was almost two-inches thick. The fuel tank was covered in ballistic nylon to ensure the truck didn't blow up. Other parts were covered in steel. Even the tires couldn't be penetrated. It cost Cam $360,000 a piece to have each of his whips customized but it was worth it. Gunfire was coming from every direction but not one bullet had breached the vehicle. Out of ammunition the men ceased fire. Cam put out his blunt in the ashtray and flared his nostrils. He wondered how much money Gunz had paid these idiots to lose their lives. They would never make it home. Their lives would end in a few short seconds. Flipping a switch, he released a smoke screen through the exhaust pipe. A cloud of smoke covered the car making it hard for the hitmen to see. The members of MCM didn't know what was happening. They didn't know if the car was about to blow up or if Cam was setting a trap. The leader of the crew decided to approach the truck to see if they'd successfully killed their targets. The windshield was practically destroyed so he couldn't see inside. Cam never took his eyes off the man as he rounded the car. The hitter was in for the shock of his life, literally. As soon as he placed his hand on the driver side door handle, he was hit with an electroshock. The zap of electricity was as painful as a taser. The man's body convulsed as he fell to the ground like a flopping fish.

"What in the Captain America Winter Soldier is going on?" Stacy asked confused.

"Nigga, why ain't we dead?" Quan's eyes darted from left to right.

"I told you to trust me." Cam smirked, pulling out his pistol. "Handle them niggas in the back. I got the front." He checked the clip, turned the safety off and hopped out.

Without further questions, Quan and Stacy leaped out with their weapons drawn. Adrenaline flooded Cam's system like an intravenous drip. In sicko mode, he pointed his gun at the man who'd been shocked head and pulled the trigger. Brain matter burst from the front of his cranium and splattered onto the concrete. Cam had one target down and three more to go. It felt weird having a gun in his hands again. It had been years since he last held or used one. The metal felt icy against his flesh. That didn't last long. With each second that passed the metal began to feel more like a part of him than a tool used for death. Like an old friend, Cam swiftly became reacquainted with his gun. He loved the way it felt in his large hands. The snug fit and flawless steadiness was all designed for him. Senses sharpened, he held his breath and strained his eyes to see through the smoke. His tactical training had prepared him for moments like this. His prickled skin calmed as he crept through the fog and trained his gun on the first man dressed in black he saw. Pulling the trigger, the bullet spat out the barrel and hit the man in the heart, thrusting him backwards. His limp body slumped to the ground. For a second, he glanced at the sky as if he was trying to take it in one last time. Then his vision faded to black and he died. Cam was so mesmerized by watching the man take his final breath that he didn't notice one of the other shooters aim his gun at him. There was one bullet left in the chamber that Cam hadn't accounted for. The hitter's intention was to shoot Cam in the heart like he'd done his friend but the sound of the bullet whipping through the air put Cam on notice. In just the nick of time he turned and dodged the shot to his heart. The bullet grazed his left arm instead. Cam didn't even feel the shot his adrenaline was pumping so hard. His heart beat fast. Thick scarlet red blood trickled from the wound, making it look worse than what it was. Extra heated, Cam quickly got his head back in the game and re-aimed. Everything around him disappeared. He felt nothing but the weight of the weapon in his hand. Inhaling, time slowed to a snail's pace. The breeze in the air reduced to a slight whisper. The contrast between it and his rapid heartbeat was vastly different. No longer playing games, he focused on his targets and squeezed the trigger. A bullet slammed into each of the men's heads. Cam watched as both guys dropped to their knees and fell forward. Blood gushed freely from their brains. The two men lay in pools of bodily fluids. The blood soaked into their black cotton clothing. If Cam didn't know any better, he'd think he was looking at a scene from an action flick, but this wasn't fake. This was real. The atmosphere reeked with the scent of slaughtered animals. These weren't animals tho. These were humans and their corpses were still warm with fresh blood.

"You straight?" Quan came to his aide.

He and Stacy had finished off the other four men with ease.

"Nah, he hit." Stacy noticed the plasma flowing from his arm. "C'mon, we gotta go." Stacy pulled him towards the truck.

Coming back to reality, Cam tucked his pistol into the back of his jeans. Police sirens were nearing, and they needed to break. Because of his arm, Cam jumped into the backseat. He couldn't drive with all the blood streaming. Just as he slammed the door shut, the sound of his phone ringing caught his attention. Cam didn't even need to check it to know it was Gray. The ringtone let him know it was her. Instead of answering, he let it go to voicemail. He had to make sure they got out of the cemetery without being caught by the cops. Once he was safe and his arm had been checked, he'd hit her back.

———

Present time

By the time Gray and the kids got to the concert, the first half of the act was coming to an end. The triplets only got to see the Wiggles perform a few songs before the intermission. The songs they got to hear brought them nothing but joy. They got their whole entire life singing, dancing and jumping around. Aoki and Press, however, were not impressed. They had outgrown the Wiggles ages ago. The only reason they were there was to help out with the little ones. The triplets couldn't take their eyes off the show. They were mesmerized by the colorful lights and the Wiggles red Beetle car that floated in front of the stage. When Wiggle Anthony came into the crowd and greeted the kids, Reign, Beaux and Sky lost their minds. Gray almost cried as she watched them smile and wave with wonder in their eyes. It truly warmed her heart that the little kids were having so much fun. This would be a moment in life she'd never forget. Cam should've been there to witness it. He better be glad Gray wasn't a mean, spiteful bitch. Even though he'd played them and didn't show up, she still captured the moment on her iPhone for him to see later.

"Mommy, I gotta go pee-pee." Reign squeezed his legs together and held his private part.

"I gotta use the bathroom too. I'll take him." Aoki rose to her feet.

"Sky and Beaux, do you have to pee too?" Gray gave them a look like you better not lie.

"No, I not have to pee, mommy." Sky shook her head while eating her cotton candy.

"Beaux?"

"Maybe. I don't know." She shrugged her little shoulders.

"Yeah, you need to go." Gray helped her out her seat. "Press, are you going too?"

"Yeah, I might as well." She pocketed her phone.

"Ya'll be careful and Aoki keep your eye on them."

"Nah, I'ma let 'em get snatched." She quipped, taking Reign and Beaux by the hand.

"Get popped in the mouth." Gary warned with a mean glare.

"Love you too dear." Aoki said sarcastically as Gray received a text message.

She hoped it was Cam hitting her up with an explanation on his whereabouts but that would be too much like right. It was Noon her boyfriend.

Noon: Ya'll having fun?

Gray: The babies are. I miss u.

Noon: I miss you too. Thursday can't get here fast enough.

Gray: Right! I'll finally get u all to myself. No work! Just me and u.

Noon: Speaking of work, I got a meeting to get to. I just wanted to check in wit' you and let you know you were on my mind.

Gray: Thank u baby.

Noon: I'ma facetime you later. Be naked!

Gray shook her head and laughed. Noon was a mess, but she was really feeling him. He was good for her. She couldn't wait for him to get into town. In a better mood, she picked Sky up and placed her on her lap. Music was still playing. Bouncing her leg up and down to the beat, she kissed Sky on the cheek and took a tiny piece of her pink cotton candy. The action reminded her of when she fed her father the same sweet candy years before at the celebrity basketball game. Gray remembered vividly him licking the sticky residue off her fingers one by one. The seductive gesture had the heartbeat in her clit on cardiac arrest. Those were the good ole days. Falling in love with Cam had been one of the best and worst experiences of her life. Before him she didn't know the meaning of true love. She'd never wanted any form of eternity with Gunz like she did with him. When she pledged her soul to him, she meant it with every inch of her heart. There wasn't a part of Cam that she didn't acknowledge or accept. She saw all of him, the joys and the burdens. None of it deterred her. She was home. With him, every ounce of breath in her lungs was taken and released into the air like midnight smoke. No one had ever been closer to her heart. Before him she felt like she'd been living in the dark. Each time they kissed time stopped. Falling in love with Cam had been easy. The hard part was admitting that the love she felt for him wasn't returned tenfold. She'd given him her all and was left questioning if he ever loved her at all. Then the scent of his Tom Ford cologne wafted up her nose, making her brown nipples erect. He was there. Sitting up straight, Gray tried to seem indifferent to his presence as she turned to face him.

"Bout time you showed up." She snapped only to get the shock of her life.

"You miss me?" Gunz stood with a devilish grin on his face.

For a second, Gray wondered had she died and gone to hell. The rapid beat against her hollow chest let her know she was alive. Everything else on her body had shut down. She'd suddenly become immobile. Gray wanted to speak but all of her words had taken flight. Gunz was the last person she thought she'd see. She hadn't heard from him in years but here he was live in the flesh. Everything about him was the same. His rich mahogany skin still shined brighter than the summer sun. Low, spinning waves, a full shimmering beard, full lips and a tall muscular frame completed the package of his panty dropping good looks. In the past, she would've been turned on by his handsome features but not anymore. She despised Gunz as much as he probably despised the glass eye he was rockin'.

"Hell, no, and what the hell are you doing here? Did you follow me?" She looked around suspiciously.

She couldn't trust Gunz for shit. The last two times she'd been in the same room with him he'd been on some foul ish. He placed a gun to her head and then kissed her while she was drunk without her consent. Gray didn't know what he had up his sleeve next. Whatever it was, nothing good would come from it.

"I see Paris did you good." Gunz trailed his brown eye from the top of her head down to the sole of her pedicured feet.

Gray looked great and she knew it. She didn't need Gunz to tell her. The last person she wanted a compliment from was him. Gunz took in her gorgeous face. Gray was just as beautiful as he remembered. Time had done her well. With age she got even prettier. Her short blonde hairdo was styled to perfection. Layers of gold necklaces decorated her décolletage. Her sumptuous perky breasts sat up without any support in a white, deep V-neck, long sleeve, ribbed crop top. A black double G Gucci belt and a gold chain belt with charms that spelled out Gucci accentuated the white midi skirt she wore. Gianvito Rossi see-through vinyl, leather slides elongated her honey colored legs. Since she left, his love for her had morphed into a twisted obsession. Gunz bought every magazine cover she graced and looked at them several times a day. He daydreamed about the moment he'd be able to ruin her life like she'd ruined his. He was determined to eliminate every aspect of her life that made her happy.

"How did you know we were gonna be here?" She held Sky close to her chest.

"C'mon, Gray. I know everything. There ain't shit that go down in this city that I don't know about. By the way, I liked that li'l outfit you had on yesterday. That li'l nude joint had your ass and titties sitting up right."

It was as if Gray retreated inside herself. Her brain had officially shut down. Her hands were a clammy, wet mess. A cold sheen of sweat glistened from her brow. The pupils of her eyes dilated to the point it hurt. Gunz had been watching her. How else would he have known what she wore? She hadn't taken any pictures the day before. She needed help. She needed to get her and her kids away from this monster as quickly as possible.

"Don't be scared. I'm not gon' hurt you . . . yet." He took a seat beside her and placed his rough hand on her thigh.

"Get your fuckin' hands off of me." She smacked it away.

The feel of him touching her made her physically ill.

"Don't be like that. You know I hate to see you upset."

"Cam is on his way. If he catches you here, he's going to kill you." She lied, hoping to scare him off.

"Now we both know that's not true." He gave her a sympathetic look.

Frightened by his expression, Gray's body began to tremble with fear.

"Introduce me to li'l mama." Gunz eased closer. "Is this Beaux or Sky?"

The fact that he knew her babies' names scared her even more. No one knew about the triplets except her friends and the girls. She knew her friends hadn't said a word and Aoki and Press wouldn't dare tell her business.

"If you don't get the fuck out my face, you one-eyed bitch. I will kill you." She gritted with malice.

"It wouldn't be the first time you killed an ex-lover."

"Fuck you. You need to go or I'ma call the police." She reached for her phone.

"And tell 'em what? That I'ma father tryin' to see his kids, after their shiesty-ass mother took them away from me."

"You got your fuckin' nerves. You know damn well I ain't keep Aoki and Press away from you. You're the one that chose not to be in their lives. You're the one that wanted to have a baby by a bitch that's damn near the same age as your daughter. You're the one that got a new family and said fuck the one you already had. What kind of man are you? Oops my bad. You're not a man. You're a fuckboy wit' a glass eye."

Gunz's nostrils flared. He didn't appreciate Gray speaking to him this way.

"Aoki and Press love you and you can't even pick up the phone and call them. They begged you to come see them and you couldn't be fuckin' bothered. But you can sit here wit' that stiff-ass eye and try to blame your shit on me. Bitch, I don't think so. The hell you're living in is of your own making. Me and my girls are good with or without you. Please believe what you won't do . . . Cam will." Gray spat indignantly.

She was tired of Gunz bullying her. If he was going to hurt her then he better aim to kill 'cause she was going to give him the fight of his life. The mere mention of Cam's name set off an anger inside of Gunz that even he didn't recognize. Before Gray could react, he snatched Sky from her arms and held her against his firm chest.

"Gunz stop." She panicked, rising to her feet.

Gray felt just like a child again, powerless, shaken and terrified. The constricted feeling inside her chest grew to a point it felt like she was being chocked by the air itself.

"She's cute, Gray. She looks just like you." Gunz caressed Sky's chubby cheek, causing her to cry.

The sound was so shrill it almost stopped Gray's heart. She'd never heard her baby cry so hard. It was like Sky knew Gunz was a bad man. She extended her small arms so her mother could rescue her but Gunz stopped Gray by blocking her with his hand.

"Gunz give me back my fuckin' daughter!" Gray raised her voice not giving a damn if she caused a scene.

She hoped someone would see her distress and come to her aide.

"Shhhhhhh it's okay." Gunz rocked Sky in his arms. "You ain't gotta cry. I won't hurt you . . . at least not today."

"You lay a hand on my daughter and I swear on my mother's grave, I will carve out your other eye." Gray sneered with hate.

"You should tell your mom I don't take too well to threats. God knows I would hate for something to happen to your pretty little face." Gunz placed a sinister kiss to Sky's forehead.

"And I would hate to have your guts splattered all over this floor." Priest pressed his Glock into the small of Gunz's back.

He'd gotten there in just the nick of time. God knows what Gunz would've done if he hadn't shown up when he did. Thank God, Cam had called him and told him to check on Gray and the kids. After getting hit at the cemetery, he wasn't taking any chances of his family being in danger. Gunz paused. He wasn't expecting Gray to have backup. He expected for Cam and his boys to be deceased. The only person he hadn't accounted for was Priest.

"Give her back to her mother." Priest removed the gun Gunz had hidden in the back of his jeans.

Unarmed Gunz had no choice but to comply. Heatedly, he gave Sky back to Gray.

"Daddy!" Press ran in his direction.

226

Gray closed her eyes. Seeing the sheer look of excitement and delight on her daughter's face tugged at her heart strings. Press had missed her daddy like crazy over the past few years. She didn't understand why he'd suddenly disappeared from their lives. Since the day she was born, she'd been raised in a two-parent home. One day she woke up and all of that abruptly changed. Gray moved on with Cam and Gunz moved on with his child bride. Press was told just because her mom and dad weren't together anymore, it didn't mean that either of them would love her any less. Gray remained the same. She continued to be a present and loving mother. When it came to Gunz, Press would call him to talk and he wouldn't answer the phone. When he did decide to answer, he would feed her a bunch of lies and make her think he was coming to see her, but he never showed. Things got even worse once they moved to Paris. While his absence did nothing but make Aoki loathe him, Press grew to yearn for him more. Cam was her Papa. She adored him and loved him dearly. He'd stepped in and filled the void that Gunz left behind but Gavin 'Gunz' Marciano was her father, the man whose last name she bore. He was the one she shared blood with. He was the one who used to kiss her boo-boo's and taught her how to ride a bike. For Press there was a major difference.

"There goes my girl." He stooped down and gave her a big bear hug.

Press hugged him back with everything she had to give. She hoped her adoration seeped into his soul and made him return to being the father she once knew.

"Let me look at you." Gunz held her at arm's length. "Wow, you got so big."

"You like my hair, daddy? I cut it." She smiled brightly, waiting her his approval.

"I love it, pretty girl. You're just as pretty as your mother." He smirked at Gray. "Aoki, come here. Give daddy a hug."

Aoki stood frozen in place. She was just as nauseous as her mother. Gunz swore that despite him not being her biological father that she'd always be his baby girl. He promised to make more of an effort to be in her life but everything he said was a lie. None of it came to fruition. Her biggest fear when she learned about her paternity was that he would turn his back on her; that's why she clung to him so strong. Now, she knew for certain that Gunz's love for her was as conditional as it was for her mother. As soon as he had no use for them, he threw them away like yesterday's trash. There were no phone calls to say hi or gifts on her birthday or Christmas to show he cared. He gave all of his time and attention to his brand-new baby boy. Tia often posted pictures of them as a family on her Instagram. They looked so happy. Gavin Jr. was the apple of Gunz's eye. She and Press were nothing but a distant memory.

"Nah, I'm good." She gave him the meanest look she could muster.

"It's like that?" Gunz scowled down at her.

"It's been like that."

"So not only did you leave me, but you turned my daughter against me?" He turned his wrath on Gray.

"You need to go." She held her children close.

"No, daddy, stay. I miss you." Press wrapped her arms around his leg.

"Nah, I can't stay baby girl. Daddy gotta shake but I promise I'ma come get you later."

"Don't hold your breath." Aoki quipped, taking hold of her sister's hand.

Press didn't wanna let go but knew she had to. Tears she'd been holding in dripped from the corner of her eyes. Gunz gave Press and Gray one last look then faced Priest who was still holding him at gunpoint.

"I'ma be seeing you soon."

"Indeed." Priest said ready for whatever.

Gray didn't let out a full breath until Gunz was out of the building.

"C'mon ya'll we about to go." She quickly grabbed her purse.

"Why, mommy? We just got here?" Beaux whined.

"Beaux, stop. We gotta go." Aoki said firmly so she knew she meant business.

"I'll walk you to your car and follow you home." Priest tried to help Gray with her things.

"Uh ah. Who are you?" She stepped back, paranoid.

"He's Pop's cousin, ma. Chill." Aoki groaned.

She'd die if Gray embarrassed her in front of her soon-to-be boyfriend. Gray looked Priest up and down. She'd seen him around, lurking in the shadows but they'd never been properly introduced.

"Where is Cam?"

"He's indisposed. Some shit just went down. He told me to tell you he'll meet you at the crib so he can explain everything. Until then, I'ma keep an eye on you."

12

"What do I say to make you understand what I'm feeling?
What do I tell you, so you know I'm way pass cloud 9 but
not that kinda high? Maybe I ain't gotta talk to ya'. Maybe
I'll just show you with the way that I walk to ya'. Maybe I
ain't gotta speak. Ain't nothin' you ain't heard. Seriously at
a loss for words."- Alex Isley, "Loss for Words"

Priest hadn't done anything but sit on the couch and
check his phone the whole time he'd been at Gray's house.
He hadn't said a peep or acknowledged the ruckus going on
around him. The triplets were running around throwing
Play-Doh at each other's head. One of them was dressed in
an Elsa costume. Press was in her room singing showtunes
on her karaoke machine. Priest was unfazed by it all, but
his presence had Aoki on ten. She couldn't stop fidgeting
with her hair, checking her appearance in the mirror or stop
poppin' Altoids to insure her breath didn't stink. She even
added some tissue to her bra to make her breasts appear
bigger. Priest, the love of her life was only a few feet away.
Now was the time to throw some game at him and see if he
bit. She knew she was thirteen and he was twenty-three, but
Aoki wouldn't be Aoki if she didn't shoot her shot. She
was fearless like that and plus he was her dream man. No
one could tell her that they wouldn't run off into the sunset
and start a family of their own someday. Her skin still
tingled from the way he wrapped his arms around her and
held her tight after the fight. Every time she came near him,
her heart beat erratically in her chest. Priest was so fine.
The white t-shirt he donned clung tight to his pecks. She

could see the print of the barbells in his nipples from across the room. Aoki imagined running her tongue across each one while moaning his name. She wanted him in the worst way. He was better looking and more dangerous than any rapper on the Billboard charts. Priest had an air of arrogance about him that made him even sexier. His physical attributes were part GQ model, part serial killer. She adored each side because he reminded her a lot of herself. The darkness around him didn't scare her. It actually drew her to him more. Aoki would cut off all her hair if she could get a glimpse inside his brain. Her 30-inch, sandy brown, curly hair was the best thing about her besides her tranquil blue eyes. Every person she came in contact with commented on her gorgeous locs. Long, brown ringlets fell perfectly around her heart shaped face, but Priest didn't notice it at all. It sucked because she noticed everything about him; like the way he counted his steps when he walked or how he washed his hands every time he touched a surface. His quirks fascinated her. She wanted to know more. She needed to know what turned him on, what made him tick, what he thought about before he pulled the trigger. The teardrops under his left eye let her know he had a few bodies under his belt. Mustering up the courage to approach him, she swayed her imaginary hips from side-to-side and stood next to the couch.

"Would you like something to drink?" She purred, trying to sound seductive.

Priest took his eyes off his phone and looked at her. Anybody else would've been frightened by his angry scowl but Aoki liked his moody behavior.

"What you got?" He asked dryly.

His gritty voice sent a chill down her spine.

"Umm . . . we got pink lemonade, apple juice, water, milk, Moscato and Henny. You look like a Henny man. Let me pour you a glass."

"Henny?" Priest drew his head back. "What you know about Henny? Ain't you like nine?"

"No!" She screwed up her face. "I'm thirteen and a half." Aoki arched her back and poked out her breasts.

"Water is fine." Priest focused back on his phone.

Not wanting to be away from him longer than a second, Aoki ran to the kitchen and grabbed him a bottle of Fiji water.

"Here." She huffed slightly out of breath.

Priest took the bottle and chugged down half of it in one long gulp. Aoki watched on in awe. *Goddamn, he's a man,* she swooned in her mind.

"*So . . .*" She sauntered slowly across the room, trying to look sexy while flicking her hair.

Her attempt was a huge fail because some of her hair got stuck to her lip-gloss. Aoki poked out her tongue and spit the pieces of hair away embarrassed. Frustrated, she pushed her curly strands away from her face and sat in an armchair opposite him.

"How old are you?" She crossed her legs.

"Old." Priest vaguely replied, watching one of Chris Smoove videos on YouTube.

"How old?"

"Old. Old."

Aoki leaned forward, hoping he'd take a look at her barely-there titties. Priest didn't look up once. Loving the sound of his raspy voice, she tried to figure out a way to get him to keep talking. Aoki was so enamored; she could drink in his words like a strong wine and enjoy feeling tipsy.

"Is Priest your real name or your nickname?" She poked out her chest some more.

The way she was sitting made it look like she was straining to breathe. The arch in her back was so deep she could do a back bend. Priest ignored her and continued to pay attention to his phone. Unwilling to give up, Aoki decided to try another approach.

"So how long you been working for Cam?"

Priest tuned her out and acted like she wasn't even there. When he didn't respond, Aoki began to think she might've hit a nerve.

"I'm sorry. Maybe I'm getting a li'l too deep. I ain't tryin' to get all in your business, ya feel me? Let's try something less intrusive. What's your favorite color?"

Silence.

"Why you chose water instead of Hennessy? You don't like to drink?" She cocked her head to the side.

More silence.

"Ohhhhh." She paused. "I get it. You don't like dark liquor. You only drink white."

Priest inwardly groaned. Cam needed to hurry up and arrive before he snapped on his stepdaughter.

"Why you ain't come to the barbeque?" Aoki twisted her shoulders back-and-forth, trying to be alluring.

The motion caused one of the balls of tissue to pop from her bra and fall to the floor. A rush of heat flushed her cheeks; she was so embarrassed. Swiftly, she picked it up and pretended like she was blowing her nose. Priest scratched the back of his head and tried not to humiliate her by laughing. For a while, silence filled the area. Aoki was mortified. Tears stung her eyes, but she played it cool. She could never let him see her sweat. If she came across like a li'l girl, she'd never be able to get him to see her as the young woman she perceived herself to be. Nervously, shaking her leg, she tried to figure out her next step. Aoki was stumped. She didn't know how to proceed. Nothing she said or did got his attention. She knew she was cute so why wasn't he feeling her?

"You don't like black people food?"

Priest tried to keep his cool, but Aoki was annoying the hell out of him. Her presence and nonstop questions buzzed around him like a fly he couldn't swat.

"I feel that vibe." She nodded her head. "I don't be liking all that fatty shit either. I'm half Korean so I gotta watch my figure." She ran her hands down her body.

Even that didn't entice him. Priest was a harder nut to crack than she thought. Biting her bottom lip, she wondered should she give up until she thought of another question.

"Do your nipple rings hurt? Cause I was thinking about getting mine done too." She touched her left titty.

"Aww fuck nah." Priest shot up from his seat. "Gray, I'ma be outside!" He rushed out of the house as Cam rushed in.

"Where you running off to?"

"Away from you weird-ass daughter." Priest jogged down the steps.

"Which one?"

"The one wit' the fucked-up name."

"Oh Aoki. Yeah, she bat shit crazy."

"You good?" Priest acknowledged his arm.

If he didn't know any better, he would've sworn Cam was fine. From the outside looking in it didn't even seem like he'd just been shot. After paying a visit to the doctor they had on the payroll, he headed home, took a quick shower and changed. There was no way he was letting Gray and the children see him covered in blood. Because of his injury, Cam wanted to be comfortable so he threw on a black dad hat, denim Bathing Ape jacket, an oversized grey t-shirt, jogging shorts, Off-White socks and zebra print Yeezy 350 boost. Even on his bummy shit, Cam still rocked pieces that cost more than your average nigga's salary.

"Wasn't nothin' a few stiches couldn't fix." He shrugged the graze wound off.

"A'ight I'm up." Priest gave him a pound and a hug. "I got security stationed on each end of the corner, in the front and back of the house."

"Good lookin' out." Cam pushed opened the door.

"Ayo Cam!"

"Yeah." He turned around before going in.

"No more playin' games. You gotta end that nigga."

"On my mama that nigga got his coming, for real." He raised his right hand to God.

Priest nodded his head and chirped the alarm on his car. Once Cam saw that his cousin had pulled off safely, he headed inside.

"Gray! Where you at?"

"She in the back throwing shit around like she Bernadine from Waiting to Exhale." Aoki wisecracked, snacking on a whole bag of Cardi B Rap Snacks.

The only thing that could fix her sour mood was carbs. She was absolutely devastated that she'd annoyed Priest so much, he got up and ran away. If she kept this up, she'd never get him to go half on a baby.

"Watch your mouth li'l girl." Cam checked her on his way to Gray's bedroom.

Under different circumstances, he would've checked on the kids first, but based off what Priest told him on the way over, Gray was freaking out and threatening to leave. If he didn't calm her down, she would be on the first flight back to France. The problem was he didn't know how to do so. In the past he could threaten her or calm her down with dick, but the dynamics of their relationship had changed. Gray didn't jump when he said how high anymore. She was on her I'ma woman, hear me roar bullshit. This conversation could either go extremely well or go left really quick. He prayed she didn't explode on him like she did the other day. Cam wasn't in the mood to be called a tall, freckled-face bitch. As soon as his feet hit the threshold of her bedroom, he started to get a migraine. Gray had shit everywhere. Several suitcases lined the bed as she frantically packed her and the kids things to go. The thought of her hopping on a plane and distancing him from their kids again almost killed him.

"I'm not letting you run again."

Gray stilled at the sound of his voice.

"You don't have a choice. He threatened my fuckin' child!" She resumed, stuffing underwear into a bag.

"He what?" Cam walked further inside the room.

He couldn't have heard right. No way was Gunz dumb enough to threaten one of his seeds.

"He threatened to hurt Sky and he's been stalking me."

Bewildered, Cam's brain stuttered for a second. He'd heard a lot of foul shit over the years, but this took the cake. Gunz had taken his disrespect to a new level. There were rules to the game. Women and children were always off limits but now that he'd taken it there the gloves were coming off. No man on earth would ever threaten the lives of his children and live to talk about it.

"Yeah. Now you see. I'm getting the fuck outta here. We're not safe. I'm taking the kids back home to Paris." Gray grabbed more things and threw them in a suitcase.

"No. You need to be here with me. Can't nobody protect you like I can."

Gray stopped and spun around. Her side swept bang covered her eyes as she glared at him.

"Well, excuse me but you're doing a shitty job of protecting us. You wouldn't even pick up the phone when I called. If you don't like me, Cam, that's fine. If you don't wanna be around me, I get it. I don't really care, but we have kids now. You can't not answer. Anything could've happened as you see. If you love the kids as much as you say you do, then no matter what you should always be there for them. Now, I don't know what was more important than spending time with your children, but if you would've been there like you said you would be, none of this shit would've happened."

Cam clenched his fist so tight his knuckles turned white.

"You love running your fuckin' mouth. Too bad you don't know what the fuck you're talkin' about. I didn't show up 'cause I was too busy getting shot at."

"What?" Gray paused, shocked.

"Yeah, nigga. Gunz sent some of his goons to kill me. Obviously, he planned on offing me, and once he figured I was dead, he'd run up on you." Cam pieced everything together.

"Oh my God." Gray shivered, holding her chest. "This is the reason why I left. I can't take this. All of this unnecessary gun violence is too much. I love Kema and I want to see her get married, but my kids come first. I can't have them around this bullshit." She restarted packing.

"You're not leaving." Cam slammed the suitcase shut.

"The hell I'm not! You don't run me! You don't dictate my life!"

"Run you? I'm tryin' to protect you. If it wasn't for me yo' dumb-ass would be at the morgue wit' a bullet in your head."

"Wooooow." Gray scoffed, appalled. "You really gon' go there? You really gon' bring that up right now?"

"I'm not talking about me holding you at gunpoint dummy. I'm talking about Victor."

"What does Victor have to do with this?" She looked him up and down confused.

"He wants you 6F."

"What?" Gray stood up straight.

She'd learned over the years 6F meant six feet deep.

"Why?"

"He thinks you're the one who got me locked up."

"But I didn't. You know I didn't and what does you getting locked up have to do with him wanting to kill me?" She tried her best not to hyperventilate.

"The shipment that was confiscated gave him unwanted attention from the FEDS. Attention that's still on him now. You know he can't have that. Somebody has to pay. Whoever got me locked up has to die. He's giving me until the wedding to find the rat, and if I can't, he's gunning for you."

"Oh my God." She held her head.

Gray felt like she was going to pass out. The walls were beginning to close in. The air in her lungs came out in small, short, spurts. Slumped over the bed, she breathed in through her nose and out of her mouth.

"I can't believe this is happening to me. This is some bullshit. I gotta get outta here." She attempted to race by him.

"You can't leave." Cam took a hold of her arm.

"The fuck I can't!" She tried to pull away.

"Stop!" He shook her in hopes of knocking some sense into her. "Listen to me, Gray! It doesn't matter where you go. He will find you. The only place you're safe is here with me."

Completely and utterly stressed, Gray's body went limp as she fell to her knees. Tears rushed her eyes like water rushing down from a waterfall. She wept loudly into her shaky hands. Covering her face, salty tears slipped through her fingers and onto the front of her skirt.

"I knew I shouldn't have come back here. I knew this was a mistake." Her words came out in ragged breaths.

Cam stooped down and took her into his big strong arms. He never liked to see Gray cry. She was more than a lover or a friend. She was the mother of his kids. The woman he'd pledged his life to. His kids' mother should never weep. Only laugher and smiles should come from her lips.

"You gotta find out who did this."

"I am. On our kids, I swear to God I will." He pulled her closer.

Gray held onto him tight. He was her human shield. Her knight in shining armor. Her

Super hero. Cam's embrace was stronger than ever before. It was as if holding her wasn't quite enough. He wrapped her up in his arms like he needed to feel every inch of her.

"You say that you'll protect me but how can you protect me when you don't trust me?"

Cam wished he could say that was a lie, but he knew that wouldn't be the truth. Trust was the foundation to all his relationships. It came first in his world. It wasn't apart of some package deal. Too much had happened between he and Gray to say he had faith in her word. The trust he had for her was broken. A few days back in each other's lives, after years of being apart, wouldn't change that. He needed time to figure things out and think things through.

"See. You don't trust me." She pushed him off her and stood back up.

What the fuck was I doing letting him hold me anyway, she thought. Cam remained seated on the floor. He was tired and the wound on his arm was starting to ache.

"Real shit. I don't wanna believe you would fuck me over but if you were in my position, you would think the same thing too. I broke up wit' you, Gray. I didn't believe you were pregnant, and I smashed a bitch I didn't even know you had beef wit' at the crib I bought for you. Hours later the FEDS show up at my door placing handcuffs on me. You can't tell me that don't look suspect as fuck."

"I know it looks crazy, but I swear I didn't do it. No matter what I was feeling at the time, I would never hurt you that way."

"I hear you but there were only six people that knew about that shipment and one of 'em is dead. I know for a fact Quan, Stacy or Priest didn't do it. That only leaves you."

"I don't know what else to tell. There's literally nothin' I can do to prove to you I didn't do so . . ." Gray shrugged, tired of explaining herself.

"We need to figure this shit out then."

"You damn right we do 'cause I'll be damned if I die behind you and your bullshit. This is exactly why I wanted you out of the life in the first place. Nothing but murder and destruction comes from it." She sat on the side of the bed.

"Until I get this shit figured out, ain't no leaving the game."

"Don't you see that there is more that God wants you to do with your life? Cam, you told me you got into Wharton. A man with your brains shouldn't be pushing narcotics."

"I know." He shifted uncomfortably.

Cam knew his mama was somewhere turning over in her grave. She would've been so disappointed in what he had become.

"Does anyone else know about this?"

"Quan and Stacy."

"Keep it that way. I don't want any of my friends to know. I've put them through enough stress over the years." Gray massaged her temples. "What are we gonna do about Gunz? He has to be stopped."

"I'ma handle it." Cam fumed with the desire to kill him with his bare hands.

"But how?"

"The less you know the better. Just know I got you. Gunz won't be a problem much longer."

It would take a lot for Gray to put all of her trust in Cam but what other choice did she have? She was no match for Gunz. She had to depend on the one man she couldn't even be in the same room with without arguing. For the first time in their relationship, she had to let go and trust Cam.

"As of today, I got armed guards everywhere. Even when I'm not around you're still safe."

"That makes me feel a li'l better but what are we gonna do about us?"

"In order for us to make it through this week and keep you alive, we're gonna have to get on the same page."

"How we gon' do that? We can barely be in the same room without arguing. Every time we're around each other, we start bickering about shit that happened three years ago." She reasoned.

Cam thought for a minute. He didn't like putting people in their business, but his back was against the wall.

"Let's go see Pastor Edris."

———

The clock read 10:40 p.m. when Cam walked in the crib. Devin sat on the couch with a fresh glass of wine in her delicate, manicured hand. A short silk robe draped across her body as she tapped her foot heatedly on the wooden floor. The television was on, but it was more so watching her than vice versa. While at work, she hadn't heard from Cam. She'd called him back-to-back. He didn't pick up once. It wasn't until nightfall that he decided to return her call. By that time, she didn't care to answer. If she answered, she was liable to say something she'd regret. Cam had her fucked up. He was out of his mind if he thought he was going to spend the whole day with his baby mama and dodge her calls. Who knows what they'd been doing this whole time? The concert had been over. Kids or no kids he had no business being over there this long.

"I come in peace." He handed her a pretty bouquet of pink roses.

Devin placed the flowers up to her nose, inhaled the floral scent then angrily threw them to the floor. Rose petals spattered everywhere.

"That's how you feel? I spent a grip on those."

"I don't care." She took a small sip from her glass.

"You ain't see me calling you. Why you ain't answer the phone?" Cam plopped down next to her.

"'Cause I wasn't in the phone answering mood." She scooted over so their skin wouldn't touch.

"Now you don't wanna talk? You was blowing me up earlier."

"That was then. This is now."

"You cook?"

Devin whipped her head in his direction.

"Oh, that got your attention." Cam grinned.

"Don't play with me." She snapped as his phone began to ring.

"Hold up. Let me take this." He walked into the kitchen to answer the call. "What you got for me?" He asked impatiently.

"Nothing yet. I got my ear to the streets but ain't nobody talkin'." Twan replied.

"So, you telling me don't nobody know shit. Even with a 100k on the line?" Cam said pissed.

"When I tell you don't nobody know shit. This muthafucka must've been a ghost. Don't get twisted tho. Niggas is lookin'. Muthafuckas is hungry. They want that bread."

Cam ran his hand down his face frustrated.

"Make it 250. I need answers like yesterday."

"Shit for 250 of them thangs, I did it." Twan joked.

"Shut up, nigga. Now is not the time."

"Real talk. I got you boss."

"A'ight. I'll get at you." Cam ended the call feeling worse than he already had.

Shit was looking dimmer and dimmer for Gray.

"You ain't been here all day then you gon' disrespect me by coming in here talkin' to them bitches." Devin quipped on ten.

"Huh? What bitches? That was business." He retook his seat.

"Mmm hmm. It's always business."

"What's wrong wit' you? Why you got an attitude?" He gripped her thigh.

"Are you fuckin' kidding me? Your baby mother and her ratchet- ass friends threw food all over me yesterday. Then you say you're going to a fuckin' Wiggles' concert but then you stay out all day and don't answer any of my calls. You don't see how disrespectful that is?"

"I talked to Gray. I told her what she did wasn't cool."

"Yeah, I heard what you said. That wasn't good enough. I need more than that. You need to get that big-bitch in check. And if you think for one second you gon' bring me some punk-ass pink flowers and everything is gon' be alright, you got another thing coming. I don't even like the color pink. That's that bitch favorite color." Devin spat.

Granted she didn't know how his day had gone, but Cam was nowhere near in the mood to argue. In order to protect his peace, it was best he bounce before he flipped out and punched Devin in her left titty.

"When you're ready to talk like you got some sense, holla at me." He pulled out his car keys.

Seeing he wasn't playing, Devin panicked and began to fake cry. She gave on an Oscar worthy performance that was so good Cam almost believed her tears.

"Why you actin' like that? I didn't even do nothin'. She's the one that came at me." She whined like a child.

"You've got to be fuckin' kidding me." He massaged his temples.

"I'm trying so hard to be understanding of your situation but it's hard. You have three kids with her."

"Five." Cam corrected her.

"See." Devin boo-hoo'd.

"Come here." Cam held out his arms.

Devin rushed over and buried her face inside his chest.

"It's a lot of things to cry about, ma, but this ain't one of 'em." He ran his long fingers through her hair.

246

Pretending to sniffle, Devin lifted her head and asked somberly, "You still fuckin' her?"

"Who? My wife? No."

"Ex-wife." Her face turned cold.

"*Wife.*" Cam corrected her. "Until the divorce is final, she's my *wife*. You need to understand and accept that. And the next time you say some slick shit about her, I'ma knock you in your shit. You understand?"

"But she—" Devin tried to argue.

"You heard what the fuck I said." Cam cut her off.

"It's not fair!" She stomped her foot like she was the triplets' age. "I was the one there for you while you were in jail. I was the one on the phone with you every day. I was the one that came to visit you. That—" She stopped herself from calling Gray a beluga whale. "*Your wife* didn't give a fuck about you. She sent you divorce papers and went on with her life, remember? I was the one that held you down." She began to cry for real this time.

"And that's why I'm here with you and not her. Me and Gray are over."

"Prove it. Sign the divorce papers."

Lying wasn't something Cam typically did but he actually cared for Devin. He couldn't tell her that he wasn't ending his marriage, until he was absolutely certain it couldn't be repaired. There was a lot of anger, trust issues, lies and infidelity between he and Gray but with time all of it could be fixed. They had a whirlwind relationship that took place over the span of seven months. Their love was so profound that they put expectations on each other they shouldn't. Looking back on things with a clear mind, he realized that they were doomed from the start. They'd moved too fast, got married too quick. He was immature and unsure. She was a wounded bird that needed time to heal her broken wings. If it was revealed, Gray wasn't the one who set him up and she could find it in her heart to forgive him for cheating, maybe, just maybe, they could give their marriage a second chance. It would be an uphill battle, but their family was worth preserving. Because of this he refused to lie to Devin. Instead, he chose not to say anything.

13

"Most men would rather deny a hard truth than face it."-
George R.R. Martin, "A Game of Thrones"

"Okay." Gray took a deep breath and popped her
back. "You can do this."

Grabbing her purse from the passenger seat, she
stepped out of her truck and chirped the alarm. New
Northside Baptist Church was a nice church. It wasn't
overly big. It was just the right size for a large congregation
without it feeling like you were at a concert every Sunday.
The building was made of old stone and stained glass. It
was beautiful but Gray wasn't excited about being there.
She didn't fully believe in organized religion. Her mother
didn't belong to a church and never forced her to go. And
after everything she'd been through, could you blame her
for not having 100% faith in God? She didn't need some
pastor she didn't know to bring her closer to him. The
aspects of him she did believe in lived inside her soul.

It was late in the day, so the parking lot was semi-
full. Walking across the concrete paved ground, she spotted
Cam standing on the top step awaiting her arrival. The
shootout at the cemetery had been all over the news. The
police had no suspects because there was no surveillance
footage in the area. Gray was thankful because the last
thing she needed was for Cam to be taken away from the
kids again. It seemed like he was trying to change. Hell,
he'd made it to the church before she did. The old Cam

would've been on Colored People Time. Maybe he was taking this marriage counseling thing more serious than she thought. He was the one who suggested it, which was an even bigger shock to Gray. Cam was the type of man that hated to be questioned and analyzed. He detested sharing his feelings. He liked keeping his emotions bottled inside. It literally took her to leave him to get him to open up about his past. She had to threaten him to seek counseling for his anxiety. The fact that he was going to willingly put his transgressions on the table took major growth.

The security Cam hired watched her walk up the steps. Gray voluptuous hips swayed. She prayed she didn't seem pressed because the inside of her stomach was churning. Cam's sex appeal was on another level. He was dipped in the color red from head to toe. A black hat with Supreme written on it in red was so low on his head, she could barely see his honeysuckle eyes. She hated when he covered his face. It was such a beautiful face to see. His pointy nose, cheek full of freckles and beard were some of her favorite things on the planet. Cam was one gorgeous man. His height and body full of tattoos overwhelmed her. She wanted to tell him to take the hat off. It covered up the tattoo of her name on his temple but Gray no longer could dish out commands when it came to Cam. He was her estranged husband. She had no say so over what he did so she kept her mouth shut and silently took in the rest of his look. A diamond encrusted Cuban link chain hung from his tattooed neck. A black and red Supreme t-shirt clung to the hard muscles of his chest. On his long legs were a pair of black track pants with a bold red stripe going down each side. A pair of red Vans with the shoe laces untied finished off his laidback look. She'd noticed since he got out of jail that he'd changed the way he dressed. He wore a lot of athleisure wear now, which she found cute. What she didn't find cute was the huge band aide on his left arm.

"What happened to you?" She took his arm in her hand and examined it closely.

"I got shot."

"What?" She panicked. "When? Yesterday?"

"Yeah."

"Why you ain't say nothin'?"

"It wasn't that big of a deal. C'mon." He turned and walked inside.

Gray stood speechless. How could he not care that he'd been shot? He could've died. If he had they wouldn't be standing there. They wouldn't have the opportunity to try and salvage their dysfunctional marriage. He and Gray had their differences, but did he not know it would crush her if she lost him, if their kids lost him? It also made her think back on their argument the day before. He'd been hurt the entire time and never let on to his pain. Instead of putting himself first he, made sure she and the kids were okay. Their safety and well-being was his only concern. The realization warmed and softened Gray's heart. It made her think she might need to ease up on him just a little bit.

Cam held the door open for her and tried to ignore the hard-on inside his pants. They were in church for God's sake. He couldn't be walking around with his dick on swole cause the scent of his wife's perfume had him dizzy with lust. This was all Gray's fault. Who told her to show up looking like she'd just stepped off the runway? She had to know the affect she had on him. Gray was a baddie to the tenth degree. She didn't let her size 18 shape stop her from being that bitch. The extra weight looked great on her. Gray had curves for days, which made her even more irresistible. Cam was more attracted to her now than he was when he met her, and he was damn near obsessed with her then. Her blonde locs were tousled to the side in wind swept curls. Black Christian Dior shades covered her eyes which he detested. Gray knew how much he adored her eyes. A white, off-the-shoulder midriff top with straps that had Christian Dior written on them showed off her full rack and arms. A long white train attached to the shirt trailed behind her. Christian Dior logo underwear peeked out the top of her ripped jeans. Black single sole Tom Ford heels with a hanging padlock decorated her pretty feet.

As soon as they entered the church the sweet sound of singing filled their ears. The church choir was in rehearsal. Their voices were like angels. High notes ascended over the clouds. Graceful notes danced over the moon as they sang for God. Cam and Gray stood in the back of the church captivated by their melodic tone. She took in the side of his face.

"Yo' li'l girlfriend know you're here?"

"No." He kept his eyes on the choir.

A sudden urge to body slam him swept over Gray. Had he not told Devin about them attending couple's therapy 'cause he actually cared about her feelings? That had to be it. There couldn't be any other reason. That left her wondering what was even the point of them being there? He didn't want to fix their marriage. He just wanted to work on their communication and nothing else. Here she was thinking they had a fighting chance at salvaging their relationship. Boy was she a fool.

"Gray." She heard a female voice call out her name.

Wondering who could possibly know her there, Gray spun around and connected eyes with a woman she hadn't seen in years.

"Mother Emilia?" She rushed over to give her a hug.

Gunz might've been a spawn of Satan but his grandmother was nothing short of a saint. Wisdom flowed and kindness seeped from her pores. She was an old woman but not the kind you pity, but the kind who could still run circles around people half her age. She stood half Gray's height with long grey hair neatly styled into a low bun. Her Latin, Italian and African roots weren't hidden behind the discrete Mary Kay makeup she wore. Wrinkles and age spots graced her light skin. Emilia was a stunning elderly woman. Gray wished she looked as good as her when she reached her age. For so long, Mother Emilia, Gunz's mother Vivian and his uncles had been her family. They were part of the reason she stayed with him so long. She didn't want to give up the only family she knew. She hoped she would build the same bond with Cam's family, but unfortunately, that never happen.

"My God. I never thought I'd see you again." She took Gray into her arms. "I missed you dear." She held her close.

"I missed you too." Gray cherished her embrace.

"Let me look at you."

Gray stepped back so she could get a good view.

"I've said it a million times. My grandson is a fool."

Gray couldn't do anything but laugh.

"Are you back for good?" Emilia hoped and prayed to God she said yes.

"No, unfortunately not." Gray winced, hating to disappoint her.

"I don't blame you. There's nothing here. Just tell me my grandbabies are doing well."

"They are."

"Are you free tomorrow? Gavin is throwing me an 80th birthday party at the Botanical Gardens. I would love for you all to come."

"We would love to be there, but unfortunately, I won't be able to attend. My best friend, Kema, is getting married this week. I'm hosting her bridal shower tomorrow."

"That girl used to be loose. I guess a lot has changed." Emilia joked.

Cam placed his hand up to his mouth and cleared his throat.

"I'm sorry. Mother Emilia this is Cam . . . my husband." Gray introduced them.

"Nice to meet you." Cam shook her hand.

"The pleasure is all mine. Now I see why you left my grandson. He's handsome." She smiled at Gray blushingly.

Instead of acknowledging Cam's good looks, Gray simply rolled her eyes.

"I didn't know you went to this church." She changed the subject.

"I joined a few months after you left. It's a wonderful congregation."

"That's good to know. We're here to see Pastor Edris."

"You'll like him. He's a lovely young man. Bishop John, his father, will be turning the church over to him soon."

"Cameron Parthens." Pastor Edris secretary called his name.

"It was nice meeting you, Miss Emilia." Cam nodded his head. "Gray, say goodbye."

"I'm so happy I got the chance to see you again Mother." Gray kissed each of her cheeks.

She wanted to tell her she'd bring the girls to come see her but with her psychotic grandson on the loose that wasn't possible.

"Can you please not tell Gunz you saw us here?" She whispered in her ear.

"No worries dear. I know how my grandson can be. Your secret is safe with me." Emilia assured.

Gray took one last look at her and followed Cam inside Pastor Edris' office. The space was painted white. It had one window which faced the parking lot. On the white Ikea desk was a laptop, notebook, files and a stack of papers sitting under a glass paperweight. The window unit air conditioner hummed softly. The sound calmed Gray's nervous spirit. A floor-to-ceiling bookshelf, bursting with books filled the wall behind Pastor Edris' desk where he sat. Gray's eyes cascaded over his tall frame. Pastor Edris was a good-looking man. He was dressed in all black. Small chains, a black tee, fitted jeans and black Chelsea boots gave him a stylish and youthful appeal. If she were younger and was into men of the cloth, she'd shoot her shot.

"Welcome to New Northside." He rose from his chair and extended his hand for both of them to shake.

"Thank you for having us on such short notice." Gray anxiously smiled.

"What's good, Preach?" Cam gave him a pound like he was on the streets.

Gray wanted to slap him upside the head. She couldn't take his hood ass anywhere.

"Let's get started." Pastor Edris grabbed his notebook and sat in a chair opposite the couch they'd sat on.

Cam sat on one end of the couch and Gray sat on the other. The session hadn't even started and the tension in the room was already thick.

"So, I know a little bit about your situation from what you told me at the park but we're going to have to dig deeper. How did you end up here?" He crossed his leg.

Neither Gray nor Cam said a word. Neither of them wanted to be the one to start things off.

"You know the enemy hits marriage hard because he hates what it represents in the kingdom of God."

"Well, the enemy must hate us." Gray chuckled.

"Facts." Cam agreed, picking a piece of invisible lint off his pants.

"Cam and I have gone through a lot. We got married after only knowing each other two and a half months."

"Wow." Pastor Edris scribbled some notes down.

"We were in love. At least I was." She took a jab at Cam.

He felt the punch in his gut.

"He moved in with me and my girls and we began learning about each other as we went on. I know. It's ass— I mean, it's backward as hell—"

"Gray." Cam cut her off.

"I'm sorry. I'm nervous."

"No need to be." Pastor Edris tried to ease her fears. "I'm here to help."

"What I'm trying to say is I loved Cam very much. I gave everything I had to give to this marriage, but he never fully trusted me. I told him everything about my past. There wasn't anything he didn't know about me, but I had to find out about his struggle with PTSD, all of his businesses and street activities from his ex-girlfriend."

"Here she go acting like she's Mother Teresa." Cam groaned. "That's part of the problem, Preach. Gray think she don't do nothin' wrong. She lie about shit— I mean, stuff all the time. She keep me in the dark about a lot of stuff too. We both wrong but she don't wanna admit that. She wanna put all of our problems off on me."

"It sounds to me like neither of you trusted the other. I mean, how could you? You barely knew each other when you said, 'I do'. Gray tell me about your family."

"I don't have any." She spoke somberly.

Cam could hear the tears rising in her throat. He wanted to stop the conversation before it even started. Any time Gray spoke on her nonexistent family she became emotional. The last thing he wanted to see was her cry.

"I was raised by my mother, but she's gone now." She fiddled with her hands to distract herself from sobbing. "We didn't have much. We were quite poor which affected me a lot growing up. I hated being poor. I got made fun of a lot for it and being mixed. My mother barely spoke English so that didn't help either. My father wasn't around to raise me. I never knew him, but I hated him. I hated him for leaving my mother alone to fend for herself. That's why I go so hard in my career. I never want to be poor again. I never ever want to depend on a man. It was hard. We struggled a lot but somehow my mother made it work."

"You never told me half of that." Cam eyed her with disdain.

"I never had the chance to."

"And you, Cam?"

"My childhood was straight." He shrugged his shoulders. "I grew up in a two-parent home. I have three brothers and a sister. We were super close when I was little but after my mom died in a plane crash, we all drifted apart."

"Tell him everything." Gray demanded.

Cam groaned. Maybe coming to couple's therapy wasn't a good idea. He hated being pressured to do things he wasn't comfortable with.

"My ole dude started cheating on my mom when I was nine. He used to take me with him over his mistress' house so he could use me as an alibi for being away from the house. The day my mother died he was supposed to be wit' her, but instead, he stayed behind to be with his side chick. I knew this. I wanted to tell my mother, but I didn't. For years, I beat myself up about it but while I was in the pen, I came to grips that it wasn't my fault my mother died.

258

It wasn't my fault that my old man cheated either. I was just as much a victim as my mother was."

"His father also had a child with his mistress that no one knows about except Cam." Gray added. "I didn't learn any of this until months after we'd been married, and he only told me 'cause he was forced to."

"This explains so much. You two have had to love each other through your brokenness, which in itself is a crazy fete. You two couldn't even tell each other about your past pain but you had to love each other in it until you saw it for yourself." Pastor Edris pointed out.

Cam and Gray let his words sink in. How could they have a successful marriage when their childhood traumas ruled the way they acted and behaved?

"Neither of you had faith in your fathers. Gray, yours was absent and Cam yours used you to dishonor your mother. You both were taught not to trust at a young age. Now that I know how you started off distrusting each other, how did that distrust morph into the deterioration of your marriage?"

"He cheated on me with his ex." Gray said with an attitude.

"Let's be clear." Cam ice grilled her. "The only reason I fucked— I mean, screwed that girl was because you knew it was my mother's death day and instead of being there for me, you took your narrow-ass to New York Fashion Week." Cam went off. "Preach, this girl begged me to open up. I go outside my comfort zone and tell her that I need her, and she couldn't be bothered."

"For the millionth time, I had to work!" Gray snapped. "Pastor Edris, my dream growing up was to have my own magazine. My dream eventually came true but when I met Cam my magazine folded. I didn't know what to do with myself. My magazine was my identity. I didn't know who I was without it. For months, I wandered around trying to figure out what I going to do with my life. During that time, I waited on Cam hand and foot. I cooked every day, washed his clothes, tried to spend time with him and he was hardly ever at home. I didn't know why he didn't want to be around me. I thought he was cheating—"

"I told you I wasn't coming home at night 'cause I didn't wanna hurt you or the girls." Cam quipped.

"I know that now, but I didn't know that then. You have to remember, at the time, I could only go off the information that was given to me which was nothing so blame yourself for putting those thoughts in my head." She rolled her eyes. "*Anyway,* after months of being out of work, an opportunity of a lifetime was placed in my lap for me to be a model. It changed my life. I got my confidence back. I would think that my *husband* would be happy for me, but he wasn't. He didn't want me to work. He wanted me to sit at home and be Suzy Fuckin' Homemaker but that's not me. I'm a working girl."

"I didn't give a damn about you working but when your career takes precedence over your man it's a problem. Plain and simple. Just like I put her first, she needs to do the same. If she would've brought her ass to L.A., I would've never have had time to cheat. She would rather rip the runway than be a wife and she wonder why I sought attention from another female. If she would've did what she was supposed to do as a wife, we wouldn't even be here."

"Bitch, are you on crack? I know damn well you ain't blaming me for you sticking your nasty dick in that big forehead, yuck mouth bitch!" If they weren't in a church, she'd kill him.

"Sister Gray." Pastor Edris interjected. "I'm gonna ask that you refrain from cursing in the house of the Lord."

"Fuck that. This nigga got me fucked up." She huffed, folding her arms.

"Let me say this." He tried to calm her down. "Many of us manipulate situations and circumstance and bend them so in fact they can be what we desire. And so, we will in fact try to convince ourselves that our will is God's will when it is not. Many men get married, only to discover too late there was no depth beyond sex. So, they wake up one morning realizing they are married to the perfect stranger. The disconnect that happens in our community is that we raise our daughters to be brides, but we raise our sons to be boyfriends. Something has happened where we coddle our sons but discipline our daughters. As a consequence we've raised our daughters to have management, to have discipline and to have focus. And we raise our sons to be spoiled. The prospect of a healthy relationship and marriage in the black community isn't pushed or championed or called to. In other ethnicities, they begin planning at birth about marriage, about life relationships yet we're just excited about dating. Nowhere in the bible does God ever provide a girlfriend or a boyfriend. He only provides mates for a life journey. God shaped Gray to be your wife. The question is are you disciplined and mature enough to be her husband?"

Cam sat dumbfounded. Pastor Edris had hit him with some shit that he wasn't prepared for. The shit made him feel some type of way. Was he ready to be a husband to Gray? In the past no. He thought he was but after much reflection he realized he was nowhere near disciplined or mature enough to be her or anyone else's husband. Back then he wanted things his way. He was controlling, self-centered and had one hell of a temper. He was the furthest thing from perfect. He was young and he was selfish. He made every woman feel like she was his and no one else's. Time away made him see the error of his ways. He truly understood now how important family is. In the past he took it for granted.

"Cheating is unacceptable. You can't place your infidelity on Gray. If you love God and yourself, you wouldn't dishonor yourself or your union in that magnitude. A man is to love his wife as Christ loves the church. Meaning that God will still love us when we are in sin. He will never leave us. When you don't love your spouse unconditionally the way the bible teaches us to, you mess up the divine order. You can't expect to have a blessed marriage going outside the foundation of love."

"BOOYAH!" Gray rolled her neck and put her hand in Cam's face.

"Move it before I break it." He warned.

Gray knew she was pushing it, so she dropped her hand by her side.

"Look, Preach, you're right." Cam placed his elbows on his knees. "What I did was wrong. I knew it was messed up when I did it, but Gray had me 38 hot. Even Quan tried to knock some sense in me, but to be honest, at the time I really didn't give a fuck. Gray hurt me so I wanted to hurt her back."

"*Wow.*" She scoffed, devastated.

"I'm happy that you have a man like Quan in your life. A real friend wants to see you faithful. He is not your boy because he covers your infidelity. Many of our brothers will not find a successful relationship because they are not around men that desire successful relationships." Pastor Edris explained.

"A woman worth having will require a sacrifice. If she is convenient, she is not worth covenant. You gotta go out of your way to find a woman who's worth something. Proverbs 31 says who can find a virtuous woman. Not who can find a woman who's fine, or dresses well or can stroke your ego but who can find a woman with character and integrity and with a prayer life. In other words, in order for you to find her, you gotta look for her. THOTS are on every street corner. Women are in the house. Understand, brother Cam, a woman worth having will be an inconvenience. These ho's out here, excuse my language, will make it easy for you. Do you want a woman that is easy or a woman like Gray who is going to challenge you?"

Cam pondered his question. All his life he dated women who tiptoed around him, didn't question his authority, and needed him financially. Women like that were easy to control. They did whatever he told them to do. With them he could come and go as he pleased. They made him feel manly. He wasn't used to women like Gray that were self-sufficient, driven and focused. She didn't take any mess from anyone. She made it known she didn't need a man for anything. She made Cam feel hella uncomfortable. Gray was of a different breed. He was in awe of her resilience but scared of her resistance to let him take care of her. Other women would die to be financially taken care of by him, but she made it known she would be good with or without him. Cam hated it. He wanted her to need him. He was raised that the man was the provider. Gray didn't want his money, leadership or control so what was his role in their marriage?

"If I wasn't under contract, I wouldn't have had any problem being there for Cam that weekend." Gray clarified. "My thing was he couldn't have been that hurt because he was going to L.A. for All Star Weekend. I'm not trying to be disrespectful but what does watching some niggas bounce a basketball have to do with your mother's death day?"

Gray was right which infuriated him. Cam sucked his teeth. Only she could get him in his bag. She was the only woman that could call him out on his shit and rattle his cage. Maybe it was because he loved her the most or because she was the only person he felt most loved by.

"Exactly. Nothing." She pursed her lips. "Cam just wanted his way and when I didn't give it to him, he acted out like he always does."

"Because morals are so low, and opportunities are so high, most men today do not know how to pursue. Because there are too many options. But a woman of God who knows her worth and knows her value, will not negotiate when she knows the price of her call. A woman who knows who she is, is not gonna put up with foolishness and will hold you into accountability. And if your mate gets upset because you hold him accountable that is not the man God has for you. He is not supposed to become bitter; he's supposed to become better because he has found someone who won't play the game."

"PERIOD!" Gray snapped her finger in a circle.

Cam wished Pastor Edris would shut the fuck up. He was making too much sense and it was pissing him off. He was beyond ready to go. He didn't like that Pastor Edris was holding his feet to the fire and not Gray. He thought therapy was supposed to be unbiased.

"You know what makes it worse?" Gray continued. "After calling me a horrible mother and saying my magazine was wack, I still came to be with him. I risked my career by breaking my contract so I could be there for him and this nigga wasn't even in L.A. 24 hours before he cheated on me."

"Women are nurtures by nature so you give credit to a man for what he could be and then try to raise him into it. But if you gotta raise him that's yo' child and not yo' man. So, we have upside down relationships where you're supposed to be covered but you're covering him. You are the favor factor. Which means the person with favor doesn't chase the one that needs the favor. If you know who you are then you better carry yourself like you're the one who's holding all the cards. If he knows what's good for him, he will run after you. Because you multiple whatever he has in concentrated form. You are the favor factor so stop distributing your favor to someone who has not factored a covenant into the equation."

Gray gasped. She'd gone about loving Cam all wrong. She thought being a good wife meant coddling him in his time of need. She thought it meant running to his aide and setting aside her own personal needs to assist him in his. She thought it meant waiting in the wings for him to grow into the man she knew he could be.

"Don't act like I'm the only one that stepped out. She fucked her weak-ass baby daddy, Preach." Cam snitched. "I caught 'em kissing on the couch. Then she gon' come to me weeks later saying she pregnant, even though her tubes were tied."

Gray spun around in her seat and faced him.

"Tell him how you cussed me out like a dog after I told you I was pregnant. This man called me everything but a child of God. He knew he'd cheated on me and still had the audacity to cuss me out like I was a bitch off the street. He stood there in my face, on his high horse pretending like he'd done nothing wrong when in fact he had. I never cheated on you, Cam. Gunz kissed me while I was drunk. I was out of my mind that night. I thought he was you. I tried explaining that, but you were so hell bent on hurting me that you wouldn't listen."

"That's the stupidest shit I ever heard." He spat, ready to choke her out.

The memory of her French kissing Gunz made him upset all over again.

"You claimed you loved me but you ain't know the difference between me and that pussy-ass nigga? Get the fuck outta here."

"At least I loved you! The only reason you told me you loved me was because you cheated!"

"If you don't think I love you than you're dumber than I thought. What nigga gon' go through all this bullshit for a woman he don't love?"

"If you love her then why can't you hear her?" Pastor Edris asked. "Based off what I'm hearing, in that moment, all she wanted from you is understanding. Love does not stop when a person disappoints you. That's when love should kick in the most. You knew of your own infidelity, yet you were still willing to shut her out. That makes me question if you really did love her or is it that you like who you are with her?"

"I play a lot of games, Preach, but what you not gon' do is question my feelings for her. If you only knew half the shit I've gone through with this girl, you wouldn't even fix your mouth to ask me no shit like that." Cam checked him. "She took my fuckin' kids! While I was locked up, she gave birth to our kids and didn't even tell me about 'em. I just found out four days ago that I got triplets! You know how fucked up that is? I don't even know my kids' middle names, their birthday, how much they weigh, when they started to walk or what their first words were!" Cam barked, furiously.

He'd had it up to here with Gray and her whoa-is-me bullshit.

"I don't give a fuck how bad things ended between us! You don't do no shit like that! She knew how bad I wanted kids and how much family meant to me! I went out of my way to love her daughters, as if they were my own, and she gon' take my biological kids away from me 'cause she got her fuckin' feelings hurt? Fuck outta here wit' that! She knew exactly what she was doing! She wanted to hurt me! It ain't have shit to do wit' me being in jail or 'cause I cussed her ass out! I cuss everybody out! That shit ain't new!"

Cam turned and faced Gray. Unknowingly, tears began to flow. An inferno of shame and rage burned underneath his skin so deep he felt empty. Cam tried to contain his composure, but he couldn't any longer. Gray had pushed him too far. She sat paralyzed in fear like his actions shocked her. She'd gutted him with her deceit. Why couldn't she see that? She'd betrayed him in the worst way possible. Gray sliced at his heart and drew blood. She was ruthless. She'd do anything to win no matter how petty the victory was. Maybe she was unable to understand human emotion. Maybe she simply didn't care when it came to him. Perhaps, she only wanted hollow victories that made her feel good in the moment. Whichever one it was it didn't matter. Her treachery severed what was left of them. They were through. It was abundantly clear now. Cam wasn't the kind of man that cried but thick salty tears slid down his freckled cheeks. His tears reminded her that he wasn't a robot that ran off logic alone. Cam had feelings like everyone else did. This was serious. She'd triggered something in him that she didn't know existed. She'd never seen him so deflated. His body was rigid. He made no attempt to conceal or even wipe his tears away. If she could, Gray would scoop him up into her arms and hold him, but she'd caused his pain. It would take more than an embrace to erase it.

"You hurt me! You happy now!" He growled, getting up in her face. "You won! This what you wanted? You wanted to see me hurt? Job well done, Gray! You got your fuckin' wish!" Cam had completely forgotten they were in church and spazzed out.

He hadn't expected to get so emotional, but Gray needed to know that she'd broken his heart. The pain she'd caused him was irreversible. He was a man. Men like him didn't get in their feelings and cry, let alone in front of another man. This was the third time she'd caused tears to flood his eyes. How could a mere woman make a man so strong weak? It seemed like she loved when he fell apart. Only she could make him behave in such a way. But why her? Why didn't LaLa or Devin have an effect on him like this? Why did *she* have so much power over him? Cam never understood how a woman could break a man down to nothing. He got it now. Only a person you truly love could cut you to your core. That level of suffering could only come from someone who held your heart in the palm of their hand. Gray was the catalyst to the greatest pain he'd ever felt. His lover. His wife. The person he thought had his back. If it were anyone else, he could bounce right back but Gray . . . she'd pulled the wool over his eyes. She was a relationship vampire and he was tired of being drained.

Gray was afraid to move, let alone speak. Therapy was supposed to help them, but it seemed to only make matters worse. Pure disgust was written on Cam's face as he looked at her. What had she done?

"I thought LaLa lying about Kamryn being mine was fucked up but you keeping the triplets away from me took the cake."

Having him compare here to LaLa was like having a stake shoved in her heart. Gray wanted to fight back. She wanted to argue her stance but there was nothing else to say but I'm sorry. Cam looked at her like she was a stranger. She was no longer the sweet, delicate soul he'd asked to marry four years before. She was his foe. They were never supposed to end up here. Their love was supposed to be the kind that transcended time and space but somehow love turned into pain, pain morphed into hate and that hatred broke them apart. This was crazy. She didn't want this to be how their story ended. Maybe with the help of Pastor Edris they could find a muster seed of the love they once shared. Prayerfully, that seed could grow into a friendship that would heal their souls. Despite everything that had been said and done, Gray still saw the good in Cam. For the most part he'd been an ideal husband. She wasn't able to acknowledge it with her words yet, but she could see the pain she'd caused him. It was written all over his face, but she wondered if he knew how much he'd hurt her too. Seeing that she wasn't going to fess up to her wrongdoings, Cam sat back depleted of all emotion. Pastor Edris sat up. He needed to take back control of the room.

"What you two need to learn is that the divine order is God and then the man which is the head of the household but without the neck the head can not turn. The woman is the neck. When your wife is not taken care of, there becomes a crook in the neck, which throws the whole household off balance. Gray, for Cam seeing you in that intimate moment with your ex was like a gunshot to the head. What happens after a person has been shot in the head? The whole body shuts down. He's affected, you're affected, the kids are affected, everything you touch is affected. It's like a cancer that spreads throughout the whole household. You, as his wife, need to aim to be his perfect peace. You need to bring him good and not harm for the rest of your life and vice versa. You said yourself that not having a father affected and hurt you greatly. Why then would you willing inflict that type of pain on your children?"

Gray's heart sank down to her white pedicured toes. If there was a cliff for her to jump off of, she would've. For the first time, she saw how much of a monster she really was.

"When someone hurts you it's not your duty to hurt them ten times worse because your feelings have been bruised. Vengeance is mine says the lord. God will make your enemy your footstool. Is Cam your enemy? Are you lovers or opponents?"

"Everything just happened so fast. I moved away, he got sentenced, I filed for divorce, then I was on bedrest for five months, then the babies were born, one of them was stillborn, the others were in NICU—"

"You steady making excuses." Cam stared at her in disbelief.

"I'm no—"

"Man, fuck this. I'm up. Deal with Victor on your own!" He charged out of the room.

"Brother Cam! Wait!" Pastor Edris tried to stop him, but was unsuccessful.

Things were really messed up now. Gray and Cam were in an even bigger mess. How were they going to fix this? They needed to get on the same page but there was so much animosity and hate between them that it was hard to function. Gray's chest heaved up and down as she started to cry. Tears ran down her face at lightening speed. Cam was leaving her alone to fend for herself. What the hell was she supposed to do now? She couldn't defend herself against Victor alone.

"This was not how I was envisioned things going when you all called." Pastor Edris passed Gray a tissue.

She sadly wiped her face and blew her nose.

"You did all you could do." She threw the Kleenex away and grabbed her purse. "Sorry we wasted your time." She prepared to leave.

"Before you go, let me leave you with this. Girlfriends have sight. Wives have vision. You don't marry for better or for better. What you manifest at your lowest is who you are at your highest. If you can't stand with this man in the bad, then why would he want to celebrate you in the good? Get that spirit of girlfriend up off you. Wives stick and stay and pray that man through until he realizes the God in him is so much greater than what the devil has whispered to him. Emotions are inconsistent, Gray. Don't trust them. Marriage is not gonna feel good all the time. You have to have it together for your husband when he doesn't have it together for himself. As his wife you're called to help, to heal and to provide peace in ways he can't get on his own. That's what your rib represents. R.I.B. Rest in the brokenness. Give that man his rib. Can you give him rest in his brokenness? Own your place as the rib. Play your position. Don't let the devil hijack your emotions and your purpose because you can't see past your anger, resentment and your failed relationship."

"I understand that, but love is supposed to make you feel good. It's been a long time since loving Cam felt good." Gray sighed, wearily.

"The law of love is not the law of emotion. It's not the law of feeling 'cause love is not a feeling. You talkin about it don't feel good. Jesus died on the cross. That was his greatest expression of love. You think that felt good?"

#14

"When people ask you what happened here, tell them the north remembers. Tell them winter came for House Frey. "- Arya Stark, "A Game of Thrones"

"Ya'll look so pretty." Selicia gushed, standing next to the photographer.

Gray used all of her connections to ensure that Kema had the best of everything for her bridal shower. She'd flown celebrity photographer David LaChapelle in to take pics. The legendary Mindy Weiss was in charge of all the décor. Dylan Monroe baked all of the desserts and cake for free as a favor for Gray since they were practically family. Heidi did all the girls' makeup. Delicious and Mina styled everyone's hair. The theme of the bridal shower was a pink wonderland. The party was being held at the Ritz Carlton hotel in their eight-room hotel suite. Guests could lounge inside the enormous suite or enjoy the festivities outdoors on the rooftop. Everything was immaculately designed. A white and blush pink flower wall served as a backdrop for photos. A table full of desserts that consisted of cupcakes, doughnut balls, cake pops, mini cakes, Miss to Mrs., ring, champagne bottle and champagne glass shaped cookies were surrounded by a gorgeous arrangement of peonies, roses and tulips. When guests arrived, they were greeted with a glass of Armand de Brignac Rosé with pink cotton candy stuffed inside the flute. Fifty bottles of the Armand de Brignac Rosé were being chilled in silver tin buckets filled with flower infused ice cubes. Square shaped tables with white tablecloths and blush colored suede chairs filled the living area. Crème and brown long stem candles, small white vases filled with flowers and feathers, gold trimmed plates and stemware, along with pink wine glasses decorated the table. Greenery and feather balls hung from the ceiling, giving the space an ethereal feel.

Gray was over the moon on how everything turned out. Her entire vision had come to life. The attire for the party was formal wear. She and all the girls wore pink gowns. After the disastrous therapy session, Gray needed to physically make a change so she decided to dye her hair black that morning. She had Delicious style her hair in a chic, choppy, shag with wispy bangs and sideburns. Her makeup consisted of a strong brow, winged liner, lashes and a bold red lip. Diamond chandelier earrings were the only jewelry she wore. A pink, ruffle, Valentino dress that stopped mid-thigh and silver metallic, 3-band, Giuseppe Zanotti, four and a half inch sandals made her legs look a mile long. Even though it wasn't her party, Gray felt like the bell of the ball. She looked gorg but Kema looked beautiful. She wore a bright pink, high-low, tulle gown that showed off her legs too. Heidi wore a dusty pink mini dress with a ruffle train. Tee-Tee rocked a pink, sheer, ruched gown with floral embellishments. The four friends were serving a new age version of the Supremes as they posed for pics.

Kema's mom, grandmothers, aunts and cousins were there beaming with pride alongside her friends Mina, Delicious, Mo, Chyna, Dylan, Billie and Selicia. They'd already dined on chicken and waffles and were about to open gifts when the doorbell rang. Gray politely excused herself to answer the door. She wondered who it could be. All of the guests were already there. Pulling open the door, she found Quan and Stacy.

"Where my wife?" Quan barged in.

"She ain't your wife yet." Gray jokingly reminded him.

Quan paused.

"Me and you ain't cool."

Gray's eyes bucked.

"Until you make things right wit' my boy, you don't get to joke around and play wit' me."

Gray was stunned. She was absolutely thunderstruck. Quan had never been so blatantly rude towards her. At the barbeque he seemed a little off, but she didn't think anything of it. Never in a million years did she think he'd treat her like she had the plague. Gray couldn't blame him tho. He had every right to be upset with her. She'd kept his best friend's kids away from him. If she were in his shoes, she'd hate her too. Somehow, some way she had to make this right. The question was how?

"Don't trip. I still fuck wit' you, Gray." Stacy gave her a friendly kiss on the cheek and a hug.

Gray gave him an awkward smile as she went to close the door, but before it was all the way shut, the door was pushed back open. Gray was damn near knocked off her feet. Thankfully, the wall broke her fall.

"Excuse you." She barked.

"You're excused." Cam gave her a quick once over glance and walked on by.

She looked good as fuck, but he wasn't going to tell her that. As far as he was concerned Gray didn't exist. Closing her eyes, she said a quick prayer to God that she didn't kick him in the back of his head. Just when she wanted to be nice, he gave her a reason to hate him all over again. The Wiggles' concert and therapy session had ended on a bad note. She didn't want to fight with him five days in a row. It seemed like lately all she did was argue. She and Cam had argued enough to last a lifetime. She needed the bridal shower to run smoothly. It was bad enough she barely got two hours of sleep. She'd been up all night tossing and turning over their session with Pastor Edris. Everything that was said and done in that room plagued her mind. She knew she'd hurt Cam when she kept him in the dark about the triplets, but the sadness stamped on his face when he cried made her fully aware of all the damage she'd caused. She was no longer the victim. She'd become the villain.

"Baby!" Kema raced into Quan's awaiting arms.

Just like in the movies, he lifted her up and held her close. All the ladies swooned. Love was written all over them.

"What are you doing here?" She smiled brightly while kissing him all over his face.

"I wanted to see you."

"*Aww!*" Every woman in the room gushed.

"I'm just here for the food." Stacy announced, going over to the dessert table.

"And why are you here?" Tee-Tee asked Cam. "You miss my friend?"

"Fuck nah." He took a seat on the couch.

"I take it therapy didn't go so well." Kema looked back-and-forth between Cam and Gray.

"It was a fuckin' disaster." Cam griped.

276

"Aww sorry to hear that."

"I know you don't want me joking and playing around wit' you, but since you're here, do you wanna play a game with Kema?" Gray asked Quan.

"What you mean he don't want you joking and playing with him? What's going on?" Kema furrowed her brows.

"Nothing babe. It's good. What's up, Gray?" Quan played it off.

"We were about to play games, but now that you're here, why don't you play a game with Kema to see how well you two know each other."

"Ooh yeah! That'll be fun." Kema clapped her hands excited.

"Great. Everyone gather around. Kema and Quan you two sit right here." Gray led them to the seats in the center of the room.

Kema and Quan sat side-by-side with a dry erase board and marker in their lap. Gray stood before them. A sheet filled with questions was in her hand as well as a glass of champagne. She needed something to ease her nerves. Cam was making her extremely nervous. Just him being in the room had her on edge. The man looked good enough to eat. His hair was freshly lined and cut. The box haircut he donned was made up of soft curls. He rocked an all denim outfit. His look consisted of a pink denim jacket, white t-shirt, light wash ripped jeans and Maroon 6 J's. Several platinum chains hung from his neck. He wasn't paying her any mind tho. His Apple AirPods were in his ears and his eyes were on his phone. Gray was the last thing on his mind which irritated her to no end. She wanted him to lust after her like she salivated over him.

"Okay. You ready?" She asked the couple-to-be.

"If you stay ready, you ain't gotta get ready." Kema snapped her finger like a real live diva.

"First question. What is your mate's favorite color?"

"That's easy." Quan said confidently.

He and Kema wrote down their answers. After a minute Gray told them it was time to reveal. Kema and Quan turned their boards around. Hers read the color orange and his Nipsey Blue.

"Rest in Peace to the West Coast King." Kema paid her respect by pouring some of her champagne on the carpet.

"Kema!" Her mother gasped aghast.

"Ma, chill. I'm paying homage." Kema guzzled down the rest of her drink.

"Was the answer right?"

"No." Quan shook his head. "Babe, my favorite color is red."

"Oh yeah." She smacked her hand against her forehead. "I forgot. We got the next one." She assured, pecking his lips.

"Next question. What is your partners favorite movie?"

Kema answered The Chronicles of Narnia and Quan answered BAPS.

"Babe!" She smacked his arm. "My favorite movie is not no damn BAPS. It's White Chicks."

"Like that's any better." Tee-Tee teased.

By the end of the game Kema and Quan got four out of the ten questions correct.

"That was fun." The happy couple lovingly kissed each other to show there were no hard feelings.

"Gray." Mo called out her name. "Why don't you and Cam play?"

"Oh, no thanks." She quickly dismissed the idea.

"Aww c'mon. Get the stick out of your ass. Both of you. Cam go play." Mo grabbed his arm and pulled him off the couch.

"Nah, Mo, chill." He tried to pull away.

"It's just a game. It's not gon' kill you."

"It might."

"Stop being mean." She made him sit down in the chair.

"A'ight. A'ight. Just get it over with." He huffed not in the mood.

"Now, Gray, sit yo' fine ass down." Kema pushed her into a seat.

Gray crossed her legs. It was taking everything in her to keep it together. Being near Cam and feeling the heat radiate off of him was making her sick. He hated her. She could feel it. She truly hated when he was mad at her. Being on the outs with Cam was like death. When they were millions of miles away from each other it didn't hit her so hard.

"Okay." Selicia took over as hostess. "First question. What is your mate's favorite color?"

"Pink." Cam answered dryly.

"Red." Gray said equally as dry.

"Is that correct?" Selicia looked at both of them.

"Yeah." They both said in unison.

"Well, perk up why don't you?" Selicia curled her upper lip. "Next question. What is your mate's favorite movie?"

"The Godfather." Gray said.

"She doesn't have one particular favorite, but The Prince and The Showgirl is one of them."

"And that is. . ." Selicia waited for their responses.

"Correct." Cam replied.

"Look at ya'll knowing each other." Tee-Tee winked his eye.

"Favorite sexual position."

"Umm, my mama is here." Kema reminded Selicia.

"How you think you got here?" She hit back.

"Exactly." Her mom agreed.

"Doggystyle." Cam and Gray said at once.

"Ughn. Ya'll nasty." Heidi smirked.

Gray's cheeks burned red. Even Cam couldn't help but grin.

"Alright. Next question. If you died today what would be your mates last meal?"

Gray cocked her head to the side uncomfortable by the question. No one except Cam knew that the query hit way too close to home. As always, he wanted to save her from anything that upset her so Cam reached over and tenderly massaged her knee.

"You good." He said as more of a statement than a question.

Gray nodded her head. The simple touch of his hand gave her the strength she needed to continue on with the game without causing a scene.

"Okay, answers please." Selicia prompted.

"Hers would be that nasty ass Kimchi Fried Rice."

"And his would be macaroni and cheese, greens and fried chicken."

"Let me guess. You got that right too?" Kema rolled her eyes.

"We sure did." Gray stuck out her tongue.

She was genuinely surprised that she and Cam knew each other so well. By the end of the game Gray and Cam had a score of eight questions right.

"I'ma get they asses this time. This question gon' be hard." Selicia went off the top of her head. "Cam . . . how many freckles does Gray have?"

"How the hell they gon' answer that?" Heidi twisted up her face.

"That's the point. Ain't no way in hell he knows the answer to that."

"Thirty." Cam arrogantly said with ease.

"Uh ah. Let me see." Kema got up and counted each freckle on Gray's nose and cheeks. "Well, I'll be damn. She does have thirty freckles."

"You sure ya'll want a divorce?" Stacy asked.

"Yep." Cam got up and returned to the couch.

Devastated by his response, it took Gray a while to find her legs. Cam truly wanted nothing to do with her and it hurt. It hurt bad.

"Well, that was mean of you to say." Mo sat next to her brother.

"It's the truth." Cam lied.

On the real, he was still reeling from the tragic counseling session. Gray had upset him by not acknowledging how she'd hurt him with her spiteful ways. In return he planned to ice her out.

"Ya'll just wasting valuable time." Mo shook her head disappointed. "But anyway, you going to see dad?"

"Fuck no. That nigga didn't reach out to me once while I was in jail."

"You shouldn't be like that. He's getting old, Cam. Life's too short for all of this animosity."

"Look, Mo. I understand that you're tryin' to help but you don't even know where my hatred for that nigga begins."

"Tell me." She urged.

She was tired of the rift between her brother and dad. Not giving a fuck about protecting his father anymore, Cam parted his lips to respond when his phone vibrated. Cam answered the call and sighed. Suddenly, he had a pounding headache. The person on the other end was the last person he wanted to talk to.

"Yes, Jefe?"

Gray spun around startled. She and Cam connected eyes. The stress on his face matched the alarmed one on hers. If Victor was calling that meant things couldn't be good.

"Where are we?" Victor cut right to the chase.

"I got a few leads but nothing solid yet."

"This is not a game, Cameron. Your wife's life is on the line."

"Don't you think I know that?" Cam forgot his place and snapped.

Holding the phone, Victor let out a sarcastic chuckle.

"Honestly, I don't give a fuck what you know. What I know is your wife is gonna be 6F in the next four days if you don't get your fuckin' head in the game. I mean . . . my kids' mother gon' still be here. That shit don't make me no difference if your bitch ends up dead. That's on you and your kids."

"I—"

Click

Gray didn't have to be on the line to know that Cam had been hung up on. Victor was upset which meant the time on her life had become even shorter. What was she to do now? She and Cam were on worse terms than they were before. She didn't even know if he still was willing to protect and help her out of this mess. Things were out of control and Gray was at her wits end.

283

"I need a drink." She picked up the first champagne flute she saw and chugged it down. "Another please." She signaled a waiter.

———

Across town Mother Emilia's 80th birthday party was in full swing. Gunz decked out the entire venue. There were ten round tables with black tablecloths, gold plates and napkins. The centerpieces consisted of floral arrangements and pictures of Emilia throughout the years. A banner that read 80 Years Young decorated the wall surrounded by black and gold balloons. Her only living son, Ronnie, his children, Gunz's mother, Vivian, and all of Emilia's friends were there to celebrate. Music and laughter filled the air as guests dined on the second course of their meal which was a split pea soup with candied bacon.

"Where is my grandson?" Mother Emilia looked around.

Gunz had missed half the party. Everyone was there except him.

"There he is." Vivian smiled. "He's walking through the door now."

All eyes were on Gunz as he strolled into the room. His powerful presence captured everyone's attention. Gunz looked like a man of means and stature. He exuded power and strength. The Tom Ford Shelton base tuxedo he donned was reminiscent of a classic 1940's tux. It fit him like a glove. The patent leather Gucci dress shoes set the entire Old Hollywood look off. Gunz was giving off daddy vibes. He wished he felt as good as he looked. Gunz wasn't even sure he was going to come. The streets were still hot after the shooting at the cemetery. He'd gotten word that Cam was coming for his head and that he had a $250,000 reward for anybody who could tell him who had him locked up. On top of that, Gavin Jr. became sick hours before the party. He'd come down with a fever that wouldn't break so Tia decided she would stay at home with him. Gunz didn't want to leave his son. Gavin Jr. was his pride and joy. He wanted to show his mini me off to the world. Mother Emilia loved when she got to spend time with her great grandson. Since he couldn't be there, Gunz didn't even want to come but Tia talked him into attending anyway. She didn't want him to miss out on celebrating with his family. Mother Emilia turning 80 was a momentous occasion. Gunz would regret it later if he didn't attend. Plus, she needed some time away from him. Gunz was obsessed with everything but her. If he wasn't grinning up in Gavin Jr.'s face, he was strategizing about how he was going to take Cam and Gray down. She was over it. Soon, she would figure out a way to get him out of her and her baby's life for good.

"Son." Gunz's mother greeted him with a hug.

"What's up, ma?" He gave her a loving embrace.

Since he'd been in hiding, Gunz didn't get to spend much time with his family anymore. This was one of the rare occasions he got to see them.

"You look good, son." She smiled brightly.

Gunz was the apple of his mother's eyes. She was extremely proud of everything he'd accomplished. He'd gone from a street king to a well-respected businessman. She partly had Gray to thank for that.

"Happy birthday, Granny." Gunz kissed Mother Emilia tenderly on the forehead.

He was so happy that she got to live to see another year. Gunz could only pray he'd get to live so long. Emilia was the best grandmother in the world. He loved her just as much if not more than his mother. His granny loved him and would get on his head when need be but put enough distance between them that she didn't seethe with anger every time he did something to disgrace their family name. Because of her chill nature and unwavering support, Gunz did everything possible to make her happy. Whenever she smiled, she made him feel higher than any morphine a doctor could prescribe. Being eighty didn't stop her beauty. She grew prettier with age. Her wrinkles were the map to her soul. The laugh lines around her lips were a gift from how much she smiled. Gunz would give her eighty more parties if it made her face light up the way it was that day.

"Thank you, baby. I was wondering where you were." She patted his back.

"The baby got sick."

"Oh no. I was looking forward to seeing him." Mother Emilia frowned, disappointed.

"I wanted you to see him too. The li'l nigga look just like me." Gunz stated proudly. "You like your party?"

"I love it."

"Good. How you doing, Uncle Ronnie?" Gunz gave him a pound.

"I can't call it. Gimme fifty dollars."

"Why every time I see you, you got yo' hand out?" Gunz reached inside his pocket and handed him a hundred-dollar bill.

"Good lookin' out nephew. I'm still waiting on you to hit the studio wit' me. We gotta do this tribute record for

286

Clyde and ya' daddy. Niggas been waiting on a remix to Smokin' Wit the Windows Up."

"They gon' keep waiting." Gunz laughed, taking a seat.

It felt good to be around his family again. He didn't realize until that moment how much he missed them. As he draped his napkin across his lap, a bowl of soup was placed before him. Gunz bowed his head and said a silent prayer before picking up a spoon to eat. Just as he was about to take a sip of the soup his grandmother said, "I saw Gray yesterday."

Gunz dropped his spoon. Fuck eating. His grandmother had his full attention now.

"Is that right?"

"She asked me not to tell you, but I know how much you miss her." Mother Emilia covered her mouth and coughed.

"I miss Gray." Vivian poked out her bottom lip.

She hated the way things ended between Gray and her son. When she learned that Gunz had put his hands on her, she cussed him out for filth and didn't speak to him for weeks.

"Have you seen the girls? I miss my grandbabies."

"Briefly." He clenched his jaw.

Gunz was still messed up that Aoki didn't want anything to do with him. She used to be his li'l rider and now she hated him. He knew he'd been out of the girls' lives. He hadn't been the best father as of late, but he figured he had time to fix the damage he'd caused. Once he got Cam out of the picture, Gray would be isolated, and he'd be able to get her to come back to him.

"Tia is a nice girl but she's a little rough around the edges. You two just don't mesh." Vivian took a gulp of water.

The soup tasted like bitter almonds. Numerous other guests started to cough and consume water as well.

"You can do better. You should try working things out with Gray."

"She's married Viv. That girl ain't taking him back." Emilia rubbed her chest.

A pain had settled there.

"I met her husband. He's a nice-looking man. They make a stunning couple."

"Thanks for having my back, Granny." Gunz said taken aback.

"You know I love you, but you didn't do right by that girl." She coughed again.

This time the cough wouldn't stop. They came hard and fast, causing her to struggle for air.

"Granny, you a'ight?" Gunz quickly came to her aide.

Mother Emilia tried to speak but couldn't. She felt like she was being choked. There was a tightness in her esophagus that felt like there was a noose around her throat. Gunz didn't know what to do. He didn't know if she was chocking or just coughing. At the end of each cough, there was a whistling sound like her airways were closing up. Gunz heart began to race.

"Somebody call 911!" He looked around frantically for help, only to see all the guests in distress too.

Everyone was holding their throats and hacking up blood. Gunz looked over to his mother and uncle. His mother was bent over as if she'd been punched in the stomach. Droplets of blood dripped from her nose and onto her lap. Gunz heart sank to his toes. Despair was like cement in his veins. The room had started to spin. Every time he tried to breathe, his body felt like it was going to stop functioning. Vivian clawed at her throat as she tried to swallow the blood that crept up her esophagus, but it was too late. Gushes of thick red plasma started to spew from her mouth. Her stomach contracted violently, forcing everything inside out. Gunz watched on in horror as his mother's angelic face turned as white as snow. Vivian lurched to her knees clutching her abdomen. At any second, she was going to die. Uncle Ronnie sat beside her coughing profusely. Each cough he released sounded loose and wet, like thick phlegmy mucus was descending up his throat. With each vicious expulsion of air, his ribs heaved up and down. The effort to breathe brought on more breathlessness. Blood surged from every orifice of his face as his organs struggled to keep him alive.

"Somebody help me!" Gunz roared.

He could feel everyone he loved slowly slipping away. He wanted to help his mother and uncle but there wasn't enough of him to go around. Bodies were dropping left and right. All he heard was loud thuds and wails of despair. Blood flowed like a lazy river throughout the room. Horrified, Gunz gawked at all the gore in fear. Blood covered his own calloused hands as he held his grandmother in his arms. Small ragged gasp escaped her throat as her face turned blue. Warm crimson liquid gushed from her eyes, nose and ears. Mother Emilia's body shook like she was having a seizure. Every vein in her face was pronounced. Her weary hands fell to her side as the last of her energy fled. Gunz's entire suit was covered in his grandmother's bodily fluid. He couldn't believe his eyes. Real blood was nothing like the shit he saw in the movies, just as death wasn't the same. No amount of time or preparation could prepare him to see the life recede from someone he loved. Hopelessness filled his grandmother's ageless eyes as she gazed upon her grandson's weeping face. No words had to be said. This was their final goodbye. Gunz locked eyes with his favorite girl and cradled her in his big strong arms. Mother Emilia's silver hair covered her eye. Gunz gently brushed it back, feeling the coldness of her skin. Then, just that quickly she was gone. Completely distraught, he kissed her forehead then closed the lids of her eyes. Unable to move he sat amongst the carnage with her tucked safely in his hold. When the police rushed in that's how they found them, his grandmother deceased and him sitting in a pool of her blood while holding her lifeless body.

Gunz cried as if his was brain had been split in half with an axe. Emotional pain flowed from every crevice of his large frame. From his mouth came a cry so raw that even the paramedics wept. He expected to bury his parents one day but never his entire family. All of his immediate family was gone. In one full swoop he was alone. It was a bloody massacre. Everyone in the room was dead, except him and the wait staff. If he had eaten the soup, he'd be heading to the morgue too. He knew exactly who'd done this. Cam had hit back and hard. He'd taken everything he loved away from him. Gunz had underestimated him. His miscalculation cost him his family. His grandmother, mother, only living uncle and cousins were dead. What was he going to do? Death had ripped away a part of him he'd never get back again. His mother's lifeless body lay on the floor a few feet away. Her black hair was stained with dried blood. Her russet eyes bore into him. He wished she would look away, but she couldn't. She'd never bat her long lashes, smile or speak again. The sight of her glaring at him rocked him to his core. He'd never get the image out of his mind. Seeing her corpse was too much for him to handle. Her body lay in the fetal position on the cold linoleum floor. And the stench that came from her was the most disturbing scent he'd ever smelled. It was obvious her bowels had released.

Gunz wanted to throw up. No son should see his mother that way. His life was over. Cam had stripped him of everything he held dear. He had no one. The only people he had left were his son and two daughters he'd practically disowned. The realization almost stopped his heart. Everything and everyone around him disappeared. All he felt was pain. His emotions turned jagged and his insides tight. This kind of pain would change him beyond recognition. This kind of pain would break what was left of him.

#15

"Oh my God, I was fine until I heard you speak. My oh my, my heart stops and my legs get weak. Used to be you were my only remedy. Tell me why you could never get it right for me. Boys like you can see when they got something really real. Girls like me will stay just cause we feel the way we feel."- Raiche, "047"

Cam was only a few feet away. Gray could smell his hypnotic cologne from the living area in which she stood. Etta Bond's *He's Mine* album played in the background, causing her hips to sway. She was in her zone. The seven glasses of Rosé she'd devoured had her floating on a cloud. All the guests were gone. Quan and Kema had snuck off to her bedroom and so had Tee-Tee and Bernard. Selicia was tired from her flight and said she was retiring for the night which prompted Stacy to follow. Heidi left to go be with her man. Melody was at home with the kids. Gray had the night to herself. She and Cam were the only ones left. Since the game, and the call from Victor, she'd been doing her best to avoid him. It was hard because everywhere she went, he was there. She couldn't escape him. Lowkey she didn't want to. The champagne made her crave him more. Cam still wasn't paying her any mind. From the moment he arrived, he acted like she didn't exist. He either chopped it up with his homeboys or was surrounded by a bevy of women. Gray was super annoyed. The thirsty bitches acted like he wasn't married. Sure, he didn't wear a ring but so. He was hers. At least on paper he was. It was only a matter of time before she became Gray

Rose again. The divorce she wanted seemed to loom closer and closer. Cam wouldn't even look at her. His denial of her existence made what was supposed to be a fun joyous day a hellhole. Gray didn't know what to do with herself. Being ignored by Cam was worse than awaiting a whooping as a child so she drank. Each glass made her feel less tense. The atmosphere became lighter. The jokes she cracked seemed funnier than what they really were. Inebriated, she could flirt and be as witty and cool as the best of them. She was the life of the party. Everyone loved her. It was a general consensus she was the best hostess ever.

With a Beyoncé level of confidence, she tugged the hem of her dress down and pushed out her boobs. She was going to get Cam's attention one way or another. No matter how mad he was, he couldn't ignore her forever. They were married. She was his wife. He had to forgive her. She never meant to make him cry. It would take a lifetime to forgive herself for what she'd done. Two wrongs didn't make a right. She should've never kept the kids away from him. Until she made amends with Cam, she'd be living in a hell of her own doing.

After finger combing her hair and applying another coat of red lipstick to her pouty lips, she grabbed another glass of Rosé and sauntered out onto the rooftop. Gray stopped once she got to the black railing. As night fell, the blue mist of day raised to reveal a sky full of stars. Sometimes, she wondered if humans were nocturnal would they appreciate the galaxy more. For Gray, nightfall was when she felt connected to the universe. Nightfall was the only time you got a glimpse into the universe beyond. Taking a sip of champagne, she took in what the night sky had to offer. The stars reminded her of salt sprinkled over black marble glass. It was such a gorgeous sight to behold. Cam used to say the same thing about her freckles. That's why he'd nicknamed her Star. Since he'd been home, he hadn't called her it once. She missed the name he'd given her. It made her feel special.

Spinning around on her heels, she turned to face him. He sat on a camel colored leather sectional with his legs spread wide. His head rested low. Not once had he looked her way. His attention stayed on his phone the entire time. The tea candles on the table before him gave light to his face. It was funny how such a thuggish man looked picture perfect amongst all the greenery planted around him. God never made a man more stunningly beautiful. Gray's throat became as dry as the summer sun. She needed to quench her thirst, but the drink was as warm as the heat on her skin. Since the champagne wouldn't give her the sustenance she needed, she decided to use Cam instead. He'd give her the nourishment she needed. On wobblily legs, she drunkenly flounced over to him. If she was sober, she would've never approached him but the endorphins in her system pushed her on.

Gray stood in-between his long legs and gazed at the top of his head. Even the coils of his hair was perfect. Cam knew she was standing there but refused to acknowledge her presence. He'd just gotten word that the massacre at Gunz grandmother's party had gone off as planned. The girls thought that he and the guys showed up just to crash the party but really, they were using the bridal shower as an alibi. Meeting Mother Emilia the day before at the church was a blessing in disguise. He'd been trying to find Gunz location and she'd served it up on a silver platter. Once he knew where her party was going to be, he paid one of the cooks to poison the soup with Cyanide. Cyanide was a rapidly acting, potentially deadly chemical that can exist in various forms. Cam was done playing with Gunz. He'd put his hand on his daughter and attempted to kill him once again. He needed the nigga dead and poisoning him and his family was the best way to do it. The only problem was Gunz was still alive. It was just his luck that everyone had eaten the soup except him. Pissed wasn't even the word to describe the way he felt. Gunz seemed to have nine lives. Why couldn't he kill him? Cam wanted to punch somebody. They'd both attempted to take each other out and failed. This war had to come to an end. Both of them couldn't survive. Plus, he had bigger things to worry about like finding out who set him up. He'd been asking around but couldn't find any information. Stress was written all over Cam's face. Gray could see it, but she wanted him to put his focus on her. Thankfully, she had Etta Bond to distract her from his rude behavior. Her sultry song *More Than A Lover* featuring SiR had begun to play. Gray closed her eyes and listened intently to the lyrics.

You never talk of forever, but ain't no need
Not with you and I
We've been through the worst of the weather
And now the sky is free for us to fly
We don't believe in love with limitations
Giving you my best is right where things begin, oh
We both benefit from our creation
Giving up on us would be my greatest sin, oh

Caught up in the song and her feelings, she unconsciously lifted her right leg and placed it on the side of him. The gesture caused the hem of her dress to rise. Cam inhaled the sweet musky scent of her arousal. He'd been doing a great job of ignoring her until now. Gray wasn't playing fair. She'd literally walked up and put her pussy in his face. Giving her the attention she so desperately wanted, he gazed up and stared at her. Her beauty was beyond measure. The lids of her eyes were closed as she lay her head to the side and pushed her red lips out. Her body swayed sensually to the soulful beat. Gray was in her element when she danced. It was when she felt most confident. Cam loved to watch her move. Her body flowed in a way that was sultry and primal.

"You're drunk." His deep voice strained with need.

Gray opened her eyes and gazed down at him.

"So." She arched her brow.

"You need to slow down."

"You can't tell me what to do. Do I look like Devin to you?"

"You look ten times better, which is why you need to slow the fuck down. But go ahead and do what you want. You grown, remember?" He focused back on his phone.

"Yeah, I am . . . so, mind your fuckin' business." She ran her fingers through his hair. "Why you so concerned with what I'm doing?"

"You the one that brought your drunk-ass over here bothering me. I don't give a fuck what you do. You ain't my problem no more."

The news passed through Gray like a hurricane. Was Cam really done with her?

"You don't give a fuck about me?" She hiked her dress up and straddled his lap.

"I thought we already established that." He continued to scroll through Instagram.

"We didn't so reestablish it, bitch." She mushed him in the head.

"Gray, I'm not for your shit. Go head dawg." He smacked her hand away.

"No . . . *biiiiiiiiiiiiiiiiiiiiitch.*" She got in his face and rolled her neck.

"You must want yo' ass beat." Cam tossed her to the side and got up.

"No!" Gray scrambled to stop him. "You gon' sit here and talk to me!" She blocked his path. "You don't love me no more, *Came-ron Archibald?*" She pronounced every syllable of his name to piss him off then hiccupped.

"Get yo' drunk-ass out my face." He tried to push her, but Gray pushed him back down onto the couch instead.

"Make me." She straddled his lap once more.

Cam's face flushed red; he was so annoyed. He knew what Gray was on. She wanted to fuck but he wasn't in the mood for her or her drunk-ass pussy. No matter how pretty her pussy was or how hard his dick might be, he wouldn't allow her to use sex as a way of saying I'm sorry. They were better than that. She was better than that.

"You gon' make me or what?"

Cam refused to respond. He simply looked at her like she was dumb.

"The fuck?" She snapped when he wouldn't answer. "You ain't gon' say nothing?"

"What you want me to say? That you're making an ass outta yourself?"

"You used to like my ass. You used to stick your tongue in it." She grinned wickedly.

"That was when I let the devil use me."

"So, you wouldn't lick my ass now? You don't wanna taste Miss Kitty." She purred like a sex kitten.

"Go head, Gray. You trippin'."

"But Miss Kitty miss you." She whined, rubbing his face.

"You and Miss Kitty better get the fuck out my face."

"Give her a kiss." She grabbed the back of his head and tried to push his face down.

"I'ma fuck you up. Stop!" He knocked her hand away.

"Give her a hug."

"No!"

"Then pat her." She begged.

"How the fuck am I supposed to pat your pussy?"

"Like this." She tapped the face of her pussy twice.

"Yo' Gray you on some shit, ma for real." Cam chuckled. "Get off me."

"No."

"Gray."

"Star. My name is Star." She reminded him.

"C'mon man. You drunk." He wrapped his muscular arms around her waist to lift her up.

"No, I'm not. I'm tipsy and I'm tryna to fuck." She whined, kissing the side of his face.

"No, you don't."

"GIVE ME THE DICK!" She demanded like a child.

"Relax, I gotta girl man. This shit is inappropriate."

"I DON'T GIVE A FUCK ABOUT THAT BITCH! THIS MY DICK AND YOU'RE MY HUSBAND! So, if I want the dick you betta give me the dick or I'm gon' take the dick!"

"So, you gon' rape me, Gray?"

The words slipped out of Cam's mouth before he even realized what he said. As if a cold bucket of water was doused on top of her head, Gray froze. The walls she built to hold herself up collapsed into a pile of rubble. She heard the sound of her cries before she felt the tears on her cheeks. That's how it was when your heart was hardened. Crying for Gray was like a theft of her soul. She hated to be vulnerable. Vulnerability led to embarrassment and she was making a complete fool out of herself. She'd lost her damn mind. She had no business throwing herself at Cam. Sure, he was her husband and the father of her kids, but he was with Devin, she was with Noon and they were on the brink of a divorce. This was a huge mistake. Whenever she got drunk bad things happened. Truth raped her and Gunz kissed her without her consent. Both events were so traumatic they altered the course of her life. If she didn't get off Cam, she was liable to make another horrible decision.

"Let me go." She attempted to shove him, but Cam only held her tighter.

"I'm sorry. I ain't even mean it like that."

"It still hurts the same." She swallowed her tears.

Without thinking, Cam tucked a piece of hair behind her ear. His night wasn't supposed to end this way. He was supposed to be rejoicing in Gunz's death, not allowing Gray to seduce him but as soon as he touched her back it was over. She was his drug. One touch and he was intoxicated. Whatever she wanted; he'd gladly give. Gray's scent alone sent him into a heady trance, one that wouldn't stop until their bodies were one. From then on he threw caution to the wind. This was the kind of stronghold she had on him. Only she could make him go back on his word.

"Only you." He whispered.

In desperate need of him, Gray opened her mouth to receive the kiss she'd been longing for. Cam sucked her bottom lip before moving his Hennessy soaked tongue into her mouth. Slowly, their tongues glided against each other with velvet ease. The kiss was everything she'd hoped for. They kissed like the world was collapsing around them, like each other were the finest thing they'd ever tasted. Cam pushed his lips into hers more firmly. A spark of electricity surged throughout Gray's body, making her head swim. Feverishly, she moved her mouth to his jaw, neck then collarbone. Cam buried his head in the crook of her neck as his hands roved all over her body.

As their breathing escalated he lifted her up. Gray eagerly wrapped her legs around his muscular back as he carried her to the bedroom. With the door closed, every pretense fell to the waist side. The façade they presented to the world drifted away. Not one bit of time was wasted. The last three years and four months had been enough. Cam peeled Gray's dress off. She helped him out of his clothes as well. Throwing her down onto the bed, his eyes roamed her naked frame with impassioned lust. The tattoo of his name was still there, branding her body as his. He'd never admit it, but he craved her touch, her skin, her scent.

He needed every piece of her. Like the song said, she was more than a lover to him. She was his everything. They'd been through the thick of it together. He could never abandon her. He loved her too much.

Gray had never felt more beautiful than when his eyes were on her. Cam gave her a look like he could eat her alive. Ready for him to feast, she spread her legs and invited him in. Cam wasted no time planting his tongue in her sopping wet hole. It had been ages since he tasted her. Upon his first lick, Gray clamped her thighs against the sides of his face. The smooth hairs of his beard tickled her skin as his tongue lapped up her juices at a speedy pace she couldn't endure. Gray was experiencing sensory overload. Sex with Noon had been good but goddamn was sex with Cam mind-blowingly great. Her sweetness was all his. Cam deepened his licks and fucked her hole with his tongue. The room started to spin. Tears dripped from the corners of her eyes. Only he could make her feel this way. Gray gripped the back of his head and pushed his face into her cunt. Her juices seeped gradually before her climatic pour. Arching her back, she palmed her breasts. Cam's tongue was making her pussy melt. A pleasure like no other erupted when he inserted his finger inside her warm hole. Gray felt like she was going to die. Cam wasn't giving her time to catch her breath, moan or scream. He hungrily lapped at her sweetened cream until her climax coated his tongue. Palming her ass, he savored the essence of her dripping cum while dipping his tongue in and out her pussy.

"Fuck, I love you." Gray cried out in extasy.

She'd regret saying the words the next day, but in the moment, she didn't care. She needed his body. Cam did something to her that no drug on earth could do. Plus, it was how she truly felt. The champagne, Etta Bond, tongue kisses and mind-numbing strokes egged her on. She was lost in him. Every nerve in her body was electrified. Her breathing sped up and so did her heart rate. As she panted breathlessly, he placed soothing kisses to her inner thighs to calm her down. On an emotional high, Gray relished his tender kisses. Then before she knew it they were face-to-face, skin-to-skin moving softly together. Thoughts of their short lived marriage danced in Cam's head. Somehow they'd fell in love then fell right out of touch but here they were in each other's arms. Gazing lovingly at her angelic face, he wiped the tears that fell from her eyes. Gray's toes dug into the mattress as their tongues intertwined. Cam held his solid body on top of hers and positioned himself between her legs. His dick pressed against her clit before he slanted his hips and gently sank inside her. For a second, he closed his eyes and didn't move. This was exactly where he should be. He was home. Gray's pussy was heaven. She was warm and painfully tight. His dick throbbed inside her as he mentally prepared himself to continue on. Once he picked up his pace, the speed of his stroke changed the speed of both their breaths. Gray had forgotten how thick and long he was. She could hardly breathe or keep up. Cam's girth was hard to get use to. He took up every inch of her insides. She was filled to maximum capacity. He was so big that all of him couldn't even fit. In and out. Out and in she breathed. Relaxing her limbs, she surrendered completely. For years, she'd wanted this. Like a glove they fit perfectly together. It was like they'd never been apart.

"You want my cum, Star?" He grunted.

She needed it. She ached for it.

"I can't sleep without your cum inside of me." She admitted.

Living without his death stroke had been hard. He'd crossed her mind a thousand times. No one could fuck her like Cam. His dick game was on another level. Every pump, thrust, stroke and grind of his hips screamed she was his. Cam held onto her wrist as he pumped fervently into her. Gray's hand snaked up his shoulders. She needed something to hold onto as he rocked into her harder. Grunting, Cam's body went into a temporary paralysis. His mind wasn't able to keep up with the pleasure she was dishing out. With each thrust, she squeezed the muscles of her pussy around his rod, sucking him deeper into her cunt. Gray's tranquil blue eyes only added to the moment. Nothing else in the world mattered but them. Pumping faster and harder, he found peace between her thighs. She made him feel like life was worth living. No one understood their dynamic. They barely did but somehow they worked. Where he ended she began. Abruptly, he pulled back for a kiss that was both soft and rough. It was just how she liked it. Their lips fit seamlessly as if they were meant to be together. Cam grabbed the back of Gray's neck 'causing her to whimper in pleasure. He was about to combust, and she was too.

"Oh my God I love you." She cried out as her body convulsed.

Cam watched her fall apart loving every second. Her pussy shuddered around his cock. Against her will Gray called out his name in English and Korean. Cam's head almost exploded as he came with her. He dumped so much cum in her that it started to seep out onto the sheets. Letting out an exasperated groan, he swallowed Gray's moans with passionate kisses. Coming up for air, he licked his lips and said, "I love you too."

———

The next morning, Cam rose from a heavy slumber and rubbed the remainder of sleep from his eyes. Upon waking, he swaddled himself inside the cool, soft sheets. He half wondered if he was still dreaming until he smelled the stomach growling scent of bacon in the air. He was fully awake now. Swinging his long legs out of the bed, he planted them on the floor and stretched his arms. Suddenly, he'd become hungry as fuck. Cam felt like he could eat a five-course meal. Grabbing his phone, he checked his call log to see that Devin had blew up his phone the entire night. He'd have to talk to her but now wasn't the time. He wasn't in the mood to hear her bitch and moan. He had to find Gray. She couldn't just leave him in bed alone like they hadn't violated each other's bodies the night before. Standing up butt naked, he searched for something to throw on. He didn't see his clothes anywhere. He couldn't leave the room completely in the nude. I mean he could, but he didn't wanna poke niggas eyes out. Grabbing Gray's pink, silk Matron of Honor robe, he slid his arms into it which were way too long and tied it around his waist. His large feet slapped against the cold floor as he made his way to the dining room. The entire crew was there already eating breakfast.

"I just lost my fuckin' appetite." Stacy threw down his fork.

Everyone looked up to see what had him so upset.

"You lyin'. Yo' fat-ass ain't gon' never lose your appetite." Cam pulled out his seat and sat next to Gray. "Why the fuck you ain't wake me up?" He ice grilled her.

"Excuse me. I'm not your alarm clock."

"Wait a minute." Kema butt in. "Ya'll slept together?"

"Mind your business." Cam scowled.

"Nigga, can you put some clothes on?" Stacy screwed up his face.

"Uh ah. We like what we see." Tee-Tee licked his lips.

"Cam, you are more than welcome to flaunt what you got. Ain't nobody judging you." Bernard winked his eye and smirked.

"Get your friend." Cam ordered Gray.

"Yo for real. We friends but you need to put some clothes on dawg." Stacy folded his arms across his chest.

"I will once I know where they are." Cam side-eyed Gray.

"I had the maid service take them down to the hotel cleaner. I got sick during the middle of the night and threw up on them." She explained, slightly embarrassed.

"I'm surprised you ain't get sick earlier. Before I went to my room you were pretty faded." Kema smacked, eating a piece of turkey bacon.

"Gimme some." Cam nodded his head in the direction of the French toast on Gray's plate.

Without thinking she cut a piece, dipped it in syrup and fed it to him. The whole crew looked at them like they were aliens from another planet. Gray felt their eyes on her. The sound of her phone ringing thankfully distracted her from their stares. Melody was Facetiming her. Gray swiftly accepted the call. She prayed nothing was wrong. She'd just talked to Melody less than an hour before when she checked on the kids.

"Hello?"

"Sorry to bother you Gray but we have a bit of a problem." Melody hesitated.

"What happened? Are the kids okay?" She panicked.

Cam scooted closer to see what was going on. If there was one scratch on either one of his kids, Melissa's weird ass was dying.

"Beaux was playing with Press' phone and hit the Emergency SOS button."

"She what?" Gray shrieked.

"Yeah. When the dispatcher answered she asked her to bring her some chicken nuggets 'cause she was hungry. Mind you, I made them egg whites, a fruit bowl and quinoa and chia seed porridge as you requested."

"I see why she called the police." Cam quipped. "Don't nobody want that nasty shit."

"It's healthy, Cam. You're the one that said they need to eat better."

"It's disgusting. You know damn well black people don't eat no fuckin' porridge. This ain't Goldilocks and The Three Bears. Melinda put my daughter on the phone." He ordered.

"Her name is Melody, jackass." Gray corrected him.

"Marissa, Michelle same thing."

"Hi mommy!" Beaux's face appeared on the screen.

Every time Gray looked at her daughter's sweet face her heart melted but she couldn't be swayed by her innocence and beauty. She had to get Beaux's bad ass together.

"Why did you call the police?" She got straight to the point.

"It was not the police."

"It was the police. You called the police, Beaux." Gray said sternly.

"Why I called the police?" She asked her mother.

"I don't know. You tell me. You the one that did it. Why did you call them?"

"Cause . . ."

"Cause what? You called the police to do what? What did you want them to come do?"

"Bring me some chicken nuggets." Beaux said it like it wasn't a big deal.

"You wanted some chicken nuggets, so you called 911?"

"Yes." Her voice squeaked.

"You getting a whoopin'."

"*Nooooooo! I don't want no whoopin'!*" Beaux immediately started to cry.

"Stop crying. Mommy not gon' whoop you." Cam quickly snatched the phone.

If he had it his way, none of his children would ever shed a tear.

"*Yes, she is!*" Beaux sobbed hysterically.

"Are you daddy's baby?" Cam began to talk in a high pitch, baby tone that made everyone look at him crazy.

"Yeah." Beaux nodded her head.

"Who's daddy's baby?"

"Umm." She stopped crying and thought about it.

"You know I'ma protect you, right?"

"Yes."

Cam examined his daughters gorgeous face and jet-black hair. Beaux was a spitfire just like Aoki. Between the two of them, by the time he was fifty, he'd have a head full of grey hair.

"Who's beautiful and strong and can do anything in the world?"

"Me?" Beaux pointed to her chest.

"Who?"

"Me!"

"And who's daddy's baby?"

Beaux stalled again.

"It's the same answer." He coached with a laugh.

"Me!" She brightened up.

"That's right. I love you."

"I love you too, daddy."

"A'ight now man up and quit crying."

Beaux didn't hesitate to wipe her eyes with the back of her hand.

"I not gon' cry no more, daddy. I pro-mise."

"That's what daddy like to hear. Now tell mommy you sorry for calling the police." He handed Gray back her phone.

"I sorry, mommy. You still gon' whoop me?"

"No. I'm not but you can't call the police no more."

"Okay but I want some nuggets."

"Daddy gon' bring you some nuggets." Cam guaranteed.

"Mommy will be home in a minute. I love you." Gray said.

"Love you." Beaux blew a kiss at the phone as Reign walked by with a fire truck in his hand.

"*Reigny.*" Cam sang.

"*Yeeeeeah!*" He sang back loudly.

"*What you doing?*"

"*Playiiiiiiin'!*"

"Daddy luuuuuuh you!"

"*I FUCKIN' LUH YOOOOU!*" Reign howled.

"Aye watch yo' mouth! You ain't supposed to be cussin'!" Cam barked.

"No, you cussin'!" Reign laughed like it was the funniest thing in the world.

"I'm grown! I can cuss li'l rock head boy."

"Okay, I'm done talkin' to ya'll." Gray waved goodbye.

"I swear yo' kids bad. You can't tell me Aoki, Beaux and Reign ain't gon' end up on the First 48." Kema joked.

"Don't be talkin' about my babies."

309

"Are ya'll fuckin'?" Tee-Tee said out of nowhere.

"Huh?" Gray eyes grew wide.

"You heard me. If you can huh you can hear."

"Yeah, ya'll acting hella weird. Last night ya'll couldn't stand each other. Now you feeding him fuckin' French toast and shit." Kema pointed out.

"As she should." Cam opened his mouth so Gray could feed him some more.

"I plead the fifth and no feed yourself." She pushed her plate in his direction.

"It's like that?"

"What you mean?" Gray played dumb.

"Oh a'ight." Cam took her plate and started eating.

"Either they fucked or she still drunk." Tee-Tee narrowed his eyes.

"I wish I was drunk. Maybe then I would've got some sleep last night." Selicia cut her eyes at Stacy.

"Oh lord what happened now?" Kema groaned.

"This fuckin' creep popped up in my room like a psycho from a Lifetime movie and wouldn't leave."

"She wanted me to leave but *I refuse to let you go!*" Stacy sang the Temptations *Ain't too Proud to Beg.*

"Yo' fat-ass wish I begged you to stay." Selicia argued.

"We have talked about this. Bitch, you fat too."

310

"Call me another one." Selicia picked up a knife and aimed it at his head. "I will carve out your insides. Keep fuckin' wit' me."

"C'mon sweetheart. We ain't Cam and Gray. We ain't gotta fight to prove our love." He tried to hug her.

"The day I love you is the day I lose my virginity." She pushed him hard.

"Well, today *is the mutha . . .fuckin'. . . day!*" Stacy pumped his crotch in the air.

"I'm leaving. I hate this nigga." Selicia threw down her napkin and left.

"Bye boo! I'ma Facetime you later!"

"Die slow muthafucka!"

"She can't get enough of me." Stacy grinned, pleased with his self.

"Ya'll niggas is crazy." Kema laughed at their foolishness. "So, friend . . .if you and yo' baby daddy didn't smash, what did you do last night? 'Cause when I left you was on one."

"Nah, she was on two." Tee-Tee joked.

"I went to sleep." She shrugged.

"Obviously not by yourself."

"Yo Quan. Get your girl. She nosey as shit." Cam pulled Gray close and kissed her cheek.

"Stop." She scooted her chair away, annoyed.

"Come back!" He yanked her towards him.

"Uh ah. Ain't gon' be no fighting up in here today." Kema warned them both.

"That's her crazy-ass."

"If ya'll didn't have sex then what the fuck is going?"

"Nothin' happened, Kema." Gray guaranteed.

"What?" Cam screwed up his face.

"It didn't." She stared directly into his whiskey colored eyes.

"Yo, don't play wit' me." He chuckled not taking her seriously.

"You let Cam eat the booty up like groceries!" Tee-Tee clapped his hands gleefully.

Everyone at the table cracked up laughing except Cam and Gray. A silent conversation was taking place between them that no one else was privy to.

"Nothing happened. We simply slept together, that's it. I would never cross the line with him again. What I look like fuckin' behind Devin? Lord knows where that pussy has been." Gray scoffed.

"You just the fuck did! You fuckin' liar!" Cam eyed her flabbergasted.

"Cam, stop playin'. We did not have sex."

Completely stunned by her behavior, he sat back and glared at her. The look on her face was as cold as winter snow.

"Oh, you dead serious?"

"We went to sleep. I threw up on your clothes. That's it."

"Before or after you begged for my dick?" He barked, furiously.

"I would never beg to fuck you. Are you dumb?"

Cam glared into her eyes, waiting for her to tell the truth but Gray never did. She sat in his face and pretended like nothing happened. Was she that ashamed of him or was she ashamed of what happened? Whichever was the question, his feelings were hurt all the same. He never intended on taking it there with Gray, but when she straddled his lap, he couldn't help but act on his desires. She was his weakness. He could never deny his self of having her, so the fact that she was trying to diss him like he didn't have her speaking in tongues blew his fuckin' mind. She'd told him she loved him, and he'd said it back. Didn't that mean anything?

"I knew you was a liar, but this shit is next level. Are you serious?"

"Dead ass. We did not fuck." Gray continued to lie to cover her ass.

"You gon' lie like that in front of all these people? Tell the truth, Gray. Don't make me fuck you up in this pink-ass robe."

"Please don't. We have seen enough." Stacy said disgusted.

"We do not need to see that baby leg he call a penis flinging around everywhere." Kema jibbed, taking a sip of coffee.

"Aye! Quit lookin' at that man dick!" Quan frowned.

"It's like a solar eclipse. I can't help but look."

"For real, Gray. Tell the truth." Cam practically begged.

"I seriously do not remember having sex with you." She lied once more.

"Damn, was it that horrible?" Tee-Tee screwed up his face.

"Shut up!" Cam shouted then turned his attention back on Gray. "You don't remember asking me to kiss Miss Kitty?"

"Miss Kitty? Ya'll freaky." Bernard chuckled.

"What? No. That don't even sound like me."

"I swear to God I'm about to kill her. On my kids I'ma snap her fuckin' neck. So, you ain't ask me to hug your pussy?" Cam shouted, angrily.

"Hug her pussy?" Stacy clutched his chest. "What kind of freaky shit are ya'll into?"

"That must be some new shit. How you do that?" Tee-Tee died to know.

"Same thing I said!" Cam threw up his hands incensed.

"Yeah, you making this shit up. I don't even talk like that." Gray shook her head.

"Gray stop cappin'. You said that shit. Kema call her pussy Miss Kitty too." Quan interjected.

"Thank you, dawg!" Cam gave him a five.

"Well, that's Kema nasty-ass. That ain't me."

"Wait a minute, bitch." Kema rolled her neck.

"Listen, I have moved on with my life. Ain't no way in hell I doubled back and fucked Cam. I would have to be stupid to fuck him again and we all know I'm not stupid."

"*Well* that's debatable friend." Tee-Tee said underneath his breath.

"I don't want him! Fuck I look like?"

"Square up." Cam rose from his seat.

"What?" Gray looked at him like he was crazy.

"Throw your hands up." He stood in a southpaw stance causing his robe to fly open.

Cam's entire body was on display for everyone to see. His thick, veiny cock curved to the left and tapped against his inner thigh.

"Aww hell naw!" Stacy ducked under the table. "My *eyes*! I'm blind! Somebody get me a cane! I can't see!" He whined.

"Holy shit." Kema gawked at Cam's python like dick.

"Uh, ah baby! Cover your eyes!" Quan blocked her view with his hand.

"Let me just see one more time." She begged.

"Ooh, Gray, now I see how you got pregnant with quads." Tee-Tee stood up to get a closer look.

"She said it was big but I ain't think it was that big. My God it's beautiful." Bernard fanned his self.

"I'll be stuck on stupid for that dick too!"

"Stand up!" Cam demanded.

"Who?" Gray drew her head back.

"You dickhead. You wanna sit up here and lie. You gon' have to fight me."

"Boy, if you don't move *and close your damn robe*!" Gray spoke through clenched teeth.

"Fuck you and this robe. Square up dawg. Real shit. I ain't gon' kill you but I'm definitely knocking yo' ass out."

"Cam, I am not fighting you."

"Yes, you is. Stand yo' husky-ass up so I can two-piece yo' jaw."

"The day you hit me is the day you gon' die." Gray warned.

"Well, we gon' die together 'cause I'm about to punch you in yo' invisible-ass neck."

"Damn Cam!" Kema groaned, covering her face. "Why you say that? You know how she feel about her neck."

"FUCK YOU! DON'T TALK ABOUT MY NECK!" Gray unconsciously rubbed it.

"No, fuck that! I done heard about niggas lying on the dick but you gon' lie on your pussy, Gray? That's some sick shit. It's cool tho. Next time you want the dick, my bad . . . *your* dick, I'ma make you beg for it."

"And that's where you got me fucked up. I would never beg for that community dick."

316

"A'ight." He pointed his finger in her face. "I guarantee you gon' eat them words! You gon' be begging me to eat Miss Kitty and I'ma be like NOPE! Fuckin' pathological liar! What the fuck is wrong wit' you? That shit ain't even normal. You are fuckin' insane. Gon' sit up here and lie wit' a straight face, knowing damn well you begged for my dick. Got me lookin' crazy walkin' around in a pink robe and shit 'cause you threw yo' pussy at me. I bet I won't fuck you again and you bet not ask 'cause the answer is gon' be HELL NO! Stupid ass!" Cam shot her the bird before he left the room.

16

"Everybody got somebody that they mess wit' on the
low."- H.E.R., "Changes"

"If I would've known we was riding bikes and shit,
I wouldn't have worn this." Gray looked down at her outfit.

Based on the activity they were about to do she was
doing the absolute most. The coed bachelor/bachelorette
party was going down. The who crew minus Cam and
Devin was there on the corner of Cherokee street. Kema
was annoyed they were late. Gray was overjoyed. She
wasn't particularly ecstatic about seeing them anyway. She
would be happy if they didn't come at all. The last thing
she wanted to do was spend the night with her husband and
his girlfriend.

"Nobody told you to come dressed like a Fly Girl
from In Living Color." Tee-Tee chuckled, giving her a
once over glance. "I mean, you cute tho bitch."

Gray was serving the kids early 90's Versace
realness. Her shag cut was styled to perfection. A pair of
Medusa head Versace earrings, necklace and bracelet
shined from her ears, neck and wrist. Cupping her breasts
was a floral and geometric print bralette that showed off her
toned stomach. A matching pair of leggings kissed every
curve of her hips and ass. The pants were so form fitting
that every time she took a step her ass jiggled. Black 4-inch
mules adorned her pretty little feet. Long story short, Gray
was killing the game. It was bad enough she felt like a third

wheel. She needed to look good. Everybody was boo'd up. Kema had Quan, Tee-Tee was with Bernard, Stacy had Selicia, Mo was with Boss, Dylan and Angel were all over each other, Heidi's boo was linking up with them later and when Cam arrived, he'd be with Devin. Even Priest was there with some chick. Gray was the odd man out. If she could've stayed back with the kids, she would've but Kema would kill her if she missed any second of her wedding week. It didn't help that every few seconds she found herself looking around expecting someone to come out of nowhere and shoot her in the head. The wedding was three days away which meant her time on earth was getting shorter by the minute. If Cam didn't get on his shit and find out who had it out for him, she'd be dead.

"Here they late asses go." Kema groaned, rolling her eyes.

Cam and Devin pulled up in his red Bugatti. Meek Mill's *Respect The Game* bumped loudly as he parked his car. A small corner of Gray's heart fluttered. Meek was Cam's favorite rapper. She'd always catch him rapping his lyrics around the house when they lived together. There wasn't a Meek Mill song he didn't know the lyrics to. Stepping out the million-dollar sportscar, he checked the oncoming traffic then walked slowly around the car. The nigga acted like he didn't have a care in the world. They were on his time. *This nigga,* Gray sucked her teeth. Cam's cocky attitude was part of the reason why she'd fell in love with him. His flashy persona was another reason. There was so much ice on his body he could start a blizzard. The nigga looked phenomenal. His tall frame fit clothes perfectly. Covering his broad shoulders and firm chest was a black t-shirt with a young Barack Obama on the front smoking a cigarette. A pair of green and white Fear of God track pants and black and white checkerboard Vans set off the Skateboard P look he donned. At least four gold chains swung from his tattooed neck and a vintage Cartier watch gleamed from his wrist. Gray wanted to kiss every freckle on his cheek and tug on his beard while massaging his dick. The feeling quickly went away when he opened the passenger side door for Devin. Sis had a freshly fucked glow on her face that irritated Kema and Gray's soul. Both of them hated her fuckin' guts. Kema didn't want the bitch anywhere around her or her wedding festivities, but on the strength of Cam and Quan's friendship, she let him bring his whore to the party anyway.

"Bout time ya'll showed up. We've been waiting a half an hour." She looked at her iced out Piguet watch.

"When you getting good dick, you lose track of time." Devin smirked, wiping the corners of her mouth.

"Eww." Heidi pretended to puke.

It took every bit of decorum Gray had not to run over and drop kick her and Cam in the throat. Mean mugging him, she tried to keep her emotions in check. Knowing he'd fucked her the night before, and then Devin the next day, was like a thousand tiny papercuts to the heart. Gray wanted to point her finger in his face and go off, but she'd created this mess. She'd played the shit out of him for her own selfish reasons. She couldn't bitch and moan now. She had to take the shit on the chin like a big girl, no matter how much it hurt.

"Quit showing out." Cam smacked Devin on the butt.

Mesmerized by the way her ass cheeks bounced, he walked right past Gray as if she didn't exist. Rocking her head from side-to-side, she tried to ease the tension in her neck before she spazzed out.

"Baby, stop." Devin giggled like a little school girl.

She loved every bit of attention Cam gave her, especially at the expense of pissing off Gray.

"My bad for being late, dawg." Cam gave Quan a pound.

"It's all good. Kema just in her feelings 'cause she came on her period."

"Damn nigga! Tell the whole block why don't you." She snapped.

"Get yo' ass on this bike before I run you over wit' it." Quan pointed to the space between the handle bars.

"You betta be glad I love you." She stomped towards the bike with her bottom lip poked out.

"Let's ride out."

The crew had a choice of riding a rented Lime Bike or a Bird scooter. Gray chose a Lime Bike. It was the safest option considering what kind of shoes she had on. Gray was super nervous. She hadn't ridden a bike since she was a kid. She hoped she still knew how. Everyone except Stacy, Cam and Priest chose a bike. Stacy hopped on a scooter. Cam and Priest bought their Boosted Boards with them. They were $1500 electric skateboards that went up to 24 mph. The weather was perfect for a night ride. It was a warm 85 degrees but there was a breeze in the air. The plan was to ride from Cherokee street to Ball Park Village.

"Be careful baby." Devin gave Cam a sensual kiss on the mouth. "I can't have you dying on me. I just got you back." She wiped her gloss off his lips.

The bike ride hadn't even started, and Gray was ready for it to be over. If she had to watch Devin and Cam suck face all night, she'd surely slit her wrist sideways. She knew Cam was being extra on purpose, but it still hurt all

321

the same. He wanted to hurt her like she'd hurt him but no part of her wanted to see him all over another woman. A woman like Devin no less. Despite her feelings and how upset with him she was, she still loved him. Whether they were together or apart, she always would.

Gradually, they all pulled off into traffic. Gray said a silent prayer to God that she'd make it home alive to her kids. The sun was beginning to set. A yellow and orange hue mixed seamlessly with the powder blue sky. Like a flock of birds, they zoomed down the busy street together. Streetlights, cars, and trees zoomed past them as fast as the speed of lightening. A cool wind whipped through their hair as the nosey sound of the city became the soundtrack of their night. At first Gray wasn't so sure about taking a ride through the city at dusk but midway into it she started to have fun. The experience was freeing in a way she hadn't expected. It was just what she needed. She felt like a kid again. They all did. Cam and Priest whizzed down the winding hill going from lane to lane. At any moment they could get hit by a car and die. Neither seemed to be scared or care. Even though they were riding down a steep hill, Cam crouched down low, holding onto the bottom of the board. He floated like he was gliding on air. The back of his t-shirt flapped in the wind. Cam was going so fast that he was keeping up with most of the cars. Like a pro, he stood back up without losing his balance and did an Ollie, Frontside 180, Backside 180, Pop Shove, Front Shove and ended with a Heelflip.

Gray was amazed. She never knew he could ride a skateboard so good. It was yet another thing she didn't know about him. Sometimes, she wondered if she even knew him at all. Judging by the newlywed game, she knew him quite well. Twenty minutes later, they pulled up to Ball Park Village. Sadly, Gray got off her bike and fixed her wind tossed hair. She wished the ride could've lasted longer.

"That was fun as fuck." Mo gushed. "I wanna do it again."

"Me too." Kema agreed, happy as hell. "Great suggestion babe." She kissed Quan sweetly on the lips.

Riding bikes and scooters at night was one of things he wanted to do. Quan, Stacy and Cam used to ride all the time before their lives became so hectic. Cam, in particular, had been skateboarding since he was seven. One by one they headed into PBR St. Louis. The club featured a large dance floor, soft-seating lounge area, private outdoor balconies, multiple bars and the world's meanest mechanical bull. Even though it was a Thursday night, Kema and Quan rented out a section just for their crew. Gray was grateful they had. The place was packed from wall-to-wall. PBR St. Louis wasn't usually the kind of place the guys would go to. They were used to hood clubs and hole in the walls, but because it was their bachelor/bachelorette party, Kema wanted to try something different. Before they even sat down, bottles of Ace of Spade, D'Usse, Hennessy, Patrón and Ciroc were brought over with buckets of ice.

"Let's take a shot." Kema said enthusiastically.

Gray wasn't a tequila girl, but she needed something extra potent to get her through the night. Cam had been paying her dust since the moment he arrived. He wouldn't even look in her direction. He and Devin sat off to the side, her on his lap, hugged up. From the outside looking in they looked like the perfect couple. You wouldn't even think Gray was the one that carried his last name. All the girls formed a semi-circle and held their shot glasses in the air.

"Who gon' make the toast?" Selicia looked around.

"You do it, Gray." Heidi suggested.

"Okay." She cleared her throat. "There are good ships and wood ships, ships that sail the sea, but the best ships are friendships, may they always be."

"Woo-hoo!" All the girls hooted while clinking their glasses.

Gray tilted her head back and gulped down the clear liquid. The tequila burned her throat something terrible, but it gave her the buzz she desired.

"Give me another one." She positioned her glass for more.

Kema eyed her skeptically. Gray wasn't a big drinker, but in the last two days, she'd been drinking heavily. The tension between her and Cam was getting to her and she didn't know how to handle it. Refusing to let her use tequila as a crutch, Kema gave her one more shot. After that she was cutting her off.

"C'mon friend. Let's go ride the bull."

Arm-in-arm the two best friends skipped down the steps and into the crowd.

"I know what you're doing and I'm not gonna allow it." Kema said firmly.

Knowing exactly what she was getting at, Gray simply leaned her head onto Kema's shoulder and sighed. Her life was a mess. She'd been doing so good until she returned to St. Louis. All she wanted to do was go back to Paris. It was her little cocoon. No one bothered her there. She didn't have to fear death or a broken heart. The only thing keeping her sane was her kids and Kema. Having her

324

by her side made her feel ten times better. Whenever she felt like shit Kema was always there to lighten the mood. Through thick and thin, she had her back.

"Fuck her . . . and him."

"I just wish I didn't love him."

"I know." Kema kissed her temple. "I know."

"C'mon, Mary Kate and Ashley!" Tee-Tee broke up the bittersweet moment. "Gray, get yo' big ass up there and ride that bull!"

Pulling herself together, she put on a brave face and handed her heels to Heidi who stood to the right of her. Gray climbed onto the squishy surface. She'd never ridden a mechanical bull before. Hiking her right leg up, she mounted the apparatus nervously and held onto the stirrup. A few feet away in their private section, Cam took a swig of Hennessy with Devin in his arms. Gray thought he wasn't paying her any attention, but he'd been watching her every move all night. He just refused to acknowledge her existence. He was still mad as hell at Gray. The stunt she'd pulled the day before was immature as fuck. He'd never admit it, especially not to her, but he was hurt. He'd allowed his self to once again open up to her, and like all the times before, she shitted on his emotions. Cam couldn't continue playing these cat and mouse games with Gray. They'd been playing the same demented game since the day they met. It was old and tired as fuck. The only problem was he had to get his dick and his heart on board with his mind. Seeing Gray in her skin tight outfit on top of a fuckin' mechanical bull was almost too much for him handle. Dawn Richard song *Sauce* filled the club as the machine started up. Gray rolled her upper body back-and-forth slowly, like she was riding a dick . . . his dick. As the machine spun around and she held on tight, she and Cam

325

linked eyes. His pride begged him to drop his gaze but with Gray he was drawn in more. He could never just get a glimpse of her. He wanted the full experience of witnessing her beauty. A wicked grin graced the corners of her lips as she wind her hips. Cam gripped Devin's thigh.

"Let me find out." She massaged his dick and stuck her tongue in his ear.

Devin thought he was aroused because of her. Cam let her think it as he enjoyed the feel of her licking his lobe. Never once did he take his off Gray. The whole time Devin licked and nibbled his ear, he imagined it was Gray. Alluringly, Gray blinked her eyes making her lashes flutter like wings. He could tell by the sensual expression on her face that she too was thinking back on their tryst. Cam's dick hardened to the point it hurt. Watching his wife ride a mechanical bull while thinking of him was the sexiest shit he'd ever seen. The song only added to her sex appeal. Up and down she bounced as Dawn sang:

It's the weekend and I'm greedy, I've been a good girl all week
So I can dirty them sheets from Friday to Sunday, no breaks
I'm ready to ride you like I'm 'bout to win a prize at the Kentucky Derby
I'm your jockey, you heard me

Red Bottoms, La Perla
Hair touching your shoulder
I'm going to work like Rihanna
told ya' 'til that sauce is all over
'Til that sauce is all over
Don't be stingy when I'm greedy

I need you to let it fall on me

Gray ran her hand slowly down her neck then across her hardened nipples. Dawn's nasty lyrics about her man coming all over her face, the powerful machine between her thighs and Cam's intense gaze was turning her on to the fullest. The conductor tried to throw her off by picking up the speed, but she held on tight the entire ride. When it was all over the crowd and her friends cheered. Grinning from ear-to-ear, she slid off the bull and took a bow.

"You did that bitch!" Kema gave her a high-five before she took her turn.

"I see how she got five kids. After witnessing that, I would nut up in her ass too and I don't even like pussy." Tee-Tee joked.

After riding the bull a few times, the girls made their way back to their section. A cloud of weed smoke hit them in the face when they returned. The rich leafy smell permeated the space. Silver smoke curled and pirouetted through the thick hazy air. The guys were good and lifted. It was the perfect time for the strippers Cam hired to arrive. One was a cute red bone chick with long blonde weave, small boobs, thick hips and a humongous ass. She basically wore neon pink dental floss as an outfit. The other girl had smooth mahogany skin, large tits and a moderately sized butt. She too was practically naked. She had on a nude bodysuit, but the thong was made out of a metal chain. *Round of Applause* by Waka Flocka Flame started to play as they stood in front of Quan and made their asses clap. Quan stood behind the chocolate dancer and gripped her waist while palming the other stripper's booty. Kema took a bottle of Ciroc to the head and watched. She loved when her nigga turned up. Ready to put on a show the chick with blonde hair laid on the ground, lifted her legs in the air and spread them into a V. The brown skinned bunny straddled her face and simulated the act of getting her pussy ate. They even got into the scissoring position and started smacking their pussies against one another. Stacy was the first to throw a stack. Cam, Priest, Boss and Angel followed up. Even the girls started throwing money in the air. In less than thirty minutes the girls made over 20 g's. The floor was covered in ones. The strippers turned out every trick in the book. They bust into splits, put their legs behind their heads and gave lap dances. When the light skinned chick shook her ass all in Cam's face, Gray wanted to snatch her up by her blonde weave but quickly checked herself. She couldn't trip. Besides, Cam and Devin seemed to be enjoying the stripper quite a bit. She wouldn't be surprised if they took her home with them that night.

When their hour was up, the girls gathered their doe and split. Gray grinned devilishly. Now that the guys entertainment was over, the real party was about to begin. It was payback time. She couldn't wait to see the look on the guys' faces when the male stripper she hired named Inferno arrived. Gray didn't have to wait long to find out. A few seconds later, he entered their section in nothing but a pair of boxer/briefs, jeans and Timbs. The nigga's body was ripped.

"Which one of ya'll getting married?" He looked around.

"*Me.*" Kema raised her hand in the air.

Quan swiftly smacked it back down.

"C'mere sweetheart." Inferno placed an empty chair in the center of the floor.

Kema giddily tiptoed over and took a seat. Tank's freaky anthem *Dirty* came through the speakers as Inferno straddled her lap, grabbed the back of her head and started grinding on her. Before Quan could blink the nigga slid down, spread her legs, placed them on his shoulders and lifted her into the air. Kema's head fell back in ecstasy as Inferno palmed her ass and acted like he was eating her out.

"You gon' take that? I know you ain't gon' let that shit ride." Stacy instigated.

"We ain't even married and I'm finna be a widower." Quan pulled out his burner.

"Don't let this nigga gas you up. Let li'l mama do her thing." Cam tried to calm his friend down.

"I know you bet not put yo' ass in that chair." Boss warned Mo.

"Boy hush." She waved him off. "I don't even like strippers." She lied.

For thirty minutes Quan had to sit and watch his fiancé be man handled by some greasy nigga that looked like a buff ass Mack Wilds. The shit was tortuous. Several times he came hella close to pulling the trigger but through the grace of God he got through it. Inferno then gave each girl a sexy lapdance except Mo. Boss would literally divorce her if she participated. Priest date and Devin even partook in the fun. Cam didn't even bat a lash at seeing her get fondled. When it was Gray's turn, Inferno had stripped down to nothing but his boxer/briefs which pissed all the men off. Gray was good and tipsy when she sat down. Inferno spread her legs and ran his hand up and down her thighs. At one point he even cupped her pussy. Laughing uncontrollably, she covered her face. Having a man rub all over her in front of a room full of people was awkward as hell. With her legs cocked open, Inferno rolled his pelvis like he was banging her pussy out. He was pounding her so hard, Gray thought she was going to fall out of the chair. They were literally simulating sex. Cam turned into an enraged panther. It was all good when it was the other ladies getting danced on, he didn't care. He didn't even trip when Devin took her turn but when it came to Gray, he saw red. No other man could touch her but him. Despite their circumstances she was his and always would be. Without effort, Inferno lifted Gray into his brawny arms and kissed all over her stomach. Gently, he laid her down on the floor and continued to assault her pussy with his pelvic thrust. Rigid with fury, Cam stood up. Gray wasn't even five minutes into her dance, and he couldn't take it anymore. The male dancer was supposed to be in good fun but the visual of him stroking his wife made Cam think of the night he caught her kissing Gunz. It was all too much. Angrily, he grabbed Inferno by the back of his neck and tossed him across the room. The poor man crashed into the metal rail.

"Get yo' ass up!" Cam looked down at Gray.

"Nah, Archibald. Let li'l mama do her thing." Stacy used Cam's words against him.

"I'm not in the mood for your dumb shit right now." He yelled at Stacy. "Gray, don't make me tell you again. Get the fuck up!"

"Oh, now you wanna speak to me?" She spat, sarcastically rising to her feet. "You ain't said shit to me all night. Keep that same energy."

"Shut the fuck up, Gray." He yelled.

"You shut the fuck up! You don't control what the hell I do!"

"Yes, I do."

"No, you don't." She rolled her neck.

"Since when? Your last name Parthens, ain't it?"

"Only for a couple more days." She hissed.

330

"Until then you gon' do what the fuck I say."

"Picture that."

"Are you fuckin' kidding me?" Devin got up in his face.

"Get the fuck out my face wit' that bullshit, man." He moved her out the way.

"No! Why the fuck you mad? You ain't give a fuck when I got a lap dance, but when her big ass get one, you wanna turn into the Incredible fuckin' Hulk!"

"That's yo' last time disrespecting me, bitch." Gray shoved her in the chest.

Before Devin could hit her back, Cam grabbed her.

"You really gon' let her put her hands on me!" Devin tried to break loose.

"Go sit yo' stupid-ass down!"

Devin stood frozen. Why was he disrespecting her and sticking up for Gray? She was the one he was in a relationship with.

"Go!" Cam roared.

Seeing he wasn't playing she begrudgingly took a seat.

"And you bet not get up!"

"You always yelling at somebody." He heard a familiar voice say from behind.

Cam would know that voice from anywhere. Sure enough, when he turned around, he found LaLa. Nothing had changed about her. She was just as fine as he remembered. Long curly weave flowed down her back. Her

331

creamy, buttery skin glowed under the amber lights. The pink crop top showed off the breast implants he bought her. The matching joggers and ankle boots gave her the Instagram baddie look she always went for. Right next to her was her friend, Alexzandria, who he also hadn't seen in years.

"I ain't know you was home." LaLa wrapped her arms around his neck and gave him a warm hug.

The smell of his Tom Ford Leather Ombre cologne had her pussy doing backflips. She'd missed him like crazy while he was away. As soon as she and Gunz got word that he'd been arrested, she regretted turning him in. It was the worst decision she'd ever made. She was caught up in her feelings and making decisions based off emotion was never good for a spiteful chick like her. Nothing would ever make up for what she did, but she thought writing him letters and putting money on his books would help. LaLa's biggest concern was making sure he never found out what she'd done. If Cam ever knew it was her and Gunz that had him locked up, she'd be 6F for sure.

"I got home a couple days ago." He kept his hands to his side.

Cam refused to hug her back. Things between he and LaLa had changed. At one point she was the love he couldn't let go of, but whenever she came around bad energy followed. His dick didn't even get hard for her anymore.

"What's up, Cam?" Alexzandria spoke.

Cam gave her a head nod.

"You look good. . . *shit*." LaLa licked her big juicy lips.

"Hold up. Who the fuck is this all friendly?" Devin sat up.

"Oooooooh chile the irony. This shit feels like déjà vu." Gray chuckled, loving the shit show that was going on before her.

Every bit of her wanted to smack the shit outta LaLa for fuckin' Cam while they were married but she was Devin's headache now.

"It's good to see you home big head. Even though last time I saw you, I was every bitch in the book." LaLa sneered.

"I mean, if the shoe fits." Cam shrugged.

"I see that mouth ain't changed."

"And the hood still know what that mouth do." He shot back.

"Whatever asshole. We need to catch up tho. It's been a minute." She ran her hand down his strong tattooed arm seductively.

"Did this bitch just ask my nigga out on a date?" Devin took off one of her earrings.

"Instead of worrying about me, you need to be worried about her. She's the real problem." Gray advised.

"I'm not you. I eliminate problems." Devin mocked, switching over to Cam. "Babe, who's your friend?"

"Didn't I tell you to sit down?"

"Who the fuck is this?" LaLa's nostrils flared.

"I'm Devin . . . his girlfriend."

"Wait a minute." LaLa stood back on one leg. "So, you left Miss Piggy for Kermit?"

"No, this buck tooth bitch didn't." Devin snatched off her other earring ready to fight.

"Damn, Cam, you love fuckin' wit' these Jim Hansen Muppet Baby lookin' bitches."

"So, I guess that makes you Gonzo? Oops my bad, you just a bitch wit' a shit stain above her lip." Devin spat.

"Girl please. I ain't worried about no bitch who nigga I can take in my sleep." LaLa flicked her wrist dismissively and pretended like Devin wasn't even there. "What ya'll getting into tonight?"

"It's Kema and Quan's bachelor/bachelorette party." Cam answered.

"Them niggas getting married. I guess the rest of us ho's do gotta chance."

On cue Kema sauntered over with a drink in her hand.

"I thought we got rid of you." She looked LaLa up and down. "But you just like herpes. You just keep poppin' up."

"Just like an outbreak." Mo cackled.

While they laughed, Kema's statement rang in Cam's mind. Mama Lucy had said the same thing to him days before. Initially, he didn't trip off it. He was too busy trying to calm Aoki down after the fight but now he was starting to think there was more behind her words. If he remembered correctly, as soon as she said it, a look of regret swept over her face. It was almost like she was afraid she'd slipped up and said something wrong. Cam wondered was LaLa the one who had him arrested. They were on bad terms after All Star Weekend. Maybe she'd had enough of his shit and decided to make him pay for hurting her time and time again. For LaLa's sake she better hope she didn't have anything to do with it. If he learned she was behind his imprisonment, he'd kill her and her whole family.

"Baby, I'll be back." He squeezed Devin's ass cheek before he left the section to go smoke.

Running into LaLa and arguing with Gray had given him a headache. Quan and Priest followed him outside. LaLa and Alexzandria followed him out of the section and headed to the dance floor. As the guys walked out, Heidi's boo thang and his boys walked in. He instantly reminded Gray of the rapper Rick Ross. They literally could've been twins.

"Babe! I'm so happy you came." Heidi held out her arms.

Gray, Kema and Tee-Tee watched on happy for their friend. Her whole mood had changed. After hugging him for what felt like an eternity, Heidi led her guy over to her friends.

"Gabe, these are my girls Kema, Gray and Tee-Tee. Girls this is my boo Gabe."

"Hey, how you doing?" He shook all of their hands except Tee-Tee's.

Gabe didn't even acknowledge his presence.

"I know you from somewhere." Gray squinted her eyes.

"Nah, we ain't never met before. I would remember you." He eyed her with lust.

335

Gray peeped his gesture and curled her upper lip. Right off the rip she didn't like Gabe. He was a creep and obviously had a problem with gay people. On top of that his friends had barely said hi and had the nerve to start drinking their liquor. If that wasn't enough, she noticed something else very incriminating about him.

"Look at this this nigga left hand." She whispered out the side of her mouth to Kema. "You see what I see?"

"Mmm hmm." Kema pursed her lips.

"This nigga married."

"He sure is." Kema crossed her legs defensively. "So, Gabe how long you been dating my friend?"

"About six months."

"Six months. Hmm. Interesting." She tapped her upper lip with her index finger.

"Ya'll spend a lot of time together?" Gray jumped in.

"Why you ask him that?" Heidi screwed up her face.

"Calm down friend. It's just a question."

"I told you, we mainly see each other on the weekends. He works the night shift, so he sleeps during the day and I work in the day so when I'm coming home, he's going to work."

"Would you say ya'll are in love?"

"Most definitely. This my baby." Gabe wrapped his arm around Heidi's neck and kissed her cheek.

"How old are you?" Kema asked.

"Damn, ya'll the FBI?" Gabe laughed anxiously.

"No disrespect. We just trying to get to know you."

"I'm thirty-eight."

"Thirty-eight. So, have you ever been married?"

"Nah."

"You're 38, work the nightshift, never been married. Got any kids?"

"Nope."

"You want some 'cause you know Heidi has a son." Gray chimed in.

"I'm cool wit' that. Li'l man almost grown anyway."

"Thirty-eight, no kids, never been married, works the night shift. Whew." Kema poked out her lips then sucked them back in. "Sheesh. It's getting hot in here."

"*So, take off all your clothes!*" Tee-Tee sang popping his ass.

Gabe and his boys looked at him like they wanted to throw up as the guys walked back in. Just like in the past, LaLa was right behind Cam following him around like a lost puppy. Cam was good and high now. His eyes were at half-mast and bloodshot red. He was so lifted that couldn't shit faze him.

"Who is these niggas in my shit?" Quan quizzed.

"This my boyfriend." Heidi squeezed Gabe's arm.

The guys could tell Heidi's nigga meant something to her. As long as they knew her, she'd never brought a man around.

"What's going on, fam?" Quan decided to be nice.

"Gabe." He introduced himself.

"Quan. What's going on?" Quan moved past him and made his way over to Kema.

Gabe shook hands with the rest of the fellas. Right off the bat Cam didn't like him. He could tell the nigga was shifty. He didn't even look him in the eye when he spoke. Real men look other men in the eye when they interacted.

"You stay by yourself?" Gray continued her investigation.

"Nah, I stay wit' my mama." Gabe wisecracked. "Yeah, I stay by myself."

Cam's antenna immediately went up. Gabe played it off like he was joking but he could hear the malice in his voice.

"You got your own crib?" Cam asked to see how he'd respond to him.

Gabe could very well be the kind of dude that didn't like for women to question him. If he did that would be a problem 'cause Gray could ask him however many questions she wanted. Nobody there going to stop her.

"I got my own everything. What you mean?" He replied callously.

"If ya'll don't leave this man alone and let him chill wit' his girl." Dylan reasoned.

"What you mean? She invited some nigga up in our shit that we ain't never seen before. Fuck you talkin' about?" Cam snapped.

He didn't even all the way like for Dylan to be around. Anybody remotely associated with Gunz was an enemy to him.

"I'ma grown ass man tho. You and the Smurfette's ain't gotta 21 question me." Gabe flexed his manhood to let niggas know he wasn't playing.

Cam sucked his teeth and chuckled. Gabe was a clown. He wasn't even worth breaking a sweat for.

"What's up with the tan print on your left ring finger, homeboy?" Kema cut straight to the chase.

Heidi looked down at his hand. Sure enough, there was a ring print there.

"I wear my class ring on that hand." Gabe put his hand in his pocket.

"Your class ring, huh?" Gray frowned.

"Is that really his answer?" Kema looked at her.

"I think he just lied to our faces." Gray cocked her head to the side.

"I think so too."

"Are we gon' have to fuck this nigga up?"

"I think we are, and I've been doing good all week." Kema cracked her knuckles.

"What is going on? What are ya'll talkin' about?" Heidi became upset.

"He's married, bitch!" Tee-Tee blurted out loud.

"Shut yo' faggot ass up!" Gabe warned.

"Bitch, please. I'm more of a man than you."

"Watch your mouth, Gabe. Don't talk to my friend like that." Heidi said with a menacing glare. "And he's not married. He couldn't be."

"Really, Heidi? Think about it? Look at his finger. You only see him on the weekend. You can barely get this nigga on the phone. Plus, you ain't never been to his house. What more evidence do you need, sis?"

"She need to meet his wife." Tee-Tee wisecracked.

"I ain't come here for your friends to be interrogating me and shit." Gabe withdrew his arm from around Heidi's neck.

"They're just overprotective of me. I know you're not married . . . right?"

"So now your friends putting shit in your head and you believing 'em? Have I ever lied to you?"

"No but babe it does look kinda sus." She argued.

"Man, if I knew you was gon' be on this type of bullshit I would've stayed at home. I called off today to spend time wit' you so I can meet your folks and you got these bitches disrespecting me."

"BITCHES?" Kema and Gray said in unison.

"Ya'll heard what the fuck I said. Bitches!"

"Oh, see now this pussy got me fucked up." Kema uncrossed her legs.

Quan held her back.

"You say what now?" Cam stepped up.

The energy in the room instantly shifted. Some shit was about to go down.

"You heard me." Gabe refused to back down.

"Stop playin' wit' me bro." Cam could feel his crazy kicking in.

"You heard me correct, nigga."

"Baby, calm down." Devin blocked his path.

"Fall back. Grown men talkin'." He moved her out the way. "On God, stop playin' wit' me. I don't even know you like that." He got up in Gabe's personal space.

"Yo' I'm about to go." Gabe shot past Cam.

"Wait!" Heidi tried to stop him as Delicious walked in.

"Gabe? What the hell you doing here?" He placed his hand on his hip.

Everyone's eyes landed on Gabe. Like a deer in headlights he stood frozen. Not a word came out of his mouth.

"Delicious, you know this fraudulent-ass nigga?" Kema asked ready to box.

"This Brooke's husband. You know Chyna's ex-friend."

"I TOLD YOU HE WAS MARRIED!" Gray stomped her foot.

"You married for real?" Heidi's bottom lip quivered.

"Going on five years." Delicious confirmed. "But wait a minute. What you doing here? Who you here wit'?"

"He's here with me. He's my boyfriend." Heidi cried. "At least I thought he was."

"Well, your boyfriend got a wife and that wife like to fight."

"And so, the fuck do we." Selicia rolled her neck and jogged in place like a prize fighter.

"I'm about tired of ya'll lonely, nosey-ass bitches. Mind your fuckin' business." Gabe shot taking Heidi into his arms. "Stop crying, babe. Let me talk to you outside."

"No, you can talk to her right here!" Gray pulled her back. "You ain't about to isolate her so you can feed her a bunch of bullshit."

"You would know about feeding wit' yo' wide load ass. Maybe if you stop eating so damn much you would have a man of your own and not be all up in our business." Gabe checked her.

"Pussy, you don't know what the fuck I got. Wit' yo' ugly dusty-ass. I don't even know what my friend see in you. You broke bitch. That's why you out here selling sperm shampoo. You need a fuckin' sports bra!" Gray embarrassed the hell out of him.

"Or a reduction." Kema clenched her fist.

"Titties bigger than both of ours. Cock-eyed bitch!"

"I've been wondering where that nigga been looking all night." Mo said out of nowhere.

"Shit, I thought that nigga was looking at me and I was behind him." Priest date announced.

"Nah, that nigga would've been 6F if he was lookin' at you." Priest confirmed.

"Fuck all ya'll." Gabe threw up the middle finger. "Heidi, lose my muthafuckin' number. You wasn't good for shit but suckin' my dick anyway and you barely did that right."

"Yo' fat-ass act like you doing her a favor." Gray shot on ten. "She don't wanna call that fuckin' iPhone 4 anyway. You can't even Facetime unless you on Wi-Fi. And she probably didn't suck your dick right 'cause she couldn't find it underneath all that stomach. I know that shit stink. Matter of fact, come to think of it, it's been smelling funky over here since you walked yo' fat-ass over here. You balled head, lazy eye, pubic hair on your face having, credit card declining, saggy titty bitch!"

No one saw it coming but the impact of Gabe punching Gray in the head could be heard around the world. He hit her so hard she saw stars. Dazed, she staggered back and fell to the ground. Rage welled up in Cam like deep water currents. The term mad barely touched the surface of how angry he was. Waves of fury soared through his veins. All he saw was red. His vision blurred as a roaring flame of rage activated in the pit of his stomach. You could practically see the fury in his eyes. His fury was so strong it took over his entire body. No way did this muthafucka think he was going to get away with putting his hands on a woman. His woman no less. Didn't niggas know by now that they would die behind fuckin' wit' Gray. Cam's long fingers curled into a fist and crashed against the side of Gabe's face. The blow was so hard blood spewed from his mouth. Gabe's round brown eyes widened as he watched Cam tilt his head back and slam it into his own. A kaleidoscope of stars burst in his vision as Cam continued to pound his head against his. It was at that moment that Gabe realized the nigga that was fucking him up was certified crazy. The headbutts caused a severe gash to open up on his forehead. A never-ending trickle of blood ran down his face. Everyone on the lower level stopped partying and clamored over to witness the fight. The DJ cut the music and signaled for security to head over to the VIP section. When the burly men reached the area and saw it was Cam and his boys making all the ruckus they eased back. Cam's name rang bell in the streets. Security in the past had learned the hard way never to lay a hand on him. They'd let the police deal with him when they arrived. The women in the crowd squealed and covered their faces as Cam brutality beat Gabe to a pulp. Nowhere near done with him, he shoved him to the ground. Gabe tried to get up but quickly realized how futile his attempt was. Cam wasn't letting him go anywhere. The psychotic look in his eyes said he wasn't going to leave there alive. Grabbing a bottle of Ace of Spade, Cam cracked it over his head. A sharp pain pierced Gabe's brain. All he could do was groan in agony. Colorful spots flashed before his eyes. It felt like his entire body had been run over by a Mack truck. Shards of glass were everywhere. It crunched under his feet as Cam used what was left of the bottle to slice his right cheek open. The sharp glass peeled apart Gabe's flesh, making a satisfying squishing sound. Gabe begged and pleaded for mercy, but Cam ignored his shrilling pleas. He wasn't going to be pleased until the color in Gabe's eyes drained away. The visual of his face being sliced open caused some of the clubgoers to vomit. Thick chunks of hot wings and fries splattered to the floor. The whole club watched on in shock with their mouths wide open. They'd never witnessed someone so severely beaten. Gabe was a bloody mess. Both his eyes were swollen, and bloody spit dripped from his slack jaw.

Wanting a piece of the action, Quan lifted his foot and kicked Gabe in the face. There wasn't a man on earth that would get away with calling Kema a bitch. Not willing to see their pot'nah get his ass beat by a psychopath, Gabe's friends jumped in and started raining down blows onto Cam's back. Stacy and Priest didn't hesitate to grab his two friends and beat the shit out of them. Stacy bearhugged one of the guys from behind, damn near breaking every bone in his body with his stronghold. Priest and Quan stomped the other dude out. They tried to stomp his head into the ground. Crimson liquid leaked from their noses and mouths. Blood splattered everywhere. At that point, people started screaming and running for the exit. The massacre that happened years before at the strip club was still fresh in everyone's mind. No one wanted to stick around and become a victim of senseless violence. It was an all-out stampede. Screams of panic echoed in the air as Heidi helped a dizzy Gray off the ground.

"You okay friend?" She checked her face for any damage.

"Yeah." Gray held the side of her head in pain.

"That's what the fuck she get." LaLa laughed. "Just 'cause she big don't mean she can talk to a man any kind of way."

"What the fuck you say? You backwards bitch?" Kema furrowed her brows on ten.

"Did I stutter?" LaLa snapped her neck.

"You know what?" Gray reared her shoulders back. "I've been meaning to fuck you up since All Star Weekend."

Before she could even get her hands on LaLa, Kema came out of nowhere and hit her with a one hitter quitter to the jaw. Kema had been itching to beat a bitch's ass. Using her right hand, she jabbed LaLa repeatedly in the face. A blood vessel burst in her eye. Blood pooled in her mouth as she tried to fight back, but to no avail. Alexzandria tried to grab Kema's hair and drag her to the ground but Gray hit her with a staggering punch to her stomach. Alexandria's guts collided together. Gray continued her assault until she fell helplessly to the floor in the fetal position. Without warning the police came charging in. Quick on their feet, Cam, Quan and Priest slipped out the side exit door. They weren't new to this. They were true to this. Cam would be damned if he went back to jail, especially for a dumb-ass fight. On their rowdy shit the girls kept banging.

"Everybody get down!" One of the officers roared with his weapon drawn.

The other officers started grabbing people one by one. When one of the officers put his hand on Gray, she was so caught up in the fight that she assumed it was someone attacking her and swung on the cop. The next thing she knew, handcuffs were being slapped on her wrists.

"Get your fuckin' hand off my friend, pig!" Kema harked up a gob of spit and spat in the officer's face.

She too was then placed in handcuffs. While everyone was focused on the cops arresting Kema and Gray, Heidi stood off to the side with her eyes on Gabe. He'd been helped off the floor by one of the officers. It was apparent by the wounds and swelling on his face that he'd need medical assistance but that wasn't bad enough. She needed him to suffer some more. He'd lied to her. He'd broken her heart. Picking up Cam's Boosted Board, she methodically broke through the crowd, reared the skateboard back like an MLB pitcher and knocked him across the face with it. All of his front teeth fell out of his mouth as his head was almost knocked off his shoulders.

"Get 'em Homicide Heidi!" Stacy congratulated her.

"That's it! You're going to jail too!" An officer placed her hands behind her back.

346

347

17

"She got my heart in a chokehold."- Emmit Fenn, "Painting Greys"

Devin folded her arms across her chest and tapped her foot repeatedly as she gazed out of the window. It had begun to rain. Trickles of rain slid down the window, matching the tears that dripped down her face. Cam was no good for her. She knew this to be true. Time and time again he betrayed her affections and left her heart in shattered pieces. There were things in life she needed to give up like carbs, caffeine, meat and loving Cam but she could never let him go. A man like him only came once in a lifetime. While staring aimlessly out the window, she wondered was it all worth it. Everything was great while Cam was locked up. They talked several times a day and began planning their future together. Since he'd been home the heartbreak she'd endured because of him came in waves, stealing her appetite and sleep. Every day it was something new with him. She could never find her footing. His kids, Gray and business always seemed to come first. Devin didn't know where or if she fit in his life. She wanted to marry Cam. She wanted to give him a baby, but Gray kept getting in the fucking way.

"I can't believe this shit." She mumbled, getting angrier by the second.

Cam gripped the steering wheel, 'causing his bruised and bloody knuckles to ache. He tried his best to ignore her tantrum but the entire car ride she kept saying slick shit under her breath.

"This nigga got me fucked up." She hissed.

"Aye yo' what's the problem?" Cam finally snapped.

"I'm not gon' answer that. You know exactly what my problem is." Devin continued to gaze out the window.

"I really don't. I ain't no fuckin' mind reader so if you got something to say I suggest you get that shit off your chest 'cause I ain't got time for all that huffin' and puffin' like you gon' blow the house down." Cam kept his eyes on the road.

"Well, since you so fuckin' clueless." Devin turned around in her seat. "Why the fuck are we picking that fat bitch up from the precinct?"

"One, we picking her up cause that's my fuckin' wife. I don't know how many times I gotta tell yo' simple-ass that. Two, you not gon' keep disrespecting her and that's the last time I'ma tell you. I find myself having to repeat shit for your dumb-ass too often and it's pissing me the fuck off!"

"And I find myself having to deal with the same bullshit over and over again. Do you wanna be wit' that bitch or wit' me?"

"The way your dumb-ass is getting on my nerves, I don't wanna be wit' neither one of ya'll."

"So, wait a minute. Gray is an option for you. Cause that's basically what you're saying."

"Any bitch that I put my dick in is still an option for me." Cam quipped, nonchalantly.

Devin's mind went blank as she stared at him in horror. At that moment, she realized she'd been misconstruing his actions and his words. She and Cam were on two totally different pages. As the days passed, he distanced himself further away from her even though she begged for his time and affection. The only emotion he seemed to conjure when it came to her was anger, annoyance or lust. What had she done to make him treat her this way? All she'd ever tried to do was love him. This wasn't how things were supposed to go when he got out of jail. He was supposed to get out and sign the divorce papers so they could live happily ever after. Gray and her raggedy-ass kids had ruined everything.

"Did you really just say that to me?" She gasped, appalled.

"Hell, yeah, and I'ma tell you some more shit since yo' ass can't comprehend." Cam placed the car into park and scowled at her. "That's my wife! We may not be good right now but that's still my wife. Not some bitch I'm just fuckin'! She's the mother of my fuckin' kids. I'm not about to have her sittin' in no cell lookin' crazy 'cause you in yo' fuckin' feelings. I been home seven days! Seven fuckin' days and I have found out I got three kids, I got Victor on my back, got shot, a nigga threatened my kid, I'm in this gay-ass wedding, I gotta write a fuckin' stupid-ass speech, I cussed in church, bodied a nigga and now I gotta go bail my baby mama outta jail. You think I got time to be going back-and-forth wit' you and dealing with your insecure bullshit?"

Devin sat emotionally bankrupt. Cam had destroyed her. Nothing she seemed to say or do was good enough.

"Ever since you came home you've been putting her before me? Why the fuck is she even so special? Are you fuckin' her?"

"I fucked her . . . yes."

Devin's heart dropped.

"Are you fuckin' kidding me?"

"Don't ask questions you don't want the answer to."

"So, you had the audacity to fuck that obese bitch after everything she's done to you. She left you, remember? She kept you from seeing your kids. Yet and still you run after her every chance you get. You know how that makes me feel? I have done everything for you, Cam. I literally put my life on hold for you—"

"I ain't ask you to do that." He cut her even deeper.

"That's not the point. I did it cause I wanted to. You ain't been coming home. You don't answer my calls. Only time we on the same page is when you wanna get your dick sucked and I'm tired of that shit. I only put up wit' your nonsense because I love you. But you obviously don't love me. You won't even say that shit back. Is it because you still love her?" Her bottom lip trembled.

As much as she tried to hold back her tears, Devin's attempts were futile. Beads of water trailed down the plains of her face with no sign of stopping. She really didn't want to know the answer, but the question was already out there. She couldn't take it back now. Cam slumped down in his seat. He didn't even need to respond. His silence was lethal in its nothingness. It showcased how vapid their conversation had become. It was useless. Cam didn't even attempt to save her feelings. His silence proved he didn't give a fuck about her. Cam ran his hand down his face, exasperated. This was not the conversation he wanted to have. He had to get inside and post Gray's bail.

"Do you love me?" Devin cried, grabbing his hand.

"Man, go head." Cam tried to take his hand from her.

"No! Answer the fuckin' question!"

Hating to be grabbed on, Cam yanked his arm away.

"Stop! Stop!" Devin tried to make him face her. "Answer the question!"

"No."

"Answer it!"

"I just did. No." Cam looked at her like she was crazy.

Devin wanted to spit in his face but knew she wouldn't survive the aftermath.

"You don't love me?" She questioned in disbelief.

"No."

"You don't love me? Really? So, you don't love me?" She tried to make sense of his words.

"Look, man. I ain't tryin' to get you upset. I appreciate everything you've done. I don't want you to think that shit went unnoticed. Why you think I copped us a crib? I'm tryin' to see what's up wit' you but you making it hard. I need peace right now. I don't wanna hear a bunch of rah-rah shit every five minutes. That shit is nerve rackin' dawg. It's too much going on in my life. I don't need you adding to it. I ain't tryin' to be selfish but if this is too much for you to handle, I can respect that. I need time to reset. On some real shit, if I'm being honest, I don't even need to be in no relationship. Every chick I fuck wit' I treat like the one that cut me deep. That's why I always end up here. I ain't tryin' to do you dirty shorty. You deserve more

352

than what I can give you. You deserve to be someone's everything, the reason their heart beats, the one a nigga come to when the world feels too tough."

"Is that what Gray is for you?"

"She used to be." Cam replied, honestly. "Look, you can have the crib. I'll move out. 'Cause at the end of the day, I wanna make sure you're happy and if I'm not making you happy then we don't need to be together."

"But I don't wanna break up wit' you." Devin wept on the brink of losing it.

"I hear you, but you need to understand, Gray is gonna be in my life forever. She ain't going nowhere and neither are my kids, so you need to figure out what you wanna do 'cause my family gon' always come first. That's the reality of this situation. The question is can you handle that?" Cam gave her one last look before he got out.

The world around Devin turned into a blur as she sat alone in the car. Nothing was the same. Everything had disappeared. The last of her tears dripped from her chin before she lost the feeling of feeling anything. Cleaning her face with a tissue she'd found in the glove compartment, she checked her face in the rearview mirror. She didn't need to think that hard. Breaking up with Cam wasn't an option. She'd continue to suck it up and deal with his shit in hopes that she'd come out on top. Gray and her brats would be gone back to Paris soon. Once she was out of sight, she'd be out of mind and then she and Cam would be able to get back on track. When she walked into the precinct the whole crew was standing around. Quan had already bailed out Kema, Stacy, Selicia and Heidi. Cam stood at the counter asking about Gray.

"She's been released on her recognizance. She should be walking out." The female officer let him know.

353

"How did that happen? We all had to post bail."
Kema questioned, confused.

"My uncle did me a favor." Some guy answered.

Everyone turned and looked at the mysterious man.
Cam had never seen the nigga before. Sizing him up, he
peeped his low-cut Caesar, small eyes, neatly lined beard,
and arm full of tattoos. The dude looked to be around six
feet tall and weighed 200 pounds. Off rip, Cam could tell
he wasn't a street nigga. The nigga looked too sweet. He
was a pretty boy that thought 'cause he worked out that
made him tough.

"Who the fuck are you?" He growled.

"He's my boyfriend." Gray stated nervously from
behind.

"And I'm the dumb-ass." Devin chuckled in
disbelief.

———

A crushing pain throbbed in the middle of Gray's
head as she watched thunder crack against the night sky.
Back and forth the windshield wiper went. The sound of
the rubber brushing against the window annoyed some
people, but Gray liked it. It soothed her. A tsunami of rain
poured from the heavens. The air was thick with humidity.
Noon kept his eye on the slick road while doing 70 on the
highway. The muscles in his arms strained as he gripped
the steering wheel. The ride home from jail had been
stressful to say the least. He was pissed and he had every
right to be. Gray had completely blindsided him with her
ratchet behavior.

"So, I guess I'ma have to start this conversation off since you not gon' say nothing." He looked at her then focused back on the highway.

Gray closed her eyes and did and internal and external sigh. She didn't know what to think or feel. So much had gone down in the last few hours. The conversation he'd broached was not one she wanted to have but knew was necessary.

"Explain to me why I haven't been in town three hours and I'm calling in favors to get you released from jail? What is going on? This is not the Gray I know. The Gray I know wouldn't be caught dead in a jail cell."

"That's exactly it. You don't understand the dynamics of my life back here. I barely understand it. That's why I didn't want to come back. It's just one thing after another. This place brings out the worst in me." She tried to focus on the discussion and not the searing pain in her head.

"I see." Noon agreed. "Why were you fighting tho?"

"A nigga disrespected me, and he got violated."

"He got what?" He glanced at her. "Who are you right now?"

"What are you talking about?"

"Do hear yourself? The Gray I know back in Paris don't talk like this. You sound like a whole nigga. Who am I dating, Griselda Blanco?"

"If you only knew." She mumbled.

"And what is going on between you and your kids father? I thought you said you were going to tell him about me?"

"That was my intention but so much has been going on that I hadn't gotten around to it yet." She lied.

Noon knew she was lying too.

"Other things like what? From my understanding you came here to do wedding shit."

"I am but other things have come up." Gray turned around in her seat and took his free hand.

My god he's beautiful, she thought.

"I know I'm asking a lot but just trust that I have your best interest at heart. I wouldn't have invited you here if I didn't care about you. I want to see where things between us will go. My life is just so hectic right now. I feel like everything is spiraling out of control."

"I'm trying to be understanding but you're right. You are asking a lot. It's a bunch of shit you not telling me and I'm not feeling it."

"I know." Gray kissed the back of his hand.

She truly felt bad that she'd put Noon in such a complicated situation. Having to explain to him why she hadn't told Cam about their relationship wasn't something she'd prepared for. It only added to her stress. Anybody with eyes knew she hadn't told Cam about seeing someone else because she was still in love with him. When she was in Paris, her feelings for Cam seemed nonexistent. She was too busy being worried about her children to think about her marriage to Cam. After the birth of the triplets it was years before she even started to date again. By the time Noon came into her life, she was more than ready to date

356

but Gray was determined to take things slow. She had five children and was still technically married. Plus, she'd rushed into her last two relationships. She didn't want to make the same mistake three times in a row. Noon was sexy as hell, successful, had great dick and treated her well. He was the total package. He knew she was married and respected the fact that her situation wasn't ideal to a budding relationship. Despite the many roadblocks ahead, he insisted on perusing her. Gray was not only beautiful but successful. She would make the perfect mate for any man. Noon wanted her bad, especially since she'd made it clear that her intention was to divorce her husband. But until she and Cam figured out their situation, there was no way she could give all of her heart to him.

"Just tell me. Have things changed? Are you having second thoughts on divorcing him? 'Cause I don't want to end up looking like a fool. It wouldn't be good for me or you." He lowkey threatened her.

The threat however went over Gray's head.

"You have nothing to worry about. I just need to get through this wedding and then I will be able to put all of my focus and attention on you."

The earnest expression on her face sucked Noon in. Gray had heartbreak written all over her, but he couldn't avoid the inevitable shredding of his heart. He wanted her and what Noon wanted he often got. He just prayed that with Gray things wouldn't be any different.

———

BAM! BAM! BAM! BAM!

After the bomb Gray dropped on him, Cam couldn't do shit but walk away. If he didn't leave, Quan and them would be watching him get placed in handcuffs. Gray had done it this time. How the fuck did she call herself having a fuckin' boyfriend? She hadn't told him shit about messing with another nigga. She'd been in town a full fucking week and hadn't said shit. He wondered if she got off on keeping shit from him. Lies slipped out of her mouth like melted butter running down a hot piece of toast. Murder was on Cam's brain as he pounded on her door. He told his self once he left the precinct, he was going to cut Gray out of his life permanently. If it didn't concern their children, he wanted nothing to do with her. He couldn't trust her. What scared him the most was that she did it with such ease and finesse. He wanted to snap her fuckin' neck. She did nothing but feed him lie after lie but here he was on her fuckin' doorstep at 4:00 a.m. Images he'd conjured up of her and her so-called boyfriend filled his head. Cam envisioned him lifting her up and throwing her down onto the bed then undressing her slow. His stomach dropped as he imagined him ogling every inch of her voluptuous frame. Cam knocked even harder as he thought about him hooking her legs in his forearms and inserting his dick inside her warm, gushy slit inch by aching inch. Gray always loved the first thrust. She'd tilt her head back, bite her bottom lip and moan out in extasy.

"GRAY OPEN THE FUCKIN' DOOR!" He punched the door like it was her face.

Each pound of his fist left smudges of his blood on the door.

"If you don't stop bamming on my fuckin' door." She undid the lock and faced him.

After taking two, extra-strength Advils, Gray had just fallen asleep. The punch she'd received from Gabe gave her a massive headache. She didn't have time to argue with Cam. She'd argued with Noon enough. Gray was tired of explaining herself to the men in her life. After their therapy session with Pastor Edris, she contemplated on telling Cam about Noon. She wanted to be honest and transparent, but she knew he'd flip. She couldn't tell him she had a man without him threatening to kill her or actually killing Noon. And yes, he had a whole girlfriend, but Gray didn't wanna risk making Cam upset with her. She hated when they were at odds. Things were already bad between them. She didn't wanna make it worse.

Cam's furious gaze wandered down to her erect nipples. The black lace trimmed silk negligee she wore had a deep slit that exposed her left thigh. Three gold chains with her wedding rings attached adorned her neck. Cam didn't know it but every night she took them off the triplets and wore them to bed. The sight warmed his heart, but it didn't take away the sting of knowing she'd omitted the truth yet again.

"That nigga here?" He eyed her with contempt.

"No." She gripped the door handle tightly.

Gray would never show it, but she was afraid for her fuckin' life.

"Where is he?"

"At the hotel he's staying at?"

Cam pushed the door open and bogarted his way inside. He was out of control with rage. He needed to smash something. Since he couldn't smash her face or slice her nigga's throat, he picked up a glass vase.

"You bet not." Gray warned.

Flexing his arms, Cam gritted his teeth and growled like a bear. Gray took the vase from his hand and sat it back down.

"What the hell are you doing? You have no business being here this late. The kids are asleep."

"He been around my kids?" Cam towered over her.

"No." Gray groaned, annoyed.

She would never introduce another man to the triplets without him knowing. Especially since he had no idea the triplets even existed until a few days ago. Things between she and Noon were still fairly new. She liked him a lot but didn't know exactly where their relationship was going. The fact that she'd even invited him to the wedding was a huge step for her.

"He bet not have." He pointed his finger in her face like a gun.

"Do it again and I'll break that fucker off." She warned, noticing the cuts and scrapes on his knuckles.

Without saying a word, she walked to the nearest bathroom and grabbed a First Aid Kit. When she returned to the living room, Cam was pacing the floor.

"Sit yo' crazy-ass down."

Cam mean-mugged her. Who the fuck was she to tell him what to do? Gray had the game fucked up.

"You heard what I said."

Groaning, he angrily took a seat on the couch. Gray sat before him on the edge of the coffee table. Lifting his hand, she examined his raw pink flesh. The bleeding had slowed to a trickle, but the damage was evident. It would take weeks for his hand to heal. Using a cotton ball, she dipped it in alcohol.

"This is gonna sting a li'l bit." She cautioned before patting his wounds.

The rubbing alcohol stung but Cam didn't flinch once. Gray still leaned forward and blew softly to ease the pain. Cam's frown deepened. He hated when she did shit like this. The way she took care of him in his time of need could only be described as admirable. Her touch carried so much passion that whatever ailed him healed. She was the sweet addiction he was born to find. Tenderly, she stretched the gauze and wrapped it around his hand then secured it so it wouldn't unravel.

"Why did you do it?" She said out nowhere.

"Do what?"

Gray took her focus off his hand and looked into his somber eyes.

"Gunz called Aoki and told her that his mother, uncle, cousins and Mother Emilia were gone. It was a massacre at her party yesterday. Everybody died except him."

"Karma's a bitch." Cam responded, coldly.

His reply was empathetic but what was he supposed to say? Was he supposed to act like he cared 'cause he didn't? The angel of death was ruthless. There was nothing you could do when it was your time to go.

"I loved them." Gray's voice cracked.

She'd cried herself to sleep when she learned the news. It was horrific. To know that Cam was behind the death of so many innocent people made her see him in a new light. He was just as psychotic as Gunz. She'd left one psychopath for another. What did that say about her? Was she crazy too?

"They were like family to me."

361

"I love my family more." Cam's deep voice reverberated throughout the room.

Knowing she wasn't going to get anywhere with him, Gray dropped the subject. Gunz had threatened their child and tried to kill Cam twice. The only way to pay for that was with death.

"Is your arm better?"

"That shit alright. Them niggas couldn't even shoot." Cam replied nonchalantly.

"Have you found out anything on who snitched?" She prayed to God he had.

"Nah." He looked the other way.

Cam didn't want to see the look of sadness on her face when he said no. Time was ticking down and things were starting to look grim for Gray and their family. The stress of not knowing how things were going to play out was stressing both of them. For a while, neither of them said a word while they pondered her fate.

"I can't believe that nigga hit you."

"I can. He's a bitch."

"You a'ight?" He massaged her head.

"I'm fine. Reign hit hard than that nigga." She savored the feel of his touch.

"How long you been wit' him?" Cam changed the subject.

"Eight months." She avoided eye contact and closed the kit.

Cam sucked his teeth.

"Eight fuckin' months." He repeated outraged. "What's his name?"

"Noon."

"What kinda stupid-ass shit is that? That nigga don't know how to tell time?"

"Shut up." Gray laughed.

"The fuck is his government?"

"Aubrey Simmons."

Cam inhaled deep and shook his head.

"You dating a nigga named Aubrey, Gray?"

"What? I think it's cute." She shrugged, sheepishly.

"So, when the fuck were you gon' tell me about this soft-ass nigga?"

"Umm . . ." Gray placed her hand on her chest. "I'm sorry but I don't I have to tell you who I date. Let's not forget you got a whole bitch that you stay with, sir. You don't get to be mad."

"I can be whatever the fuck I wanna be." He argued like a child.

"Let's not forget, you introduced the triplets to Devin and didn't even ask me how I felt about it."

"You damn right I did. You pissed me off when you apologized to Mo instead of saying I'm sorry to me."

"Whatever." She waved him off.

She was so sick of the tit-for-tat bullshit. She and Cam were in over their heads. Things had spiraled out of control. There was no way for them to get to the other side of pain without drowning. Both of them were tired. Their bodies were weak. They'd done nothing but waste each other's time with their nonstop bickering.

"How he get you released without bail?" He died to know.

"He called in a favor from a family friend."

"Has he been here the whole time?"

"He just got in from Paris tonight."

"You love him?"

The question slipped out of Cam's mouth before he could take it back. It would kill him if she said yes.

"You love her?" She countered, folding her arms underneath her breasts.

"Answer the fuckin' question." He demanded, smacking her thigh.

"You answer first." She mushed him in the head.

"I take that as a yes." He thought of ways to kill her without leaving a trace.

"Take it how you wanna take it."

"You know I'm bodying that nigga, right?"

"Haven't you done enough killing this week?" She gave a mock-glare.

Cam couldn't help but grin. Gray narrowed her eyes. She didn't find shit funny.

"If I ask you something, will you tell me the truth?" She probed, playing with his chain.

"Depends on what it is."

"Did you fuck her after you fucked me?"

Knowing Gray, he knew she wouldn't ask such a question if the thought hadn't affected her. She was jealous. He lowkey liked that he could get her riled up. Despite her steely nature it showed she cared.

"No, but I let her suck my dick."

Gray didn't know whether to be happy or offended.

"You fucked him?"

"Yep." She stood, needing space.

Cam gripped her hips and stopped her from walking away. Her words hit him hard like a freight train. Knowing she'd fucked someone other than him was a nightmare come true. He wanted to wake up, but this was his reality. Quan had warned him years before that this would happen, but he never believed him. His exact words were: *You saw what I went through wit' your sister. You know how fucked up I was when I saw her wit' Boss and the twins for the first time? I was sick. I could barely get my ass outta bed. I felt like a bitch. That shit had me laid up in the fetal position, straight up. That was supposed to be us, but because of my dumb-ass decisions, I ruined anything we could ever be. Keep it up and you gon' end up just like me. I'm tellin' you, ain't nothin' worse than seeing the woman you love, love somebody else.* Cam took it all as a joke. He'd let his ego believe that she'd never move on from him. Boy was he wrong. How was it possible that God could inflict so much pain? Gray was the love of his life. Without her, who would calm his fears? Who would hold his hand to ensure he didn't fall? Who would love him and tell him everything would be okay? Not her. She was with someone else. His best friend, his wife, his soulmate was gone. With time she'd forget all about him. Between his legs, she flushed with distress. Anytime Cam put his hands on her, the seat of her thong became slick with juices.

"Was it good?"

"Delicious." She said out of spite.

"Petty ass."

"Whatever."

"Is he better than me?" He pulled her down and made her straddle his lap.

Gray could feel his dick grow underneath her.

"Don't ask me questions you don't want the answer to."

"Yo, Gray, this night been fucked up enough. This is not the time to play wit' me."

"Who said I was playing?" She arched her brow.

"My dick, the way you was cumming all over it yesterday, but I forgot. You don't remember."

"I remember everything about yesterday." She smirked devilishly.

"You can't tell me you ain't Satan. Had me lookin' crazy in front of all our friends for nothin'."

"Oh, it was for something alright."

"Hold up. You lied cause of that nigga. You ain't want him to know I turned Miss Kitty into Miss Cat?"

"Let me go." Gray tried to push him away.

"Nah, don't run now. Keep it real wit' a nigga for once in your life."

"Keep it real about what?"

"Is he better than me?"

"Is she better than me?" Gray countered.

"Only on Tuesdays and Thursdays. And stop answering my question wit' a question." He smacked her hard on the ass.

Inhaling deep, Gray closed her eyes and sighed. Her back was up against the wall. She didn't wanna lie but she also didn't wanna tell the truth. Giving an arrogant nigga like Cam an inch was like giving him a mile.

"No." She admitted, feeling defeated.

"No what?" He quizzed, watching her every move.

Gray licked her lips and opened her eyes. They landed on his.

"No, he's not better than you."

A slow elated smile burst onto his face.

"I knew it!" He punched his bruised fist inside his other hand.

"You don't have to be an asshole about it."

"I'm just sayin'. I knew that nigga wasn't fuckin' you right."

"How you know that?"

"C'mon, Gray. The nigga had on Hush Puppies."

"No, he didn't." She playfully hit his chest.

"Yes, he did and yo' ass came like thirty times, so I know that nigga ain't been doing shit. You might as well move back here. Ain't shit in Paris, including good dick."

"Dick ain't everything. If it was, me and you would still be together." She ran her hands down the back of his head and got lost in his touch.

His hold on her ass cheeks had her insides doing summersaults. Cam's hard dick pressed against her eager clit. Flushed with desire, she grinded her hips into his steel erection.

"Is that right?" He used his long fingers to grip her waist.

Gray could feel his hardness right against her clit. Cam admired the way her heavy breasts jiggled as she rotated her hips in a clockwise motion.

"Yep. Sex between us was never the problem. We were very compatible in that area." Caught up in the moment she, placed a small kiss on his cheek.

"You like fuckin' me, Gray?" Cam savored her kisses and the way she dutty wine on his dick.

"Yep."

"You wanna fuck me now?"

"Uh huh." She licked and bit his earlobe.

"Tell me what you want then."

"I want you to fuck me." She whispered.

"And what else?" He slipped his hand under her nightie.

Gray pressed her lips against his. Cam's body instantly loosened as he kissed her back. His and Gray's lips fit together like two puzzle pieces. Finding her swollen clit, he rubbed her gently. Pleasure surged through Gray as he applied the perfect amount of pressure to her aching bud. Cam felt just as good as when she played with herself.

"I want you to make me come." She said coming up for air.

"How bad?"

"Real bad. Fuck me, Cam." She sucked his bottom lip and grinded against him like she was riding his cock.

Fully aroused, Cam took hold of her face and blessed her with a fiery, passionate kiss. Gray's hands made their way around his chest, feeling each line and muscle of his upper body. Cam explored her physique as well. There wasn't an inch of her that wasn't touched. An eternity passed by before they pulled apart and stared deep into each other's eyes. Hers were full of passion and lust.

"You look so fuckin' sexy." Cam groaned.

Gray's breathing turned labored as he started to drag her clit against his throbbing length. Back-and-forth, he applied the supreme amount of pressure to send her over the edge. Gray hadn't clothes burned since she was a teen, but damn did it feel good. Cam maneuvered her harder. Gray swore all 11-inches of him was inside her. She could feel the friction he'd created in her toes. At any second, she was going to explode.

"Fuck me, Cam. I want you inside of me now." She begged.

"Too bad. You ain't getting shit." He pushed her off his lap.

"What?" She panted bewildered.

"Told you I was gon' make you eat them words, dickhead." Cam bugged up laughing while fixing his pants.

"Get the fuck out! Now!" Gray shot angrily.

"I was leaving anyway. I'm getting the hell away from yo' freak ass." He laughed on the way to the door.

"Fuck you!" She tossed a throw pillow at his head.

"Nope. I'll pass." He dodged the hit.

"Get out!"

"*Never gonna get it. Never gonna get it.*" He sang EN Vogue's *My Lovin'* while wagging his index finger.

"*Neeeeeeeever gonna get it. Never gonna get it. Neeeeeeeever gonna get it. Never gonna get it. Never gonna get it. Woo-woo-woo-woo!*" He Crip walked out the door and left her with a bruised ego and an aching clit.

18

"You gon' miss me when I'm gone."- Iyla, "Shampoo"

The sky blazed blue. Not one cloud was in sight that sunny Friday afternoon. It was scorching hot outside. Ninety-eight degrees to be exact. It was a dry heat that made it nearly impossible to breathe. The only thing to do was stay inside or cool off in the pool all day. Aoki planned to do just that. She'd practically begged her mom to let her and Press go to the community center. The Grace Parthens Community Center was a gift for Cam from Gray. She had it built for him before they broke up. Since it's opening, the Grace Parthens Community Center had become a staple for kids and teens all over St. Louis. Everything in it was state of the art. There was a full gym, rock-climbing wall, children's garden, dance room, computer room, cafeteria and a basketball court. There was even an auditorium dedicated in memory of Diggy. Kids couldn't wait for summer. Most of them didn't have access to a pool, so when it opened, the community center was the place to be. Kids from the North side, West side and South City came to swim, play and learn. Kema, Heidi and Tee-Tee had done a phenomenal job running the place in Gray's absence. She couldn't thank them enough for all of their help. It meant the world to her that Aoki and Press wanted to kick it there, but the wedding was only two days away. Gray didn't have time to take them. Kema had her on a tight leash. There were still so many things that had to be done before the ceremony. Going to the pool wasn't one of them. Melody offered to take the girls, but when Cam

371

found out they wanted to go, he offered to not only take Aoki and Press but the triplets as well. He hadn't been to the community center since the day Gray surprised him with it. While locked up he learned from Quan that Gray's friends were the ones running the place and that it was doing exceptionally well.

Taking the kids to the center was supposed to be for them but Cam needed to blow off some steam. No one in the streets knew anything about who'd snitched, and his lawyer still hadn't gotten back from vacation. He needed his case file asap. If there was information that could help him save Gray, he needed to use that to his advantage. He couldn't leave one stone unturned. At this point it was his only hope. A good pick-up game with the fellas would do him some good. He needed something to take his mind off all the pressure in his life. Gray was unsure about him taking the kids alone. It would be the second time he took them by himself. When he took the kids to Aunt Vickie's house, she was cool. Having her around to assist him was a major stress relief. Taking them to a busy community center where there would be fifty million kids was a whole other story. She wasn't sure Cam would be able to handle it. Keeping track of three rambunctious toddlers, a curious nine-year old and a thirteen-year-old who was going on thirty was too much for Gray to handle on most days. She knew damn well Cam wouldn't be able to keep up. He was still getting used to the idea of even being a dad. After much convincing and begging from Aoki and Press, she agreed to let them go but not without packing everything they might need in case of an emergency.

It was noon by the time they arrived at the center. Cam gazed up at the building. A proud smile stretched across his face. Almost four years had passed, and the place still looked brand spanking new. Kema, Tee-Tee and Heidi had done a great job keeping the place up. He could almost guarantee that his mom and Diggy were in heaven smiling down on them. Taking the triplets out of their car seats one by one, he grabbed their diaper bag, healthy snacks, pool toys, floaties and stroller. Cam was tired already and hadn't even left the parking lot. He never realized that having kids meant carrying around so much stuff. Aoki and Press helped him carry the things he couldn't. Thank God they did because there were children everywhere. The staff was doing a great job at keeping the chaos controlled. There were computer classes, ballet lessons and art class going on, but majority of the kids were at the pool.

"I'ma be in the gym. Aoki, keep an eye on your sister."

"Ya'll act like I'm not thirteen and a half. I'm practically grown, Pop. I got this. Chill." She smacked her lips.

"Somebody change one fuckin' diaper and think they grown." Cam gave her a mock-glare. "Just do what I said, Li'l Boosie, and stay yo' bad ass outta trouble."

"I left the strap at home. I'm chillin' today." Aoki scoped the scene for any haters.

"The sad part is you're probably serious but a butter knife ain't no fuckin' strap, Aoki."

"I upgraded from butter knives a long time ago. I got the 9m on deck. Fuck wit' ya' girl."

It was at that moment that Cam realized that his daughter was a real live hood chick. He was going to have to keep a close eye on her. Aoki was more like him than he would care to admit. The girl was crazy as cat shit. Like him, she would have to learn how to contain her crazy and use it for good and not for evil.

"Me and you gon' have a talk when we get home."
He pointed his finger in her face.

"Took ya'll long enough." Ryan walked over in a
huff.

"Yeah, we been waiting on ya'll all day." Makiah
stepped by her sister's side. "Hey, Uncle Cam."

"Oh, hell nah!" Cam shouted once he saw his
nieces. "Ya'll some fake-ass Migos. Got me up here on a
mission. Ya'll got me fucked up. Ya'll think ya'll slick.
You wanted to come up here so you and your cousins could
be on some hoe shit. Not on my watch. I'm going to the
pool wit' ya'll."

"Nooooo." Aoki and Makiah wailed.

"In the kitchen, wrist twistin' like a stir-fry." Ryan
did the Chicken Head.

"See! Fuck no! She talkin' about whipping up crack
and shit! Fuck that! We going home!" Cam started pushing
the triplets towards the door.

"No, Pop. Wait." Aoki pulled him back. "I swear
we not gon' even get in the water. We on our pretty girl shit
today."

Cam squinted his eyes and shot her a frightening
glare to see if she was telling the truth. Aoki gave him the
saddest puppy dog face she could muster and hoped he'd
fall for it. He did hook, line and sinker.

"A'ight. I'ma let ya'll have fun and do ya'll but
ya'll bet not be on no fuck shit or I'm whoopin' all ya'll.
On my mama, everybody dying."

"We get it. You a shooter. *Bang-Bang*." Ryan
mocked, rolling her eyes.

"I will really fuck yo' li'l bad-ass up. Where is yo' mama at anyway?"

"She dropped us off."

"Fuckin' deadbeat. She need to stop having all them damn kids if she ain't gon' watch 'em, but that ain't none of my damn business. Ya'll go out there to that pool, sit ya'll ass the fuck down, drink some water, put on some sun screen and keep yo' fuckin' legs closed. Don't talk to none of these li'l knuckle head ass niggas around here."

"Okay, Uncle Cam. We get it." Makiah groaned.

"Uncle Cam, we get it." Cam imitated her whiny voice.

"Shut up!" He scowled. "Ya'll be good." He gave Aoki and Press a kiss on the forehead and watched as they walked off.

The girls were growing up too fast. He truly hated that he'd missed years of their lives.

"How you deal wit' him?" Makiah said to Aoki. "He get on my damn nerves."

"Aye!" He stopped them.

"Huh?" The girls and half the other kids in the common area turned around.

"Quit all that muthafuckin' cursing!"

Before Cam could embarrass them any further, the girls scurried to the entrance door that led to the pool. Feeling herself, her messy bun, Chloe shades, t-shirt and Chanel slides, Aoki prepared herself to have some big girl fun. Popping a piece of gum, she pushed open the door to heaven. The pool area was lit. The pool itself was rectangular shaped with one section for the diving board.

Beach balls were being tossed around. Some of the girls sat on inflatable doughnuts or unicorns while others played chicken or Marco Polo. The scene was just like in the movie ATL. Sheck Wes summer anthem *Mo Bamba* had everyone up on their feet swaggin' and surfin'. A sea of beautiful brown bodies were scattered around the pool or swimming in it. Aoki loved being around her people. Black culture in Paris was way different, so different she didn't wanna return after the wedding. She and Press had plans on talking to their mom about moving back to St. Louis. She missed her friends, the food, the culture and most of all she didn't wanna leave Priest. Like New-New, Star and Veda, time slowed as Aoki and her girls parted through the crowd. You couldn't tell her they weren't the shit. Like Beyoncé they were feeling themselves. The teenage boys from the neighborhood eyed them with lust. On their pretty girl shit they switched their hips like the queens they were and gave the guys their young-asses to kiss. Huddled up, Damya and her friends whispered and talked shit as they strode by. Aoki looked her up and down and laughed. Damya and her stank-ass friends were the least of her worries. She was just mad 'cause she'd gotten her ass beat by a thirteen-year-old. She better hope Aoki didn't fuck her up again. Every time she looked at the scratches on the back of her legs, she got mad.

Press tucked her towel under her arm and scanned the crowed for King. She knew wherever he was, Sanya wouldn't be far behind. She was like his shadow. Sure enough, King was in the pool playing around with some of his friends. Sanya sat on the edge of the pool watching his every move. Press' heart sank. Since the fight, King had tried calling her several times, but she didn't bother answering. She'd saw a side of him she didn't like the day of the fight. Out of all the people in the world she thought might disappoint her, King wasn't one of them. That day he proved her wrong. She was beyond mad at him. Not only did he not have her back, but he lied to her as well. He said Sanya wasn't a threat to their friendship when really, she was. Press might've been naive and sweet, but she wasn't a fool. Even though she liked King, she would not allow him to go back-and-forth between her and another girl. She'd gladly removed herself from the equation. No matter how much it hurt.

"Damn shawty! What yo' name is?" One of the boys tried to take Aoki's hand.

Aoki quickly snatched it away and kept it pushing. Not because Cam told her not to talk to any boys, but because in her mind, she was already taken.

"Girl, you trippin'. He was cute." Makiah blew a bubble with her gum.

"You holla at him then."

"My daddy ain't about to kill me." She replied as they found a set of chaise lounges.

Once they were all situated, the girls lathered themselves with sunscreen and laid out in the sun. This went on for a half an hour, until the hairs on Aoki's arm stood up. A cold shiver raced down her spine.

"He's here." She sat up and looked around.

"Who's here?" Makiah took off her shades.

"My future husband." Aoki smiled as her eyes landed on her boo.

From head to toe Priest body was covered in tattoos. There wasn't an inch of his skin that wasn't covered in ink. Every portrait was perfectly drawn onto slabs and slabs of hard muscle. Priest looked like he worked out for fun.

There wasn't an ounce of fat on his body. Every girl there had their eyes on him, but he wasn't paying them any mind. He was there to ensure all the kids safety. In his spare time, he volunteered as a lifeguard. Priest was an expert swimmer. In high school he was the captain of his swim team. He and his best friend, Yaasir, made their way to the watchtower. Aoki watched intently as he made sure he didn't physically come in contract with anyone while he walked. With a concentrated look on his face, he counted each step he took until he made it to his destination. Aoki didn't know much about being OCD, but it was apparent Priest had a severe case of it. Every second of the day and night she thought of him. He was her first crush, first love, her muse. In her notebook she drew pictures of his face. One day, she'd paint him on a canvas for the whole world to see.

"I love him." She swooned.

"Girl, give it rest." Makiah groaned, rolling her eyes.

"Right. Our cousin ain't going to jail behind you." Ryan confirmed.

"*Your cousin* and let me find out ya'll still some haters. That is bae right there."

"Sure, he is." Makiah said cynically.

"I'm tellin' ya'll. He feeling the kid. We just had a whole conversation when he was at my house the other day."

"I know that's a lie 'cause Priest don't even talk."

"Yes, he do. He talked to me."

"Prove it." Ryan dared her. "I bet you twenty dollars he pay you dust." She held out her pinky finger.

Never the one to back down from a challenge, Aoki peeled her t-shirt over her head and revealed a red, two-piece string bikini. Her mom had no idea she even owned a bikini, let alone wore one out of the house. If Gray found out, she'd surely get knocked upside the head and placed on punishment.

"You ain't said nothing but a word girlfriend." Aoki twisted her pinky with Ryan's.

On her feet, she unraveled her bun and let her long, curly hair flow down her back. Standing up straight, she pushed her boobs and butt out. All the guys licked their lips as she sashayed by. Aoki's tall, slender frame was every teenage boys fantasy. She had the perfect figure. On a scale of one to ten, she was most definitely a twelve. A lot of the older boys liked her. Because of her height, Aoki looked like she could at least be sixteen. She'd use that to her advantage when she flirted with Priest. Before she even reached him, his eyes were already on her. He didn't look pleased to see her but she couldn't let that deter her. If she punked out, the twins would never let her live it down. At the bottom of the watchtower, she placed one of her hands on her non-existent hip and looked up at him.

"Hey Priest." She said sweetly.

Hoping she'd leave as quickly as she came, he simply hit her with a head nod. He didn't even bother speaking back. The twins were right. He shot her a look like she was stupid then focused back on the kids in the pool. Aoki caught the shade but refused to back down. Her motto was go hard or go home. Priest was gon' feel her one way or another.

"Makiah and Ryan just bet me that I couldn't start a conversation with the finest nigga out here." She trifled, swaying her leg back-and-forth. "What should we do with their money?"

Yaasir bugged up laughing.

"Yo' who is this li'l girl?"

"I'm Aoki. His future everything." She sassed.

"You ain't my future shit." Priest argued back.

"This Cam stepdaughter?" Yaasir asked.

"Yeah." Priest frowned, annoyed.

"She wild as fuck."

"Yo daddy know you out here with this bullshit on?" Priest questioned.

"Oh, you like my bikini? I wore it just for you." Aoki played with the string on her hip.

"Listen, dawg. Take yo' bony, tomboy body back where the fuck you came from fore I beat yo' ass myself. I know Cam don't even know you got that skimpy-ass shit on."

"What he don't know won't hurt him."

"Yo, get the fuck on." He waved her off, done with the conversation.

"*Oww!*" She covered her eye and rubbed it.

Thinking she was hurt Priest jumped up.

"I think there's something wrong with my eyes." She pretended to cry.

"You a'ight?" He asked concerned.

"Yeah." She looked up. "I just can't take them off of you." She cracked a wryly smile.

"Get the fuck away from me, dawg." Priest snapped, pissed.

He didn't have time for Aoki and the ridiculous, school girl crush she had on him.

"I'm sayin' if you were a Transformer, you'd be Optimus *Fine*." She continued throwing out pick-up lines she'd learned on the internet to impress him.

Yaasir was laughing so hard he had to hold his stomach. Priest didn't find shit funny. He wanted Aoki far the fuck away from him.

"Yo' go take your grown-ass back over there with your friends." He ordered.

"Just tell me." She held her hand up in a mock surrender. "Is your name Google 'cause you're everything I've been searching for?"

"She's funny." Some chick said from behind.

Expecting to find a girl her age and height, Aoki turned around. Slowly, her eyes traveled up and then up some more till they landed on the 5 feet 11 Amazon's striking face. Aoki hated her instantly. The color of her skin was fascinating. Burnt Sienna never looked so good on a woman. She had the perfect everything. Perfect hair, perfect eyes, perfect cheekbones and perfect tits. If Aoki was a man, she'd fuck her. Long wavy beach curls cascaded over her C cup breasts, teeny tiny waist and modelesque ass. The tangerine tube top with matching tassels and skirt complimented her reddish-brown skin.

"And you are?" Aoki rolled her neck.

"Be nice and stay in a child's place." Priest jumped down from the watchtower. "What's up, babe?" He kissed the girl on her lips and gripped her ass.

Aoki held her breath, feeling as if she was about to die. *Did he really just kiss this bitch in front of me,* she thought. *The one day I don't bring my shank, niggas wanna act up.* Aoki wanted to spit, curse, scream and cry. He didn't even budge when she came over, but as soon as this bobble-head bitch arrived, he leaped up like a bat out of hell. The disrespect was real. Priest was her man. If she could, she'd wrap him up in her arms and never let him go. Her skin tingled whenever he came around. They were soulmates. She knew it and eventually he would too.

"What you doing here?" He pulled the girl close.

"I thought you might be hungry, so I brought you some lunch."

"Good lookin' out." He took the bag from her hand.

"Who is this cute li'l thing?" She beamed brightly at Aoki.

"Your competition." Yaasir joked.

"I'm Britten." She held out her hand gleefully.

"And I'm your worst fuckin' nightmare." Aoki gave her a handshake.

"She must be one of the inner-city kids that get bussed in?" Britten whispered to Priest.

"Nah, this my cousin daughter, Okoye."

"It's Aoki!" She fumed, balling her fist.

"She gon' fuck you up, cuz." Yaasir grinned.

"*Aw*www I get it. She has a crush on you, babe?" Britten pinched Aoki's cheek like she was a child.

Aoki's temperature rose to a scalding 106 degrees. She was getting tried on several different levels and she didn't appreciate any of it. Priest and his bitch had her messed up.

"You wanna come up in the tower with me while I eat?" He asked his girl.

"Of course. It was nice meeting you, Akira." She waved over her shoulder.

Aoki was so embarrassed all she could do was stand there. Her face reddened with anger. In order to save face, she needed to walk away but her legs wouldn't move. It was as if they were crazy glued to the cement. Across the way, Press lay on her back watching a documentary on eight incredibly clever creatures when she felt the lounge chair she lay on dip. Taking her attention off the phone, she looked to see who was interrupting her fun. It was King. His long hair was pulled up into a man bun. The style showed off all the handsome features of his face. King was too damn cute for his own good. The tan he'd gotten from the sun turned his milk chocolate skin into an onyx playground. That didn't stop her from frowning. Being cute wasn't going to get him off her shit list.

"Can I talk to you for a minute?" His raspy voice gave her goosebumps.

"No." She focused back on the screen.

"C'mon, man, please?" King took the phone from her hand.

"No. I'm not your friend anymore. I don't wanna talk to you." Press folded her arms across her chest defiantly.

"I don't care. I'm still your friend." He reached over and gently pulled one of her curls.

On the outside, Press acted like his sweet gesture didn't faze her, but on the inside, her organs were melting. King swore to keep his hands to his self, but when it came to Press, she was too pretty not to touch.

"You're Sanya's friend, remember? A real friend wouldn't have played me like you did."

"Real friends make mistakes too, right?" He returned his hand to his lap.

"Yeah, but I don't care. I'm good on you King."

"Well, I ain't good on you and I never will be. You can be mad all you want. You still my best friend and ain't nothin' gon' change that."

Press' little heart did a backflip into a split. This was the King she knew and loved. This was the King that she trusted her life with.

"You done?" She shot with an attitude.

King hung his head and chuckled. Press wasn't going to make this easy for him. If anybody else would've disrespected him, they'd be shooting a fair one.

"I'ma let you have that 'cause the way I did you was messed up."

"It was more than messed up. You hurt my feelings."

"It hurt my feelings knowing I hurt your feelings. I ain't even been able to sleep at night and you know my pretty-ass need my beauty rest." He grinned, unabashedly. "For real, I'm sorry."

"Sorry ain't good enough. Ya'll embarrassed me."

"And I already handled that."

"How?" Press challenged.

"Watch this. Sanya!" He shouted. "Come here!"

"What you callin' her over here for?" Press sat all the way up.

She needed to be ready in case things went left. No way was Sanya going to catch her slipping. *I'ma bad bitch. I'ma bad bitch,* she reminded herself.

"Just chill. Ain't nothin' gon' happen to you." King assured, rubbing her leg.

He could tell she was nervous. Stomping her feet, Sanya walked over to them. She made no effort to hide her attitude. She didn't want to talk to Press as much as Press didn't wanna talk to her.

"I'm here, now what?" She pursed her lips and stood back on one leg.

"What did we just talk about? Fix your attitude." King glared at her with disdain.

"*Huuuuuuuh* I'm sorry." Sanya whined, stomping her foot some more.

"Don't you got something to say to Press?"

"I'm sorry." She mumbled.

"What? Speak up. I ain't hear you."

"I'M SORRY, DANG!"

"Sorry for what?"

"Really, King?" Sanya pouted, wanting to cry.

"Say no more. Bye Sanya." He dismissed her by turning his back.

"Okay-okay-okay." She made him face her. "You better be glad you cute."

"Get to the point." He barked.

Looking at the sky, Sanya groaned out, "I'm sorry for being mean to you and calling you dumb."

"And what else?" King urged.

"For saying I was gon' slap you."

"And?"

"You not ugly. You're very pretty and I like your hair."

With each word Sanya felt like she was dying a slow death. She would rather eat a worm than apologize to some girl she didn't know and didn't even like.

"Keep going."

"And it will never happen again." She tried to keep it together.

"You ain't finished."

"Please accept my apology." She finally gave Press eye contact.

Not even bothering to accept her apology, Press rose to her feet and left King and Sanya behind. She would be a fool if she accepted her fake-ass I'm sorry. There

wasn't anything genuine about it. She'd only said it
because King made her.

"Where you going?" He ran after her, only to get
pushed into the pool.

Press stood back with a wicked grin, taking in her
dirty work. An apology from him and Sanya wasn't good
enough but shoving him into the pool made her feel ten
times better.

"What you push me for?" He kicked his legs and
rotated his arms to stay afloat.

"The next time you let somebody be mean to me
I'm telling my sister and yo' uncle Cam and we ain't gon'
ever be friends again. You got it?"

"C'mon, man, for real." King frowned.

The thought of not having Press in his life was too
much to bear.

"Yep." She rolled her eyes like a ghetto girl.

Wading in the water, King smiled from ear-to-ear.

"A'ight, I got you. Now jump yo' pretty-ass in this
pool."

———

Inside the indoor gym, a heated game of three on
three was taking place. Cam, Quan and Stacy played
against the homey Bigg, Koran and Kingston. Bigg and
Koran were cool people, but Kingston wasn't Cam's cup of
tea. For many reasons outside of the fact that he'd tried
coming on to Gray years before, he just didn't like the
nigga. Every time he looked at his face, he was reminded of

things from his past that he wanted to forget but circumstances wouldn't allow it. With ten seconds left on the clock the score was 86 to 90. Cam and his boys were in the lead. With his arms spread wide, Kingston tried to guard him, but Cam was quick on his feet. When he was a teenager, he was a high school basketball star with plans to go to the NBA. The sudden death of his mother sidetracked that dream and sent him on a different career path. Basketball was Cam's first love. He loved the sport. Whenever he got the chance to play, a part of him that felt empty was fulfilled. Staring Kingston square in the eye he did a dribble drive, a dribble pound that launched him into a hop then hit him with an Allen Iverson Fade Away as the buzzer sounded. Stacy and Quan ran over and chest bumped him while cheering loudly. Reign even tried to get in on the action, but he was too little.

"That's what the fuck I'm talkin' about! Ya'll niggas can't see me!" Cam boasted while holding his son. "You see daddy bust these niggas ass?"

"I wanna bust niggas ass too." Reign wrapped his arms around Cam's neck.

"Soon, young grasshopper, soon." Cam bounced him up and down as Kingston stormed out of the gym upset.

"That nigga a sore loser." Quan shook his head.

"He gon' cry when in he get in the car." Stacy chuckled.

Clap, Clap, Clap

"Good job, baby." Devin sauntered over, looking like a whole snack.

Cam hadn't expected to see her but welcomed her unexpected pop up.

"I've only been gone a few hours. You miss daddy dick already?"

"You know I do. I can't stay away from you too long. I get sad when you're gone." She trialed her finger nail down the side of his face.

"Is that right?"

"Yep, we miss you." She glanced at him then down to her pussy.

"Oh yeah? That's how you feel?" Cam's dick immediately bricked up.

"I just need a li'l taste then I'll be on my way."

Cam wanted to beat the brakes off her pussy, but he was with his kids and they were at the community center. He'd never disrespect his children or a space that Gray built in honor of his mother.

"I got you later on at the crib." He smacked her ass.

"Boooooooo." Devin gave him a thumbs down.

Ever since the foursome, her and Cam's sex life had plummeted. The only time he touched her was when he wanted his dick sucked. Devin was feenin for the dick, but it was obvious he was giving it to someone else. That someone being Gray. Devin had to find a way to get rid of her ass quick.

"Daddy?" Beaux tugged on the hem of his hooping shorts.

"Yes, doll face."

"I want ice cream."

"Ya'll kids always hungry. I'm starting to think ya'll mama don't feed you."

"She don't. She hog all the food for herself." Devin giggled.

Cam side-eyed her.

"What?" She shrugged. "It was too easy."

"Mommy said no sugar." Sky wagged her index finger like a grown woman.

Gray didn't allow them to have sugary sweets that often, so whenever they were around Cam, they begged for all the things they knew they wouldn't get at home.

"Mommy's not here and so what mommy don't know won't hurt her?" Cam arched his brow. "Who wants some ice cream?"

"*ME!*" The triplets and Stacy raised their hands.

"You gotta promise to keep it a secret tho, okay?"

"We will, daddy. We-we pro-mise." Beaux nodded her head.

"A'ight c'mon. Let's go get some ice cream from the cafeteria."

"Race you to the door." Stacy challenged Sky and Beaux.

Instantly, they took off running. Stacy pretended like he couldn't keep up by jogging at a snail's pace. As they made their way to the cafeteria, Cam noticed Kingston standing outside the entryway of the center talking to Tia.

"Ya'll go head." He urged Devin, Beaux and Sky to follow Stacy.

He and Reign stayed behind. The conversation between Kingston and Tia looked heated. He couldn't hear what they were saying because they were outside, but whatever they were discussing didn't look pleasant. She was visibly distraught. He too was angry. Fed up with the conversation, Tia tried to walk away but Kingston swiftly pulled her back and planted a firm kiss to her lips. Cam watched to see if she'd fight him off, but Tia didn't do anything but wrap her arms around his neck and lean into the kiss. Cam couldn't believe his eyes. He knew Mama Lucy had raised a family of ho's but damn. Tia was straight up messing around with her aunt's baby daddy. Normally, Cam wouldn't be on know bitch shit, but something told him to snap a picture of their tryst. The evidence might come in handy later. Quickly, he snapped several pictures and then made his way to the cafeteria with his kids.

Back at the pool, Aoki gazed absently at the rippling water in a daze. The sun beamed down onto her face, yet her mind was clouded grey. All she could think of is Priest. He'd crushed every hope and dream she had of them being together. Emotionally destroyed she had no energy or will to go on. An old song that her mom liked to play when she was sad by Brandy called *Brokenhearted* came to mind as she stood there. The song described her feelings to a T. Aoki hummed the lyrics as her sapphire eyes burned with tears.

I'm young but I'm wise
Enough to know that you
Don't fall in love overnight
That's why I thought if I
Took my time that everything
In love would be right

But as soon as I closed my eyes
I was saying to love Goodbye

Her thirteen-year-old heart had never felt a pain that cut so deep. Didn't Priest know she'd pull a star out of the sky for him? Anything he asked of her she'd do. Aoki's insides were so raw the wind could blow right through her guts. What was left of her was shattered. Any peace she harbored was now lost. She'd put her all into loving Priest and he'd thrown her love away like it was yesterday's trash. Aoki wanted to hold her head high and be tough, but her resilience had been ripped to shreds. She stood hopelessly trying to keep it together; praying that no one noticed the tears gliding down her cheeks. Priest was only a few feet away. She would die if he saw her cry. Aoki had nothing to worry about. He hadn't given her a second thought. Britten and her perfect existence was all that mattered. They sat up in the watchtower grinning up in each other's faces, kissing and hugging. Aoki balled her fist. It should've been her up there with him. Britten didn't understand him like she did. It was obvious they had more in common. She loved muscle cars just like him. His name was Priest and her sister's name was Press. What more evidence did they need? They were meant to be with each other. Britten was just a pretty face. Some arm candy for him to show off. Aoki wanted to carve both their eyes out with a dull knife so they could feel how she felt. She wanted to throw herself in front of a moving car and die. Her heart still beat, but she felt dead. It was cruel how a person's heart could keep beating even after it had been broken in half. Aoki wished she would've seen this coming, but heartbreak was always unexpected. One minute you're riding the wave of love and the next you're being drowned by it. Life was funny that way.

Wiping her face with her forearm, she looked up to see if the twins were watching her. They were. Aoki was even more embarrassed now. She couldn't go back. She refused to hear them say I told you so. Like a caged animal, she needed to escape but she didn't seek freedom. Aoki wanted to escape from reality. She wanted to exist in an alternate universe where she and Priest were one. Maybe if she did something drastic, she could get him to see how deep her feelings for him flowed. Maybe if she jumped into the pool, she could get him to save her. Visualizing him giving her mouth-to-mouth made her heart skip a beat. The thought gave her hope. Aoki was sure that once his lips touched hers, he'd fall in love. Not giving the crazy idea a second thought, she stepped to the edge of the pool and allowed herself to sink into 12 feet of water.

Aoki was a great swimmer, as long as she didn't go past six feet. After that she became ridden with anxiety. She didn't trust herself or her abilities when she couldn't feel the ground. She remembered this as her body fell further into darkness. The farther down she sank the more the water enveloped her. The coldness she felt upon entering the water vanished. A desperate heatwave washed over her slender frame. The realization that she'd willing allowed herself to drown filled her with deep dread. The frantic beat of her heart matched the fast kicks of her arms and legs. The urgency to breathe took over her body. Why hadn't Priest come to save her yet? Hadn't he seen her fall? It was his job to rescue her from death, literally and figuratively. Surely, he wouldn't let her drown. *But what if he didn't see me,* Aoki freaked out. What if she'd risked her life only to die? Her mother would kill her. *What have I done,* she tried to swim her way to the top, but her body had become too weak? She'd held her breath for as long as she could. Every cell in her body was pleading, no screaming for oxygen. Unwilling to give up, Aoki kept kicking until it felt like her head was going to implode. Black dots filled her eyes. Soon, the tiny dots morphed into huge black blotches and clouded her vision. No longer able to hold her breath the chlorine water filled her lungs. Any hope that she had to survive was gone. Lack of oxygen to the brain caused her eyes to flutter close. As everything faded to black, her heart stopped hammering against her chest. Dying wasn't as bad as Aoki thought it would be. Fear ebbed away. When they found her dead body, Priest would regret ever treating her badly. He'd regret choosing Britten over her. He'd miss her once she was gone. Accepting her fate, Aoki drifted into unconsciousness. The last few seconds of her life were peaceful. Just when she thought her time had come to an end, Aoki felt her body being pulled to the surface.

"Aoki, wake up!" Gray heard Press scream as she and Noon made their way to the pool.

She'd finished helping Kema and decided to pick the kids up early so she could spend some time with them. None of that mattered now. Her daughter was in trouble. Gray's legs started running before she knew what she was doing. All she knew was something was wrong with her baby. She had to get to her. The only problem was she wasn't prepared for what she was about to see. Her first born, her best friend, her heartbeat, one of her greatest loves lay unconscious on the ground receiving CPR from Priest. Dizzy with terror, she fell to her knees in despair. Aoki looked like a cold wet fish. She wasn't breathing and her limbs weren't functioning on their own.

"She can't be dead." Gray covered her face and howled. "God, she can't be. Please. Don't do this to me God. Please."

Noon pulled her into his embrace and held her close. If Aoki didn't wake up, Gray didn't know what she'd do. She'd gladly lay down and die right next to her. She wouldn't be able to live without her child.

"Aoki, wake up! Please." Press begged on the verge of losing her mind.

Aoki was not only her big sister but her idol. She wished she was as beautiful and fearless as she was. Where Press lacked strength and confidence, she got it from her sister. She couldn't lose her. She'd already lost her father. She couldn't lose her sister too. A mob of kids stood around in a circle watching in horror as Priest tried to resuscitate her. Even Damya and Sanya were shook. With his fingers interlocked, Priest performed thirty chest compressions then gave Aoki two rescue breaths. He repeated the steps four times before her blue eyes shot open and she gasped for air. Water sputtered out of her mouth as she coughed profusely.

"Oh, thank God." Gray curled over, relieved.

Racing over to her daughter, she took her wet body into her loving arms and showered her with kisses. Relief wasn't the word to describe how she felt. She was thankful.

"Are you okay?" She rocked Aoki back-and-forth.

"Yeah." Her voice croaked.

"What happened?" Gray continued to cry.

"She jum—" Ryan started to snitch but was cut off by Priest.

"She tripped and fell into the deep end."

Shocked by his response, Aoki guiltily connected eyes with him. The grim look he gave her let her know he knew the truth of what she'd done. Aoki thought Priest wasn't paying her any attention, but he'd been watching her the whole time. He saw her teetering around the pool like a wounded bird. He knew her feelings were hurt but never did he think her li'l crazy-ass would jump in the deep end just to get his attention. Aoki was gustier and more deranged than he thought. After the stunt she'd pulled he was going to stay far away from her. Her obsession with him had gone too far. Aoki adverted her eyes back to her mother's chest. She couldn't take the expression on Priest's face. It was one of pity and repulsion.

"Oh my God. You gotta be careful, Aoki." Gray kissed her again. "Thank you, Priest. If it wasn't for you . . . I don't even wanna think about it." She sighed.

"It's all good. Just glad I could help. " He gave Aoki one last look before returning to the watchtower and Britten.

Aoki felt like an idiot. Her plan had backfired big time. She'd almost died, and Priest was disgusted by her. She'd never get him to love her now.

"Where is Cam?" Gray helped her off the ground.

"He's in the gym." Makiah answered.

"And what the hell you got on?" Gray looked down at Aoki's barely there bikini.

Aoki sat silent. She was in big trouble now.

"I got her G." Noon took Aoki from her arms. "We need to take her to the hospital now."

Gray was happy that she had him there. If she would've been alone, God only knows how she would've reacted. His calming spirit and brute strength kept her sane. Her feelings for him grew leaps and bounds in that moment.

"Okay." She nodded bewildered. "Press, get your things and meet me at the door." Gray stormed back inside the center.

She was so mad she could spit. Her baby had almost drowned and Cam was nowhere to be found. She'd only let him take the kids 'cause he promised to keep a close eye on them. Meanwhile, Aoki and Press were at the pool alone and he was in the gym doing god knows what. Pissed to the highest extent, she snatched open the gymnasium door and found him sitting on the bleacher with Devin on his lap. Gray stopped dead in her tracks. Her eyes had to be deceiving her. No way was he hugged up with his bitch while her daughter was a few feet away drowning. Why was she even there? Didn't Cam know that bringing her there would crush her soul. The community center was sacred ground for them. She'd gifted him the place out of love and he had the gall to bring a woman he'd cheated on her with there? The same woman who'd not only slept with her husband but Gunz as well. Devin was a fuckin' viper. She shouldn't be there. She shouldn't be around her kids. Cam was clearly trying to kill her. Just when she thought she could trust him; he found a way to fail her again. Meanwhile, the triplets ran around the gym high on sugar. Refusing to act on her emotions, she turned around and left before he saw her.

"Did you find him?" Ryan asked.

"Tell your uncle to meet us at the hospital." Gray followed Noon out the door.

———

By the time Cam arrived at the hospital, Gray had already been there an hour. When he'd learned the news that Aoki had drowned he felt like a piece of him died. He knew he should've went with his first mind and accompanied them to the pool. Aoki was so mature and grown that he often forgot she was still a little girl. He should've been there. If he were there none of this would've ever happened. With the triplets in their stroller,

397

he and Devin raced into the emergency room. Cam found Gray leaning into Noon's embrace as she cried. Press sat beside her rubbing her arm quietly.

"Is she alright?" He asked in a panic.

The mere sound of his voice caused Gray to see red and black out. She hated him. It was because of him that her daughter was having test done to ensure she didn't suffer lasting effects from drowning.

"My fuckin' daughter nearly died 'cause you were in the gym playin' house with' this big face bitch!" She walked up and smacked him across the face.

Caught off guard by the hit, Cam's head snapped back from the force of the blow. Devin's mouth dropped open. She just knew that Cam was going to hit her back. He'd made it clear on more than one occasion that if she ever hit him, she wouldn't live to talk about it, but for Cam, hitting Gray was never an option.

"You gon' get enough of putting your fuckin' hands on me." He gripped her up by the collar of her shirt and shook her. "Now use your fuckin' words instead of your hands and tell me what the fuck is wrong wit' you?"

"I trusted you to keep them safe . . . to keep me safe." She broke down and sobbed. "And Aoki almost died."

"What happened?" Cam loosened his grip.

"She fell into the pool and drowned. What do you think what happened? Where were you?" Gray wept hysterically.

The stress of the week had finally gotten to her. She couldn't pretend like death wasn't knocking on her door anymore. It was smacking her dead in the face.

"Is she alright? Where is she?" Cam looked around for answers.

He would never be able to live with himself if something happened to one of the kids on his watch.

"She's being tested. No thanks to you." Gray pushed him with all her might. "You need to be thanking your lucky stars I had Noon there to help me. You were so busy with this dizzy bitch, you ain't even know what was going on."

"I was there. I was right in the other fuckin' room. Aoki told me she wasn't getting into the pool anyway." Cam scowled.

"Regardless, you should've been there. I wouldn't even have to do all of this if you would've been watching her like I told you to!" She pointed her finger in his face.

If Gray kept it up, he was going to bite her finger off.

"Aoki is 45. She's more of an adult than me and you put together! I thought I could trust her to stay out of trouble while I spent time with the little kids."

"It don't look like you were spending time with them at all! When I walked in there you were grinning up in this slut's face."

Cam could argue back that he'd fed the kids, played Ring Around The Rosy, Hide and Go Seek and Red Light/Green Light but going back-and-forth with Gray wasn't high on his list of things to do. Emotions were already high. Feeding into her anger would only make things worse. Besides, he understood her anger. She was a mother who'd almost lost her child. If he was her, he'd be erratic too.

"This is the second time you've had her around my fuckin' kids without asking me."

"What is Eleven doing here? Did you ask me if you could introduce them to him? No, so shut the fuck up with all that bullshit. Our main concern right now needs to be Aoki."

"I can't wait till this fuckin' wedding is over. Me and my kids are getting far away from this fuck-ass city, and most importantly, away from you!"

Gray knew she was being spiteful. After talking to Pastor Edris she was supposed to stop using the kids as a weapon, but she couldn't stop herself. It seemed like the only time Cam acknowledged her pain was when she connected it to their children.

"No mommy!" Press cried. "We don't wanna go back to Paris!"

Gray spun around. The look on Press's face destroyed her. She never wanted the kids to see her and Cam fight.

"Calm down, beautiful." Noon took Press into his big strong arms.

Cam's brows dipped. His eyes turned rigid and cold. This Noon cat was getting on his last nerves. The old him wanted nothing more than to strangle him with his bare hands. He was stepping in on his territory, his family. The nigga shouldn't even be around. If it were left up to Cam, his lame-ass wouldn't be around Gray or his kids. She was *his* wife. She ain't have no business dating. And he was over Noon swooping in and saving the day every time something went wrong with his girls. First it was Gray at the precinct and now it was Aoki and Press. The nigga had to go.

"Aye yo' gimme my fuckin' daughter. I got her."
He pulled Press from his hold.

"Oh, now you wanna be stepdad of the fuckin' year." Gray quipped, annoyed.

"Hold up, nigga. You can back the fuck up. You should've been there in the first place." Noon checked him.

"Mmm . . . right." Gray pursed her lips.

"What, nigga?" Cam walked up on Noon with Press in his arms.

"Nigga, did I stutter?" Noon stood firm.

"Nigga, do you know who the fuck I am?" Cam screwed up his face.

"Yeah, I do but the question is do you know who the fuck I am?"

"Yo, hold my daughter." Cam handed Press to Devin.

"Papa, please don't let her take us back. We wanna stay." She begged urgently.

Cam stopped and focused on his heart, which was Press. That quickly, he'd let his anger take over. He'd completely forgotten about his children. He couldn't fight in front of them. He'd already carved Gunz's eye out in front of Aoki and Press.

"No worries, pretty girl. You ain't going nowhere. I'ma make sure of it." Cam calmed her down with a kiss on the cheek.

"Stop making her promises you can't keep." Gray fumed.

"You ain't taking my kids, Gray."

"Wanna bet?"

#19

"You cannot pretend that I don't even matter. You and I
know better. You've been away from me for too long. It's
time for you to come on home."- Brandy, "Nothing"

After Aoki nearly died from drowning, Gray didn't
think her life could get any worse, but it did. The same day
was the dress rehearsal. She didn't even know if she'd be
able to attend. She and Cam ended up spending five hours
in the emergency room. The whole time they sat opposite
each other refusing to speak. Both of them knew if they
spoke, they'd end up arguing again. Neither of them
wanted that. Enough had already been said. Their main
concern was making sure Aoki didn't suffer any
complications. Devin and Noon offered to keep them both
company but Cam and Gray thought it was best they go
home. Having their significant others around wouldn't help
the situation. It would only make things worse. Waiting
around for the doctor's diagnosis was cruel and strenuous
enough, so Melody came to get the kids. The not knowing
and hard uncomfortable seats made the experience
unbearable. Gray sat with her arms and legs crossed,
shaking her head. Life was funny. In the past it would've
been her and Gunz in the emergency room together. For a
split second she wondered should she tell him what
happened to Aoki, but the thought quickly faded. Gunz was
the enemy. He'd done nothing but cause her and her
daughter pain. Besides that, he had enough on his plate.
Planning the funerals for the people he loved most in life
had to be overwhelming, even for a man like him that

didn't feel anything. Hours passed by before the doctor cleared Aoki and sent her home. Gray was overjoyed to learn that she didn't suffer any internal injuries. The doctor said she simply needed rest. For the rest of the day, Gray never left her side. She was afraid that if she blinked, she'd lose her. What saddened her the most was that this might've been her last time holding her child. In 48 hours, she'd probably be dead.

She thought that life couldn't be anymore fucked up. Boy did God beg to differ. That night, as she slipped on her metallic gold, spaghetti strapped, deep V-neck, pleated dress, she received a call from a real estate agent confirming the sale of her Paris home. At first, she thought it was a joke until the agent told her she'd been contacted by her husband Cameron Parthens. He was the one that put her home up for sale. Gray plopped down on the bed defeated. She'd threatened to take the kids away and he'd called her bluff. He'd figured out that she'd forged his name on the loan application, and on the deed for the house, and used it to his advantage. When she moved to Paris and learned she was pregnant with quads, Gray had to find a bigger home. Her income alone at the time wasn't great enough to get the kind of home that could house six people so she forged Cam's name on the loan so both of their incomes combined would get her the home of her dreams. Then, after having such a high risk pregnancy, she added his name to the deed to ensure he had control over the home in case something happened to her. He was in jail, so she figured he'd never find out, and once he learned of the kids, he'd realize why she'd gone behind his back in the first place.

Tired of being bullied by him, she finished dressing and grabbed her things. Gray couldn't make it to the rehearsal dinner venue fast enough. Cam was going to rue the day he ever messed with her. He had to learn that he could not control her life. If she wanted to go back to Paris, she could. She'd never keep him away from his kids again, but if she didn't wanna live in Saint Louis, he couldn't make her. Cam couldn't have his way this time. She wouldn't allow it. He couldn't tie her down. She didn't want to be dominated by him or any man for that matter. He didn't have the right to assert his will on her life when he'd thrown her and their marriage away. Confidently and furiously, she strutted into the rehearsal dinner ready for battle. If she were in a better mood she would've taken in and appreciated the ambiance of the venue. Kema and Quan's wedding would be taking place at a gorgeous winery in Edwardsville, Illinois. Guests would get to experience the stunning vineyard, tasting rooms and wine shop. The rehearsal dinner and wedding ceremony would take place in the heart of the vineyard. Along one of the dirt paths was a tent made out of amber lights. A long rectangular shaped table that seated fifty people stretched down the pathway. Lovely greenery, peach roses and candles decorated the center of the table along with white Hermes plates, silverware and custom-made napkins. The setting and weather was perfect. The wedding party looked dapper in their after-five attire. All of Kema's bridesmaid, the groomsmen, Pastor Edris and their family and friends were there.

Cam especially looked handsome. He wasn't a suit-and-tie type nigga. The only time he wore a suit was to court and the last time he'd wear one would be at his funeral. For Kema and Quan he made an exception. He didn't wanna disrespect their gathering by showing up in a t-shirt and jeans. On his grown man shit he donned a custom mint green, wide shawl Lepel, double breasted suit. The crisp white button up, black bowtie and blood orange handkerchief set the entire look off. His fresh haircut, lined edges and beard only added to his clit tingling sex appeal.

Gray's blazing eyes landed on him as soon as she stepped under the tent. He sat at the end of the table, leaned back in his seat with his legs crossed, staring right back at her. All the men looked handsome, but Cam was on a level all by his self. He was already fine as hell. From across the way she could see the flecks of gold in his brown smoldering eyes. Everything about him was perfect from his freckled cheekbones to his angular jaw. She wished he wasn't so good looking. Maybe then she would be able to hate him more. Gray wondered where Devin was. Usually, she'd be all up Cam's ass. He'd decided it was best she sit out on the rehearsal dinner. She'd be his plus one at the wedding. Noon and the children stood by Gray's side. Aoki stayed behind with Melody. The rest of the kids were there because they were a part of the wedding. Diggy's children would be too. When her children saw Mo's and Diggy's kids, they took off running to be with them. Now that they were distracted, Gray could take care of her business. All eyes were on her as she strutted in Cam's direction. Even he couldn't take his eyes off her. She looked beautiful. The corner of his mouth turned up as he looked at her. She'd parted her hair to the side and smoothed it down. Gold dangle earrings hung from her ears. A simplistic beat adorned her face. The metallic gold dress she wore flowed in the wind as she walked. Cam licked his bottom lip. He loved her curves and softness of her figure. Her eyes were just like the ocean, tranquil and emotionless. As always, she was mad about something, but Cam didn't care. He'd take mad Gray any day, as long as he could have her.

"You had no right to put my house up for sale."

"You mean *our* house." He grinned mischievously. "You gon' get enough of doing slick shit. You ain't good at it."

"You can't make me stay here."

"Wanna bet?" He used her words against her.

"I fuckin' hate you."

"There you go lying again."

"I'm not doing this with you. Sign the fuckin' papers." She slammed the divorce decree down onto the table.

"I ain't signing shit."

"Yes, you are. I don't want to be with you. Clearly, I've moved on." She looked over at Noon.

Cam rose to his feet slowly and loomed over her. Gray gazed up at him fearfully and swallowed the frog in her throat.

"You think I give a fuck about that nigga. You're wit' em 'cause I'm letting you be wit' him. We both know if I wanted you, I could have you." He took his pinky finger and traced the side of her face.

Gray shamefully savored his touch.

"Fuck me, Cam. Fuck me." He mocked. "Remember that?"

Holding her breath, Gray prayed to God Noon didn't hear him.

"Fuck you." She pushed him.

"Been there done that, I'm good."

"Sign the fuckin' papers, Archibald!" She slapped them against his hard chest and then let them fall.

Done with her and the entire conversation, Cam kept his eyes on Gray as he unbuttoned his suit jacket. Gray looked down to see what he was about to do. All she knew was he bet not hit her. Cam liked to take his clothes off before he bust somebody's ass. He had no intentions on laying a finger on her. He merely unbuckled his belt, calmly unzipped his dress pants then pulled out his 11-inch dick. Holding his python in his hands, he continued to look Gray in the eye while peeing all over the divorce papers. Urine splattered all over the ground to everyone's shock and dismay. Kema's mother and father gasped for air. Quan's mother didn't do anything but shake her head. She was used to Cam's shenanigans. Stunned by his actions, Gray jumped back so none of his pee would get on her feet.

"Aww hell nah." Stacy screwed up his face.

"Yo, you nasty." Selicia frowned, appalled. "What is wrong wit' you?"

"My lord. Jesus has risen." Kema's grandmother clutched her pearls while eyeing Cam's long erect penis.

"Cam, you nasty as fuck dawg. I was eating." Stacy pushed his plate away.

"When ain't you eating?" Cam smirked, still looking at Gray while he placed his enormous penis back inside his pants.

Her chest heaved up and down. He took joy in making her mad and miserable. It was clear. His life's mission was to bring her down. Cam knew exactly what he was doing. He was pissing her off on purpose. He gleefully rode the demonic dragon inside of him to new heights of brutality and treasured it. Cam was going to do everything in his power to keep her tethered to him. He no longer treated her like a person but a possession. How had they gotten here? Gray never saw the day she'd hate Cam. He was her soulmate. Now she was filled with bitterness she couldn't control. Hateful tears marred the cheeks of her freckled skin as she lunged towards him. Before she could get to him, Kema grabbed her by the waist and pulled her back.

"Why won't you let me go?" She sobbed, flushing in distress. "Haven't you hurt me enough?"

"You hurt me too! You ain't fuckin' innocent!" Cam roared, charging towards her only to be stopped by Quan.

In the midst of all the chaos, neither him nor Gray realized that they had everyone's full attention. Press held her weeping brother and sisters in her arms. She too had tears of her own in her eyes.

"STOP!" Quan yoked Cam up by the collar of his shirt.

"She's not taking my fuckin' kids!" He yelled so loud his lungs became sore.

"I'm not taking your kids! I'm leaving you! There's a difference!" Gray shrilled, trying to break free.

"Gray, stop!" Kema ordered.

"I hate him!"

"THAT IS ENOUGH!" Pastor Edris stepped in. "I rebuke you devil in the name of Jesus. You do not have any dominion over this couple or over this wedding. Satan, in the name of Jesus I bind you, and every principality, power, spiritual host of wickedness in heavenly places, every evil spirit, demon spirit, and every spirit that is not of God that has been, is now or will attempt to operate against us."

"Amen!" Stacy and Selicia shouted.

"You two are going to kill each other." Pastor Edris looked from Cam to Gray. "I want you both in my office tomorrow at 10:00 a.m. sharp. We're gonna fix this." He demanded, before storming off upset.

"C'mon, Gray." Kema pushed her inside the winery.

"No, Kema. No. I can't take this anymore. I wanna go home." Gray covered her face and cried.

Kema had no idea that Gray was on the verge of losing her mind. She didn't know that in 48 hours she'd probably be dead. Gray had kept her impending death from her so she wouldn't ruin the most special time of her life but somehow, she still ended up ruining everything.

"You need to pull it together friend." Kema rubbed her back.

"I'm tryin' to but I can't." Gray hiccupped.

She was a disheveled mess.

"You have to. The kids are here. They're watching you. They don't need to see you like this."

The mention of her babies got Gray's full attention. Her heart sank. For the second time in the last 24 hours her kids had seen her show out. She was turning into a monster. She didn't know if Cam had made her this way or if her circumstances had done it. It was all too much to digest. She was under a considerable amount of pressure. Her life was hanging in the balance and there was nothing that she could do to clear her name. On top of that Cam was making her life a living hell. No matter how much she wanted to give up and give into her pain, she had to put her children first. For them she had to pull it together. Sniffling the snot in her nose, she wiped the remaining tears from her face.

"That's my girl. Now let me see you smile." Kema lifted her chin with her index and thumb.

"I don't want to right now." Gray groaned.

"Well, it's my wedding. I'm the bride and what I say goes so smile."

Begrudgingly, Gray rolled her eyes and shot her a quick smirk.

"Now come sit down." Kema lead her over to an empty bench.

Gray sat by her best friend and tried to regain her composure. Kema smoothed her hair back down then took her by the hand. Before she could speak, Noon came to check on Gray.

"Babe, are you okay?" He massaged her shoulder.

"No, but I will be. I'm sorry that I've been such a terrible host and date. You must hate me now." She giggled sadly. " I told you I come with a lot of baggage."

"And I'm here to help you unpack it." He assured.

"Shit, you better keep him." Kema gushed.

"Thanks, babe. I'll be right out after I talk to Kema." Gray confirmed, rubbing the back of his hand.

"A'ight and be cool. I got you." Noon winked his eye.

Gray and Kema watched him walk until he was out of sight.

"Now I see why you wanna divorce. He can get it."

"He sure can." Gray agreed.

"Back to what I was saying tho. You know I love you but I gotta keep it real wit' you. If I don't, I'll be doing you a disservice as a friend and someone you call your sister. You've been fuckin' up friend."

"I know I have." Gray sulked.

"I didn't agree with you when you ran off to Paris, but I had your back. I didn't agree with you when you decided to keep the quads a secret. I didn't agree with you when you gave birth and kept Cam in the dark. I had your back through it all. I can't have your back anymore. This situation has gotten beyond out of control. You cannot use those kids as a weapon to hurt him every time he hurts you. It's not fair and it's not right. Ya'll need to sit down and talk. And not about no surface level bullshit but about what's really affecting the both of you. Cause ya'll aren't just hurting each other, you're hurting us as well. I'm suffering, my fiancé's suffering, your kids are suffering. We're all affected. It's not just about you and Cam anymore. This is supposed to be the best time of my life, but I've spent the entire week checking on you to make sure you're alright. You're supposed to have my back right now but here I am catering to you. That ain't cool sis."

Gray couldn't even argue back. Everything Kema said was true.

"You're right. I'm so sorry, Kema." Gray hugged her tight. "I didn't even take into consideration how this was affecting you."

"You're a horrible friend but it's okay." Kema laughed.

"No, it's not okay. I've been totally selfish. I have made this week about me and I am truly sorry for that. I pray you can forgive me because I love you. Without you I don't know where I'd be. You've not only been my best friend but my sister, my baby daddy, my kids' godmother and my shoulder to lean on. I should've been the main

412

person making sure your wedding week was stress free. That's the least I can do, considering all you've done for me. I swear, I'm going to make sure your wedding is the best day of your life. Just please, forgive me."

"Under one condition."

"Anything."

"When you talk to Pastor Edris, really take in what he's saying and apply it to your life. You and Cam have to get on the same page. This can't go on any longer."

On the outside of the wine shop, Quan shoved Cam's back into the wall. He'd had about all he could take of Cam and Gray's bullshit. The shit used to be funny but now it was nothing but a headache. They were bringing everyone down with their nonsense.

"What the fuck is wrong wit' you dawg?"

"I told you she wasn't takin' my kids." Cam huffed, trying to steady his breathing.

"So, you sell her house and piss on the divorce papers? In front of my family? In front of Kema's? What the fuck was that gon' solve?"

"I don't give a fuck what it was gon' solve, and to be honest, I ain't tryin' to hear shit you got to say right now." Cam pushed him off of him.

"Nah, nigga hold up." Quan pushed him back just as hard. "You might not wanna hear me but you gon' feel me. Ya'll done ruined our whole wedding week wit' ya'll back-and-forth bullshit. Ya'll have made every moment and every second about you and your feelings and what ya'll got going on. I almost got shot at the cemetery 'cause of you. I have taken too many L's because of you and you

413

know exactly what I'm talkin' about." He referred to Diggy.

Cam clenched his jaw. He felt like shit seeing his best friend so upset behind some shit he'd did.

"I ain't gon' let you ruin this for me. You not about to ruin my wedding, dawg. Get your shit together, talk to Pastor Edris tomor and fix this shit. 'Cause it's getting to the point where I don't even want you apart of my wedding." Quan shot before charging off.

He loved Cam but being his friend could be extremely tough at times. Alone, Cam closed his eyes and let his limbs fall loose. Tilting his head back, he let Quan's words sink in. Everything he said was right. He had to get his shit together. The war he and Gray had waged on each other had gotten out of control. They'd caused each other enough pain to last a lifetime. If for no other reason than their kids, they had to make peace with one another. Cam glanced up at the sky. Nightfall was approaching as the sun began to set. He watched in awe as a tranquil red orb of light gradually descended under the horizon. Tiny threads of light remained in the sky, blending with the clouds, staining the heavens pink, then orange and lastly blue. And just like that darkness took over the sky. Glittery stars decorated the atmosphere. It was the prettiest sunset he'd ever seen. Being out in nature without the loud noise of the city soothed his troubled spirit. Now he needed something greater than himself to help his troubled marriage.

———

The following morning, Cam interlocked his fingers and prepared to be scolded by a nigga that was damn near ten years younger than him. *This some bullshit,* he thought. Participating in an impromptu marriage counseling session was the last thing he wanted to do. The last session had gone horribly wrong. He wasn't in the mood for Pastor Edris to blame all of their problems on him. Prayerfully, this time he'd acknowledge both of their flaws so he and Gray could come to some kind of resolution.

"Please tell me what on earth were you two arguing about that would prompt you to pull out your penis in front of a room full of people, including your children?"

"She's fuckin' crazy." Cam quipped, sitting as far away from Gray as possible.

"No, you're the one that's insane." She argued back. "He put my home up for sale to keep me and the kids here in St. Louis. Like always, Cam does what he wants. Forget about how I feel. To be honest, I don't even know why we're sitting here right now. Talking to you isn't going to change anything. No amount of God and prayer can help his kind of crazy. That's why I don't believe in God now. If he's letting people like him roam around doing whatever the hell they wanna do, then I don't want nothing to do with him."

"I understand you're angry, Sister Gray, but I'ma have to check you real quick. You can't put God's character on somebody else's craziness. That's not what the word says. You don't get to put his character on Cam's bad behavior or yours for that matter. There are some things that God had nothing to do with it. We are antonymous human beings who make horrible decisions and sometimes we make great decisions. Sometimes, we submit our will to God and sometimes we submit ourselves to the devil. And right now, both of you are leaning more towards Satan. God wants you to be productive. You cannot be productive if you don't develop a partnership, a team that you don't have to fight with, argue with or compete with."

"I've been trying to get along with her, but she won't let me." Cam explained. "Every time I turn around, she's mad about something. I understand I hurt her in the past and that I did some things I shouldn't have when I got home." He referred to trying to kill her and not watching Aoki at the pool. "But her attitude is just nasty, bro. I don't even know who this woman is sitting next to me. This ain't the girl I married. It's like as soon as we said I do she switched up on a nigga. Everything I said and did was wrong. The only time she was happy was when I was kissing her ass or dicking her down. Other than that, if I breathed too hard, she was mad. If I didn't answer the phone fast enough, she was mad. If I stepped in and tried to parent her kids, she was mad. She's just *angry*. Leave it up to Gray, I can't do nothing right."

"You never gave our marriage a chance. You never came home, you lied to me, you kept secrets, you pushed me away so hell yeah, I was mad." She challenged.

"Gray, everyday Cam walks out that door he's fighting a war. When he returns home to you and the chaos of your relationship, he begins to see you as another battle that he has to deal with and his intimacy with you deteriorates because he sees you as his next job. Atmosphere for a man is everything. All we basically want is for you to be happy." Pastor Edris tried to make her understand.

"When I married you, you were happy. It was one of the reasons why I proposed. Your happiness made me happy." Cam clarified.

Hearing him say that softened a sliver of Gray's heart. She never knew he felt that way about her.

"You said the last time we met that loving Cam doesn't feel good anymore. Well, how do you think he

416

feels? Don't make your happy hard to get because, as you can see, eventually, he will stop trying to obtain it. Make your happy within his reach. If you're lucky enough to marry a Samson, bask in his love. There aren't many left. There aren't many men that are willing to take on real responsibility. Most of the men you have to choose from are mama's boys who are looking for a woman to mother them. But if you're lucky enough to find a Samson, don't just be his wife, be his Delilah."

Gray didn't know much about the bible, but she'd read that Delilah betrayed Samson by cutting his hair and turning him over to the Philistines. Why Pastor Edris was asking her to be more like an unscrupulous traitor was beyond her understanding.

"Isn't it funny how when we read about Samson and Delilah it never talks about her hips, her hair or her sex? It says she was a place he could lay his head. He saw her as rest. He could come off the battlefield and not have to battle at home. Meaning that he needs to be able to rely on that he'll be able to come home to the same you every day. No man wants to come home and try to figure out which you you're going to be today. He can't rest in something that doesn't feel stable."

"Ohhhhhhhhh." Gray leaned back blown away.

Now she got it. Delilah might've been a conspirator but the feeling she gave Samson was real. He loved her and she gave him peace that's why he was comfortable enough to tell her his secrets. Gray needed to be Cam's peace. If he could find harmony in her presence, he'd feel content enough to open up.

"I didn't realize until now how selfish I've been. All I cared about was my feelings and how he'd hurt me. I never really took the time to look at his pain. If I'm being honest, I didn't know how committed I was to loneliness until I got married. I grew up as an only child. I didn't have to share. Not even just with my things but my heart. It wasn't till Cam kept asking me what's wrong and I kept saying I'm alright, that I realized something was wrong. I wasn't okay. On the inside, I was screaming because I still felt like this little poor girl, that didn't know her father. And the feeling kept piling up and piling up. Every now and then it would manifest in certain ugly ways and he had no clue because I kept my feelings close to my chest. I had committed myself to believing that no one would understand me, and that if I ever showed him that part of me, he would leave. Sure enough, when I needed him, when things got tough and I needed him to understand me, he did exactly what I expected him to and left." She sighed, defeated.

Cam stared off into space feeling horrible. He hadn't done right by Gray. She'd begged and pleaded for him to hear her out after he caught her kissing Gunz, but he refused to listen. He'd made it up in his head that his eyes hadn't deceived him. He'd caught her red handed but the part of him that trusted Gray knew that she wasn't a cheater. He knew that she loved him. He'd allowed his insecurities to cloud his rationale. In the process, he not only pushed her out of his life but destroyed their marriage as well. If he would've never shut her out, she would've never run off to Paris and felt the need to exclude him from her and their kids' lives.

Pastor Edris saw that he was getting somewhere with them and continued on.

"It takes a long time to really be a couple because in order to be a couple you have to leave enough, to cleave enough. You don't leave and cleave in a ten-minute ceremony at the courthouse. You'll become a couple through pregnancies, through losses of babies, through getting jobs, losing family, losing friends."

The mention of losing a child made Gray think of the baby they'd lost. Cam looked her way. He could feel she was about to cry. No matter how mad they were at each other, she was still apart of him. Her pain was his pain. Reaching over he grabbed a Kleenex and handed it to her. Without giving him eye contact, Gray reached to the side and took it.

"Thank you." She whispered, dabbing the inner corner of her eyes.

"You're expecting each other to understand the nuances of your emotions and moods and then when you don't understand you get offended 'cause in your mind he or she was supposed to know you. All disappointment is controlled by expectation. If you can't control her behavior, the only thing that will give you control is your expectation. In order to know what to expect from her, you have to know her. You've built a false premise of expectation from a romanticized stranger."

"Wow." Cam said astonished.

Pastor Edris had hit him again with some shit he'd never realized. He knew Gray to an extent but to be her husband he had to know her inside and out. He'd taken the time to learn the basics but not the things that made her tick, that made her scared, that made her cry or that made her run when times got rough.

"You said you don't know who she is anymore, but you never knew her to begin with. You sitting up here mad 'cause she didn't fulfil a fantasy of this woman you conjured up in your head. Most men are angry with their wives over something they never told her they expected. Because to you, common sense should've let her know that you're emotionally unavailable, easily angered, have PTSD, expected her to be a stay-at-home wife, you didn't want her to work and that you wanted to be the sole provider. Before you met, you were skating by on grace, Cam. It wasn't until you found her that you got favor. Without her you will not have the favor of God because he who finds a wife finds a good thing and gets favor from the lord. There are a lot of men who date down to feel up. They don't want a woman who will challenge them. They want a woman that will cheer for them. Your position as a wife, Gray, is to never be a trophy wife but to be the reward for good work."

Gray wasn't just his wife. She was his blessing and until Cam treated her as such things between them would never be right. Pastor Edris turned to Cam.

"You've gotta learn how to love God because what you've done is try to change her last name to Christ, but she can't save you. The same goes for you, Gray. Too many people in relationships have made their partner their savior, but as soon as they see their humanity, they don't want anything to do with them. Your partner will never be everything you need. They're just a part of what you needed. God will always leave a God size hole inside of you that only he can fill. And out of his love he will let you try to fill it with other things so when you're done, he can be like see . . . I was here the whole time."

When Cam proposed to Gray, he thought the goodness in her would somehow magically fix his brokenness. Instead, it shined a light on everything wrong with him. What he was about to admit was hard for him to say, but in order for him and Gray to move forward, he had to be real.

"What I learned in jail was that I struggled with so much doubt and self-loathing that it was difficult, if not damn-near impossible, for me to receive the love God sent through my wife. To keep it a buck, I've struggled with the idea that I could be loved by Gray particularly in the areas I didn't love myself in."

"Gray, do you get that you have married a man who doesn't understand love?" Pastor Edris questioned. "Cam has been holding onto things that has held him hostage for years. Because of that the love you tried to give him, he looked at with suspicion. How can you love him, when he doesn't love himself?"

Gray's face dropped. There was no way Cam didn't love his self. He was one of the most confident men she'd ever met. His confidence was one of the things that made her fall in love with him. But confidence didn't equal self-love. Cam's brash attitude and cocky behavior was a mask to cover up his insecurities.

"Women have been groomed for marriage their whole lives. Men have not so here lies the problem. Men never practice being married. We played games and activities so everything for us is about scoring." He alluded to sex. "Gray, from a small child you started preparing for marriage and practiced all your life for something he never thought about. So, with that being said, the same merciful mama love that you give your kids, can you love him like that too?"

For the first time since they sat down, Gray focused her attention on Cam. She wholeheartedly believed that everyone deserved a shot at unconditional love. She truly believed that true love existed. Some people were cynics and thought that love was just an imaginary feeling people tricked themselves into believing in, much like God. The thing about love that Gray adored so much was that it was unpredictable. There was no controlling it. Love was beautiful, mysterious and magical. Everyone deserved to have a slice of magic in their life. For Gray, her magic started the day she met Cam inside Principal Glanville's office.

"Here's what scripture says. The lord test the righteous but the wicked his soul hates. Which means if he loves you, he corrects you. If he hates you, he'll leave you alone. God ain't leaving you two alone. He keeps disrupting everything in your lives because he's trying to get your attention. What would you say is the biggest problem in your relationship?"

"Trust." Gray and Cam said in unison.

"I don't think we've ever really trusted each other." She confessed.

"Trust for men is almost always about emotional safety. When a man says I cannot trust you, he means that his heart and his secrets are not kept in the bank of your love. It means when he's talking to you, he feels like he's talking to your friends and your family as well. It means, if he gets vulnerable, and in a moment of weakness, he tells you his secrets and the next time you get mad and use his vulnerabilities against him, he . . . cannot . . . trust . . . you. The first time you spook him, the first thing he'll do is take away his emotions. If he cannot make a deposit in you *emotionally*, he'll still come home *physically* but he's not in the house anymore. A man can come in the house and not come home. When he doesn't trust you, his love is homeless and most homeless people start panhandling."

"Mmm." Gray nodded her head.

She felt that word in her spirit. Pastor Edris statement was the epitome of their relationship.

"He was scared when you got him, Gray. Being emotionally scared starts early. It starts the first time someone tells you big boys don't cry, be a man. That translates to young boys that men don't have feelings. You all have a son correct?"

"Yes."

"Remember, you are either raising some woman's miracle or some woman's misery. Don't raise him to be your little boy. Raise him to be her man. Put everything in him, you wish you had."

Cam and Gray looked at one another. The last thing either of them wanted was to raise a son who was emotionally unstable and didn't know how to treat women. They wanted to raise a good man, with morals and values and that had a prayer life. Just because Gray didn't fully believe in God's power, didn't mean she didn't want her kids to believe. Pastor Edris was slowly but surely reigniting her faith in a higher power. Unlike most men, Cam didn't want his son to be a mirror image of him. His flaws had given him years of emptiness that he would never be able to get back. He didn't want that to be Reign's fate.

"When I got locked up, I put myself into solitary confinement on purpose. I didn't want the other inmates to know that I suffered from PTSD. It would make me look weak. So, for four months I sat in a dark room by myself with no one to talk to. During my journey of dealing with my anxiety, I learned a lot about myself. I realized there were places in me that had never healed. There was something in me that was empty that was connecting to something that needed to be validated from years ago. Things that happened in our marriage preceded our marriage. The brokenness in me happened when I was 9 years old and my father took me to his mistress' house. From then till now I'm still trying to find myself. I'm still trying to figure out who likes me for me. Most women just want to be associated with Killa Cam, the flashy nigga that don't give a fuck. They don't want to get to know the real me. The only woman I ever truly let my guard down for was a woman I was with before Gray."

Gray's body tensed. Cam didn't even have to say LaLa's name for her to know he was talking about her.

"So, I'm thinking she knows me. I can be myself with her, so instead of going to my wife, I went to her for comfort. I see now that wasn't right. I take full responsibility for the places where I failed. The healing is not just about my marriage, it's about my manhood. Because I'm still hurting from a father who used me and I'm trying to figure out how to be a good husband and a good father but how can I be what I've never seen?" Cam genuinely wanted to know.

"The issues and challenges in my marriage aren't three and half years old. They're 41 years old. I'm 41. What happened when my father began to cheat and lie to my mother was the beginning of my brokenness. There is a fucked up little nigga in me that doesn't know how to function in intimate places. That fear traveled into my marriage, so I found myself looking for safe places and ended up in an unsafe place instead."

Gray was so happy that he'd finally admitted his wrongdoings. Before, he'd always made it seem like it was her fault why he'd cheated.

"Because we watch so many movies, we think the emotion of love is you have to feel something in order to stay in love." Pastor Edris eyed them both. "Love is not the feeling, it's the thing you do in spite of what you feel sometimes. A healthy marriage starts with being healthy as a single. Because what you don't address within your singleness will be multiplied in your marriage. See Gray, a man can love you desperately with their feelings and still not know how to love you correctly with their actions."

Clearing her throat, Gray pushed her pride to the side and prepared to tell a truth she thought she'd never reveal.

"This might sound crazy but I'm actually happy he did what he did because this is our appointment for growth as a married couple. If Cam would've never lied and cheated, the things that needed to be healed and addressed would still be left unsaid. I'm broken and he's broken but those things didn't come up until we were tied to each other. You don't have to face yourself, when you're with yourself. I don't think either of us went into this looking to hurt the other. I really believe that there was a situation that had to happen for us to grow and to not think that marriage is all hearts and flowers. There are things about my husband that he would've never had to face and vice versa, if we weren't in each other's lives." Gray acknowledged.

To hear her refer to him as her husband warmed Cam's heart. Just the day before they were trying to claw each other's face off. Now here they were actually recognizing each other's downfalls.

"Most men end up cheating with who you used to be. So, the more wife you throw at him, you're pushing him further away. You're throwing wife and she's throwing out girlfriend. Here's what you gotta know. She's still in there but Cam what you gotta know is part of the reason she's not coming out is because you don't treat her like you used to. If you would stop making night deposits and invest in her like you do in the streets things would be different."

"Mmm." Gray waved her hand, wanting to shout.

Pastor Edris was speaking a word. The Holy Ghost was truly amongst them.

"You know the reason they have night deposits is for convenience. You used to spend time with her, hangout with her. She was the place you laid your head and got your rest. You used to invest and now you just deposit. All the while your son is watching you and here's what's worse. Your daughters are watching you too. If they see you investing into their mother, they'll know what to expect from a man. See, you can make a deposit and the bank not be open but if you're going to make an investment it has to be during business hours. So, I have to ask. Gray do you want him to invest you?"

Gray pondered his question before replying.

"That's all I've ever wanted."

"But in order for him to invest in you, you have to be open. Are you open, Gray?" Pastor Edris asked.

Was Gray open to letting Cam back in? She wished she could say yes but he'd destroyed what was left of the trust she had in men. He was supposed to be her knight in shining armor. He was supposed to be the love that out trumped them all. But he'd hurt her far worse than Gunz ever had.

"You don't even have to say it. I know you're not ready. You know why you're not open anymore? Cause he hurt you, and when he hurt you, you closed. So, this raises the question. How do you get her to open when she's closed? It's by admitting your faults, asking for forgiveness and repairing the damage you've created."

There was no more time to waste. Tomorrow would probably be the last day he got to spend with her. He didn't wanna leave off on bad terms. Cam nervously took Gray's hand. The five hearts that were tattooed onto her ring finger reminded him of the family they shared together. Whether they stayed married or not they were bonded for life.

426

Unsure of what he was about to do, she gazed at him curiously.

"I don't expect you to forgive me. I understand why you wouldn't, but I do feel bad about the way things ended between us. I'm genuinely sorry. I know it's not an excuse that I cheated because I was frustrated and upset but that's how I felt at that time. I should've talked to you and told you what I was feeling but I didn't. Because of that I hurt you. For that, I'm sorry." He sincerely apologized.

A lot of people thought forgiveness was weak, but it wasn't. It took a very strong person to forgive. Forgiveness brought freedom to love again, to heal the heart, soul and mind. It brought about the opportunity to release all negative emotion associated with the person who hurt you. Cam would never know how much his apology meant to Gray. His admission of guilt started the process of mending the cracks in her broken heart. She didn't wanna fight anymore. She didn't want to spend another second of the time she had left on earth being angry. In the end it wasn't worth it.

"Thank you. I accept your apology." She teared up again. "And I'm sorry as well. I was dead wrong for keeping Reign, Beaux and Sky away from you. I take full responsibility for any pain that I have caused you. I honestly hope that you can find it in your heart to forgive me. I want you to be in our babies lives. They need you. Aoki and Press need you." Gray wanted to say that she needed him too, but her pride wouldn't let her admit the truth.

"I will never keep them away from you again. You may not believe me right now but through my actions I'm gonna prove to you that I'm serious."

Gray didn't have to jump through hoops to get him to trust her word. He knew she was telling truth. They'd both learned their lesson.

"During my ministry, I've learned that so many people marry for passion when they need to be marrying for purpose. Cause if you marry for purpose, your passion will come but it's a lot of people that got married for passion and it didn't last cause there was no purpose attached. So, when the tickle of the physical is gone what do you have left? You all are in the space where the physical has faded and your purpose as a couple is being revealed. It's not going to be an easy journey."

Cam held Gray's hand tight. He wanted to spend every waking moment with her. They'd fucked up in the past and done things to hurt each other, but if they had time, they could work through their issues. Beneath the rubble of distrust and hurt feelings was love. With God, love, repentance and purpose, they could rebuild their foundation and start anew.

"So, love is never what you feel. It's what you do in spite of what you feel. The law of love is I will do what honors, builds and blesses *her*. Even if it cost me everything because Jesus gave that kind of love to me. And in return she'll give you a love that you can't define, a legacy you couldn't create, a hope you can't contain. That is the power of love."

Suddenly the sound of Gray's phone ringing interrupted them. It was Kema calling. Gray had to get to her final fitting. Gray reluctantly pulled her hand away from Cam's. She could tell he didn't wanna let go. Neither did she. They'd finally had a breakthrough. She didn't want that good feeling to end. But just that quickly, reality began to sink in. She and Cam were husband and wife, but he had a woman and she had a man. Things between them wouldn't just fall back into place because they'd said I'm sorry. It would take more than an apology to get them back on track. Gray was pleased tho. This therapy session had been a huge success. She and Cam were finally on the same page. It was the first step at a brighter future for them both. She just prayed she'd live to see it.

"Thank you, Pastor Edris." She shook his hand. "You've changed our lives for the better. I can't say thank you enough. We really truly needed this."

"That's what I'm here for. Don't hesitate to pick up the phone and call."

"I won't." She smiled then gave Cam one last look.

She didn't want to leave him. They'd just began to scratch the surface of their healing. There was so much more that needed to be said and revealed. What if she never got the chance to tell him everything in her heart? Cam watched as she grabbed her purse and left. Every part of him wanted to kiss her and hold her. He didn't want to spend another second on this planet without his wife. They'd been apart long enough.

"The truth of the matter is she misses you." Pastor Edris gathered his bible. "I know she's fussing and acting all crazy and getting on your nerves, but she doesn't know how to get you back. The stuff she's doing might be pushing you further away but it's only because she wants you back in her life. And in spite of how awkwardly and crazy she might go about it, see the intention. It's hard and it's a lot of work to rebuild but stop fighting the inevitable, Cam. Go home. Go . . . home."

20

"So many places I can go. None of them feel the same as home. Take me back to the surroundings that I know. It gets so lonely on the road. I'll take the one that leads to you. The corner of me and you."- Alex Isley, "Road to You"

That night sleep evaded Gray. The past week had been tumultuous. She could no longer keep up with all the chaos. The lack of sleep proved it. After their talk with Pastor Edris the rest of wedding preparation went off without a hitch. The wedding would be everything Kema hoped for. Gray was happy for her friend. She was in love and about to marry the man of her dreams. The happiness and bright smile that graced her face every time she looked at Quan was enviable. Gray remembered a time with she looked at Cam the same way. Things had changed drastically. Even after their breakthrough she wondered would they ever get back to solid ground. Before they got married, they'd developed a friendship she thought was unshakable. She wished they could get back to that place. When they were friends there was no expectations, just friendship. He'd replaced the void of male companionship that Truth left behind. He'd become her new male best friend. He'd come into her life when she was in desperate need of guidance. He'd gave her strength when her heart ached for guidance. Though bruised, his soul reached out to hers and made an eternal bond of friendship. In the midst of pain and misery their love for each other grew. Then they messed everything up when they ran off and said, 'I do.'

Their friendship ended as soon as they got married. The friendship faded and they began to play house. Instead of being friends they tried to step into the role of husband and wife but lacked trust and a solid foundation. They'd skipped all the necessary steps that led to being a married couple. Before they ran off to the courthouse, Cam and Gray had never even been on a real date. She'd taken him on a picnic and that was it. He didn't court her or learn her. They went from mortal enemies, to quick friends, to even faster lovers to husband and wife. Their marriage was doomed from day one. Cam and Gray went into their marriage lacking faith. They never sought the help of God. They thought they could do everything on their own. They had no chance of survival. It was destined to end in disaster their first go around. Their marriage had to be broken to be rebuilt. If given the chance they could build a solid foundation of love, faith and trust. Only then could they truly grow.

Frustrated with herself and lack of sleep, Gray kicked the covers off her and sighed. Her soul was restless. It was screaming out for something she didn't know she needed. Looking at the clock midnight morphed into 1:00 a.m. Time went by so fast she couldn't keep up. Gray needed to go to sleep. She'd die if she had bags under her eyes on Kema's wedding day. It would show up in photos, but her mind wouldn't settle. Where there should be dreams was one thought after another. Sitting up, she ran her hands through her hair then eased out of bed. There was no point in trying to force sleep. It wasn't coming anyway. Dressed in a grey Calvin Klein sports bra and matching panties she slipped on a grey cropped hoodie, cut-off jogging shorts and pastel colored unicorn slippers. Grabbing her keys, she decided to go on a night drive. It had been ages since she'd done so. After kissing each of the kids goodbye, she told Melody she was leaving for a minute and hit the road. She knew she'd be safe. The security Cam hired would be right behind her. For nearly an hour, she drove around aimlessly listening to Ari Lennox, Billie Eilish and Etta Bond. Her song *Teleport* stayed on repeat. Gripping the steering, she imagined she was singing her heart out to the man she loved. That man should've been Noon, but it wasn't. It was Cam.

If I could teleport (Teleport)
If I could teleport
I'd be with you tonight, mmm
If I knew magic as well
I'd cast a spell on myself
Oh, boy, if I could fly, oh

The song mixed with the dark starry night put her in a somber mood. There was so much that Gray craved that she was depriving herself of. The main thing being Cam. Her body yearned for him to touch her skin, to grip her thighs, to thrust deep until he reached her soul and she cried. If she was brave, she'd call him and tell him that she desired a feeling only he could give. Gray didn't know if she was pathetic or not for wanting him. She and Cam just had this thing she couldn't shake. Even if she could, she wasn't quite sure she would. The only thing that could make her stop loving him was death. The notion put everything in perspective. The grim reaper was creeping closer and they'd spent the last week of her life fighting over things that didn't matter in the bigger scheme of things. They should've been loving on one another and figuring out how they were going to prepare the kids for life after her death. Sadly, they hadn't done any of that. Now they had no time left.

Disturbed by the thought, Gray unknowingly realized she'd pulled in the driveway of her old home. When she'd come back to Saint Louis, staying there hadn't been an option. The house she'd purchased held too many bad memories. When she packed up her and the kids' things that fateful night in March, she had no plans of ever returning. She wanted to sell it, but her friends talked her out of it. Instead, Kema kept the house up while she was away. Gray turned off the ignition and looked at her home. Nothing about it had changed. She wondered if Mrs. Miriam still lived across the street or if she'd passed on. So many old memories flashed before her eyes. She remembered when she and the girls used to take long walks with Kilo and Gram. Press would make them all gather in the living room and sing showtunes on her Karaoke machine. Christmas Day with Cam had been one of the best Christmas' she'd ever had. She missed laying on the couch, between his legs while he watched the Godfather. He'd seen it a million times but always acted as if it was his first. She remembered the first time he came over for dinner and ordered pizza instead of eating her traditional Korean meal. She also remembered being lonely, the screaming matches and the nights he didn't come home. Deciding it was best she go; she started the ignition then noticed the living room light turn on. Her heart slammed against her chest. Had someone broken in? Then she saw a shadowy figure walk by the window.

Gray let out a sigh relief. She'd know that silhouette from anywhere. It was Cam. His car wasn't in the driveway. He must've parked in the garage. It freaked her out that they'd both ended up at the same place. It was yet another sign that their souls were tied together. Getting out she made her way to the door . . . to him. Nervously, she knocked on her own door. The key she had to the house was in Paris. Cam's brows dipped. No one should be knocking on the door at that time of morning. It was after 2:00 a.m. All he knew was it better not be Mrs. Miriam's nosey ass. He wasn't in the mood for her racist bullshit.

Pulling his piece from out of the back out of his Bathing Ape shorts, he cautiously neared the door. Looking through the peephole he was surprised to find Gray standing there. Tucking his gun away, he let her in. No words were said as his brown orbs connected to her blue ones. He wondered how she knew he was there. She was long gone when Pastor Edris told him to go home. It could only be a coincidence that they ended up in the same place. Quietly, she walked past him and entered her old home. Not one piece of furniture was out of place. For the first time in a long while, Gray's soul felt at peace. She was meant to be there. She needed this. She needed him.

"Where are the kids?"

"Melody's watching them."

"What you doing here?" He leaned against the wall and watched her walk around.

"Couldn't sleep." She trailed her hand along her furniture.

She'd took such pleasure picking out each pieces for her home.

"You?" She turned and faced him.

"Same."

"Today was a trip, right?"

"Who knew we were so fucked up." Cam chuckled, massaging his jaw.

The bottom of Gray's ass cheeks were peeking out the bottom of her shorts 'causing his dick to stir in his shorts. Visions of bending her pretty-ass over the back of the couch like he used to filled his mind. They both were restless. They both craved a release they weren't bold enough to ask for. Coming across an old photobook, she took the large booklet off the shelf and took a seat on the floor. There was a little dust on it. Gray blew it off then peeled open the first page. Tears instantly stung the brim of her eyes. How had she left this behind? Inside were baby pictures of Aoki and Press. She hadn't seen the photos in years. Seeing how small her girls once were brought back so many memories. They were such beautiful babies. Time had gone by so fast . . . too fast. She needed more. To think that in a few short hours her time on earth was done was a painful pill she didn't want to swallow.

"Have you seen these?" She traced her girls' faces with the pad of her index.

Cam pushed his body off the wall and took a seat next to her. Their shoulders touched as she pointed to a picture of Aoki when she was two and they'd gone to the Pumpkin Patch. Cam chuckled. In the pic she was taking a mini pumpkin from another toddler's hand, causing her to cry. Even at two Aoki was bad. Silently, they went through the entire photobook together. When they reached the end, they were surprised to find the one and only picture they took the day they got married. Gray had forgotten she'd stuck the photo in the book for safe keeping until she could buy a frame to house it in. Their marriage ended so quickly she never got the chance to put the pic on display. Taking the pic out, she and Cam examined it closely. Neither of them had dressed up for the occasion. Both wore jeans and a shirt. Cam's long tattooed arms were wrapped around her waist as she rested her head on his chest, looked at the camera and smiled. A tiny bouquet of pink peonies were in her hand. There was so much hope and love in their eyes. It was sad to see how they'd ended up.

Cam took the photo from her hand and eyed it. In the pic, there wasn't a trace of a smile on his face but on the inside a happiness like no other filled his soul. Marrying Gray had been one of the best days of his life. He'd married a woman his mother would've been proud to call her daughter-in-law.

"You ain't going nowhere so get that out of your head." He said out the blue.

Gray bit her bottom lip and looked everywhere but at him. She wanted to remind him that she might be dead before the day was over. Cam acted like there wasn't a price on her head. Why wasn't he as worried as she was?

"You're not leaving." He placed the picture down and took her hand in his. "You and my babies are staying."

"But Cam—"

"Shhhhhhh." He silenced her.

Cam knew exactly what she was about to say. He didn't want to hear it. There would be no talk of Victor that night. They'd done enough talking all week. They'd wasted valuable time. Time they'd never be able to get back. Cam wrapped his arm around her shoulders and pulled her close. A side hug wasn't enough. Gray turned her body to face him and wrapped her arms around his torso. Like in the picture on their wedding, she buried her face in his chest and relished the feel of him. Cam held her tight. His hold was stronger than ever before. It was as if holding her wasn't enough. He needed to feel every ounce of her pressed into him.

"See you fit too good to leave."

Gray closed her eyes and inhaled his heavenly scent. If this was how she was going to spend her last night alive she wouldn't complain. When she and Cam were good, she experienced a high no drug could supply.

"Cam." Her voice croaked.

"Yes."

"I want my friend back." She whispered.

Taking her waist into his hands, Cam pulled her onto his lap. Chest to chest, his hand traveled to her curly hair. Gently, he pushed it from her angelic face. A spark of passion flickered in her caerulean eyes. Goosebumps covered her arms. Fuck a divorce or death. Nothing else mattered except what was taking place right then and right there.

"Is that all you want?"

This was his way of asking her did she want him without putting his heart on the line. Gray placed her lips on his. Cam opened his mouth and sucked her bottom lip. Their mouths took a trip to the Dominican Republic as their tongues did the Merengue. Gray clenched her pussy muscles. Cam was one hell of a kisser. Pecking his pink lips tenderly, she gazed in his eyes and said, "That's all my heart can take."

Disappointed by her response, Cam flexed his jaw. Gray noticed the change in his exterior. Quickly, she recovered by caressing his face. Cam's hard exterior melted away at the touch of her hand. With nothing shielding him, he allowed her access to his heart once again. The rest of the world became a blur. Victor, Gunz, Devin, Noon were all exiled to the recesses of his mind. The only thing of importance was tracing her mouth, neck and heavy breasts with his tongue. Cam tried to be calm while removing her clothing but found it difficult to keep his composure. He couldn't get her naked fast enough. Gray removed his clothes as well. The Bathing Ape t-shirt, shorts, Hennessy socks and Supreme slides were all gone. Nude, Cam lay her body down then lay on top of her. This was the reason neither of them could let go. Neither of them felt complete without the other. Gray was the only woman that could break his heart a million times and he'd still find her to be perfect for him.

All night Gray had been restless, but as soon as she lay underneath his warm body, a sense of peace washed over her. All thoughts of death ceased. Her heart took over her head. All that mattered was Cam. Gray caressed his face once more. She had to prove he was real, and that this wasn't a fantasy. Sure enough, he was there with her. None of this fake. They'd found their way to each other again. A soft moan echoed as his tender lips brushed the side of her neck. Cam ran his hand through her hair. His kisses turned animalistic as he licked and sucked her caramel skin. Gray gripped his back and spread her legs wide. His woodsy scent sent her over the edge. He was making her lose her mind. Cam feasted on her body as if she was his last supper. There wasn't an inch of her body his tongue didn't explore. He sucked and kissed her neck, her breasts, fingers, stomach, pelvic bone, thighs and toes. He saved her pussy for last. A river of pleasure saturated his tongue as he lapped at her honey coated center. Gray closed her eyes and tried to hold on. She was dripping wet with desire. She was almost certain that if Cam kept eating her pussy with such reckless abandon he'd drown. Each flicker of his tongue on her clit made her weak. Her juices and his salacious kisses was too much to bear. The sweet scent of her arousal had Cam going. The longer he ate her the longer he wanted to go. He'd found home between her silky-smooth thighs.

Making love to Gray put his mind at ease. The simple touch of her hand caused him to move in ways he'd never been taught but knew so well. His dick hardened to the point it hurt as she pushed her pussy into his face. Gray's body quacked in the palm of his needy hands. Her breathing increased with each stroke of his tongue. Cam sucked the soul out of her. Gray's pussy was heaven. He'd gladly lay down and die on the altar of her lips. She felt good. Too good. Everything with her was right.

After making her come, he made his way up and locked eyes with her. Her blue orbs penetrated his soul. Gray gripped his face and planted her lips against his. Their tongues glided against each other in perfect harmony. With each lap of his tongue, Cam yearned to breathe all of her in, so he did. For hours they made love. Cam didn't stop until she couldn't take anymore. Even then he put up a fight to continue. Exhausted, but thoroughly satisfied, Gray drifted off to sleep inside the arms of the man she loved. This was what life was all about. She and Cam were one. With him she was home.

———

Yawning, Gray opened her eyes and welcomed the morning sun. Rolling over onto her back she gave her mind a moment to shed the grogginess from her brain. She needed a minute to pull herself together. She was still so tired. A soft, cushiony bed was calling her name. Sleeping on the floor after making love all night wasn't an ideal way to get rest. *Cam*, she thought popping up. Fretfully, she searched the living room for him, but she was alone. A white sheet covered her naked body. There was no trace of him. He'd apparently left. Gray's shoulders dropped from disappointment. She wished they could've said goodbye. The day was going to be hectic. They probably wouldn't get to say a word to each other. Feeling blue, she checked her phone for the time. It was going on 11:00 a.m.

"Shit." She leaped from the floor.

Gray had over twenty missed calls. Some were from Noon and Melody. Majority of them were from Kema. She was supposed to be at the hotel by 9:00 a.m. for makeup and hair. With the speed of lightning, she put on her clothes. Kema was going to kill her. The thought of death stopped Gray in her tracks. Time was up. Today was the day she'd meet her maker. A cold sweat washed over her tense body. Gray could barely breathe. Staggering backwards, she held her chest and landed on the couch. Her lungs had begun to close up on her. Breathing in and out, she took several deep breaths in hopes she didn't faint.

"God, I know we don't talk much but I need you. Please don't take me away from kids." Several tears slipped from her eyes. "Please."

Sitting up straight, she inhaled oxygen through her nose and exhaled it out of her mouth. Back on her feet she made her way to the entryway table to get her keys. Once again, Gray was thrown off track. Under her keys was the divorce decree she'd sent Cam while in jail. That could only mean one thing. Dizzy with trepidation, she flipped the pages until she got to the end. Gray froze in place. On the last page Cam had signed his name. He'd finally given her what she wanted but now that she'd gotten it, she didn't want it all.

21

"I swear to God every day. He won't take you away.
'Cause without you babe, I lose my way. "- James Arthur,
"Falling like the Stars"

      Quan stood at the altar with his groomsmen looking
out on the ceremony décor. Kema and the wedding planner
had outdone themselves. He didn't know what to expect but
the vision she had for their special day was perfect. In the
middle of the vineyard they would marry under an altar that
was made of blush feathers, foliage, and straw fans.
Wooden chairs were on each side of the pathway that was
lined with vases filled with feathers. The backdrop of the
rolling hills, olive groves and grape trees was nothing short
of picturesque. The undeveloped grapes hung low, filling
the air with a sweet smell. Quan was decked out from head
to toe. He wore a white tuxedo jacket with a black lapel
that fit perfectly over a white crisp shirt, bowtie, black vest,
fitted tuxedo pants and patent leather dress shoes. His
groomsmen that consisted of his best man Cam, Li'l Quan
and Stacy donned olive-green tuxedo jackets with black
lapels, black bowties, white shirts, black pants and suede
slip-on loafers. A seat in the front row was left empty with
a single rose in memory of Diggy. The positive, serene
energy surrounding him let Quan know he was there. With
his hands clasped in front of him, he awaited his bride.
R&B singer, Kenny Lattimore, sang his legendary wedding
song *For You* as the precession began.

For you, I'd give a life time of stability,
Anything you want of me,
Nothing is impossible,
For you, there are no words or ways to show my
love,
Or all the thoughts I'm thinking of,
'Cause this life is no good alone

Nervous butterflies fluttered in Quan's stomach. Diggy Jr. held Reign's tiny hand and helped him down the aisle. Reign wore a sign around his neck that said I can't be trusted with the rings. Everyone laughed and cooed as he made his way to his father, but Reign wasn't having it. He hated every second of being dragged down the aisle. The deep frown on his face resembled the one Cam often wore. When the boys finally made it to the altar Diggy Jr. sat Reign on Mo's lap. The bridesmaids came out next. The light from the candles highlighted their melanin skin. Tee-Tee was the first to ease down the aisle in a cross-neck, sheer gold, dress with a silk organza train. Some of the more conservative guests tuned up their faces when they saw a man dressed in a gown. Quan eyed them all with contempt. Dressing in women's clothing wasn't his thing but he respected Tee-Tee as a man and as a great friend of his wife. Heidi strolled down the aisle in a dress made out of the same material but hers was long sleeved and had a gold belt attached. She looked spectacular. All of the single men, and even some who were attached, eyed her with lust.

Since we've become one, I made a change,
Everything I do now makes sense,
All roads end,
All I do is for you

Cam clenched his jaw tight. Gray was coming out next. He hadn't seen her since he left her asleep on the floor that morning. Leaving her behind was one of the hardest things he'd ever done. If he could've, he would've stayed there with her forever. There inside their old home, they were content, they were at peace, they were safe, they were in love. Tranquility was plastered across her face as she slept on his chest. Gray seemed perfectly relaxed, even though she lay on concrete muscle. All of the stress and worries of the world were no longer evident. Her skin felt like silk against his. Her wild curly hair tickled him every time she moved but he didn't mind. Having her hooked in the curve of his arm gave him comfort. Cam toyed with a tendril of her hair and imagined himself waking up to her for the rest of his days. If they had taken their time, they could've grown old together. It was the one thing in life Cam wanted the most, but Gray didn't want that. She wanted out of their marriage. She wanted to be away from him. She'd chosen Paris and Noon over him. Could he blame her? No. He'd tried fighting the divorce tooth and nail. He'd held out for years, but time had run out. He had to except their reality. It was over. Instead of forcing her to stay with him, Cam did the one selfless thing he could do. Let her go. He wondered how she felt when she saw the divorce papers. Did she thank God? Did she shout for joy? Did she cry? Did she hurt at all? He sure as hell was in pain. The ache of letting her go stung like a million bee stings. But for once in his God forsaken life, Cam had to do the right thing instead of the selfish thing. He couldn't say that he loved her and keep her trapped. He had to let her go. Not only for her but for his own personal growth. For so long, he thought Gray would be his healer but Pastor Edris was right. She couldn't fix him. He had to fix himself. He had to pull himself up by the boot straps, dust himself off and heal the scars of his tattered heart. If he didn't, he'd just keep fucking her over.

For you, I share the cup of love that overflows,
And anyone who knows us knows,

I would change all thoughts I have,
For you, there is no low or high or in between,
Of my heart that you haven't seen

The sight of Victor sitting in the audience next to his wife reminded Cam that he and Gray didn't have much longer together anyway. They were up against something way bigger than them. Victor was the one man Cam couldn't take down. He was like Thanos or the Knight King. In his world he reigned supreme. Cam hung his head and looked off to the side. He didn't even want to look at Gray when she walked down the aisle. Knowing that he'd failed her not only in marriage but in life was too much for him to stomach. He couldn't look at her knowing he'd failed her. He'd swore before God to keep her safe. The sudden gasp for air and ooh's and ahh's from the crowd forced him to look up. What Cam's eyes landed on was nothing shy of a vision of beauty. Gray looked like a royal, Indian goddess. A thin gold headband decorated her hair while gold earrings swung from her ears. A long sheer, gold, beaded cape trailed behind her as she walked. The high neck matching dress hugged every curve of her flawless physique. The dress was so sheer that Cam could see every inch of her bronzed skin. The only thing covering her bountiful breasts and vag was the strategically placed beadwork.

Cause I share all I have and am,
Nothing I've said is hard to understand,
All I feel I feel deeper still,
And always will,
All this love is for you

Cam stood up straight and swallowed. Gray was more mesmerizing than a leaf falling from a tree on a cool autumn day. If only for a few hours more this was his wife. *God keep her with me,* he begged internally. Out of the corner of his eye he noticed Devin ice grilling him, but Cam didn't care. It would take an army to make him look away. Gray felt the same. Seeing Cam stand in a tux right next to an altar after signing the divorce papers brought up all kinds of emotions. This should've been their wedding. It should've been her walking down the aisle to him. They should've been repledging their love to one another and God. She'd hoped after a year of being a couple, they'd have a wedding of their own. That day never came and now it never would.

If she could rewind time, she'd take back every bad thing she'd ever said to him. He'd tried his best to make her happy but all she concentrated on was the things he didn't do. Because of her selfish, conceited behavior she threw out scathing digs and withdrew her affection to punish him. Now they were officially apart. He'd signed his name on the dotted line and moved on to another woman who would give him the unwavering love he desired. She'd give him kisses instead of her ass to kiss, understanding in place of disapproval. Because of this maybe Gray didn't deserve him. Her love had been too conditional. She prayed that one day he received the love she'd withheld over the last three and a half years. Locked into his gaze, she wished they could be more, but she'd messed up and realized the error of her ways too late.

Every note that I play,
Every word I might say,
Every melody I feel are only for you and your
appeal,
Every page that I write,
Every day of my life,
Would not be filled without the things,
That my love for you now brings

As the song reached its peak, the flowers girls that consisted of Diggy's daughter, Taylani, Aoki, Press, Kayla, Sky and Beaux prodded down the aisle in their pretty little Baby's Breath crowns and tulle dresses. On the way down, Aoki placed her hand on her hip and stopped and did a jailhouse pose that wasn't authorized, Sky started crying and Beaux took off running through the seats instead of walking straight. The whole thing was a disaster, but the crowd laughed. Gray and Cam had to leave their spots and round their kids up then get them settled.

For you, I make a promise of fidelity,
Now and for eternity,
No one could replace this love,
For you, I take your hand and heart and everything,
And add to them a wedding ring,
'Cause this life is no good alone,
Since we've become one you're all I know,
If this feeling should leave I'd die,
And here's why all I am is for you,

Once everything was calm again, the doors to the winery opened and out came Kema with her father. Quan placed his hand over his heart. She looked unbelievable. Kema was a beautiful woman but that day she was breathtaking. Her hair was pulled back off her face in a chignon. A small pair of diamond earrings adorned her ears. No other jewelry was on her body. Her dress wasn't white. It was an antique crème, strapless, pearl beaded, mermaid gown. A long cathedral veil was combed perfectly into the back of her hair. This was it. This was the moment they'd both been waiting for.

Everything I do now makes sense,
All roads end,
All I do is for you,
Only for you

446

Love was in the air as Kenny Lattimore finished the song. Everyone's hearts were full. Candles lit the ceremony space illuminating the wedding party and guests. It was a gorgeous night wedding. After a handshake and a hug, Kema's father handed her over to Quan. Kema handed Gray her bouquet then took hands with her husband. Pastor Edris stood in front of the microphone and began to speak.

"Dearly Beloved, we are gathered here today in the presence of these witnesses, to join Kema Miller and Jayquan Mitchell in matrimony commended to be honorable among all; and therefore, is not to be entered into lightly but reverently, passionately, lovingly and solemnly. Into this —these two persons present now come to be joined. If any person can show just cause why they may not be joined together—let them speak now or forever hold their peace."

All the guests there were in full support of their union so neither Quan nor Kema expected anyone to object.

"Friends, we have joined here today to share with Jayquan and Kema in an important moment in their lives. Their time together, they have seen their love and understanding of each other grow and blossom and now they have decided to live out the rest of their lives as one. We are here to bear witness to the miracle of love. Marriage is the beginning of a new life. A chance of fulfilling long held dreams and an opportunity for great personal growth. The journey of a thousand miles begins with a single step. For you, your wedding today is a beautiful choreographed first step in a life long journey. As Jayquan and Kema have committed themselves to one another and their hearts before me and those gathered here today, may we all rejoice in their expression of love. The couple has prepared their own vows. Kema you may recite the vows you have written."

Taking out a small piece of paper, she cleared her throat and took the microphone.

"Quan, it is with a heart full of joy that I choose you. As we stand here today before God, our family and our friends." She became choked up. "I promise you my deepest love, my fullest devotion, my most tender care throughout all of the pressures of the present and all of the uncertainties of the future. I vow to respect you, to love you, to be faithful to you, to commit myself to you and support you from today until the day I die. I promise to have the patience that love demands and a heart that is always ready to ask for forgiveness as well as forgive. Despite my feelings, I promise to always touch toes at the end of the night." She giggled which made Quan laugh too.

"I know that in you, all of my prayers have been answered. I know that our love is a gift from God and not of our own orchestration. I praise God for you. For the love that he's given us together and the constant friendship he's blessed us with. I promise to be here by your side as your partner, forever and always, from this day forward, until death parts us. Quan, from this day forward you shall not walk alone. Through the good and the bad, through sickness and in health, I vow to always be by your side. My heart will be your shelter and my arms will be your home. As I give you my hand to hold, today I give my life to keep."

There wasn't a dry eye in the audience. Gray particularly was over wrought with emotion. How could she not be? Her best friend was living out her biggest dream and her marriage and life was coming to an end. Victor's presence reminded her of this every second.

"Quan, it's your turn." Pastor Edris instructed.

"How is this day already here when I so clearly remember the day we first met. I don't know where the time went but for once I'm so glad that it passed by. I Jayquan Mitchell, take thee Kema Miller to be my wife. In front of all these witnesses I promise to be faithful and true."

Devin covered her mouth and let out a loud cough. Kema gave her the evil eye and dared her to make another sound. She would surely kick her ass at her own wedding.

"I vow to be the man you deserve. I promise to tell you with actions and with words everyday how incredible I think you are." Quan's voice cracked. "Thank you for loving my son. Thank you for stepping in and being the mother he's never had. I am your biggest fan. Only God knows what the future holds. There may be sickness and health, poverty and wealth, but I know by God's grace that I can vow to lead this family putting God first. Putting your thoughts and desires above my own. Today, Kema, I commit myself to you. I promise to love you in good times and in bad. I vow to honor you with all my actions and love you with all my heart. I promise to cherish you and always hold you in the highest regard. Today, I give you my hand, my heart and my love without conditions."

Cam exhaled a deep breath. Hearing his best friend speak so eloquently about the woman he loved made him wished he would've professed his feelings for Gray more. After the exchange of rings, Quan and Kema rejoined hands smiling gleefully.

"This is where the two of you become one." Pastor Edris beamed. "I ask that you always remember to cherish each other. Remember this moment your entire life. I now pronounce you husband and wife. Jayquan, you may kiss your beautiful bride."

There was no hesitation on Quan's part as he took his bride into his arms and laid a sweet, loving kiss on her. The bridal party and guests cheered and whistled. Beyond happy, the newly married couple faced the audience in bliss and jumped the broom. A choir appeared out of nowhere and began to sing *Oh Happy Day*. The joy amongst the guests went up ten notches. Cam held out his arm for Gray to take. Love was in his eyes as he waited for her to take her rightful place by his side. Gray held her bouquet in hand and gazed devotedly back at him. Linking her arm through his, they made their way down the aisle and into their destiny.

22

"Don't know what to say. Now I'm running out of time.
Slipping like sand, through an hour glass, in and of itself
it's making me lose my hand. On dry land, nothings
shielding me. Hold my hand. Pour into me once again. The
life that I have it depends, oh I. . . I still need you."- Alex
Isley, "Water & Air"

Various shapes of Bamboo lanterns hung from the
sky cascading a golden glow over the reception space.
Feather balls floated above like clouds. Square and round
tables were placed around for the guests to dine. Tall vases
filled with tan feathers, small floral centerpieces and rustic
wooden chairs with white cushions decorated each one.
Kema had spared no expense. There was a grass wall with
nothing, but several rows of glasses filled with champagne.
A server made sure to keep the wall stocked with fresh
drinks. The photo booth wasn't your traditional photo
booth. Kema had a metal frame built. Pieces of greenery
hung from the beam as well as a single white swing with
photo booth written above it on a piece of lumber. A
dessert table and bar finished off the area. Nursing a glass
of Armand de Brignac Rosé, Gray sat with her back facing
Noon watching as Cam and Devin danced cheek-to-cheek.
Noon's arm was draped around her shoulder. He trailed his
fingers up and down her skin blind to the fact that her
attention was on her ex. Gray knew watching Cam and
Devin dance was stupid, but she couldn't look away. She
had to take him in while she still could. No matter how
painful it was a tsunami of tears clouded her vision as she

watched on. Gray had to pull herself together, but the tears wouldn't stay at bay. She'd never felt more alone in her life. Was this really how she was going to spend her last day, mourning the death of her marriage? God was truly cruel. Why couldn't it be her in his arms? She wanted to bathe in his smile, drown in his laughter and melt from his touch. She wondered did he even notice her sitting there. After their walk down the aisle they hadn't said a word to each other. Their dates and kids kept them occupied.

Each time Cam and Devin twirled in a circle a part of her died. Gray didn't even know how she was still living. Her body had been reduced to nothing but shattered bones. The air became heavy as her will to breathe decreased. The need to cry made her want to vomit. Gray held her head back and blinked back her tears. She had to tuck her emotions away for later. It was Kema's wedding day. Nothing was more important than her.

"You a'ight babe?" Noon asked, pulling her further into him.

"Yeah. I'm just tired." She lied.

"Excuse me everyone." The DJ interrupted the music. "The bride and groom would like to call Cam and Gray up for their speeches."

"It's showtime." She forced herself to smile.

"You got this." Noon assured.

Saddened by everything that was taking place, Gray kept her eyes on the ground as she made her way to the front. If she looked at Cam, she'd turn into a big ball of mush and break down and cry. Cam peeped her odd behavior but figured it was because of Victor's impending threat. He wanted to reach out and comfort her, but things were so awkward between them that it didn't make sense.

452

She hadn't said a word about him signing the divorce papers. He found it strange. Was she pleased that she'd gotten her wish? If she was in her head over the Victor situation, she had nothing to worry about. Cam hadn't given up hope. He was going to find a way to get her out of this.

"You wanna go first or second?" He asked, taking the mic.

"I'll go first." She spoke somberly.

Cam wondered how she was going to give an encouraging speech when her mood was so sad. Gray might've been in her feelings and afraid for her life, but she was a showgirl at heart. She knew how to turn on the charm when it was time. Holding her index cards, she looked out into the crowd. All eyes were on her.

"Hello everyone. I'm Gray, the matron of honor. Before I get started, I do have a serious confession to make. Shortly after Kema and Quan started dating, she told me that he had invited her on a camping trip. And uh, this is where I gotta be honest with you, I told her to run. Black people don't go camping. I was like what kind of new-fangled nigga is this," she joked. "I told her to change her name, her address, her appearance 'cause this man had to be crazy. But in my defense, we are talking about real camping like peeing behind a tree camping. For those of you who don't know Quan all that well, he's like very out doorsy and Kema . . . well, the most out doorsy thing she does is have a glass of wine on the patio. Needless to say, she didn't listen to me so here we are. I guess I was wrong."

The audience laughed.

"Kema entered my life many years ago and by a glorious twist of fate ended up becoming one of the best things that has ever happened to me. We've lived a lot of life us two. Whether it was our daily Facetime conversations, to our countless nights watching Sex and the City, Kema has always been the Samantha to my Carrie. My constant reminder that it's not what you have it's who you have as we walk through this crazy thing called life. She's the girl I can count on to pick me up off every bathroom floor I've ever laid on, to believe in me when I struggle to believe in myself, to celebrate my greatest highs alongside me and to tell me when I'm being selfish and obnoxious. It's a very rare thing when you find someone who's happy for your happiness and sad for your sadness, but when that happens, that person breaks all friendship barriers and they become your family. It is a very humbling thing when someone asks you to stand by their side on arguably one of the most important days of their life. It is with great honor that I raise my glass to you, your new husband and a happily ever after."

While the guests cheered, Kema rushed to her feet and hugged Gray with all her might. After the disastrous rehearsal dinner, and her showing up late that morning, she and Gray were on rocky ground. Her speech, however, reminded her of how deep their friendship flowed. Sure, sometimes they argued and fought but that's what sisters do. No matter what, she and Gray would always be there for one another.

"I love you friend." She gushed.

"I love you too." Gray held onto her for as long as she possibly could.

Kema didn't know it but it would be their last hug. Quan tapping her on the shoulder is the only reason she backed away. He loved Gray's speech and wanted to give thanks. Quan hadn't been happy with her behavior as of late, but was very appreciative that she'd tried to make amends. If she could've, she would've kept hugging Kema forever. Next up was Cam. Unlike Gray, he wasn't as sure about himself or his speech. He hated public speaking. He didn't like to talk in front of crowds. He couldn't look like no punk tho. He had to represent for his friend to the fullest. Nervously, Cam pulled out his speech and cleared his throat. He prayed he'd done a good job. He'd been working on it since his release.

"There comes a time in everyone's life when they meet their one true love." He unknowingly glanced over at Gray. "Their soulmate. The person that's going to love them for the rest of their life. That moment came for Quan thirty-four years ago . . . when he met me."

An eruption of laughter and applause burst throughout the crowd. Gray cracked a smile and laughed. It wouldn't have been Cam if he didn't make his speech about himself.

"For those of you who don't know me, I'm Cam. Quan's oldest and best friend. To be asked by Quan to be his best man is an honor for me but it's also very honorable of him because he's finally admitting to each and everyone of you that I truly am the best."

"You a bad bitch, Papa!" Press clapped 'causing everyone to laugh again.

"Nah, I'ma real-ass nigga, pretty girl." Cam corrected her, making the guests chuckle some more.

Once the laughter died down, he continued.

"I would also like to say how beautiful . . . most of you look tonight. I'm glad that most of you actually made an effort. But speaking of beautiful our bride Kema looks absolutely stunning. It's clear to see how Quan has become so enchanted by her but to be honest her beauty is making Quan a little bit more handsome than he actually is."

All the guests snickered, thoroughly enjoying his speech.

"Growing up Quan and I were polar opposites. He was smart and driven. I was the funny goofball. He was athletic. I was and still am incredibly good looking."

"You sure are baby!" Devin whistled.

Gray rolled her eyes and groaned.

"If Kema and Quan were having a lowkey night going bowling or out to eat they'd invite me to tag along. See, Quan knew I was lonely and knew I didn't do well being by myself. I don't know if he ever told Kema this but regardless she never made me feel like a third wheel. I remember one night after leaving the club, Quan was laughing, smiling, having a great time, and at that moment I knew Kema was going to be around for the long haul. She made my friend happy in a way that I hadn't seen in over ten years. I can honestly say Kema, that you may be the reason Quan and I are as close as we are today. Over the last four years our friendship has gotten tighter. We do still fight but for different reasons that are way deeper than when we were kids. Through thick and thin, good or bad, you're my brother. I've always looked up to you and admired you. Kema, I could not be any happier that you are apart of our family. I wish you nothing but happiness, love and success for the rest of your years." Cam raised his glass.

Everyone followed then drank from their flutes. Quan was speechless. Cam had never spoken so kindly from the heart. He wasn't the kind of nigga that wore his heart on his sleeve. That's how he knew his words were real. Blessed by his friendship and love, Quan gave his brother, his best friend a brotherly hug.

"Thanks fool." He patted Cam's back.

"You know I got you, fam."

The rest of the wedding party, as well as some of the guests, came up to congratulate Gray and Cam on their speeches. Some of those guests included Mina and Victor Gonzalez. A fear like no other swept over Gray. Victor's presence alone shook her to the core. Cam sensed her hesitancy and pulled her by his side. She had to know she wasn't alone.

"You both did a wonderful job." Mina acknowledged them with a friendly embrace.

"Thank you, Mina." Gray tried to steady her shaky voice.

It was hard for her to even look her in the eyes, she was so nervous.

"It's good to see you again, Cam." Mina greeted him with a sweet smile.

"Same here, Mrs. Gonzalez."

"Baby, I'll be back. I want to go say hello to the bride and groom."

"Okay sweetheart." Victor waited till his wife was out of earshot before he gave Cam his attention.

"Cam." He shook his hand firmly.

"Jefe." Cam returned his strength.

Victor smirked. He liked that despite his obvious disadvantage Cam still refused to back down. His bravado, however, wouldn't help him out of this situation. He'd failed to clear his wife's name as a rat. Because of his failure she would pay with her life.

"You have until midnight."

Cam's brain formulated words, but he could not speak. His mouth parted in shock. Glancing at his toes, he looked back up again and caught Victor's eye. No way was he really going to go through with killing his wife. He wasn't the kind of man who begged but for Gray he'd do that and more.

"Victor, just give me—"

"No." He cut him off.

Cam could feel his anger snowball inside of his stomach. He couldn't concentrate on anything else. His heart beat faster and harder than ever before. It took everything in him not to smash Victor's brain in with his bare hands. Negative thoughts swarmed his mind. His heart felt as if it was going to explode. What was Cam going to do? He couldn't fail Gray. He couldn't fail their children or their family.

"Gray." Victor leaned down and gave her the kiss of death before walking away.

The skin of her forehead burned from his peck.

"What time is it?" She choked out.

Her esophagus had begun to close up. Cam checked his watch. It was 10:50 p.m. He didn't wanna tell her the time but knew she would find out one way or another.

"Fifteen minutes to eleven."

Gray held her stomach as if she'd been kicked with a steel-toe boot. This could not be happening. She knew it was coming, but now it wasn't just a threat anymore, her death was a guarantee.

"Will the bridal party take to the dance floor. Grab a partner! It's time to dance!" The DJ announced.

"Fuck nah. Ya'll got me fucked up." Stacy shook his head.

There were only three bridesmaids to choose from. Cam would certainly pick Gray so that only left Heidi and Tee-Tee. There was no way in hell he was dancing with him.

"Shut up, Stacy. I'll dance wit' you." Selicia took him by the hand.

"I ain't wanna dance with his fat-ass no way." Tee-Tee tooted his lips and took to the floor with Bernard.

Heidi danced with Li'l Quan. Slow dancing was the last thing that Gray or Cam wanted to do. Not dancing would cause too much attention. They didn't wanna upset the flow of the night or Kema and Quan. They'd upset them enough that week. They also didn't want to draw attention from the kids. They'd been having a good time feasting on sweets and playing with their cousins and friends. Well, everyone was having fun except Aoki. Gray noticed that she'd spent majority of the night at the table alone on her phone sulking. She caught her several times eying Priest and his girlfriend with pure hate. Gray figured she'd developed a crush on him. She'd planned on asking her about it after the wedding but now that time would never come.

"C'mon." Cam led her shaking body out onto the custom-made dance floor.

The thought of taking Gray and the kids and running crossed his mind but there was no use. Victor hadn't come to the wedding with just his wife. He would bet his life that he had his own personal security planted inside the venue and around it. There was no place for them to go. Even if they could escape, running was useless. Victor would find them wherever they went. Chest to chest, everything slowed down to nothing as the DJ spinned the gut-wrenching Luther Vandross classic *Superstar*.

Don't you remember you told me you loved me baby
You said you'd be coming back this way again baby
Baby, baby, baby, baby, oh, baby, I love you, I
really do

Gray's entire body became one giant salty teardrop as she and Cam eased into a slow rhythm. Silently, they danced and spinned. The lights above twinkled with each step they took. She used to love to slow dance. The weight of a strong hand on the small of her back and the feel of her light feet gliding across the floor made her think she could fly. All she had to do was stretch out her wings and take wind. That feeling was long gone. Gray no longer felt like a bird. She was trapped. She didn't feel anything but grief. Emptiness stretched across her heart. Nothingness took hold of her weary body. The only thing keeping her upright was Cam. Without him she'd surely collapse to the floor. The weight of the world rested on her exhausted shoulders.

Long ago and oh so far away

I fell in love with you before the second show

And your guitar, it sounds so sweet and clear

But you're not really here

It's just the radio

Despite the heaviness in his stomach, Cam tried his best to comfort Gray. Gently, he rubbed her back as his chin rested on the top of her head. Gray sank into the warmth of his hold, appreciative of his touch. Neither of them cared that their significant others were watching them from afar in shock and horror. None of that mattered. The only thing of importance was him and her. Who would've thought when they became one that this is where they'd end. Resting her head on his chest, Gray swayed her body as they went round and round in a circle. Between Luther's velvety voice, the moody piano and heavenly violins neither she nor Cam would be able to keep it together much longer. Numbness pounded in Cam's brain. Several times his knees wanted to buckle but he held it together for her. Mountains of heaviness threatened to expose the disgusting truth he'd been harboring. He'd failed her. He'd failed their kids. He'd failed them. As the depressing music played on, Cam's tough façade cracked, and he began to cry.

Loneliness is a such a sad affair, sad affair
And I can hardly wait to be with you again

Gray closed her eyes. In Cam's hold she was cushioned better than any butterfly-to-be. He bathed her in his warmth and enthralling cologne. When the song ended it would be too soon. She'd want more but this was it for them. They'd hit the end of the road. There was so much that needed to be said and so little time. Apprehensively, Gray looked up into his whiskey brown eyes and cried.

"Why do you love me?" She died to know.

Cam was shocked by her question. He thought she knew.

"Cause I see you." He answered truthfully.

Now was not the time for a bunch of faking and fronting. He had to clear up anything that might've been misconstrued.

"Well, if you see me then why won't you leave me?"

"Cause I *see* you." He made it clear.

She was a mirror image of him. Even with all of her flaws his love would never waiver.

"You're an organ in my body, Gray. If you fail, I fail."

Gray dropped her head and let her tears fall where they may. Cam wasn't playing fair. He had no right to say these things to her now.

"Look at me." He demanded.

Doing as she was told; Gray gave him eye contact.

"I've been operating from a place of fear and not love. Fear of losing you. Losing the kids. Fear of the ramifications that come along with all that shit, but I refuse to let it happen. I need you to understand that you, me and the kids are gonna always be alright. I got you, just have me."

And what to say, to say, to make you come again, oh honey

Come back to me again
I wanna be, I wanna be anywhere you are

Every part of Gray wanted to believe that he'd come to her rescue not just physically but emotionally, but the stakes were higher this time. Time wasn't on their side. It was already 11:00 p.m. She only had an hour left. Unless Cam pulled a rabbit out of his hat, she was done.

"I didn't do it." She professed.

"I know you didn't." Cam hugged her so tight, she could barely breathe.

A sense of relief washed over Gray. She didn't know how much she needed to hear that until he'd said it. Pushing him back some, she held her head high and went into mommy mode. She'd never written a will so Cam would need to know how to proceed after she was gone.

"My insurance policy information is in my office back at home in Paris. Along with all of my banking info. Each of the kids have a trust fund set up in their names that they can't touch until they're 21—"

"Gray." Cam felt his face growing hot.

"No, Cam. Let me finish."

Cam didn't want to. Every part of him wanted to shut her up. He didn't want to have this conversation. It wouldn't help anything. It would only make him sadder but reluctantly he closed his mouth.

"The triplets turn three next month on August 1st."

Shocked, Cam stopped swaying to the beat. His babies were born four days before him and shared the same zodiac sign. He had no idea.

"They'll be starting preschool in the fall so you have to get them registered. Aoki will be going to the seventh grade this year and Press will be going to the fourth." Gray became distraught with tears.

Don't you remember you told me you loved me baby
You said you'd be coming back this way again baby
Baby, baby, baby, oh, baby, yes, I love you, I really do

"Sky can't go to sleep without having her Elsa costume on. Sometimes, when she can't sleep, I'll give her a cup of warm milk to put her to bed. And she's allergic to strawberries." One tear after another slipped from her blue eyes.

Cam could barely look at her. Seeing Gray in so much agony was killing him.

"Gray, stop. It's gon' be alright."

"Beaux is very sneaky." She ignored his plea. Don't let her cute face fool you. She likes to hide Sky and Reign's toys around the house to make them mad. Even though she's mischievous, she's such a great little helper. She loves to ask questions. She wants to know everything. When it rains, she likes to come in my room and get in the bed with me so remember that, okay?"

"No. I won't. You're gonna be fine. I don't wanna hear this shit."

"Beaux will only wear her hair in pigtails. Sky likes to wear her hair down. Reign had the most problems breathing when he was born so he stayed in the NICU the longest. His breathing has gotten a lot better but sometimes I still have to give him breathing treatments. Melody and Aoki will teach you. And Cam please don't fire Melody. The kids love her and she's great with them." She begged.

Cam bit his upper lip to suppress his cry. Love and sorrow was all he felt as she continued to talk. The love he felt for her was saccharine. Decades after she was gone it would remain strong. He'd never love another woman after her. Gray was the end all be all. The realization that they would never be together again filled him with great sorrow. Cam could only pray that God would throw him a bone and reunite them in the afterlife or the next lifetime. For in that

464

moment the loss of losing Gray was more than his fragile heart could take. *God please,* he pleaded.

"I'm sorry I kept your son away from you so long. I thought because he was so little that he'd be fine without you, but I was wrong. He needed you just as much as I did. As I do." Gray wept uncontrollably.

The tears that poured from her stormy irises were heart wrenchingly painful to watch. Why was God doing this to them . . . to him? Cam hadn't felt this helpless since his mother died. He couldn't endure that kind of torture again. He'd barely made it through the first time. Losing Gray would be the end of his existence.

"Baby, I got you. You don't have to tell me any of this." He pleaded.

"I know you think that Press is delicate but believe or not she's stronger than Aoki. Press is levelheaded and nurturing. It's going to take her a while to find her voice, but she'll get there. Just continue to encourage her to be herself. The kids her age make fun of her cause she wears reading glasses, likes to learn and watches musicals. They call her a weirdo cause she doesn't have many friends and rarely speaks. She's a loner Cam and Press needs to know that's okay."

Hearing that Press was going through so much in school ripped Cam's heart apart. He had no idea all of this was going on. Press hadn't let on one bit that she'd been bullied. He guessed Gray was right. She was stronger than she led him to believe or maybe he was the one who perceived her as weak.

"You're gonna have to keep a close eye on Aoki. She's gonna take this the hardest. Once I'm gone, she'll be like me. She'll have no one." Gray cried harder than she ever had before.

Her body shook violently. Cam cradled her in his arms. His fists were clenched so tight they'd begun to turn blue. The sound of heartbreak echoed with each grief ridden whimper that passed Gray's dry lips. Her heartbreak brought on the disturbing reality that death was around the corner. He would live life raising their children alone. This awareness hit him hard, so as he watched Gray tremble with sorrow, a part of him died too.

When are you gonna say "it's alright, it's alright,
ooh baby"
"It's alright, it's alright, oh right now"
Keep like that, keep it like that

"Mama." Aoki tugged on her dress.

"Yes baby." Gray quickly wiped her face.

It was of no use. Her face was sodden with tears. Aoki had watched her mother cry long enough. She'd tried to stay in a child's place and stay out of it but she refused to let anyone bring her mother down.

"You a'ight?"

"No, but I will be." Gray lied, kissing the tip of her nose.

She wouldn't be okay, but she'd never tell her daughter that. She wanted Aoki to remember her at her best, not her worse.

"You sure? Cause if you crying over that Devin bitch, I'll bust her ass." Aoki glowered.

"Watch your mouth and what you talkin' about?"

"She was over there talkin' mad shi—I mean mad crap about you. I guess she mad 'cause you and Pop back in love again."

"What?" Cam drew his head back. "How you figure that?"

Aoki smacked her lips.

"I ain't blind. Anybody with eyes can see it. You was holding ma like she was the last piece of chicken."

"Go sit down." Gray laughed.

"Nah for real. Love looks good on you two."

Gray and Cam looked at one another. Aoki was right. This version of them was a wonderful sight to see.

"Aye yo." Quan interrupted their familial moment. "I need to holla at you for a minute."

Cam saw the manila folder in his hand. His lawyer had finally come through with his case file.

"Here I come. Gray, go clean yourself up and meet me back here."

"Baby, it doesn't even matter." She sighed, not even realizing she'd called him baby.

"Yes, it does. We still have time."

Gray checked her watch.

"Not much."

It was 11:23. Cam took her hand in his.

"Have I ever let you down?"

"Is that a trick question?" Gray smirked, arching her brow.

"I got you." Cam said seriously.

Gray swallowed her anxiety. If she had any chance at survival, she had to open her heart and allow herself to trust him again.

"You believe me?" Cam's earnest eyes prayed she said yes.

Her answer would define their future.

Gray breathlessly said, "Yes."

A sense of relief washed over Cam's tall frame.

"Bet. Meet me back here in ten minutes." He hesitantly let her go.

Loss consumed Gray as soon as their fingers untwined. She didn't want to leave Cam's side. She felt safest when she was with him. Then, she noticed Noon across the room frowning at her. Gray honestly was shocked he was still there. She'd invited him to attend the wedding with her and hadn't spent hardly any time with him.

"Keep a close eye on your brother and sister while I go to the restroom." She told Aoki.

"Yes ma'am."

Gray headed to the ladies room. She was sure her makeup looked a mess. Sure enough, tear stains streaked her foundation. Taking a paper towel, she used it to blot the spots where her makeup was messed up. As she pulled herself together in the mirror, the sound of the door opening caught her attention. On high alert, Gray's heart thudded in her chest as she turned to see who had entered. A look of annoyance crossed her face when she realized it was her arch nemesis, Devin.

"What do I have to do to get rid of you?" She approached Gray with venom.

She'd had about all she could take of her and her bad-ass kids. The way Gray had practically threw herself at Cam on the dance floor was pathetic. Devin had to make it clear, once and for all, that he was her man. She might've lost the battle when it came to Gunz, but she'd be damned if she didn't win the war for Cam's heart.

"Excuse me?" Gray looked at her like she was stupid.

"My life was perfect until you and your ashy-ass kids came back."

Gray scoffed and gave Devin her back. She didn't have time to verbally decimate her.

"Devin, you better get the fuck out my face. Now is not the time to play wit' me. Trust me this is not what you want girlfriend." Gray continued to fix her makeup.

"Just 'cause you swole don't mean I'm scared of you."

That did it. Gray turned around and shot daggers at Devin with her eyes. If she wanted to fight, it was go time. She was about to die anyway. She might as well go out with a bang. This confrontation was thirteen years overdue.

"You know, I would slap you, but animal cruelty is against the law." Gray quipped, leaning against the sink.

"Ha-ha-ha." Devin mocked. "You know what I don't like about you big bitches?" She stepped closer.

"You feel like somebody owes you something. Cam don't owe you shit but to be a father to his kids, that's it. Whatever ya'll had three years ago is over. He's with me now. We live together. I'm the one that's been there for him this whole time. Where were you?" She placed her hand on her chin and pondered the question. "Oh yeah, you were in Paris eating croissants getting bigger . . . and bigger . . . and bigger . . . and bigger."

Truly unaffected by her jab, Gray continued to lean against the sink with a blank expression on her face. Seeing she hadn't gotten under her skin, Devin continued to talk shit.

"You were in Paris holding his kids hostage like a fuckin' psychopath and you wonder why he don't want you. Yet you still make it a point to be desperate and chase behind him knowing he's in a whole relationship. Crying won't make him love you, Gray. Those kids won't make him love you either and that wack-ass marriage certificate really ain't gon' make him love you. He loves me. Not you so get that through that obese brain of yours. It's over. You and your illegitimate, dusty, forever hungry, soon to be on Weight Watchers, chinky eyed, contact wearing, I eat dogs for fun, Bebe's kids need to go back where ya'll came from and leave me and my man the fuck alone."

Totally unfazed by her rant, Gray cocked her head to the side and simply stared at Devin. Before her was a woman so insecure and delusional it was almost sad to take witness of.

"You done?" She yawned and checked the polish on her nails.

"No, bitch. I'm just getting started."

———

With a new found determination to keep Gray alive, Cam followed Quan inside a conference room inside the winery. Gray was only a few feet away in the restroom. He could get to her quickly in case any crazy shit went down. Victor was a man that held true to his word. It wasn't midnight yet so she should be fine. Once inside the conference room, Quan closed the door behind them and faced Cam with trepidation.

"Are those the papers?" He questioned eagerly.

Cam didn't have a second to waste.

"Yeah, but ain't no point in getting your hopes up, bruh. The informants name is blacked out." Quan handed him the file.

Cam flipped through the paperwork frantically. Sure enough, the person's name had a bold black bar over it.

"Fuuuuuuuuuck!" He threw the entire folder across the room.

Papers went flying everywhere. This was his last shot at saving Gray. What was he going to do now? Outraged, he grabbed the conference table and flipped it over. In a huff, he undid his bowtie and unbuttoned his shirt. Cam couldn't breathe. He felt like his lungs were filling with water and he couldn't come up for air.

"I'm sorry, man." Quan wanted to say more but there were no words in the English dictionary that would comfort his friend in his greatest time of need.

"What you gon' do?"

"I don't know."

Cam truly felt helpless.

"I'm down for whatever." Quan revealed the gun holster inside his tuxedo jacket.

This was why they were brothers. Even on his wedding day Quan was ready to shoot it out but Cam couldn't allow him to take it there. He'd just married the love of his life. He finally had the family he'd always wanted. There was no way he was going to allow his friend to lose his life. Besides, this wasn't Quan's fight. It was his.

"I appreciate it but I gotta handle this on my own."

"You can't take Victor alone."

"Shit, even if I did have you by my side, it would still be a suicide mission."

Cam's shoulders slumped. He was truly fucked.

"All I know is if she leaves this earth, I'm leaving with her. That's how much she means to me bro. That's my baby. She's the other half of me. The better half of me. She's my best friend, my wife, my heart, my soul, my life."

"I get it, bro. I feel the same way about Kema."

"You got my kids?"

Cam couldn't think of anyone else he'd want to raise his children in his absence.

"Do you even have to ask?"

———

Feeling her cunt, Devin continued her tirade against Gray. She was filled with so much animosity, she couldn't contain herself. Gray checked the time. It was 11:37. She was late meeting Cam. She didn't have time for this. She had to get out of there.

472

"You got a whole nigga you ain't even tell Cam about. Who's to say them Rugrats are even his. They might be Three O'Clock's or whatever his name is. We all know you a hoe." Devin looked Gray up and down. "You'll fuck any nigga that'll give yo' big ass a cheeseburger and you'll really get freaky if he supersize it. You are a bitch, Gray. You left that man for dead when he needed you most. What kind of wife does that? And you set him up! How is it the day after you found out he was with me; he ends up in jail. Girl bye, you ain't fooling nobody but the mirror you look into every day."

Instead of being upset, Gray snorted with laughter.

"This bitch is so delusional. You funny tho." She wagged her finger in Devin's face.

"I'ma give you that. You should take this circus act of yours on the road. But before you do let me explain something to you li'l girl. You gon' always play second fiddle to me. You've been the side hoe since we met. None of these niggas wanna claim you bitch. You was only good for letting Gunz nut on your forehead. Cam only moved you in 'cause he felt sorry for you. If you think for one second that *my* husband loves you then you're dumber than I fuckin' thought. You're a pet dog. A mutt. Cam tolerates you. You're nothing but a place for him to drop his cum at night. Nothing more, nothing less. You will never be me." Gray got all the way in Devin's face.

"You will never have his last name. You wanna know why? Cause I'm not going no fuckin' where. I'ma be here forever . . . and ever. . . and ever. . . and ever." Gray got her second wind.

Fuck that. She wasn't dying. In the words of Arya Stark not today.

"Cause guess what? I'm his fuckin' wife. He chose me. He will choose me time and time again. You wanna know why? 'Cause that man loves me from the top of my head to the bottom of my feet. You will never know how it feels to be loved by him 'cause his heart belongs to me. You were just the intermission. I'm the whole fuckin' movie."

Devin flushed in distress. She'd come in there with the intention of going off on Gray and ended up receiving the read of a lifetime.

"Let's be clear, the only reason you're even in this so-called girlfriend position is because I allowed you to be but that's over now. Your services are no longer needed and your position has been terminated effective immediately. Wifey's home and I'm reclaiming my time and my man. I ain't going nowhere." Gray spoke her life into existence.

"And just so you know how serious I am, where do you think he was last night?"

Devin's eyes nearly popped out of her head. She'd feared when Cam left the house during the middle of the night that he'd gone to her.

"Eating my pussy. After an hour I begged him to stop but he wouldn't. He kept going . . . and going . . . and going." Gray grinned devilishly. "Poor you. You really thought you had a chance. None of these niggas will ever love you. But you know, maybe if you keep having foursomes or whatever it is that you do, you'll find somebody. It just won't be Cam. Now you have a nice night. I'm about to go find my husband." Gray bumped her shoulder as she walked by.

"Oh, and be careful when you walk out. I don't want you to hurt yourself stepping on that." Gray held onto the door handle.

"Stepping on what?" Devin looked down.

"Your face."

———

As midnight approached, Cam sat inside the conference room alone. He should've been meeting up with Gray but how could he face her when he'd failed her? Checking his watch, he only had fifteen minutes left. Time was against him. He'd exhausted every option in his playbook. Cam needed to face the music, but he couldn't. He couldn't watch his rib be taken away to die. If that made him a pussy, then so be it. Cam held his head back and groaned. He'd hate himself forever if he let her face death alone. Fuck that. They'd face it together. For the sake of their children, one of them needed to stay behind but Cam couldn't honestly see himself living without Gray. He wouldn't cower out at the last minute and choose himself like his father did. He was going to ride it out with her. That's what a husband should do. And sure, his father didn't know his mother would die in a plane crash, but if he'd been there, she wouldn't have had to face her last minutes on earth alone. Unlike Cam Sr. he'd be there to hold her hand. They'd take their last breaths together. Rising to his feet, Cam pulled back his shoulders. He'd never been afraid of death. He was surprised he hadn't died sooner. Defeated, one by one he walked around the room picking up the papers from his case file. As he lifted one of the sheets, he couldn't help but notice how the light from the overhead bulb seeped through the blacked-out areas. Standing up straight, Cam raised the sheet of paper over his head and aimed it towards the light. A slow smile crept upon his face as he realized he could see through the blacked-out area. And there it was. The name of the person who'd snitched on him was there in plain sight.

"LaPorsha Angelique Wright." He read LaLa's government name loud. "You gotta be fuckin' kidding me." Cam balled the paper up in his fist, he was so mad.

The whole time he'd been locked up, she never even crossed his mind. His focus had been on Gray the whole time. *How the fuck did she even know,* he thought. Cam racked his brain until the night at the club during All Star Weekend popped in his head. She'd overheard his and Quan's entire conversation while they were outside the restroom arguing. She'd overheard everything. He was so drunk and high off his ass that he'd completely forgotten she was in there. Because of her, he'd missed out on the birth of his kids. Nothing would be able to save her. She'd crossed a line that couldn't be forgiven. His wife's life hung in the balance because of her. Cam wasn't going to rest until she was beaten down then dead. He was on her ass. There wasn't a corner of the earth she'd be able to hide. He had to get to Gray and then reveal what he'd learned to Victor.

"Thank you, God." Cam gathered up the last of the paperwork and headed towards the door.

It was 11:50. He only had ten minutes to spare before all hell broke loose. As he was leaving out the conference room, Pastor Edris came in.

"Brother Cam." He stopped him. "Are you okay? I saw you and Sister Gray were very emotional on the dance floor. Did you two have another breakthrough?"

"Something like that but hold up, Preach, I gotta go." Cam tried to step past him.

476

"Calm down. You letting your anxiety get the best of you. Remember patience is a virtue. What's going on? Maybe I could be of service."

"I just learned my ex was the one who dropped a dime on me. I gotta get to Gray and tell her."

"And what do you plan to do, now that you have that information? Remember, vengeance is mine said the lord."

"Well, God knows my heart. That bitch is good as dead." Cam tried to push past him.

"I can't let you do that, Brother Cam." Pastor Edris blocked his path and closed the door behind him.

"I know you on your Jesus shit right now but now is not the time."

"I'm truly sorry it has to come to this." Pastor Edris pulled something from his pocket.

"Wha—" Cam looked down to see he'd been stabbed.

The butcher knife he'd stolen from the kitchen plunged into Cam's chiseled flesh and made a sickening squishing sound. Cam held his stomach in shock. Scarlet red blood formed a never-ending circle, staining his stark white shirt. Confusion was written on his face as he looked back at Pastor Edris. He didn't understand what was happening.

11:52 p.m.

"The Marciano's send their regards." Pastor Edris twisted the knife some more.

With each turn, the blade sunk deeper and deeper tearing Cam's gut to shreds. Blood gushed in a steady flow from his wound. It was strong and thick and flowed through his shaking fingers as he gripped his stomach. Cam gasped for air as he stared helplessly into Pastor Edris' cold brown eyes. He'd always thought his eyes held kindness but now all he saw was hate. There was no trace of the man who'd counseled him all week. Boy what a fool he'd been. He'd fallen right into Gunz's trap. Cam knew he was would retaliate for the murder of his family but never in a million years did he expect Pastor Edris to be a mole. Once again, he'd underestimated how far Gunz would go to take him down. Then, it dawned on Cam that Pastor Edris had been a spy the whole time. All the signs were there. He'd wondered how Gunz knew he'd be at the cemetery that day he'd ambushed him. He knew because he'd mentioned it in front of Pastor Edris at the barbeque. Why hadn't he done a thorough investigation when he said he was a former street dude? Cam was slipping. It all made sense now. Pastor Edris was a former member of MCM. Cam wondered if it was by happenstance that he'd officiated the wedding. Had that been apart of the plan the whole time? Why had his father pulled out at the last minute? Gunz had probably had his father removed on purpose. Cam would have to figure that part out later. The angel of death was sitting on his shoulder.

11:53 p.m.

Death wasn't kind. Cam knew this. He'd seen so many people die that he couldn't keep count. His battle buddies had died right in front of him. He still struggled with the gruesome memory. Death didn't pretend to care about the innocent. It snatched your soul without remorse or hesitation, but Cam refused to die. July 11th would not be the day he died.

Without warning, Pastor Edris ripped the knife from his injured flesh. A guttural roar mixed with the sound of

478

suffering came from Cam's mouth as he sank to his knees. Blood seeped from the gaping hole in his abdomen. This wasn't just any old stab wound; this one was fatal. He was losing blood at a rapid speed. If he didn't get help, he'd surely die but first he had a preacher to kill.

"Repeat after me, Brother Cam." Pastor Edris circled around his bloody body. "Yea though I walk through the valley of the shadow of death, I will fear no evil: for thou *art* with me; thy rod and thy staff they comfort me."

11:54 p.m.

Cam slumped over holding his stomach. His vision was starting to blur. Pastor Edris crouched down behind him with the blood-stained knife in his hand. He had to get the job done before someone walked in. A clean swipe to the throat would end it all. Pastor Edris hated what he was doing but it was either Cam's life or his. His plan was never to counsel him and Gray, but their troubled marriage ended up working out in his favor. Gunz had threatened the lives of him and his entire family if he didn't takeout Cam on his behalf. Ten years before, when Pastor Edris was a part of MCM, Gunz had saved his life when he'd gotten gunned down. He'd handled the niggas that shot him and had them all murdered. For that, Pastor Edris owed him his life. Even though he was a man of the cloth, now that Gunz needed him, he had to return the favor. Gripping the butcher knife tight, he held the blade to Cam's sweaty neck.

"Forgive me lord." He pulled the knife back to slice his throat.

11:57 p.m.

Before he could, Cam used one of the tactical moves he'd learned in the army and snapped his wrist which caused the knife to fall. Holding his broken wrist,

Cam yanked his arm and flipped his body over his back. Pastor Edris now lay before him screaming in pain. Swiftly, Cam slipped off his bowtie and wrapped it around Pastor Edris' neck. Using all his strength he pulled. Pastor Edris' eyes grew wide with fear. Ragged gasps for air fled his throat. An immense amount of pressure from the tie caused his lungs to ache. His eyes bulged as he tried to take in air, but to no avail. Cam wasn't letting up. He'd die by strangulation.

11:58 p.m.

Clawing at his neck, Pastor Edris kicked his legs in hopes of breaking loose. Cam's grip was just too strong. He held the bowtie so tight that the skin of his hand began to peel. Sweat poured from Cam's face. Every vein in his neck protruded as he pulled with all his might. Pastor Edris wasn't making it out of that conference room alive. He'd die making sure of it. Using the little strength that he had, Pastor Edris tried clawing at Cam's face. That only infuriated Cam and made him tug on the tie some more. Using all of his might, he yanked Pastor Edris back. Unable to keep up the fight, Pastor Edris felt his soul begin to leave his body and go to a peaceful place. His heart rate slowed so did his breaths. Seconds later, he blacked out and met his maker. Once he was gone and his body went limp, Cam released his hold and eased back out of breath. He too was about to lose consciousness. Death wasn't on his agenda tho. He had to get to Gray. He prayed to God he wasn't too late.

————

With a new found confidence, Gray stepped out of the restroom prepared to face death right in the eye. She wasn't giving up that easily. She had her kids and her man

480

to live for. She wanted her family back. Victor was not going to take that from her. She'd kill him before she allowed him to kill her. Rushing outside, she searched the crowd with her eyes for Cam but didn't see him anywhere. Wondering where he could be she walked around the whole area. Gray's heart was racing so fast she thought she was going to past out. *Where is he,* she wondered.

"Press." She stopped her daughter. "Have you seen Papa?"

"No." She answered then took off running behind King.

Bewildered, Gray started to sweat. This couldn't be happening to her. Cam swore he would protect her. He promised to be there. No way was he letting her down again.

"Quan!" She ran over to him in a panic. "Where is Cam?"

"Last time I saw him, he was in the conference room."

Gray didn't even have time to say thank you. Quickly, she raced back inside but as she stepped across the threshold, she bumped right into the man she hoped to avoid. Victor stood there in all his frightening glory with a gold-plated pistol in hand. A silencer was attached to the barrel. The last thing Gray expected was for him to get his hands dirty and kill her his self. Adrenaline flooded her system as they linked eyes. Her body wanted to flee but there was no place for her to go. It was midnight. Time had officially run out. She was so scared she wanted to vomit. Saliva thickened in her mouth as beads of sweat trickled down her spine. Victor raised the gun and aimed it at her forehead. Gray slowly closed her eyes and prayed that her kids wouldn't walk into the winery as her body fell lifeless to the ground.

"Can you please tell Cam and my kids I love them?" She wept.

Victor didn't say a word as he took his gun off safety. Just as he was about to pull the trigger and blow Gray's brains out, the sound of a door opening from across the way caught their attention.

"Gray!" Cam called out her name wearily.

Simultaneously, she and Victor looked his way. Cam could barely stand. He stumbled out of the conference room with blood seeping from his mouth and stomach. With great effort, he tried to make his way to her, but all of his strength was gone. The pain in his abdomen burned like fire. A cloud of black swarmed his vision. The only thing he could concentrate on was the sound of his decreasing heartbeat. His breaths had shallowed to virtually nothing.

"Cam!" Gray pushed Victor out of the way to get to him.

Before she could, Cam's body hit the ground with a loud thud. Gently, she took him into her arms.

"Baby, what happened?" She asked, wiping the blood from his mouth away.

"It was . . ." His eyes fluttered closed.

"It was who baby? Who did this to you?" She held him near as Victor concealed his weapon and called 911.

Cam wanted to tell her it was LaLa who'd set him up, but the sound of Gray's cries grew fainter by the second. She wanted to save him, but it was of no use. It was too late for him . . . for them. If it came down to him or her,

482

he'd gladly lay down his burdens and die. Besides, he'd be joining his mother and their baby girl soon. He could die happily now. Black filled the edges of his vision as Cam's eyes fluttered closed. His breaths came out in short, ragged, gasp as he faintly heard Gray call his name.

"Cam." She shook his face. "You have to wake up . . . Cam!" She cried out and trembled with grief.

She wanted to save him, but it was too late. His time was up. Cam's tired human heart beat one last time before everything faded to black.

"Cam! No-no-no-no! You can't do this to me!" Gray shook him hard. "Somebody help me!" She screamed.

Gray's life might as well have been over. Cam's dying would be her undoing.

"Baby." She ran her hand across his face. "You have to wake up! Baby!" She shook him again. "Please Cam! Wake up! PLEASE!"

Afterword

At the end of Beast Mode, I was prepared for you all to hate Cam, but as I close Sicko Mode, I know you all hate my guts!!! I always tell you guys to expect the unexpected. Pastor Edris . . . you didn't see that coming did you? LMAO!!!! I got ya'll asses. Did I lie when I said this book is a rollercoaster ride of nonstop action? There are so many freakin' layers to Cam and Gray's chaotic love story. Lord only knows where they'll go now. Will Cam survive? Will Victor still kill Gray? Will LaLa and Gunz ever get their just do? These answers and more will be answered in their next book. I don't have a title yet, but I do have a release date. Am I telling ya'll? Nope, lol. Mama needs some rest. I have been pushing myself to the brink for the last few years. Now it's time for me to take some time for myself. I know you all will understand. If you don't, oh the fuck well. I love you guys from the moon and back. I pray that you enjoyed Sicko Mode as much as I enjoyed writing it. Until next time . . .

XoXo

Keisha R. Ervin

About The Author

Keisha Ervin is the critically-acclaimed, best-selling author of numerous novels, including: The Untold Stories by Chyna Black, Cashmere Mafia, Material Girl 3: Secrets & Betrayals, Paper Heart, Pure Heroine, Emotionally Unavailable, Heartless, Radio Silence, Smells Like Teen Spirit Vol 1: Heiress, Mina's Joint 2: The Perfect Illusion, Cranes in the Sky, Postcards from the Edge, Such A Fuckin' Lady and First Wives Club Vol.1 Melanin Magic, Beast Mode and Sicko Mode.

For news on Keisha's upcoming work, to buy books and merch keep in touch by following her on any of the social media accounts listed below.

WEBSITE>> https://authorkeishaervin.com/

INSTAGRAM>>@keishaervin/https://www.instagram.com/keishaervin/?hl=en

SNAPCHAT >> kyrese99

TWITTER >> www.twitter.com/keishaervin

FACEBOOK >> www.facebook.com/keisha.ervin

Please, subscribe to my YouTube channel, to watch all my hilarious reviews on your favorite reality shows and drama series!!!

YOUTUBE >> https://www.youtube.com/colormepynk